THE FORCE

DON WINSLOW

WILLIAM MORROW
An Imprint of HarperCollins*Publishers*

THE FORCE. Copyright © 2017 by Samburu, Inc. All rights reserved. Printed in the United States of America. No part of this book may be used or reproduced in any manner whatsoever without written permission except in the case of brief quotations embodied in critical articles and reviews. For information address HarperCollins Publishers, 195 Broadway, New York, NY 10007.

HarperCollins books may be purchased for educational, business, or sales promotional use. For information please e-mail the Special Markets Department at SPsales@harpercollins.com.

FIRST EDITION

DESIGNED BY WILLIAM RUOTO

Library of Congress Cataloging-in-Publication Data has been applied for.

ISBN 978-0-06-266441-9 (hardcover)
ISBN 978-0-06-268428-8 (international edition)

17 18 19 20 21   LSC   10 9 8 7 6 5 4 3 2 1

During the time that I was writing this novel, the following law enforcement personnel were murdered in the line of duty. This book is dedicated to them:

Sergeant Cory Blake Wride, Deputy Sheriff Percy Lee House III, Deputy Sheriff Jonathan Scott Pine, Correctional Officer Amanda Beth Baker, Detective John Thomas Hobbs, Agent Joaquin Correa-Ortega, Officer Jason Marc Crisp, Chief Deputy Sheriff Allen Ray "Pete" Richardson, Officer Robert Gordon German, Master-at-Arms Mark Aaron Mayo, Officer Mark Hayden Larson, Officer Alexander Edward Thalmann, Officer David Wayne Smith Jr., Officer Christopher Alan Cortijo, Deputy Sheriff Michael J. Seversen, Trooper Gabriel Lenox Rich, Sergeant Patrick "Scott" Johnson, Officer Roberto Carlos Sanchez, Trooper Chelsea Renee Richard, Master Sergeant John Thomas Collum, Officer Michael Alexander Petrina, Detective Charles David Dinwiddie, Officer Stephen J. Arkell, Officer Jair Abelardo Cabrera, Trooper Christopher G. Skinner, Special Deputy Marshal Frank Edward McKnight, Officer Brian Wayne Jones, Officer Kevin Dorian Jordan, Officer Igor Soldo, Officer Alyn Ronnie Beck, Chief of Police Lee Dixon, Deputy Sheriff Allen Morris Bares Jr., Officer Perry Wayne Renn, Patrolman Jeffrey Brady Westerfield, Detective Melvin Vincent Santiago, Officer Scott Thomas Patrick, Chief of Police Michael Anthony Pimentel, Agent Geniel Amaro-Fantauzzi, Officer Daryl Pierson, Patrolman Nickolaus Edward Schultz, Corporal Jason Eugene Harwood, Deputy Sheriff Joseph John Matuskovic, Corporal Bryon Keith Dickson II, Deputy Sheriff Michael Andrew Norris, Sergeant Michael Joe Naylor, Deputy Sheriff Danny Paul Oliver, Detective Michael David Davis Jr., Deputy Sheriff Yevhen "Eugene" Kostiuchenko, Deputy Sheriff Jesse Valdez III, Officer Shaun Richard Diamond, Officer David Smith Payne, Constable Robert Parker White, Deputy Sheriff Matthew Scott Chism, Officer Justin Robert Winebrenner, Deputy Sheriff Christopher Lynd Smith, Agent Edwin O. Roman-Acevedo, Officer Wenjian Liu, Officer Rafael Ramos, Officer Charles Kondek, Officer Tyler Jacob Stewart, Detective Terence Avery Green, Officer Robert Wilson III, Deputy U.S. Marshal Josie

Wells, Patrolman George S. Nissen, Officer Alex K. Yazzie, Officer Michael Johnson, Trooper Trevor Casper, Officer Brian Raymond Moore, Sergeant Greg Moore, Officer Liquori Tate, Officer Benjamin Deen, Deputy Sonny Smith, Detective Kerrie Orozco, Trooper Taylor Thyfault, Patrolman James Arthur Bennett Jr., Officer Gregg "Nigel" Benner, Officer Rick Silva, Officer Sonny Kim, Officer Daryle Holloway, Sergeant Christopher Kelley, Corrections Officer Timothy Davison, Sergeant Scott Lunger, Officer Sean Michael Bolton, Officer Thomas Joseph LaValley, Deputy Sheriff Carl G. Howell, Trooper Steven Vincent, Officer Henry Nelson, Deputy Sheriff Darren Goforth, Sergeant Miguel Perez-Rios, Trooper Joseph Cameron Ponder, Deputy Sheriff Dwight Darwin Maness, Deputy Sheriff Bill Myers, Officer Gregory Thomas Alia, Detective Randolph A. Holder, Officer Daniel Scott Webster, Officer Bryce Edward Hanes, Officer Daniel Neil Ellis, Chief of Police Darrell Lemond Allen, Trooper Jaimie Lynn Jursevics, Officer Ricardo Galvez, Corporal William Matthew Solomon, Officer Garrett Preston Russell Swasey, Officer Lloyd E. Reed Jr., Officer Noah Leotta, Commander Frank Roman Rodriguez, Lieutenant Luz M. Soto Segarra, Agent Rosario Hernandez de Hoyos, Officer Thomas W. Cottrell Jr., Special Agent Scott McGuire, Officer Douglas Scott Barney II, Sergeant Jason Goodding, Deputy Derek Geer, Deputy Mark F. Logsdon, Deputy Patrick B. Dailey, Major Gregory E. "Lem" Barney, Officer Jason Moszer, Special Agent Lee Tartt, Corporal Nate Carrigan, Officer Ashley Marie Guindon, Officer David Stefan Hofer, Deputy Sheriff John Robert Kotfila Jr., Officer Allen Lee Jacobs, Deputy Carl A. Koontz, Officer Carlos Puente-Morales, Officer Susan Louise Farrell, Trooper Chad Phillip Dermyer, Officer Steven M. Smith, Detective Brad D. Lancaster, Officer David Glasser, Officer Ronald Tarentino Jr., Officer Verdell Smith Sr., Officer Natasha Maria Hunter, Officer Endy Nddiobong Ekpanya, Deputy Sheriff David Francis Michel Jr., Officer Brent Alan Thompson, Sergeant Michael Joseph Smith, Officer Patrick E. Zamarripa, Officer Lorne Bradley Ahrens, Officer Michael Leslie Krol, Security Supervisor Joseph Zangaro, Court Officer Ronald Eugene Kienzle, Deputy Sheriff Bradford Allen Garafola, Officer Matthew Lane Gerald, Corporal Montrell Lyle Jackson, Officer Marco Antonio Zarate, Corrections Officer Mari Johnson, Correctional Officer Kristopher D. Moules, Captain Robert D. Melton, Officer Clint Corvinus, Officer Jonathan De Guzman, Officer José Ismael Chavez, Special Agent De'Greaun Frazier, Corporal Bill Cooper, Officer John Scott Martin, Officer Kenneth Ray Moats, Officer Kevin "Tim" Smith, Sergeant Steve Owen, Master Deputy Sheriff Brandon Collins, Officer Timothy James Brackeen, Officer Lesley Zerebny, Officer Jose Gilbert Vega, Officer Scott Leslie Bashioum, Sergeant Luis A. Meléndez-Maldonado, Deputy Sheriff Jack Hopkins, Correctional Officer Kenneth Bettis, Deputy Sheriff Dan Glaze, Officer Myron Jarrett, Sergeant Allen Brandt, Officer Blake Curtis Snyder, Sergeant Kenneth Steil, Officer Justin Martin, Sergeant Anthony Beminio, Sergeant Paul Tuozzolo, Deputy Sheriff Dennis Wallace, Detective Benjamin Edward Marconi, Deputy Commander Patrick Thomas Carothers, Officer Collin James Rose, Trooper Cody James Donahue.

"Cops are just people," she said irrelevantly.
"They start out that way, I've heard."
—RAYMOND CHANDLER, *FAREWELL, MY LOVELY*

The last guy on earth anyone ever expected to end up in the Metropolitan Correctional Center on Park Row was Denny Malone.

You said the mayor, the president of the United States, the pope—people in New York would have laid odds they'd see them behind bars before they saw Detective First Grade Dennis John Malone.

A hero cop.

The son of a hero cop.

A veteran sergeant in the NYPD's most elite unit.

The Manhattan North Special Task Force.

And, most of all, a guy who knows where all the skeletons are hidden, because he put half of them there himself.

Malone and Russo and Billy O and Big Monty and the rest made these streets their own, and they ruled them like kings. They made them safe and kept them safe for the decent people trying to make lives there, and that was their job and their passion and their love, and if that meant they worked the corners of the plate and put a little something extra on the ball now and then, that's what they did.

The people, they don't know what it takes sometimes to keep them safe and it's better that they don't.

They may think they want to know, they may say they want to know, but they don't.

Malone and the Task Force, they weren't just any cops on the Job. You got thirty-eight thousand wearing blue, Denny Malone and his guys were the 1 percent of the 1 percent of the 1 percent—

the smartest, the toughest, the quickest, the bravest, the best, the baddest.

The Manhattan North Special Task Force.

"Da Force" blew through the city like a cold, harsh, fast and violent wind, scouring the streets and alleys, the playgrounds, parks and projects, scraping away the trash and the filth, a predatory storm blowing away the predators.

A strong wind finds its way through every crack, into the project stairwells, the tenement heroin mills, the social club back rooms, the new-money condos, the old-money penthouses. From Columbus Circle to the Henry Hudson Bridge, Riverside Park to the Harlem River, up Broadway and Amsterdam, down Lenox and St. Nicholas, on the numbered streets that spanned the Upper West Side, Harlem, Washington Heights and Inwood, if there was a secret Da Force didn't know about, it was because it hadn't been whispered about or even thought of yet.

Drug deals and gun deals, traffic in people and property, rapes, robberies and assaults, crimes hatched in English, Spanish, French, Russian over collard greens and smothered chicken or jerk pork or pasta marinara or gourmet meals at five-star restaurants in a city made from sin and for profit.

Da Force hit them all, but especially guns and drugs, because guns kill and drugs incite the killings.

Now Malone's in lockup, the wind has stopped blowing, but everyone knows it's the eye of the storm, the dead quiet lull that comes before the worst of it. Denny Malone in the hands of the feds? Not IAB, not the state's attorneys, but the feds, where no one in the city can touch him?

Everyone's hunkered down, shitting bricks and waiting for that blow, that tsunami, because with what Malone knows, he could take out commanders, chiefs, even the commissioner. He could roll on prosecutors, judges—shit, he could serve the feds the mayor on the proverbial silver platter with at least one congressman and a couple of real estate billionaires as appetizers.

So as the word went out that Malone was sitting in the MCC, people in the eye of the hurricane got scared, real scared, started to seek shelter even in the calm, even knowing that there are no walls high enough, no cellars deep enough—not at One Police, not at the Criminal Courts Building, not even at Gracie Mansion or in the penthouse palaces lining Fifth Avenue and Central Park South—to keep them safe from what's in Denny Malone's head.

If Malone wants to pull the whole city down around him, he can.

Then again, no one's ever really been safe from Malone and his crew.

Malone's guys made headlines—the *Daily News,* the *Post,* Channels 7, 4 and 2; "film at eleven" cops. Recognized-on-the-street cops, the-mayor-knows-your-name cops, comped seats at the Garden, the Meadowlands, Yankee Stadium and Shea, walk-into-any-restaurant-bar-or-club-in-the-city-and-get-treated-like-royalty cops.

And of this pack of alphas, Denny Malone is the undisputed leader.

Walks into any house in the city, the uniforms and the rookies stop and stare, the lieutenants give him a nod, even the captains know not to step on his shoes.

He's earned their respect.

Among other things (Shit, you want to talk about the robberies he stopped, the bullet he took, the kid in that hostage situation he saved? The busts, the takedowns, the convictions?), Malone and his team, they made the biggest drug bust in the history of New York.

Fifty kilos of heroin.

And the Dominican who was trafficking it gone.

Along with a hero cop.

Malone's crew laid their partner in the ground—bagpipes, folded flag, black ribbons over shields—and went right back to work because the slingers and the gangs and the robbers and the rapists and the wiseguys, they don't take time off to grieve. You wanna keep your streets safe, you gotta be on those streets—days, nights, weekends, holidays, whatever it takes, and your wives, they knew what they signed up for, and your kids, they learn to understand that's what Daddy does, he puts the bad guys behind bars.

Except now it's him in the cage, Malone sitting on a steel bench in a holding cell like the dirtbags he usually puts there, bent over, his head in his hands, worrying about his partners—his brothers on Da Force—and what's going to happen to them now that he's put them neck deep in shit.

Worrying about his family—his wife, who didn't sign up for this, his two kids, a son and a daughter who are too young to understand now, but when they're old enough are never going to forgive why they had to grow up without a father.

Then there's Claudette.

Fucked up in her own way.

Needy, needing him, and he's not going to be there.

For her or for anybody, so he doesn't know now what's going to happen to the people he loves.

The wall he's staring at doesn't have any answers, either, as to how he got here.

No, fuck that, Malone thinks. At least be honest with yourself, he thinks as he sits there with nothing in front of him but time.

At least, at last, tell yourself the truth.

You know exactly how you got here.

Step by motherfucking step.

Our ends know our beginnings but the reverse isn't true.

When Malone was a kid, the nuns taught him that even before we're born, God—and only God—knows the days of our lives and the day of our death and who and what we'll become.

Well, I wish he'd fucking shared it with me, Malone thinks. Given me a word, a tip, dimed me out, ratted on me to myself, told me something, anything. Said, Hey, jerkoff, you took a left, you should have gone right.

But no, nothing.

All he's seen, Malone isn't a big fan of God and figures the feeling is mutual. He has a lot of questions he'd like to ask him, but if he ever got him in the room, God'd probably shut his mouth, lawyer up, let his own kid take the jolt.

All this time on the Job, Malone lost his faith, so when the moment came when he was looking the devil in the eye, there was nothing between Malone and murder except ten pounds of trigger pull.

Ten pounds of gravity.

It was Malone's finger pulled the trigger, but maybe it was gravity that pulled him down—the relentless, unforgiving gravity of eighteen years on the Job.

Pulling him down to where he is now.

Malone didn't start out to end up here. Didn't throw his hat in the air the day he graduated the Academy and took the oath, the happiest day of his life—the brightest, bluest, best day—thinking that he'd end up here.

No, he started with his eyes firmly on the guiding star, his feet planted on the path, but that's the thing about the life you walk— you start out pointed true north, but you vary one degree off, it doesn't matter for maybe one year, five years, but as the years stack up you're just walking farther and farther away from where you started out to go, you don't even know you're lost until you're so far from your original destination you can't even see it anymore.

You can't even get back on the path to start over.

Time and gravity won't allow it.

And Denny Malone would give a lot to start over.

Hell, he'd give everything.

Because he never thought he'd end up in the federal lockup on Park Row. No one did, except maybe God, and he wasn't talking.

But here Malone is.

Without his gun or his shield or anything else that says what and who he is, what and who he was.

A dirty cop.

THE RIP

Lenox Avenue,
Honey.
Midnight.
And the gods are laughing at us.

—LANGSTON HUGHES, "LENOX AVENUE: MIDNIGHT"

Harlem, New York City
July 2016

Four A.M.

When the city that never sleeps at least lies down and closes its eyes.

This is what Denny Malone thinks as his Crown Vic slides up the spine of Harlem.

Behind the walls and windows, in apartments and hotels, tenements and project towers, people are sleeping or can't, are dreaming or are beyond dreams. People are fighting or fucking or both, making love and making babies, screaming curses or speaking soft, intimate words meant for each other and not the street. Some try to rock infants back to sleep, or are just getting up for another day of work, while others cut kilos of heroin into glassine bags to sell to the addicts for their wake-up shots.

After the hookers and before the street cleaners, that's the window of time you have to make a rip, Malone knows. Nothing good ever happens after midnight, is what his old man used to say, and he knew. He was a cop on these streets, coming home in the morning after a graveyard shift with murder in his eyes, death in his nose and an icicle in his heart that never melted and eventually killed him. Got out of the car in the driveway one morning and his heart cracked. The doctors said he was dead before he hit the ground.

Malone found him there.

Eight years old, leaving the house to walk to school, he saw the blue overcoat in the pile of dirty snow he'd helped his dad shovel off the driveway.

Now it's before dawn and already hot. One of those summers when God the landlord refuses to turn the heat down or the air-conditioning on—the city edgy and irritable, on the brink of a flameout, a fight or a riot, the smell of old garbage and stale urine, sweet, sour, sickly and corrupt as an old whore's perfume.

Denny Malone loves it.

Even in the daytime when it's baking hot and noisy, when the gangbangers are on the corners and the hip-hop bass beats hurt your ears, and bottles, cans, dirty diapers and plastic bags of piss come flying out of project windows, and the dog shit stinks in the fetid heat, he wouldn't be anywhere else in the world.

It's his city, his turf, his heart.

Rolling up Lenox now, past the old Mount Morris Park neighborhood and its graceful brownstones, Malone worships the small gods of place—the twin towers of Ebenezer Gospel Tabernacle, where the hymns float out on Sundays with the voices of angels, then the distinctive spire of Ephesus Seventh-Day Adventist and, farther up the block, Harlem Shake—not the dance but some of the best damn burgers in the city.

Then there are the dead gods—the old Lenox Lounge, with its iconic neon sign, red front and all that history. Billie Holiday used to sing there, Miles Davis and John Coltrane played their horns, and it was a hang for James Baldwin, Langston Hughes and Malcolm X. It's closed now—the window covered with brown paper, the sign dark—but there's talk about opening it again.

Malone doubts it.

Dead gods don't rise again except in fairy tales.

He crosses 125th, a.k.a. Dr. Martin Luther King Jr. Boulevard.

Urban pioneers and the black middle class have gentrified the area, which the Realtors have now christened "SoHa," a blended acronym always being the death knell of any old neighborhood, Malone thinks. He's convinced that if real estate developers could buy properties in the bottom levels of Dante's *Inferno* they'd rename it "LoHel" and start throwing up boutiques and condos.

Fifteen years ago, this stretch of Lenox was empty storefronts; now it's trendy again with new restaurants, bars and sidewalk cafés where the better-off locals come to eat, the white people come to feel hip and some of those condos in the new high-rise buildings go for two and a half mil.

All you need to know about this part of Harlem now, Malone thinks, is that there's a Banana Republic next to the Apollo Theater. There are the gods of place and the gods of commerce, and if you have to bet who's going to win out, put your money on money every time.

Farther uptown and in the projects it's still the ghetto.

Malone crosses 125th and passes the Red Rooster, where Ginny's Supper Club resides in the basement.

There are less famous shrines, nonetheless sacred to Malone.

He's attended funerals at Bailey's, bought pint bottles at Lenox Liquors, been stitched up in the E-room at Harlem Hospital, played hoops by the Big L mural in Fred Samuel Playground, ordered food through the bulletproof glass at Kennedy Fried Chicken. Parked along the street and watched the kids dance, smoked weed on a rooftop, watched the sun come up from Fort Tryon Park.

Now more dead gods, ancient gods—the old Savoy Ballroom, the site of the Cotton Club, both gone long before Malone's time, ghosts from the last Harlem Renaissance haunting this neighborhood with the image of what it once was and can never be again.

But Lenox is alive.

It actually throbs from the IRT subway line that runs directly underneath its entire length. Malone used to ride the #2 train, the one they called "The Beast" back then.

Now it's Black Star Music, the Mormon Church, African American Best Food. When they get to the end of Lenox, Malone says, "Go around the block."

Phil Russo, behind the wheel, turns left onto 147th and drives around the block, down Seventh Avenue and then another left onto 146th, and cruises past an abandoned tenement the owner gave back to the rats and the roaches, chasing the people out in the hope that some junkie cooking up will burn it down and he can collect the insurance and then sell the lot.

Win-win.

Malone scans for sentries or some cops cooping in a radio car, bagging a little sleep on the graveyard shift. A sole lookout stands outside the door. Green bandanna, green Nikes with green shoelaces make him a Trinitario.

Malone's crew has been watching the heroin mill on the second floor all summer. The Mexicans truck the smack up and deliver it to Diego Pena, the Dominican in charge of NYC. Pena breaks it down from kilos into dime bags and distributes it to the Domo gangs, the Trinitarios and DDP (Dominicans Don't Play), and then to the black and PR gangs in the projects.

The mill is fat tonight.

Fat with money.

Fat with dope.

"Gear up," Malone says, checking the Sig Sauer P226 in the holster on his hip. A Beretta 8000D Mini-Cougar rests in a second holster in the small of his back just below the new ceramic-plate vest.

He makes the whole crew wear vests on a job. Big Monty complains his is too tight, but Malone tells him it's a looser fit than a coffin. Bill Montague, a.k.a. Big Monty, is old school. On his head, even in summer, is his trademark trilby, with its stingy brim and a red feather on the left side. His concession to the heat is an XXXL guayabera shirt over khaki slacks. An unlit Montecristo cigar perches in the corner of his mouth.

A Mossberg 590 pump-action 12-gauge shotgun with a twenty-inch barrel loaded with powdered ceramic rounds sits at Phil Russo's feet by his high-polished red leather shoes with the skinny guinea toes. The shoes match his hair—Russo is that rare redheaded Italian and Malone jokes that there must have been a bogtrotter in the woodpile. Russo answers that's impossible because he isn't an alcoholic and he don't need a magnifying glass to find his own dick.

Billy O'Neill carries an HK MP5 submachine gun, two flash-bang grenades and a roll of duct tape. Billy O's the youngest of the crew, but he has talent, street smarts and moves.

Guts, too.

Malone knows Billy ain't gonna cut and run, ain't gonna freeze or hesitate to pull the trigger, if he needs to. If anything, it's the opposite—Billy might be a little too quick to go. Got that Irish temper along with the Kennedy good looks. Got some other Kennedy-esque attributes, too. The kid likes women and women like him back.

Tonight, the crew is going in heavy.

And high.

You go up against narcos who are jacked on coke or speed, it helps to be pharmacologically even with them, so Malone pops two "go-pills"—Dexedrine. Then he slips on a blue windbreaker with NYPD stenciled in white and flips the lanyard with his shield over his chest.

Russo orbits the block again. Coming back around on 146th, he hits the gas, races up to the mill and slams the brakes. The lookout hears the tires squeal but turns around too late—Malone's out the door before the car stops. He shoves the lookout face-first into the wall and sticks the barrel of the Sig against his head.

"*Cállate, pendejo,*" Malone says. "One sound, I'll splatter you."

He kicks the lookout's feet out from under him and puts him on the ground. Billy is already there—he duct-tapes the lookout's hands behind him and then slaps a strip over his mouth.

Malone's crew press themselves against the wall of the building. "We all stay sharp," Malone says, "we all go home tonight."

The Dex starts to kick in—Malone feels his heart race and his blood get hot.

It feels good.

He sends Billy O up to the roof to come down the fire escape and cover the window. The rest go in and head up the stairs. Malone first, the Sig in front of him, ready. Russo behind him with the shotgun, then Monty.

Malone don't worry about his back.

A wooden door blocks the top of the stairs.

Malone nods at Monty.

The big man steps up, jams the Rabbit between the door and the sill. Sweat pops on his forehead and runs down his dark skin as he presses the handles of the tool together and cracks the door open.

Malone steps through, swings his pistol in an arc, but no one's in the hallway. Looking to the right, he sees the new steel door at the end of the hall. *Machata* music plays from a radio inside, voices in Spanish, the whir of coffee grinders, the clack of a money counter.

And a dog barking.

Fuck, Malone thinks, all the narcos got 'em now. Just like every chick on the East Side has a yapping little Yorkie in her handbag these days, the slingers got pit bulls. It's a good idea—the spooks are scared shitless of dogs and the *chicas* working in the mills won't risk getting their faces chewed off for stealing.

Malone worries about Billy O because the kid loves dogs, even pit bulls. Malone learned this back in April when they hit a warehouse over by the river and three pit bulls were trying to jump through the chain-link fence to rip their throats out but Billy O, he just couldn't bring himself to pop them or let anyone else do it, so they had to go all the way around the back of the building, up the fire escape to the roof and then down the stairs.

It was a pain in the ass.

Anyway, the pit bull has made them but the Domos haven't. Malone hears one of them yell, "*Cállate!*" and then a sharp whack and the dog shuts up.

But the Hi-Guard steel security door is a problem.

The Rabbit ain't gonna crack it.

Malone gets on the radio. "Billy, you in place?"

"Born in place, bro."

"We're gonna blow the door," Malone says. "When it goes, you toss in a flashbang."

"You got it, D."

Malone nods to Russo, who aims at the door's hinges and fires two blasts. The ceramic powder explodes faster than the speed of sound and the door comes down.

Women, naked save for plastic gloves and hairnets, bolt for the window. Others crouch under tables as money-counting machines spit cash onto the floor like slot machines paying off with paper.

Malone yells, "NYPD!"

He sees Billy through the window to his left.

Doing exactly shit, just staring through the window. Jesus Christ, throw the grenade.

But Billy doesn't.

The fuck's he waiting for?

Then Malone sees it.

The pit bull's got puppies, four of them, curled up in a ball behind her as she runs to the end of her metal chain, snapping and growling to protect them.

Billy doesn't want to hurt the puppies.

Malone yells through the radio. "Goddamn it, do it!"

Billy looks through the window at him, then he kicks in the glass and lobs the grenade in.

But he throws it short, to avoid the goddamn dogs.

The concussion shatters the rest of the glass, spraying shards into Billy's face and neck.

Bright, blinding white light—screams, yells.

Malone counts to three and goes in.

Chaos.

A Trini staggers, one hand to his blinded eyes, the other shooting a Glock as he moves toward the window and the fire escape. Malone hits him with two rounds in the chest and he topples into the window. A second gunman aims at Malone from beneath a counting table but Monty hits him with a blast from his .38 and then a second one to make sure he's DOA.

They let the women get out the window.

"Billy, you okay?" Malone asks.

Billy O's face looks like a Halloween mask.

Gashes on his arms and legs.

"I been cut worse in hockey games," he says, laughing. "I'll get stitched up when we're done here."

Money's everywhere, in stacks, in the machines, spilled on the floor. Heroin is still in coffee grinders where it was being cut.

But that's the small shit.

La caja—the trap—a large hole carved into the wall, is open.

Stacked, floor to ceiling, with bricks of heroin.

Diego Pena sits calmly at a table. If the deaths of two of his guys bother him, it doesn't show on his face. "Do you have a warrant, Malone?"

"I heard a woman scream for help," Malone says.

Pena smirks.

Well-dressed motherfucker. Gray Armani suit worth two large, the gold Piguet watch on his wrist five times that.

Pena notices. "It's yours. I have three more."

The pit bull barks wildly, straining against her chain.

Malone is looking at the heroin.

Stacks of it, vacuum wrapped in black plastic.

Enough H to keep the city high for weeks.

"I'll save you the trouble of counting," Pena says. "One hundred kilos even. Mexican cinnamon heroin—'Dark Horse'—sixty percent pure. You can sell it for a hundred thousand dollars a kilo. The cash you're seeing should amount to another five million. You take the drugs and the money. I get on a plane to the Dominican, you never see me again. Think about it—when's the next time you can make fifteen million dollars for turning your back?"

And we all go home tonight, Malone thinks.

He says, "Take your gun out. Slow."

Pena slowly reaches into his jacket for his pistol.

Malone shoots him twice in the heart.

Billy O squats and picks up a kilo. Slicing it open with his K-bar, he dips a small vial into the heroin, gets a pinch and dumps it into a plastic pouch he takes from his pocket. He crushes the vial inside the test bag and waits for the color to change.

It turns purple.

Billy grins. "We're rich!"

Malone says, "Hurry the fuck up."

There's the sound of a pop as the pit bull breaks the chain and lunges toward him. Billy falls back, throwing the kilo into the air. It mushroom-clouds and then falls like a snow shower into his open wounds.

Another blast as Monty kills the dog.

But Billy's flat on the floor. Malone sees him go rigid, then his legs start to spasm, jerking uncontrollably as the heroin speeds through his bloodstream.

His feet pound on the floor.

Malone kneels beside him, holds him in his arms.

"Billy, no," Malone says. "Hold on."

Billy looks up at him with empty eyes.

His face is white.

His spine jerks like an uncoiling spring.

Then he's gone.

Freakin' Billy, beautiful young Billy O, as old now as he's ever gonna get.

Malone hears his own heart crack, and then dull explosions and at first he thinks he's been shot, but he doesn't see any wounds so then he thinks it's his head blowing up.

Then he remembers.

It's the Fourth of July.

PART 1

WHITE CHRISTMAS

Welcome to da jungle, this is my home,
The birth of the blues, the birth of the song.

—CHRIS THOMAS KING, "WELCOME TO DA JUNGLE"

CHAPTER 1

Harlem, New York City
Christmas Eve

oon.

Denny Malone pops two go-pills and steps into the shower.

He just got up after a midnight-to-eight and needs the uppers to get him going. Tilting his face toward the showerhead, he lets the sharp needles sting his skin until it hurts.

He needs that, too.

Tired skin, tired eyes.

Tired soul.

Malone turns around and indulges in the hot water pounding on the back of his neck and shoulders. Running down the tattooed sleeves of his arms. It feels good, he could stand there all day, but he has things to do.

"Time to move, ace," he tells himself.

You have responsibilities.

He gets out, dries off, wraps the towel around his waist.

Malone is six two and solid. Thirty-eight now, he knows he has a hard look to him. It's the tats on the broad forearms, the heavy stubble even when he shaves, the short-cropped black hair, the don't-fuck-with-me blue eyes.

It's the broken nose, the small scar over the left side of his lip. What can't be seen are the bigger scars on his right leg—his Medal of Valor scars for being stupid enough to get himself shot. That's the NYPD, though, he thinks. They give you a medal for being stupid, take your badge for being smart.

Maybe the badass look helps him stay out of the physical confrontations, which he does try to avoid. For one thing, it's more professional to talk your way through. For another, any fight is going to get you hurt—even if it's just your knuckles—and he doesn't like getting his clothes messed up rolling around in God only knows what nasty shit is down there on the concrete.

He's not so much on the weights, so he hits the heavy bag and does the running, usually early morning or late afternoon depending on work, through Riverside Park because he likes the open view of the Hudson, Jersey across the river and the George Washington Bridge.

Now Malone goes into the small kitchen. There's a little coffee left from when Claudette got up, and he pours a cup and puts it into the microwave.

She's pulling a double at Harlem Hospital, just four blocks away on Lenox and 135th, so another nurse can spend time with family. With any luck, he'll see her later tonight or early in the morning.

Malone doesn't care that the coffee is stale and bitter. He's not after a quality experience, just a caffeine kick to jump-start the Dexedrine. Can't stand the whole gourmet coffee bullshit anyway, standing in line behind some millennial asshole taking ten minutes to order a perfect latte so he can take a selfie with it. Malone dumps in some cream and sugar, like most cops do. They drink too much of it, so the milk helps soothe their stomachs while the sugar gives them a boost.

An Upper West Side doctor writes Malone scrip for anything he wants—Dex, Vicodin, Xanax, antibiotics, whatever. A couple of years ago, the good doc—and he is a good guy, with a wife and three kids—had a little something on the side who decided to blackmail him when he decided to break it off.

Malone had a talk with the girl and explained things to her.

Handed her a sealed envelope with $10K and told her that was it. She should never contact the doc again or Malone would put her in the House of D where she'd be giving up her overvalued cooch for an extra spoonful of peanut butter.

Now the grateful doctor writes him scrip but half the time just gives him free samples. Every little bit helps, Malone thinks, and anyway, it's not like he could have speed or pain pills show up on his medical records if he got them through his insurance.

He doesn't want to phone Claudette and bother her at work, but texts to let her know that he didn't sleep through the alarm and to ask how her day is going. She texts back, Xmas crazy but OK.

Yeah, Christmas Crazy.

Always crazy in New York, Malone thinks.

If it ain't Christmas Crazy, it's New Year's Eve Crazy (drunks), or Valentine's Day Crazy (domestic disputes skyrocket and the gays get into bar fights), St. Paddy's Crazy (drunk cops), Fourth of July Crazy, Labor Day Crazy. What we need is a holiday from the holidays. Just take a year off from any of them, see how it works out.

It probably wouldn't, he thinks.

Because you still got Everyday Crazy—Drunk Crazy, Junkie Crazy, Crack Crazy, Meth Crazy, Love Crazy, Hate Crazy and, Malone's personal favorite, plain old Crazy Crazy. What the public at large doesn't understand is that the city's jails have become its de facto mental hospitals and detox centers. Three-quarters of the prisoners they check in test positive for drugs or are psychotic, or both.

They belong in hospitals but don't have the insurance.

Malone goes into the bedroom to get dressed.

Black denim shirt, Levi's jeans, Doc Marten boots with steel-reinforced toes (the better to kick in doors), a black leather jacket. The quasi-official Irish-American New York street uniform, Staten Island division.

Malone grew up there, his wife and his kids still live there, and if you're Irish or Italian from Staten Island, your career choices are basically cop, fireman or crook. Malone took door number one, although he has a brother and two cousins who are firefighters.

Well, his brother, Liam, *was* a firefighter, until 9/11.

Now he's a twice-annual trip to Silver Lake Cemetery to leave flowers, a pint of Jameson's and a report on how the Rangers are doing.

Usually shitty.

They always used to joke that Liam was the black sheep of the family, becoming a "hose-monkey"—a firefighter—instead of a cop. Malone used to measure his brother's arms to see if they'd gotten any longer lugging all that shit around and Liam would shoot back that the only thing a cop would heft up a flight of stairs was a bag of doughnuts. And then there was the fictional competition between them about who could steal more—a firefighter on a domestic blaze or a cop on a burglary call.

Malone loved his little brother, looked after him all those nights the old man wasn't home, and they watched the Rangers together on Channel 11. The night the Rangers won the Stanley Cup in 1994 was one of the happiest nights in Malone's life. Him and Liam in front of the TV set, on their knees the last minute of the game when the Rangers were holding on to a one-goal lead by their fingernails and Craig MacTavish—God bless Craig MacTavish—kept getting the puck down deep in the Canucks' zone and time finally ran out and the Rangers won the series 4–3 and Denny and Liam hugged each other and jumped up and down.

And then Liam was gone, just like that, and it was Malone who had to go tell their mother. She was never the same after that and died just a year later. The doctors said it was cancer but Malone knew she was another victim of 9/11.

Now he clips his holster with the regulation Sig Sauer onto his belt.

A lot of cops like the shoulder holster but Malone thinks it's just an extra move to get your hand up there and he prefers his weapon where his hand already is. He clips his off-duty Beretta to the back of his waistband, where it nestles into the small of his back. The SOG knife goes into his right boot. It's against regs and illegal as shit, but Malone doesn't care. He could be in a situation some skels take his guns and then what's he supposed to pull, his dick? He ain't going down like a bitch, he's going out slashing and stabbing.

And anyway, who's going to bust him?

A lot of people, you dumb donkey, he tells himself. These days, every cop's got a bull's-eye on his back.

Tough times for the NYPD.

First, there's the Michael Bennett shooting.

Michael Bennett was a fourteen-year-old black kid who was shot to death by an Anti-Crime cop in Brownsville. The classic case: nighttime, he looked hinky, the cop—a newbie named Hayes—told him to stop and he didn't. Bennett turned, reached into his waistband and pulled out what Hayes thought was a gun.

The newbie emptied his weapon into the kid.

Turned out it wasn't a gun, it was a cell phone.

The community, of course, was "outraged." Protests teetered on the edge of riots, the usual celebrity ministers, lawyers and social activists performed for the cameras, the city promised a complete investigation. Hayes was placed on administrative leave pending the result of the investigation, and the hostile relationship between blacks and the police got even worse than it already was.

The investigation is still "ongoing."

And it came behind the whole Ferguson thing, and Cleveland and Chicago, Freddie Gray down in Baltimore. Then there was Alton Sterling in Baton Rouge, Philando Castile in Minnesota, on and on.

Not that the NYPD didn't have its own cops killing unarmed black men—Sean Bell, Ousmane Zongo, George Tillman, Akai Gurley, David Felix, Eric Garner, Delrawn Small . . . And now this rookie had to go and shoot young Michael Bennett.

So you got Black Lives Matter up your ass, every citizen a journalist with a cell-phone camera at the ready, and you go to work each day with the whole world thinking you're a murdering racist.

Okay, maybe not everybody, Malone admits, but it's definitely different now.

People look at you different.

Or shoot at you.

Five cops gunned down by a sniper in Dallas. Two cops in Las Vegas shot to death as they sat at a restaurant eating lunch. Forty-nine officers murdered in the United States in the past year. One of them, Paul Tuozzolo, in the NYPD, and the year before the Job lost Randy Holder and Brian Moore. There have been too many over the years. Malone knows the stats: 325 gunned down, 21 stabbed, 32 beaten to death, 21 deliberately run over by cars, 8 blown up in explosions, and none of that counts the guys dying from the shit they sucked down on 9/11.

So yeah, Malone carries something extra, and yeah, he thinks, there'd be any number of people ready to string you up, they found you with illegal weapons, not the least of which would be the cop-hating CCRB, which Phil Russo insists stands for "Cunts, Cock-suckers, Rats and Ballbusters," but is actually the Civilian Complaint Review Board, the mayor's chosen stick for beating up on his police force when he needs to deflect attention from his own scandals.

So the CCRB would hang you, Malone thinks, IAB—the god-damn Internal Affairs Bureau—would sure as shit hang you, even your own boss would cheerfully put a noose around your neck.

Now Malone sucks it up to call Sheila. What he doesn't want is a fight, what he doesn't want is the question, Where are you calling from? But that's what he gets when his estranged wife answers the phone. "Where are you calling from?"

"The city," Malone says.

To every Staten Islander, Manhattan is and will always be "the city." He doesn't get more specific than that, and fortunately she doesn't press him on it. Instead she says, "This better not be a call telling me you can't make it tomorrow. The kids will be—"

"No, I'm coming."

"For presents?"

"I'll get there early," Malone says. "What's a good time?"

"Seven thirty, eight."

"Okay."

"You on a midnight?" she asks, a tinge of suspicion in her tone.

"Yeah," Malone says. Malone's team is on the graveyard, but it's a technicality—they work when they decide to work, which is when the cases tell them to. Drug dealers work regular shifts so their customers know when and where to find them, but drug *traffickers* work their own hours. "And it isn't what you think."

"What do I think?" Sheila knows that every cop with an IQ over 10 and a rank over rookie can get Christmas Eve off if he wants, and a midnight tour is usually just an excuse to get drunk with your buddies or bang some whore, or both.

"Don't get it twisted, we're working on something," Malone says, "might break tonight."

"Sure."

Sarcastic, like. The hell she thinks pays for the presents, the kids' braces, her spa days, her girls' nights out? Every guy on the Job relies on overtime to pay the bills, maybe even get a little ahead. The wives, even the ones you're separated from, gotta understand. You're out there busting your hump, all the time.

"You spending Christmas Eve with her?" Sheila asks.

So close, Malone thinks, to getting away. And Sheila pronounces it "huh." *You spending Christmas Eve with huh?*

"She's working," Malone says, dodging the question like a skel. "So am I."

"You're always working, Denny."

Ain't that the large truth, Malone thinks, taking that as a good-bye and clicking off. They'll put it on my freakin' headstone: *Denny Malone, he was always working.* Fuck it—you work, you die, you try to have a life somewhere in there.

But mostly you work.

A lot of guys, they come on the Job to do their twenty, pull the pin, get their pension. Malone, he's on the Job because he loves the job.

Be honest, he tells himself as he walks out of the apartment. You had to do it all over again you wouldn't be nothin' but a New York City police detective.

The best job in the whole freakin' world.

Malone pulls on a black wool beanie because it's cold out there, locks up the apartment and goes down the stairs onto 136th. Claudette picked the place because it's a short walk to her work, and near the Hansborough Rec Center, which has an indoor pool where she likes to swim.

"How can you swim in a public pool?" Malone has asked her. "I mean, the germs floating around in there. You're a nurse."

She laughed at him. "Do you have a private pool I don't know about?"

He walks west on 136th out to Seventh Avenue, a.k.a. Adam Clayton Powell Jr. Boulevard, past the Christian Science Church, United Fried Chicken and Café 22, where Claudette doesn't like to eat because she's afraid she'll get fat and he doesn't like to eat because he's afraid they'll spit in his food. Across the street is Judi's, the little bar where he and Claudette will get a quiet drink on the odd occasions their downtimes coincide. Then he crosses ACP at 135th and walks past the Thurgood Marshall Academy and an IHOP where Small's Paradise used to be down in the basement.

Claudette, who knows about these things, told Malone that Billie Holiday had her first audition there and that Malcolm X was a waiter there during World War II. Malone was more interested that Wilt Chamberlain owned the place for a while.

City blocks are memories.

They have lives and they have deaths.

Malone was still wearing the bag, riding a sector car, when a

THE FORCE / 27

mook raped a little Haitian girl on this block back in the day. This was the fourth girl this animal had done, and every cop in the Three-Two was looking for him.

The Haitians got there before the cops did, found the perp still on the rooftop and tossed him off into the back alley.

Malone and his then partner caught the call and walked into the alley where Rocky the Non-Flying Squirrel was lying in a spreading pool of his own blood, with most of the bones in his body broken because nine floors is a long way to fall.

"That's the man," one of the local women told Malone at the edge of the alley. "The man who raped those little girls."

The EMTs knew what was what, and one of them asked, "He dead yet?"

Malone shook his head and the EMTs lit up cigarettes and leaned on the ambulance smoking for a good ten minutes until they went in with a stretcher and came back out with the word to call the medical examiner.

The ME pronounced the cause of death as "massive blunt trauma with catastrophic and fatal bleeding," and the Homicide guys who showed up accepted Malone's account that the guy had jumped out of guilt over what he'd done.

The detectives wrote it off as a suicide, Malone got a lot of stroke from the Haitian community, and most important, no little girls had to testify in court with their rapist sitting there staring at them and some dirtbag defense attorney trying to make them look like liars.

It was a good result but shit, he thinks, we did that today we'd go to jail, we got caught.

He keeps walking south, past St. Nick's.

A.k.a. "The Nickel."

The St. Nicholas Houses, a baker's dozen of fourteen-story buildings straddled by Adam Clayton Powell and Frederick Douglass Boulevards from 127th to 131st, make up a good part of Malone's working life.

Yeah, Harlem has changed, Harlem has gentrified, but the projects are still the projects. They sit like desert islands in a sea of new prosperity and what makes the projects is what's always made the projects—poverty, unemployment, drug slinging and gangs. Mostly good people inhabit St. Nick's, Malone believes, trying to live their lives, raise their kids against tough odds, do their day-to-day, but you also have the hard-core thugs and the gangs.

Two gangs dominate action in St. Nick's—the Get Money Boys and Black Spades. GMB has the north projects, the Spades the south, and they live in an uneasy peace enforced by DeVon Carter, who controls most of the drug trafficking in West Harlem.

The border between the gangs is 129th Street, and Malone walks past the basketball courts on the south side of the street.

The gang boys aren't out there today, it's too freakin' cold.

He goes out Frederick Douglass past the Harlem Bar-B-Q and Greater Zion Hill Baptist. It was just down the street where he got the rep as both a "hero cop" and a "racist cop," neither of which tag is true, Malone thinks.

It was what, six years ago now, he was working plainclothes out of the Three-Three and was having lunch at Manna's when he heard screaming outside. He went out the door and saw people pointing at a deli across the street and down the block.

Malone called in a 10-61, pulled his weapon and went into the deli.

The robber grabbed a little girl and held a gun to her head.

The girl's mother was screaming.

"Drop your gun," the robber yelled at Malone, "or I'll kill her! I will!"

He was black, junkie-sick, out of his fucking mind.

Malone kept his gun aimed at him and said, "The fuck do I care you kill her? Just another nigger baby to me."

When the guy blinked, Malone put one through his head.

The mother ran forward and grabbed her little girl. Held her tight against her chest.

It was the first guy Malone ever killed.

A clean shooting, no trouble with the shooting board, although Malone had to ride a desk until it was cleared and had to go see the departmental shrink to find out if he had PTSD or something, which it turned out he didn't.

Only trouble was, the store clerk got the whole thing on his cell-phone camera and the *Daily News* ran with the headline JUST ANOTHER N****R BABY TO ME with a photo of Malone with the log line "Hero Cop a Racist."

Malone got called into a meeting with his then captain, IAB and a PR flack from One Police, who asked, "'Nigger baby'?"

"I had to be sure he believed me."

"You couldn't have chosen different words?" the flack asked.

"I didn't have a speechwriter with me," Malone said.

"We'd like to put you up for a Medal of Valor," said his captain, "but . . ."

"I wasn't going to put in for one."

To his credit, the IAB guy said, "May I point out that Sergeant Malone *saved* an African American life?"

"What if he'd missed?" the PR flack asked.

"I didn't," Malone said.

Truth was, though, he'd thought the same thing. Didn't tell it to the shrink, but he had nightmares about missing the skel and hitting the little girl.

Still does.

Shit, he even has nightmares about hitting the skel.

The clip ran on YouTube and a local rap group cut a song called "Just Another Nigger Baby," which got a few hundred thousand hits. But on the plus side, the little girl's mother came to the house with a pan of her special jalapeño cornbread and a handwritten thank-you card and sought Malone out.

He still has the card.

Now he crosses St. Nicholas and Convent and walks down 127th until it merges where 126th takes a northwest angle. He crosses Amsterdam and walks past Amsterdam Liquor Mart, which knows him well, Antioch Baptist Church, which doesn't, past St. Mary's Center and the Two-Six House and into the old building that now houses the Manhattan North Special Task Force.

Or, as it's known on the street, "Da Force."

CHAPTER 2

The Manhattan North Special Task Force was half Malone's idea to begin with.

A lot of bureaucratic verbiage describes their mission, but Malone and every other cop on Da Force know exactly what their "special task" is—

Hold the line.

Big Monty put it somewhat differently. "We're landscapers. Our job is to keep the jungle from growing back."

"The fuck are you talking about?" Russo asked.

"The old urban jungle that was Manhattan North has been mostly cut down," Monty said, "to make room for a cultivated, commercial Garden of Eden. But there are still patches of jungle—to wit, the projects. Our job is to keep the jungle from reclaiming paradise."

Malone knows the equation—real estate prices rise as crime falls—but he could give a shit about that.

His concern was the violence.

When Malone first came on the Job, the "Giuliani Miracle" had transformed the city. Police commissioners Ray Kelly and Bill Bratton had used "broken windows" theory and CompStat technology to reduce street crime to an almost negligible level.

Nine/eleven changed the department's focus from anticrime to antiterrorism, but street violence continued to fall, the murder rate plummeted and the Upper Manhattan "ghetto" neighborhoods of Harlem, Washington Heights and Inwood started to revive.

The crack epidemic had largely reached its tragic Darwinian

conclusion, but the problems of poverty and unemployment—drug addiction, alcoholism, domestic violence and gangs—hadn't gone away.

To Malone, it was like there were two neighborhoods, two cultures grouped around their respective castles—the shiny new condo towers and the old project high-rises. The difference was that the people in power were now literally invested.

Back in the day, Harlem was Harlem, and rich white people "just didn't go there" unless they were slumming or looking for a cheap thrill. The murder rate was high, muggings and armed robberies and all the violence that came with drugs was high, but as long as blacks were raping, robbing and murdering other blacks, who gave a fuck?

Well, Malone.

Other cops.

That's the bitter, brutal irony about police work.

That's the root of the love-hate relationship cops have with the community and the community with the police.

The cops see it every day and every night.

The hurt, the dead.

People forget that the cops see first the victims and *then* the perpetrators. From the baby some crack whore dropped into the bathtub to the kid beat into stupefaction by his mother's eighteenth live-in boyfriend, the old lady whose hip gets broken when a purse snatcher knocks her to the sidewalk, the fifteen-year-old wannabe dope slinger gunned down on the corner.

The cops feel for the vics and hate the perps, but they can't feel too much or they can't do their jobs and they can't hate too much or they'll become the perps. So they develop a shell, a "we hate everybody" attitude force field around themselves that everyone can feel from ten feet away.

You gotta have it, Malone knows, or this job kills you, physically or psychologically. Or both.

So you feel for the old lady victim, but hate the mutt who did it;

you sympathize with the storeowner who just got robbed, but despise the mope who robbed him; you feel bad for the black kid who got shot, but hate the nigger who shot him.

The real problem, Malone thinks, is when you start hating the victim, too. And you do—it just wears you down. Their pain becomes yours, the responsibility for their suffering weighs on your shoulders—you didn't do enough to protect them, you were in the wrong place, you didn't catch the perp earlier.

You start blaming yourself and/or you start blaming the victim—why are they so vulnerable, why so weak, why do they live in those conditions, why do they join gangs, sling drugs, why do they have to shoot each other over nothing . . . why are they such fucking animals?

But Malone still fucking cares.

Doesn't want to.

But does.

Tenelli ain't happy.

"Why does this dick have to bring us in Christmas Eve?" she asks Malone as he comes through the doors.

"I think you answered your own question," Malone says.

Captain Sykes is a dick.

Speaking of dicks, the prevailing opinion is that Janice Tenelli has the biggest one on Da Force. Malone has watched the detective repeatedly kick a heavy bag right where the nuts would be and it made his own package shrivel.

Or expand. Tenelli has a mane of thick black hair, a won't-quit rack and a face straight out of an Italian movie. Every guy on Da Force would like to have sex with her, but she's made it very clear she don't shit where she eats.

All evidence to the contrary, Russo insists on insisting, to Tenelli's face, that the married mother of two is a lesbian.

"Because I won't fuck you?" she asked.

"Because it's my dearest-held fantasy," Russo said. "You and Flynn."

"Flynn *is* a lesbian."

"I know."

"Knock yourself out," Tenelli said, jerking her wrist.

"I haven't wrapped a single gift," she tells Malone now, "the in-laws are coming over tomorrow, I have to sit and listen to this guy make speeches? Come on, straighten him out, Denny."

She knows what they all know—Malone was here before Sykes came and he'll be here after he leaves. The joke is that Malone would take the lieutenant's exam except he couldn't take the pay cut.

"Sit and listen to his speech," Malone says, "then go home and make . . . What are you making?"

"I dunno, Jack does all the cooking," she says. "Prime rib, I think. You doing your annual Turkey Run this year?"

"Hence the term 'annual.'"

"Right."

They're filing into the briefing room when Malone spots Kevin Callahan out of the corner of his eye. The undercover—tall, skinny, long red hair and beard—looks baked out of his mind.

Cops, undercover or otherwise, aren't supposed to do dope, but how else are they supposed to make buys and not get made? So sometimes it turns into a habit. A lot of guys come off undercover straight into rehab and their careers are fucked.

Occupational hazard.

Malone walks over, grabs Callahan by the elbow and walks him out the door. "Sykes sees you, he'll piss-test you straightaway."

"I have to log in."

"I'll sign you out on a surveillance," Malone says. "You get asked, you were up at the Ville for me."

The Manhattan North Special Task Force house is conveniently located between two projects—Manhattanville, just across the street uptown, and Grant, across 125th Street below them.

Come the revolution, Malone thinks, we're surrounded.

"Thanks, Denny."

"Why are you still standing here?" Malone asks. "Get your ass up to the Ville. And, Callahan, you mess up again, I'll piss you myself."

He goes back in and takes a folding metal chair in the briefing room next to Russo.

Big Monty turns around in his chair and looks at them. He holds a steaming cup of tea, which he manages to sip even though his unlit cigar is jammed in the corner of his mouth. "I just want to enter my official protest regarding this afternoon's activities."

"Noted," Malone says.

Monty turns back around.

Russo grins. "He ain't happy."

He is *un*happy, Malone thinks, happily. It's good to shake the otherwise unflappable Big Man up every once in a while.

Keeps him fresh.

Raf Torres walks in with his team—Gallina, Ortiz and Tenelli. Malone doesn't like that Tenelli is with Torres, because he likes Tenelli and thinks that Torres is a piece of shit. He's a big mother-fucker, Torres, but to Malone he looks like a big, brown, pock-marked Puerto Rican toad.

Torres nods to Malone. It somehow manages to be a gesture of acknowledgment, respect and challenge at the same time.

Sykes walks in and stands behind the lectern like a professor. He's young for a captain, but then again he has rabbis at the Puzzle Palace, brass looking out for his interests.

And he's black.

Malone knows that Sykes has been tagged as the next big thing, and that the Manhattan North Special Task Force is a high-profile box for him to tick on his way up.

To Malone he looks like some precocious Republican Senate candidate—very crisp, very clean, his hair cut short. He sure as hell don't have any tattoos, unless there's an arrow pointing up his ass-hole reading *This Way to My Brain*.

That isn't fair, Malone thinks, checking himself. The guy's record is solid, he did some real police work on Major Crimes in Queens and then became the Job's designated precinct janitor—he cleaned up the Tenth and the Seven-Six, real dumping grounds, and now they've moved him here.

To check another box on his sheet? Malone wonders.

Or to clean us up?

In either case, Sykes brought that Queens attitude with him.

Squared away, by the book.

A Queens Marine.

Sykes's first day on command he had the whole Task Force— fifty-four detectives, undercovers, anticrime guys and uniforms— come in, sat them down and made a speech.

"I know I'm looking at the elite," Sykes said. "The best of the best. I also know I'm looking at a few dirty cops. You know who you are. Soon, *I'll* know who you are. And hear this—I catch any of you taking as much as a free coffee or a sandwich, I'll have your shield and gun, I'll have your pension. Now get out, go do your jobs."

He didn't make any friends, but he made it clear that he wasn't there to make friends. And Sykes had also alienated his people by taking a vocal stand against "police brutality," warning them he wouldn't tolerate intimidation, beatings, profiling or stop and frisk.

How the fuck does he think we maintain even a semblance of control? Malone thinks, looking at the man now.

The captain holds up a copy of the *New York Times*.

"'White Christmas,'" Sykes reads. "'Heroin Floods the City on the Holidays.' Mark Rubenstein in the *New York Times*. And not just one article, he's doing a series. The *New York Times,* gentlemen."

He pauses to let that sink in.

It doesn't.

Most cops don't read the *Times*. They read the *Daily News* and the *Post,* mostly for the sports news or the T&A on Page Six. A few read the *Wall Street Journal* to keep up on their portfolios. The *Times* is strictly for the suits at One Police and the hacks in the mayor's office.

But the *Times* says there's a "heroin epidemic," Malone thinks.

Which is only an epidemic, of course, because now white people are dying.

Whites started to get opium-based pills from their physicians—oxycodone, Vicodin, that shit. But it was expensive and doctors were reluctant to prescribe too much for exactly the fear of addiction. So the white folks went to the open market and the pills became a street drug. It was all very nice and civilized until the Sinaloa Cartel down in Mexico made a corporate decision that it could undersell the big American pharmaceutical companies by raising production of its heroin, thereby reducing price.

As an incentive, they also increased its potency.

The addicted white Americans found that Mexican "cinnamon" heroin was cheaper and stronger than the pills and started shooting it into their veins and overdosing.

Malone literally saw it happening.

He and his team busted more bridge-and-tunnel junkies, suburban housewives and Upper East Side madonnas than they could count. More and more of the bodies they'd find slumped dead in alleys were Caucasian.

Which, according to the media, is a tragedy.

Even congressmen and senators pulled their noses out of their donors' ass cracks long enough to notice the new epidemic and demand that "something has to be done about it."

"I want you out there making heroin arrests," Sykes says. "Our numbers on crack cocaine are satisfactory, but our numbers on heroin are subpar."

The suits love their numbers, Malone thinks. This new "management" breed of cops are like the sabermetrics baseball people—they believe the numbers say it all. And when the numbers don't say what they want them to, they massage them like Koreans on Eighth Avenue until they get a happy ending.

You want to look good? Violent crime is down.

You need more funding? It's up.

You need arrests? Send your people out to make a bunch of bullshit busts that will never get convictions. You don't care—convictions are the DA's problem—you just want the arrest numbers.

You want to prove drugs are down in your sector? Send your guys on "search and avoid" missions where there aren't any drugs.

That's half the scam. The other way to manipulate the numbers is to let officers know they should downgrade charges from felonies to misdemeanors. So you call a straight-up robbery a "petit larceny," a burglary becomes "lost property," a rape a "sexual assault."

Boom—crime is down.

Moneyball.

"There's a heroin epidemic," Sykes says, "and we're on the front lines."

They must have really cracked Inspector McGivern's nuts at the CompStat meeting, Malone thinks, and he passed the pain along to Sykes.

So he hands it off to us.

And we'll pass it down to a bunch of low-level dealers, addicts who sell so they can score, and fill the house with a bunch of arrests so Central Booking will flow with puke from junkies jonesing, and bog down the court dockets with quivering losers pleading out and then going back to jail to score more smack. Come out still addicted, and start the whole cycle all over again.

But we'll make par.

The suits at One Police can say as much as they want that there are no quotas, but every guy on the Job knows there are. Back in the "broken windows" days, they were writing summonses for everything—loitering, littering, jumping a subway stile, double-parking. The theory was if you didn't come down on the small stuff, people would figure it was okay to do the big stuff.

So they were out there writing a lot of bullshit C-summonses, which forced a lot of poor people to take time off work they couldn't afford to go to court to pay fines they couldn't pay. Some just skipped their court days and got "no-show" warrants, so their misdemeanors escalated to felonies and they were looking at jail time for tossing a gum wrapper on the sidewalk.

It provoked a lot of anger toward the police.

Then there were the 250s.

The stop and frisks.

Which basically meant that if you saw a young black kid on the street, you stopped him and shook him down. It caused a lot of resentment, too, and got a lot of negative media, so we don't do that anymore, either.

Except we do.

Now the quota that isn't is heroin.

"Cooperation," Sykes is saying, "and coordination are what makes us a task force and not just separate entities officed in the same space. So let's work together, gentlemen, and get this thing done."

Rah fuckin' rah, Malone thinks.

Sykes probably doesn't realize that he's just given his people contradictory instructions—work their sources and make heroin arrests—doesn't even get that you work your sources by popping them with drugs and then *not* arresting them.

They give you information, you give them a pass.

That's the way it works.

What's he think, a dealer is going to talk to you out of the goodness of his heart, which he doesn't have anyway? To be a good citizen? A dealer talks to you for money or drugs, to skate on a charge or to fuck a rival dealer. Or maybe, *maybe,* because someone is fucking his bitch.

That's it.

The guys on Da Force don't look too much like cops. In fact, Malone thinks as he looks around, they look more like criminals.

The undercovers look like junkies or dope slingers—hoodies, baggy pants or filthy jeans, sneakers. Malone's personal favorite, a black kid called Babyface, hides under a thick hood and sucks on a big pacifier as he looks up at Sykes, knowing the boss isn't going to say shit about it because Babyface brings home the bacon.

The plainclothes guys are urban pirates. They still have tin shields—not gold—under their black leather jackets, navy peacoats and down vests. Their jeans are clean but not creased, and they prefer Chelsea boots to tennis shoes.

Except "Cowboy" Bob Bartlett, who wears shitkicker boots with skinny toes, "the better to go up a black ass." Bartlett's never been farther west than Jersey City, but he affects a redneck drawl and aggravates the shit out of Malone by playing country-western "music" in the locker room.

The "uniforms" in their bags don't look like your run-of-the-mill cops either. It ain't what they wear, it's in their faces. They're badasses, with the smirks as pinned on as the badges on their chests. These boys are always ready to go, ready to dance, just for the fuck of it.

Even the women have attitudes. There ain't many of them on Da Force, but the ones who are take no prisoners. You got Tenelli and then there's Emma Flynn, a hard-drinking (Irish, go figure) party girl with the sexual voracity of a Roman empress. And they're all tough, with a healthy hatred in their hearts.

The detectives, though, the gold shields like Malone, Russo, Montague, Torres, Gallina, Ortiz, Tenelli, they're in a different league altogether, "the best of the best," decorated veterans with scores of major arrests under their belts.

The Task Force detectives aren't uniforms or plainclothes or undercovers.

They're kings.

Their kingdoms aren't fields and castles but city blocks and project towers. Tony Upper West Side neighborhoods and Harlem projects. They rule Broadway and West End, Amsterdam, Lenox, St. Nicholas and Adam Clayton Powell. Central Park and Riverside where Jamaican nannies push yuppies' kids in strollers and start-up entrepreneurs jog, and trash-strewn playgrounds where the gangbangers ball and sling dope.

We'd *better* rule, Malone thinks, with a strong hand, because our subjects are blacks and whites, Puerto Ricans, Dominicans, Haitians, Jamaicans, Italians, Irish, Jews, Chinese, Vietnamese, Koreans, who all hate each other and who, in the absence of kings, would kill each other more than they already do.

We rule over gangs—Crips and Bloods and Trinitarios and Latin Lords. Dominicans Don't Play, Broad Day Shooters, Gun Clappin' Goonies, Goons on Deck (seems to be a theme), From Da Zoo, Money Stackin' High, Mac Baller Brims. Folk Nation, Insane Gangster Crips, Addicted to Cash, Hot Boys, Get Money Boys.

Then there's the Italians—the Genovese family, the Lucheses, the Gambinos, the Ciminos—all of which would get *totally* out of control if they didn't know there were kings out there who would cut off their heads.

We rule Da Force, too. Sykes thinks he does, or at least pretends to think he does, but it's the detective kings who really call the shots. The undercovers are our spies, the uniforms our foot soldiers, the plainclothes our knights.

And we didn't become kings because our daddies were—we took our crowns the hard way, like the old warriors who fought their way to the throne with nicked swords and dented armor and wounds and scars. We started on these streets with guns and nightsticks and fists and nerve and guts and brains and balls. We came up through our hard-won street knowledge, our earned respect, our victories and even our defeats. We earned our reps as tough, strong, ruthless and fair rulers, administering rough justice with tempered mercy.

That's what a king does.

He hands down justice.

Malone knows it's important they look the part. Subjects expect their kings to look tight, to look sharp, to wear a little money on their backs and their feet, a little style. Take Montague, for instance. Big Monty dresses like an Ivy League professor—tweedy jackets, vests, knit ties—and the trilby with a small red feather in the band. It goes against the stereotype and it's scary because the skels don't know what to make of him, and when he gets them in the room, they think they're being interrogated by a genius.

Which Monty probably is.

Malone has seen him go into Morningside Park where the old black men play chess, contest five boards at a time and win every one of them.

Then give back the money he just took from them.

Which is also genius.

Russo, he's old school. Sports a long red-brown leather overcoat, a 1980s throwback that he wears well. Then again, Russo wears everything well, he's a sharp dresser. The retro overcoat, custom-tailored Italian suits, monogrammed shirts, Magli shoes.

A haircut every Friday, a shave twice a day.

Mobster chic, Russo's ironic comment on the wiseguys he grew up with and never wanted to be. He went the other way with it; as a cop, he likes to joke, he's the "white sheep of the family."

Malone always wears black.

His trademark.

All Da Force detectives are kings, but Malone—with no disrespect intended to our Lord and Savior—is the King of Kings.

Manhattan North is the Kingdom of Malone.

Like with any king, his subjects love him and fear him, revere him and loathe him, praise him and revile him. He has his loyalists and rivals, his sycophants and critics, his jesters and advisers, but he has no real friends.

Except his partners.

Russo and Monty.

His brother kings.

He would die for them.

"Malone? If you have a moment for me?"

It's Sykes.

CHAPTER 3

A s I'm sure you know," Sykes says in his office, "just about every-thing I said in there was bullshit."

"Yes, sir," Malone says. "I was just wondering if *you* knew it."

Sykes's tight smile gets tighter, which Malone didn't think was possible.

The captain thinks that Malone is arrogant.

Malone doesn't argue with that.

A cop on these streets, he thinks, you'd better be arrogant. There are people up here, they see you don't think you're the shit, they will kill you. They'll cap you and fuck you in the entry wounds. Let *Sykes* go out on the streets, let him make the busts, go through the doors.

Sykes doesn't like it, but he doesn't like a lot about Detective Sergeant Dennis Malone—his sense of humor, his tat sleeves, his encyclopedic knowledge of hip-hop lyrics. He especially doesn't like Malone's attitude, which is basically that Manhattan North is his kingdom and his captain is just a tourist.

Fuck him, Malone thinks.

There's nothing Sykes can do because last July Malone and his team made the largest heroin bust in the history of New York City. They hit Diego Pena, the Dominican kingpin, for fifty kilos, enough to supply a fix for every man, woman and child in the city.

They also seized close to two million in cash.

The suits at One Police Plaza weren't thrilled that Malone and his team did the whole investigation on their own and didn't bring anyone else in. Narcotics was furious, DEA was pissed, too. But fuck 'em all, Malone thinks.

The media loved it.

The *Daily News* and the *Post* had full-color screaming headlines, every TV station led with it. Even the *Times* put a story in the Metro section.

So the suits had to grin and bear it.

Posed with the stacks of heroin.

The media also lifted its dress over its head in September when the Task Force made a major raid into the Grant and Manhattanville projects and busted over a hundred gangbangers from the 3Staccs, the Money Avenue Crew and the Make It Happen Boys, the latter of which youth-at-risk capped an eighteen-year-old star woman basketball player in retaliation for one of their own getting shot. She was on her knees in a stairwell begging for her life, pleading for the chance to go to that college where she had a full ride, but she didn't get it.

They left her on the landing, her blood dripping down the steps like a little crimson waterfall.

The papers were full of pictures of Malone and his team and the rest of the Task Force hauling her killers out of the projects and toward life without parole in Attica, known in the street as the Terror Dome.

So my team, Malone thinks, brings in three-quarters of the quality arrests in "your command"—serious arrests with serious weight that result in convictions with serious time. It doesn't show up in your numbers, but you know goddamn well that my team has made assists in just about every drug-related homicide arrest—resulting in conviction—not to mention muggings, burglaries, robberies, domestic assaults and rapes committed by junkies and dealers.

I've taken more real bad guys off the street than cancer, and it's my team that keeps the lid on this shithole, keeps it from exploding, and you know it.

So even though you're threatened by me, even though you know it's really me and not you that runs the Task Force, you ain't gonna reassign me because you need me to make you look good.

And you know that, too.

You may not like your best player, but you don't trade him. He puts points on the board.

Sykes can't touch him.

Now the captain says, "That was a dog-and-pony show to satisfy the suits. Heroin makes headlines, we have to respond."

The fact is that heroin use in the black community is down, not up, Malone knows. The retail sale of heroin by black gangs is down, not up; in fact, the young bangers are diversifying into cell-phone theft and cybercrime—identity theft and credit card fraud.

Any cop in Brooklyn, the Bronx and Manhattan North knows that the violence isn't around heroin, it's about weed. The corner boys are fighting over who gets to sell peaceful marijuana, and where they get to sell it.

"If we can take down the heroin mills," Sykes says, "by all means, let's take them down. But what I really care about is the guns. What I really care about is stopping these young idiots from killing themselves and other people on my streets."

Guns and dope are the soup and sandwich of American crime. As much as the Job is obsessed with heroin, it's more obsessed with getting guns off the streets. And for good reason—it's the cops who have to deal with the murders, the wounded, cops who have to tell the families, work with them, try to get them some justice.

And, of course, it's guns on the street that kill cops.

The NRA assholes will tell you that "guns don't kill people, people do." Yeah, Malone thinks, people with guns.

Sure, you have stabbings, you have fatal beatings, but without guns the homicide figures would be negligible. And most of the congressional whores who go to their NRA meeting smelling nice and wearing something frilly have never seen a gunshot homicide or even a person who's been shot.

Cops have. Cops do.

It ain't pretty. It don't look or sound (or smell) anything like in the movies. These asshats who think that the answer is to arm everyone so they could, for instance, shoot it out in a dark theater have never had a gun pointed at them and would shit themselves if they did.

They say it's all about the Second Amendment and individual rights but what it's about is the money. The gun manufacturers, who make up the vast bulk of the NRA's funding, want to sell guns and make their cash.

End of motherfucking story.

New York City has the strictest gun laws in the country but that doesn't make any difference because all the guns come in from the outside, up the "Iron Pipeline." Dealers make straw purchases in states with weak gun laws—Texas, Arizona, Alabama, the Carolinas—and then bring them up I-95 to the cities of the Northeast and New England.

The goobers love to talk about crime in the big cities, Malone thinks, but either don't know or don't care that the guns come from their states.

To date, at least four New York cops have been killed with guns that came up the Iron Pipeline.

Not to mention the corner boys and the bystanders.

The mayor's office, the department, everyone is desperate to get guns off the streets. The Job is even buying them back—a no-questions-asked cash-and-gift-card offer: you bring in your guns, we smile at you and give you $200 bank cards for handguns and assault rifles and $25 for rifles, shotguns and BB guns.

The last buyback, at the church over on 129th and Adam Clayton Powell, netted forty-eight revolvers, seventeen semiautomatic pistols, three rifles, a shotgun and an AR-15.

Malone has no problem with it. Guns off the streets are guns off the streets, and guns off the streets help a cop achieve job number one—go home at end of shift. One of the old hairbags taught him that when he first came on the Job—your first job is to go home at end of shift.

Now Sykes asks, "Where are we with DeVon Carter?"

DeVon Carter is the drug lord of Manhattan North, a.k.a. the Soul Survivor, the latest in a line of Harlem kingpins that came down from Bumpy Johnson, Frank Lucas and Nicky Barnes.

He makes most of his money through the heroin mills that are really distribution centers, shipping to New England, the small towns up the Hudson, or down to Philly, Baltimore and Washington.

Think Amazon for smack.

He's smart, he's strategic and he's insulated himself from the day-to-day operations. He never goes near the drugs or the sales, and all his communications are filtered through a handful of subordinates who go talk to him personally, never over the phone, text or e-mail.

Da Force hasn't been able to get a CI inside Carter's operation because the Soul Survivor only lets old friends and close family into his inner circle. And if they get busted, they choose doing the time over flipping on him, because doing the time means they're still alive.

It's frustrating—the Task Force could bust as many street-level dealers as they want. The undercovers do numerous buy-and-bust ops, but it's a revolving door, a few gangbangers go to Rikers and there are others in line to take their place slinging the dope.

But so far, Carter has been untouchable.

"We have CIs out on the street," Malone says, "sometime we get a twenty on him, but so what? Without a wiretap, we're fucked."

Carter owns or has pieces of a dozen clubs, bodegas, apartment buildings, boats and God knows what else and he spreads his meetings out. If they could get a wire into one of those places, they might get enough to move on him.

It's the classic vicious circle. Without probable cause, you can't get a warrant, but without the warrant, you can't get probable cause.

Malone doesn't bother saying this. Sykes already knows.

"Intel," Sykes says, "indicates that Carter is negotiating a major firearms purchase. Serious weapons—assault rifles, automatic pistols, even rocket launchers."

"Where are you getting this?"

"Despite your opinion," Sykes says, "you're not the only one who does police work out of this building. If Carter is looking for that kind of weaponry, it means he's going to war against the Dominicans."

"I agree."

"Good," Sykes says. "I don't want that war fought on my turf. I don't want to see that level of bloodshed. I want that shipment stopped."

Yeah, Malone thinks, you want it stopped, but you want it stopped your way—"no cowboy bullshit, no illegal wires, no booming, no dropping your own dime." He's heard the whole speech before.

"I grew up in Brooklyn," Sykes says. "In the Marcy projects."

Malone knows the story—it's been in the papers, paraded on the Job's website: "From the projects to the precinct—black officer fights his way from the gangs to the upper echelon of the NYPD." How Sykes turned his life around, got a scholarship to Brown, came home to "make a difference."

Malone ain't about to burst into tears.

But it has to be tough, being a black cop in a high position. Everyone looks at you different—to the people in the precinct you ain't quite black, to the cops in the house you ain't quite blue. Malone wonders which Sykes is to himself, or if he even knows. So, it's gotta be tough, especially these days, all the racial shit going down.

"I know what you think of me," Sykes says. "Empty suit. Token black careerist. 'Move on and move up'?"

"Pretty much, we're being honest, sir."

"The suits want to make Manhattan North safe for white money," Sykes says. "I want to make it safe for black people. Is that honest enough for you?"

"Yeah, that'll do."

"I know you think you're protected by the Pena bust, your other heroics, by McGivern and the Irish-Italian Club downtown at One Police," Sykes says. "But let me tell you something, Malone; you have enemies down there just waiting for you to slip on the banana peel so they can walk all over you."

"And you're not."

"Right now I need you," Sykes says. "I need you and your team to keep DeVon Carter from turning my streets into a slaughterhouse. You do that for me, I'll, yes, move on and move up and leave you with your little kingdom here. You don't do that for me, you're just a white pain in my black ass and I will have you moved so far from Manhattan North you'll be wearing a fucking sombrero to work."

Try it, motherfucker, Malone thinks.

Try it, see what happens.

The fucked-up part, though, is they both want the same thing. They don't want those guns getting on the streets.

And they're *my* streets, Malone thinks, not yours.

He says, "I can stop that shipment. I don't know if I can stop that shipment by the book."

So how bad do you want them stopped, Captain Sykes?

He sits there and watches Sykes consider his own deal with the devil.

Then Sykes says, "I want reports, Sergeant. And everything you report to me had better be by the book. I want to know where you are and what you're doing there. Do we understand each other?"

Perfectly, Malone thinks.

We're all corrupt.

Just each in our own way.

And it's a peace offering—if this turns into a big bust, I bring you with me this time. You star in the movie, get your picture in the *Post*, a boost in your career. And no one gives a fuck about Manhattan North's numbers until you're up and out.

"Merry Christmas, Captain," Malone says.

"Merry Christmas, Malone."

CHAPTER 4

Malone started the Turkey Run, what, five years ago, when the Task Force came into being and he thought they needed a little positive PR in the neighborhood.

Everyone up here knows the detectives from Da Force anyway, and it doesn't hurt to spread a little love and goodwill toward men. You never know when some kid who ate turkey instead of going hungry on Christmas is going to decide to cut you a break, give you a tip.

It's a point of pride with Malone that the turkeys come out of his own pocket. Lou Savino and the wiseguys over on Pleasant Avenue would cheerfully donate turkeys that fell off the backs of trucks, but Malone knows the community would get wind of that right away. So he accepts a discount on the turkeys from a food wholesaler whose double-parked trucks don't get ticketed, but he pays the rest of the freight himself.

Shit, one decent bust more than makes up for it.

Malone doesn't kid himself that the same people who take his turkeys won't be dropping "airmail"—bottles, cans, dirty diapers—on him from the upper floors of the project buildings the day after tomorrow. One time someone dropped an entire air-conditioning unit from the nineteenth floor that missed Malone's head by about an inch.

Malone knows the Turkey Run is just a truce.

Now he goes down to the locker room where Big Monty is getting into the Santa costume.

Malone laughs. "You look good."

Well, actually ridiculous. A big black man, normally reserved and dignified, with a red Santa cap and a big beard. "A black Santa?"

"Diversity," Malone says. "I read it on the Job's website."

"Anyway," Russo says to Montague, "you're not Santa Claus, you're *Crack* Claus. Who would be black up here. And you got the belly."

Montague says, "Ain't my fault every time I fuck your wife she makes me a sandwich."

Russo laughs. "More than she makes me."

Used to be it was Billy O played Santa, even though he was skinnier than a rail. He freakin' loved it, shoving a pillow under the suit, joking with the kids, handing out the turkeys. Now it's fallen on Monty, even though he's black.

Monty adjusts the beard and looks at Malone. "You know they *sell* those turkeys. We might as well just cut out the middleman and hand them crack."

Malone knows every turkey ain't gonna make it to the table, that a lot of them will go straight to the pipe or into arms or up noses. Those turkeys will go to the dealers, who'll sell them to the bodegas, who'll put them on the shelves and make a profit. But most of the turkeys will make it home, and life is a numbers game. Some kids will get Christmas dinner because of his turkeys, others won't.

Has to be good enough.

DeVon Carter doesn't think it's even close to good enough. Carter, he laughed at Malone's Christmas Turkey Run.

This was a month or so ago.

Malone, Russo and Monty were having lunch at Sylvia's, each of them digging into some stewed turkey wings, when Monty looked up and said, "Guess who's here."

Malone glanced over at the bar and saw DeVon Carter.

Russo said, "You want to get the check and go?"

"No reason to be unfriendly," Malone said. "I think I'll slide over and say hello."

As Malone got up, two of Carter's guys moved to step in the way, but Carter waved them off. Malone took the stool next to Carter and said, "DeVon Carter, Denny Malone."

"I know who you are," Carter said. "Is there a problem?"

"Not unless you have one," Malone said. "I just thought, hey, we're in the same place, we might as well meet in person."

Carter looked good, like he always does. Gray cashmere Brioni turtleneck sweater, charcoal Ralph Lauren slacks, large Gucci eyeglass frames.

It got a little quiet in the place. There was the biggest drug slinger in Harlem and the cop trying to bust him sitting down with each other. Carter said, "As a matter of fact, we were just laughing about you."

"Yeah? What's so funny about me?"

"Your 'Turkey Run,'" Carter said. "You give the people drumsticks. I give them money and dope. Who do you think is going to win that one?"

"The real question," Malone said, "is who's going to win between you and the Domos?"

The Pena bust slowed the Dominicans down a little, but it was just a setback. Some of Carter's gangs were starting to look at the Dominicans as an option. They're afraid they're outnumbered and outgunned and are going to lose the marijuana business.

So Carter is a polydrug merchandiser—he has to be. In addition to the smack that mostly leaves the city or at least goes to a mostly white customer base, he markets coke and marijuana as well, because to run his moneymaking heroin business he needs troops. He needs security, mules, communications people—he needs the gangs.

The gangs have to make money, they have to eat.

Carter doesn't have a choice but to let "his" gangs deal weed—he has to, or the Dominicans will and they'll take his business. They'll either buy Carter's gangs outright or just wipe them off the map, because without the weed money, the gangs couldn't buy guns and they'd be helpless.

His pyramid would crumble from the bottom.

Malone wouldn't care that much about the weed slinging except that 70 percent of the murders in Manhattan North are drug related.

So you have Latino gangs fighting each other, you have black gangs fighting each other and, increasingly, you have black gangs fighting Latino gangs as the battle between their big-money heroin bosses escalates.

"You took Pena off the count for me," Carter said.

"And not as much as a muffin basket."

"I heard you were well compensated."

It sent a jolt up Malone's spine but he didn't flinch. "Every time there's a big bust, the 'community' says the cops ripped some off the top."

"That's because every time they do."

"Here's what you don't understand," Malone said. "Young black men used to pick cotton—now you *are* the cotton. You're the raw product that gets fed into the machine, thousands of you every day."

"The prison-industrial complex," Carter said. "I pay your salary."

"Don't think I'm not grateful," Malone said. "But if it's not you, it would be someone else. Why do you think they call you the 'Soul Survivor'? Because you're black and you're isolated and you're the last of your kind. Used to be, white politicians would come kiss your ass looking for your votes. You don't see that so much anymore because they don't need you. They're sucking up to Latinos, Asians, the dotheads. Fuck, even the Muslims have more swag than you do. You're on your way out."

Carter smiled. "If I had a nickel for every time I heard that . . ."

"You been to Pleasant Avenue lately?" Malone asked. "It's *Chinese.* Inwood and the Heights? More Latinos every day. Your people in the Ville and Grant are starting to buy from the Domos; you're even going to lose the Nickel soon. The Domos, the Mexicans, the PRs—they speak the same language, eat the same food, listen to the same music. They'll sell to you, but partner with you? Forget it. The Mexicans give the local spics a wholesale price they don't give you, and you just can't compete, because a junkie ain't got no loyalty to nothin' but his arm."

"You betting on the Domos?" Carter asked.

"I'm betting on me," Malone said. "You know why? Because the machine keeps grinding."

Later that day a basket of muffins arrived at Manhattan North for Malone with a note saying that it cost $49.95, a nickel under the legal cost of a gift that a cop can accept.

Captain Sykes was not amused.

Now Malone rolls up Lenox, sitting in the back of a van with the doors open as Monty shouts, "Ho, ho, ho!," while Malone tosses out turkeys with the benediction, "May Da Force be with you!"

The unit's unofficial motto.

Which Sykes also don't like because he thinks it's "frivolous." What the captain don't understand is that being a cop up here is part show business. It's not like they're undercovers—they work with UCs, but undercovers don't make busts.

We make busts, Malone thinks, and some of them get in the papers with our smiling faces and what Sykes don't get is that we have to have a presence here. An image. And the image has to be that Da Force is *with* you, not against you.

Unless you're slinging dope, assaulting people, raping women, doing drive-bys. Then Da Force is coming for your ass, and we're going to get it.

One way or the other.

And the people up here know us anyway.

Yelling back, "Fuck Da Force," "Give me my motherfucking turkey, motherfuckers," "You pigs, why you ain't giving out pork?" Malone just laughs, it's just busting balls, and most of the people don't say anything or just a quiet "Thank you." Because most of the people here are good people, trying to make a living, raise their kids, like most everyone else.

Like Montague.

The big man carries too much on his shoulders, Malone thinks, living in the Savoy Apartments with a wife and three sons, the oldest almost that age when you keep him or lose him to the streets—and more and more Montague worries about spending too much time away from his boys. Like tonight, he wants to be home with his family on Christmas Eve, but instead he's out making their college money, handling his business as a father.

Best thing a man can do for his kids—handle his motherfucking business.

And they're good boys, Montague's boys, Malone thinks. Smart, polite, respectful.

Malone is their "Uncle Denny."

And their named legal guardian. Him and Sheila are the guardians to Monty's kids *and* Russo's kids, should something happen. If the Montagues and the Russos go out to dinner together, like they sometimes do, Malone jokes they shouldn't ride in the same car so he doesn't inherit six more kids.

Phil and Donna Russo are the named guardians for the Malone children. Denny and Sheila go down in a plane crash or something—an increasingly unlikely scenario—John and Caitlin go live with the Russos.

It isn't that Malone don't trust Montague—Monty might be the best father he's ever seen and the kids love him—but Phil is his brother. Another Staten Island boy, he's not only Malone's partner, he's his best friend. They grew up together, went through the Academy together. The slick guinea has saved Malone's life more times than he can count and Malone has returned the favor.

He'd take a bullet for Russo.

For Monty, too.

Now a little kid, maybe eight, is giving Monty a hard time. "Santa don't smoke no motherfuckin' cigar."

"This one does. And watch your mouth."

"How come?"

"You want a turkey or not?" Monty asks. "Quit busting balls."

"Santa don't say 'balls.'"

"Let Santa be, take your turkey." The Reverend Cornelius Hampton walks up to the van and the crowd parts for him like the Red Sea he's always preaching about in his "let my people go" sermons.

Malone looks at the famous face, the conked silver hair, the placid expression. Hampton is a community activist, a civil rights leader, a frequent guest on television talk shows, CNN and MSNBC.

Reverend Hampton has never seen a camera he didn't like, Malone thinks. Hampton gets more airtime than Judge Judy.

Monty hands him a turkey. "For the church, Reverend."

"Not *that* turkey," Malone says. "This one."

He reaches back and selects a bird, hands it to Hampton. "It's fatter."

Heavier, too, with the stuffing.

Twenty large in cash stuck up the turkey's ass, this courtesy of Lou Savino, the Harlem capo for the Cimino family and the boys on Pleasant Avenue.

"Thank you, Sergeant Malone," Hampton says. "This will go to feed the poor and the homeless."

Yeah, Malone thinks, maybe some of it.

"Merry Christmas," Hampton says.

"Merry Christmas."

Malone spots Nasty Ass.

Junkie-bopping at the edge of the little parade, his long skinny neck tucked into the collar of the North Face down jacket Malone bought him so he don't freeze to death out in the streets.

Nasty Ass is one of Malone's CIs, a "criminal informant," his special snitch, although Malone's never filed a folder on him. A junkie and a small-time dealer, his info is usually good. Nasty Ass got his street name because he always smells like he has a round in the chamber. If you can, you want to talk to Nasty Ass in the open air.

Now he comes up to the back of the van, his thin frame shivering, because he's either cold or jonesing. Malone hands him a turkey, although where the hell Nasty is going to cook it is a mystery, because the man usually flops out in shooting galleries.

Nasty Ass says, "218 One-Eight-Four. About eleven."

"What's he doing there?" Malone asks.

"Gettin' his dick wet."

"You know this for sure."

"Dead ass. He told me hisself."

"This pans out, it's a payday for you," Malone says. "And find a fuckin' toilet, for Chrissakes, huh?"

"Merry Christmas," Nasty Ass says.

He walks away with the turkey. Maybe he can sell it, Malone thinks, score a fix-up shot.

A man on the sidewalk yells, "I don't want no cop turkey! Michael Bennett, he can't eat no fucking turkey, can he!?"

Well, that's true, Malone thinks.

That's the cold truth.

Then he sees Marcus Sayer.

The boy's face is swollen and purple, his bottom lip cut open as he asks for a turkey.

Marcus's mother, a fat lazy idiot, opens the door a crack and sees the gold shield.

"Let me in, Lavelle," Malone says. "I have a turkey for you."

He does, he has a turkey under his arm and eight-year-old Marcus by the hand.

She slides the chain lock off and opens the door. "Is he in trouble? Marcus, what you do?"

Malone nudges Marcus in front of him and steps inside. He sets the turkey on the kitchen counter, or what he can see of it under the empty bottles, ashtrays and general filth.

"Where's Dante?" Malone asks.

"Sleepin'."

Malone pulls up Marcus's jacket and plaid shirt and shows her the welts on his back. "Dante do this?"

"What Marcus tell you?"

"He didn't tell me nothin'," Malone says.

Dante comes out of the bedroom. Lavelle's newest man is brolic, has to go six seven, all of it muscle and mean. He's drunk now, his eyes yellow and bloodshot, and he looms over Malone. "What you want?"

"What did I tell you I was going to do if you beat this boy again?"

"You was going to break my wrist."

Malone has the nightstick out and twirls it like a baton, bringing it down on Dante's right wrist, snapping it like a Popsicle stick. Dante bellows and swings with his left. Malone ducks, goes low and brings the stick across Dante's shins. The man goes down like a felled tree.

"So there you go," Malone says.

"This is police brutality."

Malone steps on Dante's neck and uses his other foot to kick him up the ass, hard, three times. "You see Al Sharpton here? Television crews? Lavelle here holding up a cell phone? There ain't no police brutality if the cameras aren't running."

"The boy disrespected me," Dante groans. "I disciplined him."

Marcus stands there wide-eyed; he's never seen big Dante get jacked up before and he kind of likes it. Lavelle, she just knows she's in for another ass-kicking when the cop leaves.

Malone steps down harder. "I see him with bruises again, I see him with welts, I'm going to discipline *you*. I'm going to shove this stick up your ass and pull it out your mouth. Then Big Monty and me are going to set your feet in cement and dump you in Jamaica Bay. Now get out. You don't live here anymore."

"You can't tell me where I can live!"

"I just did." Malone lets his foot off Dante's neck. "Why you still laying there, bitch?"

Dante gets up, holds his broken wrist and grimaces in pain.

Malone sees his coat and tosses it to him.

"What about my shoes?" Dante asks. "They in the bedroom."

"You go barefoot," Malone says. "You walk barefoot in the snow to the E-room and tell them what happens to grown men who beat up little boys."

Dante stumbles out the door.

Malone knows everyone will be talking about it tonight. The word will get passed—maybe you beat little kids in Brooklyn, in Queens, but not in Manhattan North, not in the Kingdom of Malone.

He turns to Lavelle. "What's wrong with you?"

"Don't I need love, too?"

"Love your kid," Malone says. "I see this again, you go to jail, he goes in the system. Is that what you want?"

"No."

"Then straighten up." He takes a twenty from his pocket. "This ain't for Little Debbies. There's still time for you to go shopping, put something under the tree."

"Ain't got a tree."

"It's an expression."

Jesus Christ.

He squats down in front of Marcus. "Anybody hurts you, anybody threatens to hurt you—you come to me, to Monty, Russo, anyone on Da Force. Okay?"

Marcus nods.

Yeah, maybe, Malone thinks. Maybe there's a chance the kid don't grow up hating every cop.

Malone's no fool—he knows he isn't going to stop every child beating in Manhattan North or even most of them. Or most of any other crime. And it bothers him—it's his turf, his responsibility. Everything that happens in Manhattan North is on him. He knows that isn't realistic either, but it's the way he feels.

Everything that happens in the kingdom is on the king.

He finds Lou Savino at D'Amore over on 116th in what they used to call Spanish Harlem.

Before that it was Italian Harlem.

Now it's on the way to becoming Asian Harlem.

Malone edges his way back to the bar.

Savino is a capo in the Cimino family with a crew based on the old Pleasant Avenue turf. They're into construction rackets, unions, shylocking, gambling—the usual mob shit—but Malone knows Lou also slings dope.

But not in Manhattan North.

Malone has assured him that if any of his shit ever shows up in the hood, all bets are off—it will blow back on his other businesses. It's pretty much always been the police deal with the mob—the wiseguys wanted to run hookers, to run gambling—card games, backroom casinos, the numbers racket before the state took it over, called it the lottery and made it a civic virtue—they gave a monthly envelope to the cops.

It was called the "pad."

Usually one cop from every precinct was the bagman—he'd collect the payoff and distribute it out to his fellow officers. The patrolmen would kick up to the sergeants, the sergeants to the lieutenants, the lieutenants to the captains, the captains to the inspectors, the inspectors to the chiefs.

Everyone got a taste.

And most everybody considered it "clean money."

Cops in those days (shit, Malone thinks, cops in these days) made a distinction between "clean money" and "dirty money." Clean money was mostly from gambling; dirty money was from drugs and violent crimes—the rare occasions when a wiseguy would try to buy off a murder, an armed robbery, a rape or a violent assault. While almost every cop would take clean money, it was the rare one who took money that had drugs or blood on it.

Even the wiseguys knew the difference and accepted the fact that the same cop who'd take gambling money on Tuesday would arrest the same gangster on Thursday for dealing smack or committing a murder.

Everyone knew the rules.

Lou Savino is one of those mob guys who thinks he's at a wedding and doesn't realize it's actually a wake.

He prays at the altar of dead false gods.

Tries to hold up an image of what he thinks used to be but in fact didn't exist except maybe in the movies. The fuckin' guy wants so bad to be something that never was, even the ghost image of which is now fading into black.

The guys of Savino's generation liked what they saw in the movies and wanted to be *that*. So Lou ain't trying to be Lefty Ruggiero, he's trying to be Al Pacino being Lefty Ruggiero. He ain't trying to be Tommy DeSimone, he's going for Joe Pesci being Tommy DeSimone, not being Jake Amari but James Gandolfini.

Those were good shows, Malone thinks, but Jesus, Lou, they were *shows*. But people point to the spot a couple of blocks away from here where Sonny Corleone beat up Carlo Rizzi with a trash can lid like it really happened, not to the spot where Francis Ford Coppola filmed James Caan pretending to beat up Gianni Russo.

Yeah well, Malone thinks, every institution survives on its own mythology, the NYPD included.

Savino wears a black silk shirt under a pearl-gray Armani jacket and sits sipping a Seven and Seven. Why the hell anyone would dump soda into good whiskey is a mystery to Malone, but to each his own.

"Hey, it's the cop *di tutti* cops!" Savino gets up and hugs him. The envelope slides effortlessly from Savino's jacket into Malone's. "Merry Christmas, Denny."

Christmas is an important time in the wiseguy community—it's when everyone gets their yearly bonuses, often in the tens of thousands of dollars. And the weight of the envelope is a barometer as to your standing in the crew—the heavier the envelope, the higher your status.

Malone's envelope has nothing to do with that.

It's for his services as a bagman.

Easy money—just meet a person here and there—a bar, a diner, the playground in Riverside Park—slip them an envelope. They already know what it's for, it's all been worked out; Malone is just the delivery guy because these good citizens don't want to take a chance they're seen with a known wiseguy.

They're city officials—the kind who award contract bids.

That's where the Cimino profit center is.

The Cimino *borgata* gets a piece of everything—a kickback from the contractor for getting him the bid, then the concrete, the rebar, the electrical, the plumbing. Otherwise, these unions find a problem and shut the project down.

Everyone thought the mob was done after RICO, Giuliani, the Commission case, the Windows case.

And they were.

Then the Towers came down.

Overnight, the feds shifted three-quarters of their personnel into antiterrorism and the mob made a comeback. Shit, they even made a fortune overcharging for debris removal from Ground Zero. Louie used to brag they took in sixty-three million.

Nine/eleven saved the Mafia.

It's not clear now who's in charge of the Cimino family, but the smart money is on Stevie Bruno. Did ten years on a RICO case, been out three now and is moving up fast. Very insulated, lives out in Jersey, rarely comes into the city, even for a meal.

So they're back, although they'll never be what they were.

Savino signals the bartender to get Malone a drink. The bartender already knows it's a Jameson's straight up.

They sit back down and go through the ritual dance—how's the

family, fine, how's yours, all good, how's business, you know another day another dollar behind, the usual bullshit.

"You touch the good reverend?" Savino asks.

"He got his turkey," Malone says. "A couple of your people tuned
up a bar owner on Lenox the other night, guy named Osborne."

"What, you got a monopoly on beating up moolies?"

"Yeah, I do," Malone says.

"He came up light on his vig," Savino says. "Two weeks in a
row."

"Don't show me up and do it on the street, where everyone sees,"
Malone says. "Things are tense enough in the 'community.'"

"Hey, just because one of your guys capped a kid means I gotta
issue some kind of hall pass?" Savino asks. "This dumb shit bets on
the Knicks. The *Knicks,* Denny. Then he don't pay me my money.
What am I supposed to do?"

"Just don't do it on my beat."

"Jesus fuck, Merry Christmas, I'm glad you came in tonight,"
Savino says. "Anything else squeezing your shoes?"

"No, that's it."

"Thank you, St. Anthony."

"You get a good envelope?"

Savino shrugs. "You want to know something . . . you and me?
The bosses these days, they're cheap cocksuckers. This guy, he has
a house in Jersey overlooks the river, a tennis court . . . He barely
comes into the city anymore. He did ten inside, okay, I get it . . . but
he thinks that means he gets to eat with both hands, no one minds.
You know something? I mind."

"Lou, shit, there are ears in here."

"Fuck them," Savino says. He orders another drink. "Here's
something might interest you, you know what I heard? I heard that
maybe all the smack from that Pena bust made you a rock star didn't
make it to the evidence locker."

Jesus Christ, is everyone talking about this? "Bullshit."

"Yeah, probably," Savino says. "Because it would have shown up on the street already, and it hasn't. Someone went French Connection, I guess they're sitting on it."

"Yeah, well, don't guess."

"You're fucking sensitive tonight," Savino says. "I'm just saying, someone's sitting on some weight, looking to lay it off . . ."

Malone sets down his glass. "I gotta go."

"Places to be, people to see," Savino says. "*Buon Natale,* Malone."

"Yeah, you too."

Malone walks out onto the street. Jesus, what has Savino heard about the Pena bust? Was he just fishing, or did he know something? It's not good, it's going to have to be dealt with.

Anyway, Malone thinks, the wops won't be beating up any deadbeat *ditzunes* out on Lenox.

So that's something.

Next.

Debbie Phillips was three months pregnant when Billy O went down.

Because they weren't married (*yet*—Monty and Russo were all over the kid to do the right thing and he was headed in that direction), the Job wouldn't do shit for her. Didn't give her any recognition at Billy's funeral—the fucking Catholic department wouldn't give the unwed mother the folded flag, the kind words, sure as shit no survivor's benefits, no medical. She'd wanted to do a paternity test and then sue the Job, but Malone talked her out of it.

You don't turn the Job over to lawyers.

"That's not the way we do things," he told her. "We'll take care of you, the baby."

"How?" Debbie asked.

"You let me worry about that," Malone said. "Anything you need, you call me. If it's a woman thing—Sheila, Donna Russo, Yolanda Montague."

Debbie never reached out.

She was an independent type anyway, not really that attached to Billy, never mind his extended family. It was a one-night stand that went permanent, despite Malone's constant warnings that Billy should double-wrap the groceries.

"I pulled out," Billy told him when Debbie called with the news.

"What are you, in *high school*?" Malone asked.

Monty cuffed him in the head. "Idiot."

"You going to marry her?" Russo asked.

"She don't want to get married."

"It doesn't matter what you or she *wants*," Monty said. "It only matters what that child *needs*—two parents."

But Debbie, she's one of those modern women doesn't think she needs a man to raise a baby. Told Billy they should wait and see how their "relationship developed."

Then they didn't get the chance.

Now, she opens the door for Malone, she's eight months and looks it. She's not getting any help from her family out in western Pennsylvania and she don't have anyone in New York. Yolanda Montague lives the closest so she checks in, brings groceries, goes to the doctor's appointments when Debbie will let her, but she don't deal with the money.

The wives never deal with the money.

"Merry Christmas, Debbie," Malone says.

"Yeah, okay."

She lets him in.

Debbie is pretty and petite, so her stomach looks huge on her. Her blond hair is stringy and dirty, the apartment is a mess. She sits down on the old sofa; the television is on to the evening news.

It's hot in the apartment, and stuffy, but it's always either too hot or too cold in these old apartments—no one can figure out the radiators. One of them hisses now, as if to tell Malone to fuck off if he doesn't like it.

He lays an envelope on the coffee table.

Five grand.

The decision was a no-brainer—Billy keeps drawing a full share, and when they lay off the Pena smack, he gets his share of that, too. Malone is the executor, he'll lay it out to Debbie as he sees she needs it and can handle it. The rest will go into a college fund for Billy's kid.

His son won't want for anything.

His mom can stay at home, take care of him.

Debbie fought him on this. "You can pay for day care. I need to work."

"No, you don't."

"It isn't just the money," she said. "I'd go crazy, all day here alone with a kid."

"You'll feel different once he's born."

"That's what they say."

Now she looks at the envelope and then up at him. "White welfare."

"It's not charity," Malone says. "It's Billy's money."

"Then give it to me," she says. "Instead of doling it out like Social Services."

"We take care of our own," Malone says. He looks around the small apartment. "Are you ready for this baby? You got, I dunno, a bassinette, diapers, a changing table?"

"Listen to you."

"Yolanda can take you shopping," Malone says. "Or if you want, we can just bring the stuff by."

"If Yolanda takes me shopping," Debbie says, "I'll look like some rich West Side bitch with a nanny. Maybe I can get her to speak in a Jamaican accent, or are they all Haitian now?"

She's bitter.

Malone don't blame her.

She has a fling with a cop, gets knocked up, the cop gets killed and there she is—alone with her life totally fucked up. Cops and their wives telling her what to do, giving her an allowance like she's a kid. But she is a kid, he thinks, and if I gave her Billy's full share in one whack, she'd blow it and where would Billy's son be?

"You have plans for tomorrow?" he asks.

"*It's a Wonderful Life*," she says. "The Montagues asked me, so did the Russos, but I don't want to intrude."

"They were sincere."

"I know." She puts her feet up on the table. "I miss him, Malone. Is that crazy?"

"No," Malone says. "It's not crazy."

I miss him, too.

I loved him, too.

The Dublin House, Seventy-Ninth and Broadway.

You go into an Irish bar on Christmas Eve, Malone thinks, what you're going to find are Irish drunks and Irish cops or some combination thereof.

He sees Bill McGivern standing at the crowded bar, knocking one back.

"Inspector?"

"Malone," McGivern says, "I was hoping to see you tonight. What are you drinking?"

"Same as you."

"Another Jameson's," McGivern says to the bartender. The inspector's cheeks are flushed, making his full head of white hair look even whiter. McGivern's one of those ruddy, full-faced, glad-handing, smiling Irishmen. A big player in the Emerald Society and Catholic Guardians. If he weren't a cop, he'd have been a ward healer, and a damn good one.

"You wanna get a booth?" Malone asks when the drink comes. They find one in the back and sit down.

"Merry Christmas, Malone."

"Merry Christmas, Inspector."

They touch glasses.

McGivern is Malone's "hook"—his mentor, protector, sponsor. Every cop with any kind of career has one—the guy who runs interference, gets you plum assignments, looks out for you.

And McGivern is a powerful hook. An NYPD inspector is two ranks higher than a captain and just below the chiefs. A well-placed inspector—and McGivern is—can kill a captain's career, and Sykes knows that.

Malone's known McGivern since he was a little boy. The inspector and Malone's father were in uniform together in the Six back in the day. It was McGivern talked to him a few years after his dad passed, explained a few things to him.

"John Malone was a great cop," McGivern said.

"He drank," Malone said. Yeah, he was sixteen, knew fucking everything.

"He did," McGivern said. "Your father and I, back in the Six, we caught eight murdered kids, all under four years of age, inside two weeks."

One of the children had all these little burn marks on his body, and McGivern and his dad couldn't figure out what they were until they finally realized they matched up exactly with the mouth of a crack pipe.

The child had been tortured and bitten his tongue off in pain.

"So, yes," McGivern said, "your father drank."

Now Malone takes an envelope from his jacket and slides it across the table. McGivern hefts the heavy envelope and says, "Merry Christmas, indeed."

"I had a good year."

McGivern shoves the envelope into his wool coat. "How's life treating you?"

Malone takes a sip of his whiskey and says, "Sykes is busting my hump."

"I can't get him transferred," McGivern says. "He's the darling of the Puzzle Palace."

One Police Plaza.

NYPD headquarters.

Which has troubles of its own right now, Malone thinks.

An FBI investigation of high-ranking officers taking gifts in exchange for favors.

Stupid shit like trips, Super Bowl tickets, gourmet meals at trendy restaurants in exchange for getting tickets fixed, building citations squashed, even guarding assholes bringing diamonds in from overseas. One of these rich fucks got one of the marine commanders to bring his friends out to Long Island on a police boat, and an air unit guy to fly his guests to a Hamptons party in a police chopper.

Then there's the thing with the gun licenses.

It's hard to get a gun permit in New York, especially a concealed carry license. It generally requires deep background checks and personal interviews. Unless you're rich and can lay out twenty grand to a "broker" and the "broker" bribes high-ranking cops to shortcut the process.

The feds have one of these brokers by the nuts and he's talking, naming names.

Indictments pending.

As it is, five chiefs have been relieved of duty already.

And one killed himself.

Drove to a street by a golf course near his house on Long Island and shot himself.

No note.

Genuine grief and shock waves have blasted through the upper rank of the NYPD, McGivern included.

They don't know who's next—to be arrested, to swallow the gun.

The media's humping it like a blind dog on a sofa leg, mostly because the mayor and the commissioner are at war.

Yeah, maybe not so much a war, Malone thinks, more like two guys on a sinking ship fighting for the last seat in the lifeboat. They're each facing down major scandals, and their one play is to throw each other to the media sharks and hope the feeding frenzy lasts long enough to paddle away.

Not enough bad things can happen to Hizzoner to make Malone happy, and most of his brother and sister cops share this opinion because the motherfucker throws them under the bus every chance he gets. Didn't back them on Garner, on Gurley, on Bennett. He knows where his votes come from, so he panders to the minority community and he's done everything but toss Black Lives Matter's collective salad.

But now his own ass is in a sling.

Turns out his administration has done some favors for major political donors. There's a shocker, Malone thinks. There's something new in this world, except the allegations claim that the mayor and his people took it a little further—threatening to actively harm potential donors who *didn't* contribute, and the New York state investigators pushing the case had an ugly word for it— extortion.

A lawyer word for "shakedown," which is an old New York tradition.

The mob did it for generations—probably still do in the few neighborhoods they still control—forcing shopkeepers and bar owners to make a weekly payment for "protection" against the theft and vandalism that would otherwise come.

The Job did it, too. Back in the day, every business owner on the block knew he'd better have an envelope ready for the beat cop on Friday, or, failing that, free sandwiches, free coffee, free drinks. From the hookers, free blow jobs, for that matter. In exchange, the cop took care of his block—checked the locks at night, moved the corner boys along.

The system worked.

And now Hizzoner is running his own shakedown for campaign funds and he's come out with an almost comical defense, offering to release a list of big donors that he *didn't* do favors for. There's talk of indictments, and of the 38,000 cops on the Job, about 37,999 have volunteered to show up with the cuffs.

Hizzoner would fire the commish, except it would look like

what it is, so he needs an excuse, and any shit the mayor can throw on the Job, he's going to shovel with both hands.

And the commissioner, he'd be winning his fight against the mayor on points going away, if it weren't for this scandal ripping through One P. So he needs better news, he needs headlines.

Heroin busts and lower crime rates.

"The mission of the Manhattan North Special Task Force hasn't changed," McGivern is saying. "I don't care what Sykes tells you, you run the zoo any way you need to. I wouldn't want to be quoted on that, of course."

When Malone first went to McGivern and proposed a task force that would simultaneously address the guns and the violence, he didn't get as much resistance as he expected.

Homicide and Narcotics are separate units. Narcotics is its own division, run directly from One Police, and they usually don't mix. But with almost three-quarters of homicides being drug related, that didn't make sense, Malone argued. Same with a separate Gangs unit, because most of the drug violence was also gang violence.

Create a single force, he said, to attack them simultaneously.

Narcotics, Homicide, and Gangs screamed like stuck pigs. And it was true that elite units have stink on them in the NYPD.

Mostly because they've been prone to corruption and over-the-top violence.

The old Plainclothes Division back in the '60s and '70s gave rise to the Knapp Commission, which damn near destroyed the department. Frank Serpico was a naive asshole, Malone thinks—*everyone* knew you took money in Plainclothes. He went into the division anyway. He knew what he was getting into.

Guy had a Jesus complex.

No wonder that not a single officer in the NYPD donated blood after he was shot. Damn near destroyed the city, too. For twenty years after Knapp, the Job's priority was fighting corruption instead of crime.

Then it was the SIU—the Special Investigative Unit—given a

free hand to operate at will throughout the city. Made some good busts, too, and made a lot of good money, ripping off dealers. They got caught, of course, and things cleaned up for a while.

The next elite unit was SCU—the Street Crimes Unit—whose principal task was to get the guns off the street that the Knapp Commission had allowed to get there in the first place. One hundred and thirty-eight cops, all white, so good at what they did that the Job expanded the unit by a factor of four and did it too fast.

The result was that on the night of February 4, 1999, when four SCU officers were patrolling the South Bronx, the senior man had been with the unit for only two years, the other three for three months. They had no supervisor with them, they didn't know each other, they didn't know the neighborhood.

So when Amadou Diallo looked like he was pulling a gun, one of the cops started firing and the others joined in.

"Contagious shooting," the experts call it.

The infamous forty-one shots.

SCU was disbanded.

The four cops were indicted, all were acquitted. Something the community remembered when Michael Bennett was shot.

But it's complicated—the fact is that SCU was effective in getting guns off the street, so more black people were probably killed as a result of the unit being disbanded than were shot by cops.

Ten years ago there was the predecessor to the Task Force—NMI, the Northern Manhattan Institute—forty-one detectives working narcotics in Harlem and Washington Heights. One of them ripped over $800,000 from dealers; his partner came in second with $740,000. The feds got them as collateral damage from a money-laundering sting. One of the cops got seven years, the other six. The unit commander got a year and change for taking his cut.

Puts a chill on everyone, seeing cops led out in cuffs.

But it doesn't stop it.

Seems about every twenty years there's a corruption scandal and a new commission.

So creating the Task Force was a hard sell.

It took time, influence and lobbying, but the Manhattan North Special Task Force was created.

The mission is simple—take back the streets.

Malone knows the unspoken agenda—we don't care what you do or how you do it (as long as it doesn't make the papers), just keep the animals in their cage.

"And what can I do for you, Denny?" McGivern asks now.

"We got a UC named Callahan," Malone says, "going down the rabbit hole. I'd like to get him pulled out before he hurts himself."

"Did you go to Sykes?"

"I don't want to hurt the kid," Malone says. "He's a good cop, he's just been under too long."

McGivern takes a pen from his jacket pocket and draws a circle on a cocktail napkin.

Then he put two dots inside the circle.

"These two dots, Denny, that's you and me. Inside the circle. You ask me to do a favor for you, that's inside the circle. This Callahan . . ." He makes a dot outside the circle. "That's him. Do you understand what I'm telling you?"

"Why am I asking a favor for someone outside the circle."

"This *once,* Denny," McGivern says. "But you need to understand that if it comes back on me, I drop it on you."

"Got it."

"There's an opening in Anti-Crime in the Two-Five," McGivern says. "I'll call Johnny over there, he owes me a favor, he'll take your kid."

"Thank you."

"We need more heroin arrests," McGivern says, getting up. "The chief of Narcotics is all over me. Make it snow, Denny. Give us a white Christmas."

He makes his way through the crowded bar, glad-handing and slapping shoulders on his way out the door.

Malone feels sad all of a sudden.

Maybe it's the adrenaline dump.

Maybe it's the Christmas blues.

He gets up and goes over to the jukebox, drops in some quarters and finds what he's looking for.

The Pogues' "Fairytale of New York."

A Christmas Eve tradition of Malone's.

It was Christmas Eve, babe, in the drunk tank,
An old man said to me, "Won't see another one."

Malone knows that Sykes is the bright-eyed boy down at Police Plaza, but he wonders exactly with who and how deep. Sykes is out to hurt him, no question.

But I'm a hero, Malone thinks, mocking himself.

Now at least half the cops in the bar start singing along with the chorus. They should be home with their families, those that still have them, but instead they're here, with their booze, their memories, with each other.

And the boys of the NYPD Choir were singing "Galway Bay"
And the bells are ringing out for Christmas Day.

It's a freezing night in Harlem.

Dumb cold.

The kind of cold where the dirty snow crunches under your feet and you can see your breath. It's after ten and not a lot of people on the street. Even most of the bodegas are closed, the heavy metal gates, graffiti-strewn, pulled down and the bars over the windows shut. A few cabs prowl for business, a couple of junkies move like ghosts.

The unmarked Crown Vic rolls north on Amsterdam and now they're not handing out turkeys, they're about to dish out the pain. Pain's nothing new to the people up here, it's a condition of life.

It's Christmas Eve and cold and clean and quiet.

Nobody's expecting anything to happen.

Which is what Malone's counting on, that Fat Teddy Bailey is fat, happy and complacent. Malone's been working for weeks with Nasty Ass to pin the midlevel smack dealer with shit on him when he's not expecting it.

Russo's singing.

You better not shout, you better not cry,
You better not pout, I'm tellin' you why.
Santa Smack is coming to town.

He turns right on 184th, where Nasty Ass said Fat Teddy would be coming to get his rocks off.

"Too cold for the lookouts," Malone says, because he doesn't see the usual kids and no one starts whistling to let anyone interested know that Da Force is on the street.

"Black people don't do cold," Monty says. "When's the last time you saw a brother on a ski slope?"

Fat Teddy's Caddy is parked outside 218.

"Nasty Ass, my *man*," Malone says.

He knows when you are sleeping.
He knows when you're awake.
He knows when you're just nodding out . . .

"You want to take him now?" Monty asks.

"Let the guy get laid," Malone says. "It's Christmas."

"Ahh, Christmas Eve," Russo says as they sit in the car. "The eggnog spiked with rum, the presents under the tree, the wife just tipsy enough to give up *la fica*, and we sit here in the jungle freezing our asses off."

Malone pulls a flask out of his jacket pocket and hands it to him.

"I'm on duty," Russo says. He takes a long draw and hands the flask to the backseat. Big Monty takes a hit and passes it back to Malone.

They wait.

"How long can that fat fuck fuck?" Russo asks. "He take Viagra? I hope he didn't have a heart attack."

Malone gets out of the car.

Russo covers him as Malone squats beside Fat Teddy's Caddy and lets the air out of his left rear tire. Then they go back into the Crown Vic and wait for fifty more cold minutes.

Fat Teddy goes six three and two eighty. When he finally comes out, he looks like the Michelin man in his long North Face coat. He starts walking toward his car in his $2,600 LeBron Air Force One basketball shoes with the satisfied swagger of a man who just got his rocks off.

Then he sees his tire. "Mothuh-fuckuh."

Fat Teddy opens the trunk, gets out the jack and bends over to start taking off the lug nuts.

He doesn't hear it coming.

Malone puts his pistol barrel behind Fat Teddy's ear. "Merry Christmas, Teddy. Ho, ho, motherfucking ho."

Russo holds his shotgun on the dealer as Monty starts to search the Caddy.

"Y'all some thirsty motherfuckers," Fat Teddy says. "Ain't you ever take a day off?"

"Does cancer take days off?" Malone pushes Fat Teddy up against the car and searches through the thick padding of the dealer's coat, relieving him of a .25 ACP. The dope slingers do love these weird-caliber weapons.

"Uh-oh," Malone says. "Convicted felon in possession of a con-cealed firearm. That's a pound zip-bit right there."

Five-year minimum sentence.

"It ain't mine," Fat Teddy says. "Why you stop me for? Walking while black?"

"Walking while *Teddy*," Malone says. "I distinctly saw a bulge in your jacket that appeared to be a handgun."

"You checkin' out my *bulge*?" Fat Teddy asks. "You gone faggot on me right now, son?"

In response, Malone finds Fat Teddy's cell phone, tosses it to the sidewalk and stomps on it.

"C'mon, son, that was a Six. You OD'd."

"You have twenty of them," Malone says. "Hands behind your back."

"You ain't takin' me in," Fat Teddy says tiredly, complying. "You ain't gonna sit there filling out no DD-5's on no Christmas fucking Eve. You got drinking to do, Irish. You got 'ackahol' to get to."

Malone asks Monty, "Why is it your people cannot pronounce 'alcohol'?"

"Don't 'acks' me." Monty reaches under the passenger seat and comes out with a sleeve of smack—a hundred glassine envelopes grouped in tens. "Oh, what have we here? Christmas at Rikers. You better bring mistletoe, Teddy, hope they let you kiss them on the mouth."

"You flaked me."

"I flaked your ass," Malone says. "This is DeVon Carter's heroin. He ain't gonna be happy you lost it."

"You need to talk to your people," Fat Teddy says.

"Which people?" Malone slaps him in the face. "Who?"

Fat Teddy shuts up.

Malone says, "I'll hang a snitch tag on you at Central Booking. You won't make it out of Rikers."

"You do that to me, man?" Fat Teddy asks.

"You're either on my bus or under it."

"All I know," Fat Teddy says, "is that Carter said he had protection in Manhattan North. I thought it was you guys."

"Well, it ain't."

Malone is *pissed*. Either Teddy is blowing smoke or someone in Manhattan North is on Carter's pad. "What else you got on you?"

"Nothin'."

Malone digs into his coat and comes out with rolls of cash wrapped in elastic bands. "This nothin'? Has to be thirty grand here, that's some serious guap. Loyal customer rebate from Mickey D's?"

"I eat *Five Guys,* motherfucker. Mickey D's."

"Well, you're eating bologna tonight."

"Come on, Malone," Fat Teddy says.

"Tell you what," Malone says, "we'll just confiscate the contraband, cut you loose. Call it a Christmas present."

It ain't an offer, it's a threat.

Teddy says, "You take my shit, you gotta arrest me, give me a five!"

Fat Teddy needs the arrest report to show Carter as proof the cops took it and he didn't just rip him off. SOP—you get busted, you better have a DD-5 to show or you're gonna get your fingers cut off.

Carter has done it.

The legend is he has one of those office paper cutters, and slingers who don't have his dope, his money or a 5 get their hand laid in there and then *whomp*—no fingers.

Except it ain't a rumor.

Malone found a guy staggering on the street one night, dripping blood all over the sidewalk. Carter left him with his thumb, though, so when he pointed the blame, he had no one to point at but himself.

They leave Teddy sitting against his car and go back to the Crown Vic. Malone cuts the cash up five ways, one for each of them, one share for expenses, and one piece for Billy O. Each guy puts his cash in a self-addressed envelope they always carry.

Then they go back and get Teddy.

"What about my ride, man?" Fat Teddy asks as they haul him to his feet. "You ain't gonna take that, are you?"

"You had smack in it, asshole," Russo says. "It is now property of the NYPD."

"You mean property of Russo," Fat Teddy says. "You ain't drivin' my Caddy out the Jersey Shore with that smelly guinea fish in it."

"I wouldn't be caught dead in this coonmobile," Russo says. "It's going to the pound."

"It's Christmas!" Fat Teddy whines.

Malone juts his chin toward the building. "What's her number?"

Fat Teddy tells him. Malone punches the number and holds his phone up to Fat Teddy's mouth.

"Baby, get down here," Fat Teddy says. "Take care my car. And it better be here when I get out. And detailed."

Russo leaves Fat Teddy's keys on the hood and they haul him toward their car.

"Who dimed me?" Fat Teddy asks. "It was that grimy little bitch Nasty Ass?"

"You wanna be one of those Christmas Eve suicides?" Malone asks. "Jumps off the GW Bridge? Because we can make that happen for you."

Fat Teddy starts in on Monty. "Workin' for the man, brothuh? You they house nigger?"

Monty slaps him across the face. Fat Teddy is big, but his head snaps back like a tetherball. "I'm a black man, you grape-soda-drinking, bitch-beating, smack-slinging projects monkey."

"Motherfucker, I didn't have these cuffs on—"

"You want to take it there?" Monty says. He drops his cigar in the street and grinds it with his heel. "Come on, just you and me."

Fat Teddy don't say nothin'.

"That's what I thought," Monty says.

On the way to the Three-Two they stop at a mailbox and put in the envelopes. Then they take Fat Teddy in and book him on the gun and the heroin. The desk sergeant is less than thrilled. "It's Christmas Eve. Task Force assholes."

"May Da Force be with you," Malone says.

I'm dreaming of a white Christmas,
Just like the ones I used to know . . .

———————

Russo drives down Broadway toward the Upper West Side.

"Who was Fat Teddy talking about?" Russo asks. "Was he just mouthing, or does Carter have someone on the pad?"

"Has to be Torres."

Torres is a wrong guy.

Does rips, sells cases, even runs whores, low-end crack addicts, mostly, and runaways. He works them hard. Keeps them in line with a car radio antenna—Malone has seen the welts.

The sergeant's a real thumper, has a well-earned reputation for brutality, even by Manhattan North standards. Malone does what he can to keep Torres sweet. They're all Task Force, after all, and have to get along.

But Malone can't have lowlifes like Fat Teddy Bailey telling him he's protected, so he's going to have to work something out with Torres.

If it's even true.

If it's even Torres.

Russo pulls off at Eighty-Seventh and finds a parking space across the street from a brownstone at 349.

Malone rents the apartment from a Realtor they protect.

The rent is zero.

It's a small pied-à-terre, but it suits their purposes. A bedroom to crash in or take a girl, a sitting room and a little kitchen, a place to take a shower.

Or hide dope, because in the shower stall there's a false platform with a loose tile under which they stored the fifty kilos they ripped from the late, unlamented Diego Pena.

They're waiting to lay it off. Fifty kilos is enough to make an impact on the street, cause a stir, even lower prices, so they have to let the Pena rip fade before they bring it out. The heroin has a street value of five million dollars, but the cops will have to lay it off at a discount to a trusted fence. Still, it's a huge score, even split four ways.

Malone has no problem letting it all sit.

The largest score they've ever made or are ever likely to make, it's their security, their 401(k)'s, their futures. It's their kids' college tuitions, a wall against catastrophic illness, the difference between retiring in a Tucson trailer park or a West Palm condo. They cut up the three million in cash right away, with Malone's warning that no one should go out on a spending spree—buy a new car, a lot of jewelry for the wife, a boat, a trip to the Bahamas.

That's what the Internal Affairs pricks look for—a change in lifestyle, work habits, attitude. Put the money away, Malone told his guys. Stash at least $50K where you can lay your hands on it inside an hour, in case IAB comes and you have to go on the lam. Another fifty for bail money if you didn't get out in time. Otherwise, spend a little, put the rest away, do your twenty, pull the pin, have a life.

They've even talked about retiring right now. Spacing it a few months apart, but quitting while they're ahead. Maybe we should, Malone thinks now, but coming so close after the Pena rip, it would raise suspicions.

He can see the headline now: HERO COPS QUIT AFTER BIGGEST BUST. IAB would come for sure.

Malone and Russo go into the sitting room and Malone grabs a bottle of Jameson's from behind the little bar and pours each of them two fingers into squat whiskey glasses.

Red hair, tall, wiry, Russo looks about as Italian as a ham sandwich with mayonnaise. Malone looks more Italian, and they used to joke when they were kids that maybe they got switched at the hospital.

And the truth is Malone probably knows Russo better than he knows himself, mostly because he keeps everything *to* himself and Russo don't. If it's on Russo's mind, it's going to come out his mouth—not to everybody, just to his brother cops.

First time he had sex with Donna, classic prom night shit, Russo didn't even have to say it the next day, it was written all over his goofy face, just like his heart was on his sleeve.

"I love her, Denny," he said. "I'm gonna marry her."

"The fuck are you, Irish?" Denny asked. "You guys don't have to get married just because you did it."

"No, I want to," Russo said.

Russo's always known who he was. A lot of guys, they wanted to get out of Staten Island, be something else. Not Russo, he knew he was going to marry Donna, have kids, live in the old neighborhood, and he was happy with being an East Shore stereotype—cop in the city, wife, kids, three-bedroom house, one and a half baths, cookouts on the holidays.

They took the exam together, joined the department together, went to the Academy together. Malone, he had to help Russo gain five pounds to make the minimum weight—force-fed him milkshakes, beer and hoagies.

Even still, Russo wouldn't have gotten through without Malone. Russo could hit anything on the target range but he couldn't fight for shit. He was always that way, even when they were playing hockey, Russo had soft hands that could tip a puck into the net, and he'd drop the gloves but then it was a catastrophe, even with his long arms, and Malone would have to come in and bail him out. So in the hand-to-hand PT at the Academy, they usually worked it out to get partnered up and Malone would let Russo flip him, get him into wristlocks and choke holds.

The day they graduated—will Malone ever forget the day they graduated?—Russo, he had this shit-eating grin he couldn't wipe off his face for nothing, and they looked at each other and knew what their lives were going to be.

When Sheila pissed two blue lines, it was Russo that Malone went to first, Russo who told him there were no questions, only one right answer and he wanted to be best man.

"That's old-school shit," Malone said. "That was our parents, our grandparents, it don't necessarily work that way anymore."

"The fuck it don't," Russo said. "We *are* old school, Denny, we're

East Shore Staten Island. You may think you're modern and shit, but you ain't. Neither is Sheila. What, don't you love her?"

"I dunno."

"You loved her enough to fuck her," Russo said. "I know you, Denny, you can't be one of them jackoff absentee father sperm donors. That's not you."

So Russo was his best man.

Malone learned to love Sheila.

It wasn't so hard—she was pretty, funny, smart in her way, it was good for a long time.

He and Russo were still in bags—uniforms—when the Towers came down. Russo, he ran *toward* those buildings, not away, because he knew who he was. And that night, when Malone learned Liam was under Tower Two and was never coming back up, it was Russo who sat with him all night.

Just like Malone sat with Russo when Donna miscarried.

Russo cried.

When Russo's daughter, Sophia, was born premature, two pounds something and the doctors said it was touch-and-go, Malone sat in the hospital with him all night, saying nothing, just sitting, until Sophia was out of the woods.

The night Malone was stupid enough to get himself shot, running too far out in front to tackle a B&E perp, if it wasn't for Russo that night, the Job would have given Malone an inspector's funeral and Sheila a folded flag. They'd have played the bagpipes and had a wake and Sheila could have been a widow instead of a divorcée, if Russo hadn't shot the perp and driven the car to the E-room like he stole it, because Malone was bleeding out internally.

No, Phil put two in the perp's chest and a third in the head because that's the code—a cop shooter dies on the scene or in the "bus" on a slow ride to the hospital, with detours if necessary and the most possible potholes.

Doctors take the Hippocratic oath—EMTs don't. They know

that if they take extraordinary measures to save a cop shooter's life, the next time they call for backup it might be slow getting there.

But Russo hadn't waited for the EMTs that night. He raced Malone to the hospital and carried him in like a baby.

Saved his life.

But that's Russo.

Stand-up, old-school guy with a Grill Master apron, an unaccountable taste for Nirvana, Pearl Jam and Nine Inch Nails, smarter than shit, clanging fucking balls, loyal like a dog, be there for you anywhere anytime Phil Russo.

A cop's cop.

A brother.

"You ever think we should quit?" Malone asks.

"The Job?"

Malone shakes his head. "The other shit. I mean, how much more do we need to earn?"

"I have three kids," Russo says. "You have two, Monty three. All smart. You know what college costs these days? They're worse than the Gambinos, they get their hooks in you. I don't know about you, I need to keep earning."

So do you, Malone tells himself.

You need the money, the cash flow, but it's more than that, admit it. You love the game. The thrill, the taking off the bad guys, even the danger, the idea that you might get caught.

You're a sick bastard.

"Maybe it's time we moved the Pena smack," Russo is saying.

"What, you need money?"

"No, I'm good," Russo says. "It's just that, you know, things have cooled down, it's just sitting there not earning. That's retirement money, Denny. That's 'fuck you I'm out of here' money. Survival money, anything should happen."

"You expecting something to happen, Phil?" Malone asks. "You know something I don't?"

"No."

"It's a big step," Malone says. "We took money before, we never dealt."

"Then why did we take it if we weren't going to sell it?"

"It makes us dope slingers," Malone says. "We been fighting these guys our whole careers, now we'll be just like them."

"If we'd turned it all in," Russo says, "someone else would have taken it."

"I know."

"Why not us?" Russo asks. "Why does everyone else get rich? The wiseguys, the dope dealers, the politicians? Why not us for a change? When is it our turn?"

"I hear you," Malone says.

They sit quietly and drink.

"Something else bothering you?" Russo asks him.

"I dunno," Malone says. "Maybe it's just Christmas, you know?"

"You going over there?" Russo asks.

"In the morning, open presents."

"Well, that'll be good."

"Yeah, that'll be good," Malone says.

"Swing by the house, you get a chance," Russo says. "Donna's going full guinea—macaroni with gravy, the *baccalata,* then the turkey."

"Thanks, I'll try."

Malone drives up to Manhattan North, asks the desk sergeant, "Fat Teddy get on the bus yet?"

"It's Christmas Eve, Malone," the sergeant says. "Things are backed up."

Malone goes down to the holding cells where Teddy sits on a bench. If there's any place more depressing on Christmas Eve than a holding cell, Malone doesn't know about it. Fat Teddy looks up when he sees Malone. "You gotta do something for me, bruvah."

"What are you going to do for me?"

"Like what?"

"Tell me who's on Carter's pad."

Teddy laughs. "Like you don't know."

"Torres?"

"I ain't know nothin'."

There it is, Malone thinks. Fat Teddy is scared to rat on a cop.

"Okay," Malone says. "Teddy, you're not an idiot, you only play one on the street. You know with two convictions on your sheet, the gun alone, you're going to do five. We trace it back to some straw purchase in Gooberville, the judge is going to be pissed, could throw you a double. Ten years, that's a long time, but look, I'll come visit, bring you ribs from Sweet Mama's."

"Don't be clowning me, Malone."

"Dead-ass serious," Malone says. "What if I could get you a walk?"

"What if you had a dick 'stead of what you got?"

"You're the one wanted to be serious, Teddy," Malone says. "If you don't . . ."

"What you want?"

Malone says, "I'm hearing that Carter has been negotiating for some serious weaponry. What I want to know is, who is he negotiating with."

"You think I'm stupid?"

"Not at all."

"No, you must, Malone," Teddy says, "because if I get a walk and you bust them guns, Carter he puts that together and I end up facedown."

"You think *I'm* stupid, Teddy? I work out the walk so it looks like business as usual."

Fat Teddy hesitates.

"Fuck you," Malone says. "I have a beautiful woman waiting, I'm sitting here with an ugly fat guy."

"His name is Mantell."

"Whose name is Mantell?"

"Cracker runs guns for the ECMF."

Malone knows the East Coast Motherfuckers are a motorcycle club deep in weed and weapons. Affiliate charters in Georgia and the Carolinas. But they're racist, white supremacists. "ECMF would do business with black?"

"I guess black money spend the same." Fat Teddy shrugs. "And they don't mind helping black kill black."

What Malone is more surprised about is Carter doing business with white. He has to be desperate. "What can the bikers offer him?"

"AKs, ARs, MAC-10s, you name it," Teddy says. "S'all I know, son."

"Carter didn't get you a lawyer?"

"Can't get hold of Carter," Teddy says. "He in the Bahamas."

"Call this guy," Malone says, handing him a card. "Mark Piccone. He'll get it squared away for you."

Teddy takes the card.

Malone gets up. "We're doing something wrong, aren't we, Teddy? You and me freezing our asses off, Carter sipping piña coladas on the beach?"

"Trill."

Trill.

True and real.

Malone cruises in his unmarked work car.

There's only so many places the snitch can be. Nasty prefers the area just north of Columbia but below 125th Street and Malone finds him skulking along the east side of Broadway, doing the junkie bop.

Pulling over, Malone rolls down the passenger window and says, "In."

Nasty Ass looks around nervously and then gets in. He's a little surprised, because normally Malone don't let him in his car because he says he stinks, although Nasty don't smell it.

He's jonesing hard.

Nose running, hands trembling as he hugs himself and rocks back and forth. And Nasty tells him, "I'm hurtin'. Can't find no one. You gotta help me, man."

His thin face is drawn, his brown skin sallow. His two upper front teeth stick out like a squirrel's in a bad cartoon, and if it weren't for his smell, he'd be called Nasty Mouth.

Now the man is sick. "Please, Malone."

Malone reaches under the dash to a metal box attached with a magnet. He opens the box and hands Nasty an envelope, enough to fix and get well.

Nasty opens the door.

"No, stay in the car," Malone says.

"I can fix in here?"

"Yeah, what the fuck. It's Christmas."

Malone takes a left and then heads south down Broadway as Nasty Ass shakes the heroin into a spoon, uses a lighter to cook it, then draws it into a syringe.

"That thing clean?" Malone asks.

"As a newborn baby."

Nasty Ass sticks the needle in his vein and pushes the plunger. His head snaps back and then he sighs.

He's well again. "Where we goin'?"

"Port Authority," Malone says. "You're getting out of town for a while."

Nasty's scared. Alarmed. "Why?!"

"It's for your own good." Just in case Fat Teddy is pissed enough to track him down and do him.

"I can't leave town," Nasty Ass says. "I got no hookups out of town."

"Well, you're going."

"Please don't make me," Nasty Ass says. He actually starts crying. "I can't jones out of town. I'll die out there."

"You want to jones at Rikers?" Malone asks. "Because that's your other choice."

"Why are you being a dick, Malone?"

"It's my nature."

"Never used to was," Nasty Ass says.

"Yeah, well, this ain't the used to was."

"Where should I go?"

"I don't know. Philly. Baltimore."

"I got a cousin in Baltimore."

"Go there, then," Malone says. He peels out five hundred-dollar bills and hands them to Nasty Ass. "Do not spend all of this on junk. Get the fuck out of New York and stay there awhile."

"How long I gotta stay?" He looks desperate, really scared. Malone doubts that Nasty Ass has ever been to the East Side, never mind out of town.

"Call me in a week or so and I'll let you know," Malone says. He pulls up in front of Port Authority and lets Nasty out. "I see you in New York, I *am* going to be mad, Nasty Ass."

"Thought we was friends, Malone."

"No, we're not friends," Malone says. "We're not going to be friends. You're my informer. A snitch. That's all."

Driving back uptown, Malone leaves the windows open.

Claudette opens the door.

"Merry Christmas, baby," she says.

Malone loves her voice.

It was her voice, low and soft, even more than her looks, that first drew him to her.

A voice full of promises and reassurance.

You'll find comfort here.

And pleasure.

In my arms, in my mouth, in my pussy.

He walks in and sits down on her little couch—she has a different word for it he can never remember—and says, "Sorry I'm so late."

"I just got home myself," she says.

Even though she's wearing a white kimono and her perfume smells like heaven, Malone thinks.

She just got home and she got herself ready for me.

Claudette sits on the couch beside him, opens a carved wooden box on the coffee table and takes out a thin joint. She lights it, takes a hit and hands it to him.

Malone sucks down a hit and says, "I thought you were four to twelve."

"I thought I was, too."

"Tough shift?" he asks.

"Fights, suicide attempts, ODs," Claudette says, taking the joint back from him. "Man came in barefoot with a broken wrist, said he knows you."

An E-room nurse usually on the night or the graveyard shift, so she's seen it all. She and Malone met when he drove a junkie CI who had accidentally shot half his foot off straight to the hospital.

"Why didn't you call an ambulance?" she'd asked him.

"In Harlem?" Malone asked. "He'd have bled out while the EMTs were at Starbucks. Instead he bled all over my interior. I just got the thing detailed, too."

"You're a cop."

"Guilty."

Now she leans back and stretches her legs across his. The kimono slides up to reveal her thighs. There's a spot just below her pussy that Malone thinks is the softest place on earth.

"Tonight," she says, "we had an abandoned crack baby. Left right on the front steps."

"Wrapped in swaddling clothes?"

"I get the irony, Malone," she says. "How was your day?"

"Yeah, good."

Malone likes that she doesn't press him, that she's satisfied with what he tells her. A lot of women aren't, they want him to "share," they want details he'd rather forget than recount. Claudette gets it— she has her own horrors.

He strokes that soft spot. "You're tired. You probably want to sleep."

"No, baby, I want to fuck."

They finish their drinks and go into her bedroom.

Claudette undresses him, kissing skin as she bares it. She goes to her knees and takes him into her mouth and even in the dark bedroom, with light coming in only from the street, he loves the look of her full red lips on his cock.

She's not high tonight, it's just the weed, although it's very good weed, and he loves that, too. He reaches down and feels her hair, then slides his hand down into the kimono and feels her breast, teases it and feels her moan.

Malone puts his hands on her shoulders to stop her. "I want to be in you."

She gets up, goes to the bed and lies down. Draws her knees up like an invitation and then issues one. "Come here, then, baby."

She's wet and warm.

He slides back and forth across her body, across the full breasts and the dark brown skin and reaches down with a finger to feel that soft spot as outside sirens blare and people shout and he doesn't care, doesn't have to care right now, only has to slide in and out of her and hear her say, "I love that, baby, I *love* that."

When he feels himself about to come, he grabs her ass—Claudette says she has no ass for a black girl—but he grabs her small tight ass and pulls her close and pushes himself as deep in her as he can go until he feels that little pocket in her and she grabs his shoulder and she bucks up and comes just before he does.

He comes like he always does with her, from the tips of his toes through the top of his head, and maybe that's the dope but he thinks it's her, with that low soft voice and warm brown skin, slick and sweaty now, mixing with his, and maybe it's a minute or maybe it's an hour when he hears her say, "Oh, baby, I'm tired."

"Yeah, me too."

He rolls off her.

She sleepily squeezes his hand and then she's out.

He lies on his back. Across the street the liquor store owner must have forgotten to turn off his lights, and their reflection blinks red on Claudette's ceiling.

It's Christmas in the jungle and for this short time, at least, Malone is at peace.

CHAPTER 5

Malone sleeps for just an hour, because he wants to be out in Staten Island before the kids get up and start ripping open the presents under the tree.

He doesn't wake Claudette when he gets up.

He gets dressed, goes into the little galley kitchen, makes himself an instant coffee and then goes to his jacket and takes out the present he got her.

Diamond earrings from Tiffany's.

Because she's crazy about that Audrey Hepburn movie.

Malone leaves the box on the coffee table and goes out. He knows she'll sleep until noon and then make it to her sister's for Christmas dinner.

"Then I'll probably hit a meeting at St. Mary's," she said.

"They have them on Christmas?" Malone asked.

"Especially on Christmas."

She's doing well, she's been clean for almost six months now. Hard for an addict working in a hospital around all those drugs.

Now he drives down to his pad, on 104th between Broadway and West End.

When he separated from Sheila, a little over a year ago now, Malone decided to be one of those few cops who lives on his beat. He didn't go all the way up to Harlem, but settled for the outskirts on the Upper West Side. He can take the train to work or even walk if he wants, and he likes the neighborhood around Columbia.

The college kids are annoying in their youthful arrogance and certitude, but there's something about that he likes, too. Likes going into the coffeehouses, the bars, hearing the conversations. Likes to walk uptown, let the dealers and the addicts know he's around.

His place is a third-floor walk-up—a small living room, a smaller kitchen, an even smaller bedroom with a bathroom attached. A heavy bag hangs from a chain in the living room. It's all he needs; he's not there much anyway. It's a place to crash, shower, make a cup of coffee in the morning.

Now he goes up, showers and changes clothes. It wouldn't do to go back to the house in the same clothes because Sheila would sniff it out in a second and ask him if he's been with "huh."

Malone doesn't know why it bugs her so much, or at all—they separated almost three months before he even met Claudette—but it was a serious mistake to have answered Sheila's question "Are you seeing anyone?" honestly.

"You're a cop, you should know better," Russo said when Malone told him about Sheila freaking out. "*Never* give an honest answer."

Or an answer at all. Other than "I want a lawyer, I want my delegate."

But Sheila had freaked. "'Claudette'? What is she, French?"

"As a matter of fact, she's black. African American."

Sheila laughed in his face. It just cracked her up. "Shit, Denny, when you said at Thanksgiving you liked the dark meat, I thought you meant the drumstick."

"Nice."

"Don't get all PC with me," Sheila said. "With you it's always 'moolie' this and 'ditzune' that. Tell me something, do you call her a nigger?"

"No."

Sheila couldn't stop laughing. "You tell the *sistuh* how many *bro-thuhs* you tuned up with your nightstick back in the day?"

"I might have left that out."

She laughed again, but he knew it was coming. She'd had a couple of pops so it was only a matter of time before the hilarity turned to rage and self-pity. And it came. "Tell me, Denny, she fuck you better than I did?"

"Come on, Sheila."

"No, I want to know. Does she fuck better than me? You know what they say, once you try black, you never go back."

"Let's not do this."

Sheila said, "Because usually you cheat on me with *white* whores."

Well, that's true, Malone thought. "I'm not cheating on you. We're separated."

But Sheila was in no mood for legalisms. "It never bothered you when we were married, though, did it, Denny? You and your brother cops tapping everything with a pussy. Hey, do *they* know? Russo and Big Monty, they know you're stirring tar?"

He didn't want to lose his temper but he did. "Shut the fuck up, Sheila."

"What, are you going to hit me?"

"I've never laid a goddamn hand on you," Malone said. He's done a lot of bad things in his life, but hitting a woman is not one of them.

"No, that's right," she said. "You stopped touching me altogether."

Problem was, she had a point about that.

Now he shaves carefully, first down and then up against the grain, because he wants to look clean and refreshed.

Good luck with that, he thinks.

Opening the medicine cabinet, he pops a couple of 5 mg Dexes to give him a little boost.

Then he changes into a pair of clean jeans, a white dress shirt and a black wool sports coat to look like a citizen. Even in the summer, he usually wears long sleeves when he goes home because the tats piss off Sheila.

She thinks they were a symbol of his leaving Staten Island, that he was getting all "city hipster."

"They don't have tattoos on Staten Island?" he asked her. Hell, there's a parlor every other corner now and half the guys walking around the neighborhood have ink. About half the women, too, come to think of it.

He likes his tattoo sleeves. For one, he just likes them, for another, they scare the shit out of the mopes because they're not used to seeing them on cops. When he rolls up his sleeves to go to work on a mope, they know it's going to be bad.

And it's hypocritical, because Sheila has a little green shamrock down by her right ankle, as if you couldn't tell she was Irish just by looking at her, with the red hair, green eyes and freckles. Yeah, it doesn't take a $200-an-hour shrink to tell me that Claudette is the exact opposite of my soon-to-be ex-wife, Malone thinks as he clips the off-duty gun to his belt.

I get it.

Sheila is everything he grew up with, no surprises, the known. Claudette is a different world, a constant unfolding, the other. It's not just race, although that's a big part of it.

Sheila is Staten Island, Claudette is Manhattan.

She *is* the city to him.

The streets, the sounds, the scents, the sophisticated, the sexy, the exotic.

Their first date, she showed up in this retro 1940s dress with a white Billie Holiday gardenia in her hair and her lips a vivid red and perfume that made him almost dizzy with want.

He took her to Buvette, down in the Village off Bleecker, because he figured with a French first name she might like that, and anyway, he didn't want to take her anywhere in Manhattan North.

She figured that right out.

"You don't want to be seen with a 'sistuh' on your beat," she said as they sat down at the table.

"It's not that," he said, telling a half-truth. "It's just that when I'm up there, I'm always on duty. What, you don't like the Village?"

"I love the Village," Claudette said. "I'd live down here if it weren't so far from work."

She didn't go to bed with him that date or the next or the next, but when she did, it was a revelation and he fell in love like he didn't think was possible. Actually, he was already in love, because she challenged him. With Sheila it was either a resentful acceptance of whatever he did or an all-out, red-haired Irish brawl. Claudette, she pushed him on his assumptions, made him see things in a new way. Malone was never much of a reader, but she got him to read, even some poetry, a little bit of which, like Langston Hughes, he even liked. Some Saturday mornings they'd sleep in late and then go get coffee and sometimes prowl bookstores, something else he never thought he'd do, and she'd show him art books, tell him about the vacation to Paris she took all by herself and how she'd like to go back.

Shit, Sheila won't come to the city by herself.

But it isn't just the contrast to Sheila that makes Malone love Claudette.

It's her intelligence, her sense of humor, her warmth.

He's never met a kinder person.

It's a problem.

She's too kind for the work she does—she hurts for her patients, bleeds inside from the things she sees—and it breaks her, makes her reach for the needle.

It's good she's hitting the meetings.

Dressed, Malone grabs the wrapped presents he bought for the kids. Well, he bought all the presents for the kids, but Santa gets the cred for the ones under the tree. These are Malone's gifts to them—the new PlayStation 4 for John and a Barbie set for Caitlin.

Those were easy; finding a present for Sheila was a bitch.

He wanted to get her something nice, but nothing romantic or remotely sexy. He finally asked Tenelli for advice and she suggested a nice scarf. "Nothing cheap, from a street vendor like you assholes usually do last minute. Take a little time, go to Macy's or Bloomie's. What's her coloration?"

"What?"

"What does she look like, dummy?" Tenelli asks. "Is she dark, pale? What color is her hair?"

"Pale. Red."

"Go with gray. It's safe."

So he went down to Macy's, fought the crowd, and found a nice gray wool scarf that set him back a hundred. He hopes it sends the right message—I'm not in love with you anymore, but I'll always take care of you.

She should know it already, he thinks.

He's never late with the child support, he pays for the kids' clothes, John's hockey team, Caitlin's dance classes, and the family is still covered on his PBA health insurance, which is very good and includes dental.

And Malone always leaves an envelope for Sheila because he doesn't want her working and he doesn't want her to have a what-do-you-call-it, a "diminution" of her lifestyle. So he does the right thing and leaves a fat envelope, and she's grateful and hip enough never to ask where the money comes from.

Her dad was a cop, too.

"No, it's good you do the right thing," Russo said one time when they were talking about it.

"What else am I going to do?" Malone asked.

You grow up in that neighborhood, you do the right thing.

The prevailing attitude on Staten Island is that men can leave their wives, but only black men leave their kids. Which isn't fair, Malone thinks—Bill Montague's probably the best father he knows—but that's what people think, that black men go around knockin' they bitches up and then stick white people with the welfare bill.

A white guy from the East Shore tries something like that, he's got everyone up his ass—his priest, his parents, his siblings, his cousins, his friends—all telling him what a degenerate he is and showing him up by picking up the slack themselves.

"You did that," the guy's mother would say, "I couldn't hold my head up going to Mass. What would I say to Father?"

That specific argument don't cut much weight with Malone.

He hates priests.

Thinks they're parasites, and he won't go near a church unless it's a wedding or a funeral and he has to. But he won't give the church any money.

Malone, who also won't pass a Salvation Army bell ringer without putting at least a five in the bucket, won't give a dime to the Catholic Church he grew up in. He refuses to donate money to what he thinks is an organization of child molesters that should be indicted under the RICO statutes.

When the pope came to NYC, Malone wanted to arrest him.

"That wouldn't go down so well," Russo said.

"Yeah, probably not." With every cop over the grade of captain elbowing each other aside to kiss the pontiff's ring or his ass, whichever was presented first.

Malone ain't crazy about nuns, either.

"What about Mother Teresa?" Sheila asked him, when they were arguing about it. "She fed starving people."

"If she passed out condoms," Malone said, "she wouldn't have had so many starving people to feed."

Malone even hates *The Sound of Music.* It was the only movie he ever saw, he rooted for the Nazis.

"How could anyone hate *The Sound of Music?*" Monty asked him. "It's nice."

"What kind of shitty black man are you?" Malone asked him. "Listen to the fucking *Sound of Music.*"

"That's right," Monty said. "You listen to that rap shit."

"What you got against rap?"

"It's racist."

It's been Malone's experience that no one hates rap and hip-hop more than black men above the age of forty. They just can't stand the attitude, the pants hanging off their asses, the backward baseball caps, the jewelry. And most black men of that age aren't going to let their women be called bitches.

That just ain't gonna happen.

Malone's seen it. Once, back before it fell apart, he and Sheila and Monty and Yolanda were on a double date, driving up Broadway on a warm night with the windows open, and this rapper on the corner of Ninety-Eighth saw Yolanda and yelled out, "You got one sweet bitch, brother!" Monty stopped the car in the middle of Broadway, got out, walked over and clocked the kid. Walked back to the car, didn't say a word.

Nobody did.

Claudette, she doesn't hate hip-hop, but she listens to mostly jazz and makes him go to the clubs with her when one of the musicians she likes is playing. Malone likes it okay, but what he really likes are the *older* rap and hip-hop guys—Biggie, Sugarhill Gang, N.W.A. and Tupac. Nelly and Eminem are all right, too; so is Dr. Dre.

Malone stands in his living room and realizes that he's been spacing out, so the Dexedrine hasn't kicked in yet.

He locks up and walks to the garage where they park his car.

Malone's personal vehicle is a beautifully restored 1967 Chevy Camaro SS convertible, black with Z-28 stripes, 427-cubic-inch engine, four-speed manual transmission, tricked out with a new Bose sound system. He never takes it to the precinct, rarely even drives it in Manhattan. It's his indulgence—he uses it to go to the Island or on joyrides to escape the city.

Now he takes the West Side Highway downtown and then crosses Manhattan near the 9/11 site. It's been more than fifteen years and he still gets mad when he doesn't see the Towers. It's a hole in the skyline, a hole in his heart. Malone, he don't hate Muslims but he sure as hell hates those jihadist cocksuckers.

Three hundred and forty-three firefighters died that day.

Thirty-seven Port Authority and New Jersey police officers.

Twenty-three cops ran into those buildings and didn't come out.

Malone will never forget that day and wishes that he could. He was off-duty but responded to the Level-4 mobilization call. Him and Russo and two thousand other cops went, and he saw the second tower fall, not knowing at the moment that his brother was in it.

That endless day of searching and waiting and then the phone call that confirmed what he already knew in his gut—Liam wasn't coming back. It was Malone had to go tell his mother and he'll never forget the *sound*—the shrill scream of grief that came out of her mouth and still echoes in his ears in the gray hours when he can't sleep.

The other gift that keeps on giving is the smell. Liam once told him that he could never get the smell of burning flesh out of his nose, and Malone never really believed him until 9/11. Then the whole city smelled like death and ash and scorched flesh and rot and rage and sorrow.

And Liam was right—Malone never has gotten the smell out of his nose.

He puts Kendrick Lamar on the sound system and blasts it as he goes through the Battery Tunnel.

The phone rings when he's on the Verrazano Bridge.

It's Mark Piccone. "You got a couple of minutes today for me?"

"It's Christmas."

"Five minutes," Piccone says. "My new client wants to get this taken care of."

"Fat Teddy?" Malone asks. "Shit, his trial won't come up for months."

"He's nervous."

"I'm headed for the Island," Malone says.

"I'm already there," Piccone says. "Big family thing, I thought I'd try to make my escape late afternoon."

"I'll call you."

Malone comes off the bridge near Fort Wadsworth, where the New York marathon starts, gets off on Hylan and drives down through Dongan Hills, past Last Chance Pond, and then takes a left onto Hamden Avenue.

The old neighborhood.

Nothing special about it, just your basic East Shore block of nice single-family homes, mostly Irish or Italian, a lot of cops and firefighters.

A good place to raise kids.

The truth is he just couldn't stand it anymore.

The incredible freakin' boredom.

Couldn't stand coming back from busts, the stakeouts, the roofs, the alleys, the chases to what, Hylan Plaza, Pathmark, Toys "R" Us, GameStop. He'd come home from a tour jacked up from speed, adrenaline, fear, anger, sadness, rage, and then go to someone's cookie-cutter house to play Mexican Train or Monopoly or nickel poker. And they were nice people and he'd feel guilty sitting there sipping their wine coolers and making small talk when what he really wanted was to be back on the street in hot, smelly, noisy, dangerous, fun, interesting, stimulating, infuriating Harlem with the real people and the families and the hustlers, the slingers, the whores.

The poets, the artists, the dreamers.

He just loved the fuckin' city, man.

Watching them ball at Rucker, or standing up on the terrace in Riverside Park watching the Cubans play baseball down below. Sometimes he'd go up to the Heights and Inwood to check out the Dominican scene—the domino games on the sidewalks, the *reggaetón* music blaring out of car stereos, the street merchants hacking coconuts open with machetes. Go into Kenny's for a *café con leche* or stop at a street stand for the sweet bean soup.

It's what he loves about New York—you want it, it's there.

The sweet, fetid richness of this city. He never really got it until he left his Irish-Italian blue-collar, cop-fireman Staten Island ghetto and moved to the city. You hear five languages walking a single street, smell six cultures, hear seven kinds of music, see a hundred kinds of people, a thousand stories and it's all New York.

New York's the world.

Malone's world, anyway.

He'll never leave it.

No reason to.

He tried to explain it to Sheila, but how do you do that without bringing her into a world you don't want to put on her? How do you go from a tenement where the mommy-daddy combo is so fucked up on crack, and you find a baby dead for a week, her feet chewed by rats, and then take your own kids to Chuck E. Cheese's? You supposed to tell her about that? "Share" that? No, the right thing to do is put a smile on your face and talk to the tire salesmen about the Mets or what-the-fuck-ever because no one wants to hear about that and you don't want to talk about it, you just want to forget it, and good luck with that, ace.

That time Phil and Monty and him get an anonymous tip, go to this address in Washington Heights and they find this guy tied to a chair, his hands had been cut off for skimming some smack off the top of a shipment and he was still alive because the people who punished him also perfectly cauterized the wounds with a blowtorch, his eyes were bulging out of his skull, his jaw broken from clenching it so hard, and then they had to go back to a cookout and stand around by the grill with the host like guys do and he and Phil looked at each other over the grill and knew what the other was thinking. You don't talk to other cops about that shit because you don't have to. They already know. They're the only ones who know.

Then there was the birthday party.

Malone don't even remember which kid's birthday it was—some friend of Caitlin's maybe—and it was another one of those backyard parties and they had a piñata strung from the clothesline and Malone was sitting there watching them whack the thing and he'd spent all week in court on a heroin dealer named Bobby Jones and the jury came back not guilty because they just wouldn't believe that Malone had seen "Bobby Bones" slinging smack from across the street. So Malone was sitting there and the kids were swinging this stick at the donkey over and over and over again and they couldn't break it and finally Malone got up, took the stick from a kid, smashed the fucking donkey into smithereens and candy came flying out all over the place.

Everything stopped.

The whole party stared at him.

"Eat your candy," Malone said.

He was embarrassed and went into the bathroom and Sheila followed him in and said, "Jesus, Denny, what the *fuck?*"

"I don't know."

"You don't know?" she asked. "You embarrass us in front of all our friends and you don't *know?*"

No, you don't know, Malone thought.

And I don't know how to tell you.

I can't do this anymore.

Go from one life to another, and this life, *this* life, feels . . .

Stupid.

Phony.

This is not who I am.

Sorry, Sheila, but it's not who I am.

So this Christmas morning a sleepy Sheila meets Malone at the door in a blue flannel robe, her hair disheveled, no makeup on yet, and a coffee cup in her hand.

Still, he thinks she's beautiful.

He always has.

"Are the kids up?" Malone asks.

"No, I slipped them some Benadryl last night." Seeing the look on his face, she says, "That was a joke, Denny."

Malone follows her into the kitchen, where she pours him a cup of coffee and then sits down on a stool at the breakfast bar.

He asks, "How was Christmas Eve?"

"Great," she says. "The kids argued over which movie to watch and we settled on *Home Alone* and then *Frozen*. What did you do?"

He says, "A tour."

Sheila looks at him like she doesn't believe him, her expression accusing him of being with "huh."

"You on today?" she asks.

"No."

"We're going to Mary's for dinner," she says. "I'd invite you, but, you know, they fucking hate you."

Same old Sheila—the subtlety of a sledgehammer. Actually, it's one of the things he's always liked about her. She's black and white, you always know where you stand with her. And she's right—her sister Mary and her whole family hate him since the separation.

"That's okay," he says. "I might swing by Phil's. So how *are* the kids?"

"You're going to have to have 'the talk' with John soon."

"He's eleven."

"He'll be going into middle school," Sheila says. "You wouldn't believe what goes on these days. The girls are giving blow jobs in seventh grade."

Malone works Harlem, Inwood, Washington Heights.

Seventh grade is late.

"I'll talk to him."

"Not today, though."

"No, not today."

They hear voices from upstairs.

"Game time," Malone says.

He's standing at the bottom of the stairs when his kids come pounding down, their eyes lit up at the sight of the presents under the tree.

"Looks like Santa came," Malone says. He isn't hurt that they squeeze past him to get to the loot. They're kids, and anyway, they come by it honest.

"PlayStation 4!" John screams.

Well, there goes *my* present, Malone thinks, knowing no kid needs two PlayStations.

How could they have grown so much in two weeks, he wonders. Sheila, she probably don't notice because she's with them every day, but John is shooting up, just starting to get a little gangly. Caitlin has her mother's red hair, although it's still really curly, and those green eyes. I'm going to have to build a guard tower on the house, keep the boys away.

His heart hurts.

Shit, he thinks, I'm missing my kids growing up.

He sits down in the same easy chair he used to every Christmas when they were still together and Sheila sits on the same cushion on the sofa.

Traditions are important, he thinks. Habits are important; they give the kids a measure of stability. So he and Sheila sit and try to establish some order and make the kids take turns so their Christmas isn't over in thirty seconds, and Sheila enforces a torturous break for cinnamon rolls and hot chocolate before they go back to the presents.

John opens Malone's gift and feigns enthusiasm. "Oh, wow, Dad!"

He's a kind kid, Malone thinks. Sensitive. Can't let him go into the family trade, it would eat him alive.

"I didn't know Santa was handling this," Malone says, a subtle dig at Sheila.

"No, it's great," John says, improvising. "I can have one upstairs and one downstairs."

"I'll take it back," Malone says. "Get you something different."

John springs up and wraps his arms around Malone.

It means everything.

Gotta keep this boy off the Job, he thinks.

Caitlin loves her Barbie set. Comes over and gives her dad a big hug and a kiss on the cheek. "Thank you, Daddy."

"You're welcome, honey."

She still has that kid smell.

That sweet innocence.

Sheila is a great mom.

Then Caitlin breaks his heart. "Are you staying, Daddy?"

Crack.

John's looking up at him like he didn't even know this was a possibility but now he's hopeful.

"Not today," Malone says, "I have to work."

"Catching the bad guys," John says.

"Catching the bad guys."

You're not going to be me, Malone thinks. You're not going to be me.

Caitlin, she ain't giving up. "When all the bad guys are caught, will you come home?"

"We'll see, honey."

"'We'll see' means no," Caitlin says, giving her mother a sharp look.

"Don't you guys have presents for *us*?" Sheila says.

The excitement deflects them and they hustle to get their gifts from under the tree. John gives Malone a New York Rangers knit cap, Caitlin has a coffee mug she decorated in art class.

"This goes on my desk," Malone says. "And this goes on my head. I love them, guys, thanks. Oh, and this is for you."

He hands Sheila a box.

"I didn't get you anything," she says.

"Good."

"Macy's." She holds up the scarf for the kids to see. "This is beautiful. And it will keep my neck so warm. Thank you."

"You're welcome."

Then it gets awkward. He knows she needs to start the kids getting dressed to go over to her family's, the kids know it too. But they also know that if they move, he'll leave and the family will be broken again, so they sit still as statues.

Malone looks at his watch. "Oh, wow. I can't keep the bad guys waiting."

"That's funny, Daddy," Caitlin says.

Except her eyes are all teary.

Malone gets up. "You guys be good for Mom, okay?"

"We will," John says, already adopting the role of the man of the family.

Malone pulls both of them to his legs. "I love you."

"Love you, too." Sadly. In chorus.

He and Sheila don't hug because they don't want to give the kids false hope.

Malone goes out the door thinking that Christmas was invented to torture divorced parents and their children.

Fuck Christmas.

It's way too early to show up at Russo's, so Malone drives out to the shore.

He wants to time his arrival for after dinner to avoid the death-by-pasta ordeal that Donna is planning. The idea is to get there just for the cannoli and the pumpkin pie and some laced coffee.

Malone parks in a lot across the road from the beach and sits in the car with the motor running and the heat on. He's tempted to go for a walk but it's too cold out.

Taking a pint bottle out of the glove compartment, he sips on it. Malone is a heavy drinker but nowhere near being an alcoholic and normally wouldn't drink this early except the whiskey warms him up.

Maybe I would be an alkie, Malone thinks, except I have too big an ego to be a stereotype.

The alcoholic divorced Irish cop.

Who was it, yeah, Jerry McNab, drove out here one Christmas afternoon and put the gun under his chin. His off-duty weapon. Alcoholic divorced Irish cop blows his own brains out.

Another stereotype.

The guys from the One-Oh-One made sure it went down he was cleaning his gun so there'd be no problem with the insurance or the pension and the claims guy knew better than to fuck with them so he pretended to believe a guy was cleaning his gun at the beach on Christmas.

Except McNab, he was scared of going to jail, doing time. They had him, too, dead to rights, on video taking money from a crack dealer in Brooklyn. They were going to take his shield, his gun, his pension, put him behind bars, and he couldn't face it. Couldn't face the shame his family would go through, his ex-wife and kids seeing him in handcuffs, so he ate the gun.

Russo had a different interpretation. They were discussing it in the car one night, killing time on a surveillance, and Russo said, "You *stunatzes* got it all wrong. He did it to save his pension, for his family."

"Didn't he put anything away?" Malone asked.

"He was in a sector car," Russo said. "He couldn't have been making that much, even in the Seven-Five. He dies in an accident, his family keeps the pension and the benefits. McNab did the right thing."

Except he didn't save, Malone thinks.

Malone does.

He has cash stowed away, investments, bank accounts where the feds can never lay their paws on it.

And he has another account, over on Pleasant Avenue with the guineas, what's left of the old Cimino family crew in East Harlem. Those guys are better than banks. They won't rob you or throw your money away on bad mortgage loans.

I'll take an honest mobster over those Wall Street cocksuckers any day, Malone thinks. What the general public doesn't get—they think the Mafia are crooks? The guineas only wish they could steal like the hedge fund guys, the politicians, the judges, the lawyers.

And Congress?

Forget about it.

A cop takes a ham sandwich to look the other way, he loses his job. Congressman Butthole takes a few million from a defense contractor for his vote, he's a patriot. The next time a politician blows his brains out to save his pension will be the first time.

And I'll pop a champagne bottle, Malone thinks.

But I ain't going the way of Jerry McNab.

Malone, he knows he's not the suicide type.

I'm going to make them shoot *me,* he thinks, looking out at the dune grass and the weathered hurricane fence. Hurricane Sandy did a number on Staten Island. Malone made sure to be home that night, sat with Sheila and the kids in the basement and played Go Fish. Went out the next day and did what he could to help.

They nail me, I'll do my time and fuck you and your pension.

I can take care of my family.

Sheila don't even have to go up to Pleasant Avenue, they'll come to her. A fat envelope every month.

They will do the right thing.

Because they're not in Congress.

He gets on the phone and calls Claudette.

"You up?" he asks when she answers.

"Just," she says. "Thank you for my earrings, baby. They're beautiful. I have something for you."

"You gave me my present last night."

"That was for *us,*" she says. "I have the four to midnight. You want to come through after?"

"I do. You going to your sister's today, right?"

"I can't think of a way out of it," Claudette says. "It will be nice to see the children, though."

He's glad she's going, he worries about her being alone.

The last time she used, he gave her a choice—you get into a car with me and I take you to rehab or I put you in bracelets and you can detox in Rikers. She was furious at him but got in the car and he drove her up to the Berkshires in Connecticut, this place his West Side doctor found for him.

Sixty grand for the rehab, but it was worth it.

She's been clean since.

"I'd like to meet your family sometime," he says now.

She laughs softly. "I'm not sure we're ready for that, baby."

Which is code for she's not ready to bring a white cop home to her family in Harlem. Be about as welcome as a Klan member at a black home in Mississippi.

"Sometime, though," Malone says.

"We'll see. I need to hop in the shower."

"Hop," he says. "I'll see you later."

He pulls the Rangers cap over his head, zips up his jacket and shuts the motor off. The car will stay warm for a few minutes. He sits back and closes his eyes, knows the Dexedrine won't let him drop off, but his eyes are sore.

Perfect timing at Phil's.

They're just clearing the dinner plates, the house is Italian-American chaos with about fifty-seven cousins running around, the men gossiping by the television, the women chattering in the kitchen, and Phil's dad somehow managing to sleep through all of it in the big easy chair in the den.

"The fuck you been?" Phil asks. "You missed dinner."

"Got a late start."

"Bullshit," Phil says, showing him in. "You been out doing that Irish brooding thing, you dumbass donkey. Come on, Donna will fix you a plate."

"I'm saving room for the cannoli."

"Yeah, well, you're going home with Tupperware, don't even try."

Phil's twin boys, Paul and Mark, come up to say hello to their uncle Denny. They're typical South Staten Island Italian teenage boys with the gelled haircuts and the muscle shirts and the attitude.

"They're spoiled assholes is what they are," Russo once said to

Malone. "Spend half their time in the mall, the other half playing video games."

Malone knows that isn't true, that Donna spends all her time chauffeuring them around to hockey and soccer and baseball. The boys are good athletes, maybe scholarship good, but Russo won't brag about them.

Maybe because he misses so many of their games.

Their daughter, Sophia, is something else. Russo has even talked about moving across the river because she wouldn't have a chance of winning Miss New York, but she might have a crack at Miss New Jersey.

Seventeen, she looks like Donna, tall and leggy and with charcoal-black hair and surprising blue eyes.

Freakin' gorgeous.

And she knows it. She's a sweet kid, though, Malone thinks, not as conceited as she could be, and she adores her dad.

Russo downplays it. His line is "I just gotta keep her off the stripper pole."

"Yeah, I don't think that's a concern," Malone said.

"And not knocked up," Russo said. "It's easier with a boy, you just got one dick to worry about."

Sophia comes up and gives Malone a kiss on the cheek and with a disarming show of maturity asks, "How are Sheila and the kids?"

"They're good, thanks for asking."

She gives his hand a sympathetic squeeze to show she's a woman and understands his pain, then she goes into the kitchen to help her mother.

"It go okay this morning?" Russo asks.

"Yeah."

"We should grab a minute to talk." Russo shouts, "Hey, Donna! I'm taking Denny down to the basement, show him that tool kit you got me!"

"Don't be long! Dessert's coming out!"

The cellar's as clean as an operating room, a place for everything

THE FORCE / 113

and everything in its place, although Malone doesn't know when Russo finds the time to actually be down here.

"It's Torres," Russo says. "On Carter's pad."

"How do you know?"

"He called this morning."

"To wish you a Merry Christmas?" Malone asks.

"To bitch about Fat Teddy," Russo says. "I'm betting that fat pig went crying to Carter, who jerked Torres's chain. Torres says we need to let him eat."

"We don't keep him from earning," Malone says.

If a guy earns outside the borough, he keeps 100 percent. But if he or his team earn inside Manhattan North, they kick ten points into a fund that everyone shares.

Kind of like the NFL.

Any of the teams can range anywhere, but as a matter of practicality, Washington Heights and Inwood are Torres's team's profit center.

But now it looks like he's on Carter's pad.

Malone won't go on a pad. He'll rip drug dealers, work the system with them, but he don't want to be an employee or a wholly owned subsidiary.

Still, he ain't going to war with Torres. Life is good right now, and when life is good, you leave it the fuck alone.

Malone says, "Piccone will take care of Fat Teddy. I'm meeting him later."

Malone has this random thought that Torres is setting them up, wearing a wire, but tosses it out of his head. They could squeeze his shoes until his bones break and Torres wouldn't give up a brother officer. He's a wrong, brutal cop and a greedy prick, but he's not a rat.

A rat is the worst thing in the world.

They're quiet for a second, then Russo says, "Christmas, it don't feel the same without Billy, does it."

"No."

It was always a thing at Christmas, to see what woman Billy would bring over that year.

A model, an actress, always some hottie.

"We better get upstairs before they think you're sucking my joint," Russo says.

"How come they won't think you're sucking mine?"

"Because no one would believe that," Russo says. "Come on."

The cannoli is as good as advertised.

Malone has two of them and sits out a debate about the relative merits of the Rangers, Islanders and Devils, because Staten Island is right in that triangle where you could legitimately root for any of them.

He's always been a Rangers guy, always will be.

Donna Russo catches him in the kitchen scraping his plate and takes the opportunity to ambush him. She's no fucking bullshit. "So, your wife and kids. You going back?"

"Yeah, I don't see that in the cards, Donna."

"Get a fresh deck," Donna says. "They need you. Believe it or not, you need them. You're a better person with Sheila."

"She don't think so."

Malone doesn't know if that's true. They've been separated for over a year, and while Sheila says she's good with getting divorced, she keeps dragging her feet on the paperwork. And he's just been too busy to push it.

What you tell yourself, anyway, Malone thinks.

"Give me that plate," Donna says. She takes it and jams it into the dishwasher. "Phil says you got something on the side in Manhattan."

"It's not on the side," Malone says. "It's in the center, I'm not married anymore."

"In the eyes of the church—"

"Don't give me that bullshit."

Malone loves Donna, known her all his life, would die for her, but he's not in the mood for her housewife hypocrisy. Donna Russo

knows—she has to know—that her husband has a *gumar* on Columbus Avenue and gets strange every chance that comes up, which it
does a lot. She knows and she chooses to ignore it because she wants
the nice house and the clothes and the kids in college.

Malone don't blame her, but let's keep it real.

"I'm sending food home with you," Donna says. "You look thin,
are you eating?"

"Italian women."

"You should be so lucky," Donna says. She starts filling large
plastic containers with turkey, mashed potatoes, vegetables and
macaroni. "Sheila and I are taking pole-dancing classes, she tell
you?"

"She left that out."

"It's great cardio," Donna says, filling his hands with the containers, "and can be very sexy, too, you know? Sheila might have
some new tricks you don't know about, buddy boy."

"It wasn't all about the sex," Malone says.

"It's always all about the sex," Donna says. "Go back to your
wife, Denny. Before it's too late."

"You know something I don't?"

"I know *everything* you don't," she says.

He says good-bye to Russo on his way out.

"She bust balls about you and Sheila?" Russo asks.

"Of course."

"Listen, she busts *my* balls about you and Sheila," Russo says.

"Thanks for having me."

"Fuck you, thanks."

Malone puts the food in the backseat and calls Mark Piccone.
"You got time now?"

"For you, always. Where?"

Malone has a wild hair. "How about the Boardwalk?"

"It's freezing."

"All the better." Won't be a lot of people out there.

116 / DON WINSLOW

It's empty, all right. The day has turned gray and a fierce wind is coming off the bay. Piccone's black Mercedes is already there, a couple of cars, people escaping their family dinners, an old van looks like it was dumped there.

He pulls up alongside Piccone's driver's side from the opposite direction and rolls down the window. Malone don't know why every lawyer has to drive a Mercedes, but they do.

Piccone hands him an envelope. "Your finder's fee on Fat Teddy."

"Thank you."

The way it works—you bust a guy, you give him a defense lawyer's card. If he goes ahead and hires that lawyer, the lawyer owes you a taste.

But it gets better.

"Can you straighten it out?" Piccone asks.

"Who's riding?"

"Justin Michaels."

Malone knows Michaels is a player. Most ADAs—assistant district attorneys—aren't, but enough are that a cop who's well connected, and Malone is, can get two licks at the spoon. "Yeah, I can probably straighten that out."

By slipping an envelope to ADA Michaels, who will find that the chain of evidence got jacked up.

"How much?" Piccone asks.

"Are we talking a reduction or a *nol pros*?" Malone asks.

"A walk."

"Ten to twenty K."

"And that includes your cut, right?"

Why is Piccone busting balls? Malone wonders. He knows as well as I do that I take my taste from Michaels. It's what I get for being the cutout, so two fucking lawyers don't have to embarrass themselves by acknowledging to each other they're for sale. Also, it's safer for them, because a cop talking to a prosecutor in the hallway is a daily event and doesn't look suspicious. "Yeah, of course."

"Make the deal."

New York, New York, Malone thinks—the town so nice they pay you twice.

And anyway, he owes Teddy for the tips on the gun source.

Malone pulls out of the parking lot.

He's gone three blocks when he sees the car tailing him.

It ain't Piccone.

Fuck, is it IAB?

The car gets closer and Malone sees it's Raf Torres. Malone pulls over and gets out. Torres pulls in behind him and they meet on the sidewalk.

"The fuck, Torres?" Malone asks. "It's Christmas. Shouldn't you be with your family, or your whores or something?"

"You get this straightened out with Piccone?" he asks.

"Your boy will be okay," Malone says.

"That bust should have been over the second he mentioned my name," Torres says.

"He didn't mention your fucking name," Malone says. "And what makes you think you can provide cover for one of Carter's people?"

"Three grand a month," Torres says. "Carter isn't happy. He wants his money back."

"The fuck I care he's happy?" Malone says.

"You have to let other people eat."

"Help yourself," Malone says. "Just dine outside Harlem."

"You're a royal prick, Malone, you know that?"

"The question is, do *you* know that?"

Torres laughs. "Piccone kicking to you?"

Malone don't answer.

"I should get a taste of that," Torres says.

Malone reaches to his crotch. "You can have a taste of this."

"Nice," Torres says. "Nice talk on Christmas."

"You want to take Carter's money, that's your business," Malone says. "Knock yourself out. But he needs to know he's bought you, not me. He slings on my turf, he's open season."

"If that's how you want it, brother."

"And you're betting on the wrong horse," Malone says. "If I don't bring Carter down, the Domos will."

"Even after losing a hundred keys of smack?" Torres asks.

"Fifty," Malone says.

Torres smirks. "Whatever you say."

It's fucking freezing out.

Malone gets back in his car and pulls out.

Torres doesn't follow him.

On the drive back to Manhattan, Malone puts Nas on and pumps it up loud. Sings along—

I'm out for presidents to represent me / Say what?
I'm out for presidents to represent me / Say what?
I'm out for dead presidents to represent me.
Whose world is this?
The world is yours.

It's mine, it's mine, it's mine.

If I can hold on to it, Malone thinks.

If DeVon Carter taps into the Iron Pipeline, he's going to leave Domo bodies strewn all over Manhattan North. The Domos will retaliate and we'll be freaking Chicago before we know it.

That ain't all.

Carter was talking about the Pena rip, then Lou Savino, and now Torres is making noise about it?

It's too risky now to try to move the Pena shit.

And the Pena shit could put you right where Jerry McNab was.

Maybe you'll luck out and go sudden from a heart attack or a stroke or an aneurysm, but if not, when the time comes you can't take care of yourself . . .

Jesus, you're a morbid piece of shit today.

Man the fuck up.
You got a job you love.
Money.
Friends.
An apartment in the city.
A beautiful sexy woman who loves you.
You own Manhattan North.
So they can't touch you.
No one can touch you.

Dwellin' in the Rotten Apple
You get tackled or caught by the devil's lasso . . .

PART 2

THE EASTER BUNNY

Over my forty-year career as a defense attorney, I regularly came into contact with people who lied, cheated, and tried to bend the system so that they would come out on top.

Most of them worked for the government.

—OSCAR GOODMAN, *BEING OSCAR*

CHAPTER 6

A dead kid kills an old lady.

The woman is ninety-one and small.

Smaller yet in death.

The entry wound, like most entry wounds, is neat and in the center of her left cheek, below the eye. The exit wound, like most exit wounds, isn't small or neat—blood, brains and white hair are blown onto the back of a plastic-covered wingback chair.

"They shouldn't look out the window when they hear shit," Ron Minelli says. "But that was probably her whole life. She probably spent her whole day looking out the window."

Fourth floor of Building Six in the Nickel, the elderly lady catches a stray round. Malone walks over to the window and looks down. The shooter is in the courtyard, his gun hand outstretched, finger still on the trigger as it was when he fell backward and squeezed off a shot. He was probably already croaked and it was an automatic muscle reaction.

"Thanks for the call," Malone says.

"I figured it was drug related," Minelli says.

It is. The DOA down in the courtyard is Mookie Gillette, one of DeVon Carter's slingers.

Monty is looking around the small apartment—photographs

of adult kids, grandchildren, great-grandchildren. China teacups, a collection of souvenir spoons from Saratoga, Colonial Williamsburg, Franconia Notch—gifts from her family.

"Leonora Williams," Monty says. "Rest in peace."

He lights a cigar, even though the body hasn't started to smell yet. The old woman is past minding.

A sector car rolls up in the courtyard and Sykes gets out. The captain walks over to the dead kid and shakes his head. Then he looks up at the window.

Malone nods.

Russo says, "I got the bullet. It's in the wall here."

"Wait for the Crime Scene guys," Malone says. "I'll be downstairs."

He takes the elevator down to the courtyard.

Half of St. Nick's is out there, kept away from the body by uniforms from the Three-Two and yellow crime tape. One of the kids says, "Hey, Malone, it true Mrs. Williams dead?"

"Yeah."

"That too bad."

"Yes, it is."

He walks over to Sykes.

Sykes looks at him. "What a world."

"But it's ours."

"Four deadly shootings in six weeks," Sykes says.

Yeah, your numbers are fucked, Captain, Malone thinks. Monday's CompStat meeting, they're going to do a flamenco on your chest. Then he regrets thinking it. He doesn't like the captain, but the man is sincerely saddened about the deaths in the projects.

It bothers Sykes.

Bothers Malone, too.

He's supposed to be protecting people like Leonora Williams. It's one thing when the slingers gun each other down, another when an innocent old lady gets hit in the cross fire.

The media will be rolling up any second.

Torres walks over.

Their arrangement has held for three months. Torres has stayed on Carter's pad while Malone and his team haven't let up. But now the tit-for-tat killings in the projects between Carter and the Dominicans, threatening an out-and-out turf war, also threaten the uneasy truce.

And now a civilian has been killed.

"Here's a shock," Torres is saying. "No one saw anything."

"It had to be a Trinitario," Sykes says. "Retaliating for DeJesus."

Raoul DeJesus was gunned down in the Heights last week. Prior to his demise, he was the chief suspect in the murder of a Get Money Boy shot and killed on 135th.

"Gillette here was GMB, right?" Sykes asks.

"Born and bred."

And GMB slings for Carter.

"Round up Trinis," Sykes says to Torres. "Bring them in for questioning, pop them for weed, outstanding warrants, I don't care. Let's see if any of them want to talk instead of going to Rikers."

"You got it, boss."

"Malone, run down your sources, see if anyone's talking," Sykes says. "I want a suspect, I want an arrest, I want these killings closed."

The circus arrives. Reporters, television news trucks. And with them, Reverend Hampton.

Of course, Malone thinks—lights, cameras, Hampton.

Actually, it's not the worst thing. Hampton at least pulls some of the media off the cops, and Malone can hear him talking . . . "community" . . . "tragedy" . . . "cycle of violence" . . . "economic disparity" . . . "what are the police doing to" . . .

To his credit, Sykes takes on the rest of the reporters. "Yes, we can confirm two homicides. . . . No, we have no suspects at the moment. . . . I can't confirm that this was drug or gang related. . . . The Manhattan North Special Task Force will be heading up the investigation. . . ."

A reporter breaks off from the gaggle and approaches Malone. "Detective Malone?"

"Yeah?"

"Mark Rubenstein, *New York Times*." Tall, thin, a neatly trimmed beard. A sports coat with a sweater underneath, glasses, smart.

"Captain Sykes is handling all the questions," Malone says.

"I get that," Rubenstein says. "I'm just wondering if there's a time you and I could get together and talk. I'm doing a series of articles about the heroin epidemic—"

"You understand I'm a little busy at the moment."

"Sure." Rubenstein hands him a card. "I'd love to talk to you if you're ever interested."

I'll never be interested, Malone thinks, taking the card.

Rubenstein goes back to the impromptu press conference.

Malone walks over to Torres. "I want to sit down with Carter."

"You think, huh?" Torres says. "You're not his favorite police officer."

"I'm taking care of Bailey for him."

His trial is coming up, the fix will go in.

"Fucking Dominicans," Torres says. "I'm Spanish and I hate those greasy cocksuckers."

Tenelli comes over. "The GMBs are already talking payback."

"Hey, Tenelli, give us a second, yeah?" Malone asks. She shrugs and moves off. "Get me with Carter?"

"You guarantee his safety?"

"You think the Trinis are going to come in when—"

"Not from the Domos," Torres says. "From *you*."

"Set it up," Malone says. He walks back to where Sykes is just finishing with the media.

A plainclothes cop stands beside him.

"Malone, this is Dave Levin," Sykes says. "He just came on the Task Force. I'm assigning him to your team."

Levin's maybe in his early thirties. Thin, tall, full black hair, a sharp nose. He shakes Malone's hand. "It's an honor to meet you."

Malone turns to Sykes. "Captain, can I have a moment?"

Sykes nods to Levin, who steps away.

"If I wanted a puppy, I'd go to the pound," Malone says.

Sykes says, "Levin's a smart guy, comes out of Anti-Crime in the Seven-Six. Had some good collars, did a lot of heavy jobs, got a lot of guns off the street."

Great, Malone thinks. Sykes is bringing his old team over from the Seven-Six. Levin's primary loyalty will be to Sykes, not the team. "That's not the point. I have a smooth-functioning team. We work well together—a new guy throws it off balance."

"Task Force teams are made up of four people," Sykes says. "You need to replace O'Neill."

Nobody can replace Billy, Malone thinks. "Then give me a Spanish guy. Give me Gallina."

"I can't fuck Torres like that."

Torres is fucking *you* like a prison bitch, Malone thinks. "Okay, I'll take Tenelli."

Sykes seems amused. "You want a woman?"

Better than a fucking spy, Malone thought.

"Tenelli just scored very high on the lieutenant's exam," Sykes says. "She's going to be out of here soon. No, you're taking Levin. You're shorthanded and, as I might have mentioned, I want these cases closed. Are you making any progress on Carter's gun hookup?"

"It's gone dead."

"Easter's coming," Sykes says. "Revive it. No guns, no war."

Malone walks over to Levin. "Come on."

He leads him toward the building where Leonora's apartment is. Was.

Levin says, "I can't believe I'm working Manhattan North with Denny freaking Malone."

"You don't need to suck my dick," Malone says. "What you need to do is listen more than you talk and at the same time not hear anything. You get that?"

"Sure."

"No, you don't," Malone says. "And you won't for a while. Then, if you're as smart as Sykes says, you'll get it."

The question is, whose spy are you? Sykes's? IAB's? One of their own people or a "field associate," a cop they use?

Are you wearing a wire?

Is this about Pena?

"What made you want to transfer to the Task Force?" Malone asks.

"It's where the action is," Levin says.

"Plenty of action in the Seven-Six." Busiest precinct in the city. Leading the league in shootings and robberies. And heavy with gangs—the Eight Trey Crips, Folk Nation, the Bully Gang. What more action does the kid want?

"Well, 'be careful what you wish for.' Sometimes boring is good," Malone says. Then he asks, "Married? Kids?"

"I have a girlfriend. We're, you know, exclusive."

Yeah, we'll see how long that lasts, Malone thinks. Da Force ain't exactly Promise Keepers. "This girl have a name?"

"Amy."

"Nice."

Good luck, Amy, Malone thinks.

Unless Dave here is IAB, then he keeps his dick as clean as his nose. Something to watch for. You can't trust a guy won't drink with you, do a little blow or a little weed, won't get laid on the side. That guy don't want to have to explain that shit to his bosses.

"So, Sykes, he's your hook?" Malone asks.

"I don't know if I'd say that."

"Well, Manhattan North is a hook house," Malone says. "The Task Force is a plum assignment. You got what, an uncle at One P?"

"I think Captain Sykes appreciated my work in the Seven-Six," Levin says. "But if you're asking if I'm his boy, I'm not."

"Does he know that?"

Levin bristles a little. The puppy has some teeth, Malone thinks.

"Yeah, I think he knows that," Levin says. "Why? Do you and he have some kind of a beef?"

"Let's just say we see things different."

"He's by the book," Levin says.

"He is that."

Levin says. "Look, I know you aren't thrilled to have a new guy, and I know I can't replace Billy O'Neill. I just want you to know I appreciate it and I won't get under your feet."

You're already under my feet, Malone thought. Or up my ass.

The elevator stinks of urine.

Levin gags.

"They use them for toilets," Malone says.

"Why don't they use the toilets?"

"Most of them are broken," Malone says. "Plumbing gets ripped out and sold. We're lucky it's just piss today."

They get out on four and walk into Leonora's apartment. The Crime Scene guys are in there now, doing their thing, although the case is obvious.

"This is Dave Levin," Malone said. "He's coming on the team."

Russo looks at Levin like he's inspecting produce at the supermarket. "Phil Russo."

"Nice to meet you."

Montague looks up from where he's straightening his argyle socks. "Bill Montague."

"Dave Levin."

"He came over from the Seven-Six," Malone says.

Now they're thinking the same thing he is—even if Levin isn't Sykes's spy, the last thing they need is a newbie, someone they don't know they can trust to have their backs.

"Let's go work the streets," Malone says.

The street is always good.

It's where Malone feels at home, in charge, in control of himself and his environment.

No matter what the problem is, the answer is always in the street.

Russo turns left off Frederick Douglass onto 129th, through the center of the project, then pulls over by a large three-story building.

"This is the HCZ," Malone tells Levin. "The Harlem Children's Zone, a charter school. There's not too much slinging around here because the boys don't want the extra sentencing for trafficking in a school zone."

Drug slinging has become largely an indoor trade because it's safer out of the eyes of the cops and it's just easier to phone or text your dealer and go to an apartment in one of the buildings or into the stairwells and make the buy. And it's virtually impossible for the cops to make a raid in the buildings because the slingers post kids as lookouts who warn them and they've scattered before you can even get through the door.

They drive east to the end of the block and Salem Methodist Church, then turn north on Seventh toward the St. Nick's playground.

"Two playgrounds in the project," Malone says, "North and South. This is North. Heavy betting on the b-ball games, the losers have been known to shoot instead of pay. What are you doing?"

"Taking notes."

"This look like college to you?" Malone asks. "You see coeds, Frisbees, man buns? You don't take notes, you don't write anything down. Only thing you ever write are your 5s. Notes you take on duty are discoverable. Some defense attorney shithead will deliberately misinterpret them and ram them up your ass on the stand."

"I get it."

"Keep everything in your head, College," Russo says.

A couple of Spades shooting hoops see the car and start to hoot. "Malone! Hey, Malone!"

Whistles pierce the air as the lookouts warn the slingers. Bangers disappear behind buildings. Malone waves to the kids on the court. "We'll be back!"

"When you do, Malone, bring your wife some clean panties! The ones she got on stink!"

Malone laughs. "Lend her a pair of yours, Andre! Those red silk ones I like!"

It gets more hoots and hollers.

"Oh No Henry" is walking along the sidewalk with that guilty but ecstatic "I just scored" look on his face.

Oh No Henry got his tag the first time they popped him, what, going on three years now. They put him against a wall and asked if he was carrying heroin.

"Oh, no," Henry said with shocked innocence.

"You shoot smack?" Malone asked.

"Oh, no."

Then Monty found the envelope of smack in his pants pocket, with fixings, and Henry just said, "Oh, no."

Monty told the story in the locker room that night and the name stuck.

Now Malone waits until Oh No Henry turns into an alley where he's going to cook up and lay out. He, Russo and Levin go in behind him, Henry turns and sees them and says, with wonderful predictability, "Oh, no."

"Henry, don't you run on me," Malone says.

"Don't you run, Henry," says Russo.

They grab him up and quickly find the smack.

"Don't say it, Henry," Malone says. "I'm begging you, don't say it."

Henry doesn't know what he means. He's a skinny white guy in his late twenties but he could easily pass for fifty. He wears a denim jacket that used to be wool-lined, jeans and sneakers, and his hair is long and filthy.

"Henry, Henry, Henry," Russo says.

"That's not mine."

"Well, it's not *mine*," Malone says. "And I don't think it's Phil's. But let me ask him. Phil, is this your heroin?"

"No, it is not."

"No, it is not," Malone says. "So if it's not mine and it's not Phil's, it must be yours, Henry. Unless you're calling us liars. You're not calling us liars, are you?"

"Give me a break, Malone," Henry says.

"You want a break," Malone says, "give *me* a break. You hear anything about that shooting in St. Nick's?"

"What did you *want* me to hear?"

"No, we're not doing that, Henry," Malone says. "If you heard something, tell me what you heard."

Henry looks around, then he says, "I heard it was Spades."

"You're full of shit," Malone says. "The Spades are with Carter, too."

"You asked me what I heard," Henry says. "That's what I heard."

If it's true, it's bad news.

The Spades and the GMB have had an uneasy but viable truce, enforced by Carter, for a year or so now. If that's broken, St. Nick's is going to tear itself apart. A war inside the project, with 129th as no-man's-land, will be a catastrophe.

"You hear anything more," Malone says, "you call me."

"Who's he?" Henry asks, pointing at Levin.

"He's with us," Malone says.

Henry looks at him funny.

He don't trust him either.

They meet Babyface up in Hamilton Heights behind the Big Brother Barber Shop.

The undercover sucks on his pacifier as Malone tells him what Henry said about the Spades.

"It's not crazy," Babyface says. "The shooter was definitely a brother."

"Not a dark Dominican?" Monty asks.

"A *brother*," Babyface says. "Could have been a Spade. They're sure as shit gunning up."

He looks at Levin.

"Dave Levin," Malone says. "He came over from Brooklyn."

Babyface nods at him. About as much of a welcome as Levin's going to get. Babyface says, "Shame about that lady."

"What are you hearing about the guns?"

"Silence," Babyface says.

"Anyone talking about a white guy?" Monty asks. "A cracker named Mantell?"

"Biker?" Babyface asks. "I've seen that dude around, but no one's talking about him. You think we're looking for an Iron Pipeline gun?"

"Could be."

"I'll keep an ear."

"Be careful, huh?" Malone says.

"Always."

"Anybody hungry?" Russo asks.

"I could eat," Monty says. "Manna's?"

Russo says, "When in Nairobi . . ." He drives down to 126th and Douglass and parks in front of the Unity Funeral Chapel across the street. A kid who looks about fourteen is standing on the sidewalk.

"Why aren't you in school?" Monty asks him.

"Suspended."

"What for?"

"Fighting."

"Dumbass." Monty slips him a ten. "Look after the car."

They go into Manna's.

The place is long and narrow—a checkout counter in front by the windows, then double cafeteria racks with trays of food. Malone takes a large Styrofoam container and fills it with jerked chicken, fried chicken, macaroni and cheese, some greens and banana pudding.

"Take what you want," he tells Levin. "They charge by the pound."

Most of the other customers, all black, either look away or give them hostile, empty looks. Contrary to myth, most cops don't eat in their own precincts, especially the predominantly black or Hispanic ones, because they're afraid the staff will spit in their food or do something worse.

Malone likes Manna's because the food's already made and he can control what he eats, and, well, he just likes the food.

He gets in line.

The counter guy asks him, "Four of you?"

Malone takes out two twenties but the guy ignores them. He hands Malone a receipt anyway. Malone walks to a table in the back. The rest of the team get their food and sit down with him.

Stares follow them all the way to the table.

It's gotten worse since the Bennett shooting. It was bad after Garner, but now it's worse.

"We don't pay?" Levin asks.

"We *tip*," Malone says. "And we tip large. These are good people up here, they work hard. And we don't come more than once a month—you don't want to beat a guy to death."

"What, you don't like your food?" Russo asks.

"Are you kidding? It's dumb good."

"Dumb good," Monty says. "Are you trying to sound hood, Levin?"

"No, I just—"

"Eat," Russo says. "You want a soda or something, you buy it because they have to account for that."

They all know it's a test. If Levin is Sykes's boy, or an IAB field agent, this will come back on them. But Malone has a receipt ready and can say that Levin is full of shit.

Unless Levin's out for bigger game, Malone thinks. He pushes it a little to feel the guy out. "We alternate tours—days, nights, graveyards—but that's just a technicality. The cases define the hours. We're flexible, you need lost time, call me, don't put it through at the house. We make good overtime, some good side jobs, you're interested. But don't take any off-duty work you don't clear through me."

"Okay."

Malone goes into teaching mode. "Those projects towers, you *never* go in alone. The roof and the top two floors are combat zones—the gangs always take them over. The stairways are where the bad shit happens—dealing, assaults, rapes."

"But we do mostly narcotics, right?" Levin asks.

"You ain't 'we' yet, College," Malone says. "Yeah, our main mission is dope and guns, but the Task Force teams do what-the-fuck-ever we want, because it's all related. Most of the robberies are junkies and crackheads. The rapes and assaults are mostly gang-bangers who are also slinging."

"We play them back and forth," Russo says. "A guy you bust on a drug charge might give you a murderer for a lesser charge or a walk. An accessory to a homicide might give you a major dealer if you'll let him plead down."

"Any Task Force team can follow a case anywhere in Manhattan North," Malone says. "This team mostly works the Upper West Side and West Harlem. Torres and his people work Inwood and the Heights.

"We work all the streets and the projects—St. Nick's, Grant and Manhattanville, Wagner. You'll learn our turf and theirs—OTV, 'Only the Ville'; Money Avenue crew; Very Crispy Gangsters; Cash Bama Bullies. The big thing we got goin' on now is the Domos up in the Heights—the Trinitarios—aren't content with just wholesale anymore. They're moving in on the black slingers down here."

"Vertical integration," Monty says.

"So where are you from, Levin?" Russo asks.

"The Bronx."

"The Bronx?" Monty asks.

"Riverdale," Levin admits.

The crew cracks up.

"Riverdale isn't the Bronx," Russo says. "It's the suburbs. Rich Jews."

"Tell me you didn't go to Horace Mann," Monty says, naming the expensive private school.

Levin doesn't answer.

"I thought so," Monty says. "And then where?"

"NYU. Majored in criminal justice."

"You might as well have majored in Bigfoot," Malone says.

"Why's that?" Levin asks.

"Because it don't exist, either. Do us all a favor, forget everything they taught you," Malone says. He gets up. "I gotta make a call."

Malone walks outside and gets on the phone. "Did you see him?"

Larry Henderson, a lieutenant in IAB, sits in a car parked in front of the funeral home. "Levin's the tall one? Black hair?"

"Jesus shit, Henderson," Malone says. "He's the one who's not *us*."

"He's not ours, either."

"You're sure."

"I'd pull your coat if I heard anything," Henderson says. "IAB doesn't have you up."

"You're sure about that, too."

"What do you want from me, Malone?"

"For a thousand a month?" Malone asks. "Some assurance."

"Go in peace," Henderson says. "You have a force field around you since the Pena bust."

"Check this Levin out, though, right?"

"You got it."

Henderson pulls out.

Malone goes back inside and sits down.

"Levin here," Russo says, "doesn't know about the Easter Bunny."

"I *know* about the Easter Bunny," Levin says. "What I mean is I don't understand the connection between your savior being nailed to a cross and then resurrected, which is a doubtful premise to begin with, and a rabbit coming around and burying candy eggs, especially as a rabbit is a mammal that does live births."

"This is what they teach them in college," Russo says. "What do you want us to bury, candy crosses?"

"It would make more sense," Levin says.

Monty kicks in. "The Easter Bunny comes from a German pagan tradition that the Lutherans adapted as a judge to determine whether children had been good or bad."

"Sort of like Santa Claus," Russo says.

"Which also doesn't make any sense," Levin says.

"You're just bitter," Russo says, "because Jewish kids get fucked over at Christmas."

"That's probably true," Levin says.

"An egg," Monty says, "is a symbol of birth, new life. When you bury and then recover it, it's a symbol of new life resurrected. But a rabbit can no more lay an egg than a man can come back from the dead. Both require miracles. So the Easter Bunny is a symbol of hope, that miracles—resurrection, a new life, redemption—are possible."

"Hey, check it out," Russo says, pointing to the television bracketed to the wall.

The mayor is standing out in front of St. Nick's talking to the press.

"My administration will not tolerate," he's saying, "and this city will not tolerate, violence in our public housing."

An old man sitting near the television laughs.

The mayor says, "I have instructed our police force to spare no effort in finding the guilty party or parties, and I promise you, we will. The people of Harlem, the people of New York City can know, and can trust, that this administration believes that black lives matter."

"Bull*shit!*" the old man yells.

A couple of customers nod in agreement.

A few more stare at Malone and the team.

"You heard the man," Malone says. "Let's get to work."

Back in the car, Malone sees the Sig Sauer P226 in Levin's shoulder holster.

"What else do you carry?" Malone asks.

"This is it."

"It's a good weapon," Malone says, "but you'll need more."

"It's regulation," Levin says.

"Tell that to some skel who just took it off you and is about to shoot you with it," Malone says.

"You need a backup weapon," Russo says. "And then something that's not a gun."

"Like what?" Levin asks.

Russo takes a leather sap out of one pocket and brass knuckles out of another and holds them up. Montague has a sawed-off baseball bat handle with lead poured down the center.

"Jesus Christ," Levin says.

"This is Manhattan North," Malone says. "The Task Force. We have one job—hold the line. The rest of it's just details."

His phone rings.

It's Torres.

DeVon Carter will sit down with Malone today.

CHAPTER 7

Malone and Torres sit across a table from DeVon Carter above a hardware store on Lenox the dope slinger uses as one of his many offices. He'll abandon it after this meeting, won't come back for months, if at all.

So it tips Malone that Carter has something to gain from the meeting, if he's willing to burn a location.

"You wanted to talk," Carter says. "Talk."

"You just took out an innocent old lady," Malone says. "What's it going to be the next time? A kid? A pregnant girl? A baby? You strike back for Mookie, sooner or later, that's what it's gonna be."

"If I don't answer back for Mookie," Carter says, "I will lose respect."

"I don't want a war on my turf," Malone says.

"Tell that to the Dominicans," Carter says. "You know who they sent up here? Cat named Carlos Castillo, a certified headhunter."

"It wasn't a Dominican who shot Mookie," Malone says. "It was a brother, maybe a Spade."

"What are you talking about?"

"I'm talking about your Spades flipping on you and going over to the Dominicans," Malone says. "Maybe they punched their ticket by doing Mookie."

Carter is good at holding himself in, but there's just a momentary look in the eye that tells Malone it's the truth.

"What do you want me to do?" Carter asks.

"Call off the deal with the bikers," Malone says. "Tell them you won't be needing any more of their guns."

Carter's voice takes on an edge. "You stay out of that."

He looks over at Torres.

So Torres knows all about the gun deal, Malone thinks. "No, I'm going to be all up in that."

"I can't fight the Domos without weapons," Carter says. "What do you want me to do, just die?"

"Let us handle the Domos."

"Like you handled Pena?"

"If that's what it takes."

Carter smiles. "And what do you want for these services? Three thousand a month, five, a flat fee? Or just the ability to rip as much as you can get your hands on?"

"I want you out of the business," Malone says. "Go to Maui, the Bahamas, I don't care, but you retire and no one comes after you."

"I just give up my business and sail away."

"How much more money do you need to live?" Malone asks. "How many cars can you drive? How many houses can you live in? How many women can you fuck? I'm giving you an out."

Carter says, "You know better than that, Malone. You of all people should know that kings don't retire."

"Be the first."

"And leave you king?"

"Diego Pena killed your boy Cleveland and his entire family," Malone says. "You didn't do shit about it. That ain't the DeVon Carter of legend. I think you're past it already."

"You know what I hear?" Carter asks. "I hear you're dipping your pen in the inkwell. And I hear you ain't the only white horse she ride, your Miss Claudette."

He taps the back of his hand on his forearm.

Malone says, "You or any of your chimps go near her I'll kill you."

"I'm just saying"—Carter smiles—"if she gets sick, I can get her well."

Malone gets up. "My offer stands."

Torres follows Malone down the stairs. "What the fuck, Denny?!"

"Go back to your boss."

"You leave the guns alone," Torres says. "I'm warning you."

Malone turns around. "Warning me or threatening me?"

"I'm telling you," Torres says. "Leave the fucking guns alone."

"What, you got a piece of that deal, too?"

He knows the bikers—white don't like to deal with black, but they'll deal with brown to deal with black.

Torres says, "For the last time, stay in your lane."

Malone turns and goes down the stairs.

Manhattan North is a zoo.

You got the usual animals, but you also got a herd of suits up from One P, and a pack of functionaries from the mayor's office.

McGivern is there.

He meets Malone at the door.

"Denny," he says, "we have to get this under control."

"Working it, Inspector."

"Work it harder," McGivern says. "The *Post,* the *Daily News* . . . the 'community' is all over us."

From two directions, Malone thinks. On the one hand, they want the violence in the projects to stop; on the other, they're out there protesting against the police sweep of the gangs that's been going on since the Gillette-Williams murders this morning.

Well, which do they want, because they can't have both.

Malone works his way through the crowd to the briefing room where Sykes leads a meeting of the Task Force.

"What do we have?" Sykes asks.

Tenelli says, "The Domos are denying right, left and center they had anything to do with the Gillette shooting."

"But they would," Sykes said. "They didn't anticipate the Williams killing and the heat from that."

"I get it," Tenelli says, "but this is more than the usual 'I din't have nothin' to do with it.' They proactively sent people to tell us it wasn't one of them."

"It wasn't," Malone says. "They subcontracted it out to the Spades."

"Why would the Spades take that job?"

"Price of admission to join the Dominicans," Malone says. "They figure that Carter can't supply them with high-quality product, guns or people. They jump off now or get stuck on the sinking boat."

Babyface takes his pacifier from his mouth. "Concur."

"The question is why now?" Emma Flynn asks. "The Domos have been quiet since the Pena bust. Why do they want to start a shooting war now?"

Sykes throws a surveillance photo on the screen.

"I reached out to Narcotics and DEA," Sykes says. "Their best information is that this man, Carlos Castillo, has come up from the Dominican to get the organization back in shape. Castillo is a full-blooded narco. He was born in Los Angeles, like a lot of the narcos of his generation, so he has dual Dominican and American citizenship."

Malone looks at the grainy image of Castillo, a small, suave man with caramel skin, thick dark hair, a hawk nose and thin lips, clean-shaven.

Sykes says, "DEA's had him on the radar for years but has never had enough for an indictment. But it all makes sense—Castillo is here to get the NYC heroin market straightened out. Vertical integration, from the DR to Harlem, from factory to customer. They want it all now. Castillo is here to lead the final charge on Carter."

Flynn looks over at Malone. "You really think the Dominicans have coopted the Spades?"

Malone shrugs. "It's a workable theory."

"Or the truce between the Spades and the GMB simply broke down," Flynn says.

"But we're not hearing that on the street," Babyface says.

Sykes asks, "What information do we have linking this shooting to the Spades?"

A lot.

The holding cells in the Three-Two, Three-Four and Four-Three are full of gangbangers—GMB, Trinitarios and Dominicans Don't Play. They've been picked up for everything from littering to outstanding warrants, parole and probation violations, simple possession. Those that are saying anything are telling the same story that Oh No Henry did: the shooter—a few say it was shooters, plural—was—or were—black.

"I don't imagine anyone is giving up names," Sykes says.

He knows the GMB bangers wouldn't give up a Spade shooter to the cops because they want to handle it themselves.

"All right," Sykes says, "tomorrow we do verticals in the North buildings. Shake out the Spades, start hauling them in, see what falls out of the trees."

"Verticals" are random patrols of project stairwells that the uniforms usually reserve for winter nights when they want to get out of the cold.

Malone can't blame them—it's dangerous and you never know when you might get shot or shoot some kid in the dim light, like that poor cop Liang who panicked and killed an unarmed black guy and claimed at his trial that his "gun just went off."

The jury didn't believe him and came back with a manslaughter conviction.

At least they didn't send him to jail.

Yeah, the verticals are treacherous. And now they're going to roust the Spades.

One of the mayor's hacks says, "The community is not going to like that. They're already up in arms about the last round of arrests."

"Who dat?" Russo, eyeballing the guy who just spoke, asks Malone.

"Yeah, we seen him before," Malone says, trying to dredge up a name. "Chandler somebody, somebody Chandler."

"Some people in the community are not going to like it," Sykes answers. "Other people in the community are going to pretend not to like it. But most of them want the gangs shut down. They want—and deserve—safety in their own homes. Is the mayor's office really going to argue against that?"

Good for you, Malone thinks.

But the mayor's office is apparently going to argue against it. Chandler says, "Couldn't we do something more surgical?"

"If we had a named suspect, possibly," Sykes says. "In the absence of that, this is the best option."

"But the community is going to perceive arresting a large group of young black men as profiling," Chandler says.

Babyface laughs out loud.

Sykes glares at him and then turns to the mayor's guy. "You're the one profiling here."

"How so?"

"By assuming all black people are going to object to this operation," Sykes says.

He and everyone else know why the mayor's office is playing both sides against the middle—minorities are his voter base and he can't afford to alienate them.

He's in a tough spot—on the one hand he has to be seen to be trying to suppress the violence in the community; on the other hand, he can't be allied with what will be termed heavy-handed police tactics against that same community.

So he pushes for an arrest while preserving for the record that he argued against the tactics that might best produce that arrest. At the same time, he'll use the issue to deflect attention from his scandal onto the police department.

Chandler is saying, "After the Bennett shooting, we can't afford to further alienate—"

McGivern, standing in the back of the room, says, "Do we really want to have this discussion in front of the entire Task Force? It's a command matter, and these officers have work to do."

"If you'd prefer," Chandler says, "we can take this discussion to—"

"We're not taking this discussion anywhere," Sykes says. "We invited you to this briefing as a courtesy and to keep you in the loop, not to participate in decisions that are the department's to make."

"All police decisions are political decisions," Chandler says.

He's done his job.

If the operation results in an arrest on the Williams murder, the mayor's office will claim credit. If it doesn't, the mayor will blame the commissioner, preach against racial profiling and hope the papers cover the Job's problems instead of his.

"Get some rest," Sykes says to his cops. "We'll go in tomorrow morning."

The meeting breaks up.

The mayor's rep comes over to Malone and hands him a card. "Detective Malone, Ned Chandler. Special assistant to the mayor."

"Yeah, I got that."

"Would you have a minute for me?" Chandler asks. "But maybe not here?"

"What about?" It's fucking treacherous, being seen with a guy his captain just took on.

"Inspector McGivern thought you might be the person to talk to."

So that's that. "Yeah, okay. Where?"

"You know the Hotel NYLO?"

"Seventy-Seventh and Broadway."

"I'll meet you there," Chandler says. "Soon as you're done here?"

McGivern is standing next to Sykes, waving Malone over.

Chandler walks away.

"You just put your neck in the noose," McGivern tells Sykes. "You think these Gracie Mansion sons of bitches will hesitate to pull the trap?"

"I'm under no such illusion," Sykes says.

He isn't under any illusion, either, Malone thinks, that if there's a hanging, McGivern won't be in the crowd cheering, glad it's not him. That's why he had Sykes running the meeting instead of himself. If things go right, McGivern will take the credit for his talented subordinate; if it goes sick and wrong, he'll be in there whispering, "Well, I tried to tell him . . ."

Now McGivern says, "Sergeant Malone, we're counting on you."

"Yes, sir."

McGivern nods and walks out.

"How's Levin doing?" Sykes asks.

"I've had him for about seven hours," Malone says, "but so far, fine."

"He's a good cop. He has a career in front of him."

So don't fuck him up, is what Sykes is saying.

"What progress have you made on the guns?" Sykes asks.

Malone fills him in on what he knows about Carter, Mantell and the ECMF deal. No shipment has come up yet, but negotiations are ongoing. Carter is fronting the deal through Teddy from an office over a nail shop on Broadway and 158th. But without a wiretap . . .

"We don't have enough for a warrant," Malone says.

Sykes looks at him. "Do what you need to do. But remember we'll need probable cause."

"Don't worry," Malone says. "If they hang you, I'll pull on your legs."

"I appreciate that, Sergeant."

"My pleasure, Captain."

The team is waiting for Malone out on the street.

"Levin," Malone says. "Why don't you go home and take a nap. The grown-ups need to talk."

"Okay." He's a little miffed, but he walks away.

"What do you think?" Malone asks.

Russo says, "Seems like a good kid."

"Can we trust him?"

"To do what?" Monty asks. "His job? Probably. Some of the other things? I don't know."

"Speaking of which," Malone says, "I got the go for a wire on Carter."

"Did you get a warrant with that?" Monty asks.

"Yeah, a nod warrant," Malone says. "We'll set it up after tomorrow's op. I gotta go see this guy from the mayor's office."

"What about?" Russo asks.

Malone shrugs.

Malone sits in the bar of a trendy West Side boutique hotel called NYLO and sips a club soda. He'd have a real drink except the guy he's there to meet is from the mayor's office and you never know.

Ned Chandler bustles in a minute later, looks around, spots Malone and sits down at his table. "I'm sorry I'm late."

"No problem," Malone says. He's annoyed. Chandler is the one with the ask, so he should be there on time if not early, he thinks. You don't come for a favor and then make the guy you want something from wait for you.

But Chandler is from the mayor's office, Malone thinks, so I guess the rules don't apply to him. The guy tilts his chin at the waitress as if that's going to get her immediate attention, which in fact it does.

"What do you have for single malt?" Chandler asks.

"We have a Laphroaig Quarter Cask."

"Too smoky. What else?"

"A Caol Ila 12," the waitress says. "Very light. Refreshing."

"I'll do that."

Malone has known Ned Chandler for maybe forty seconds and already wants to smack the elitist asshole. Guy has to be in his early thirties, wears a checked shirt with a knit tie under a gray cardigan sweater and tan cords.

Malone hates him just for that.

"I know your time is precious," Chandler says, "so I'll get right at it."

Anytime someone tells you that your time is precious, Malone thinks, what they really mean is that *their* time is precious.

"Bill McGivern recommended you," Chandler said. "Of course, I know you by reputation—I'm impressed, by the way—but Bill said you were professional, competent and discreet."

"If you're looking for a spy in Sykes's command, that's not me."

"I'm not looking for a spy, Detective," Chandler says. "Do you know Bryce Anderson?"

No, Malone thinks, I don't know a billionaire real estate developer on the city's Development Commission. Fuck yes, I know who he is. He's planning to inhabit Gracie Mansion once the current resident moves on to the governor's office.

"I know the name, I don't know him personally," Malone says.

"Bryce has a problem," Chandler says, "that requires discretion."

He stops talking because the waitress comes over with his light and refreshing single malt.

"I'm sorry," Chandler says to Malone. "I should have asked. Do you want—"

"No, I'm good."

"On duty."

"There you go."

"Bryce has a daughter," Chandler says. "Lyndsey. Nineteen, smart, beautiful, apple of her father's eye, all that happy crap. Dropped out of Bennington to build her 'lifestyle brand' by being a YouTube celebrity."

"What's her lifestyle brand?"

"Damned if I know," Chandler says. "She probably doesn't, either. Anyway, little Lyndsey has a boyfriend, a real mook. Of course she goes for him to get back at Daddy for giving her everything."

Malone hates it when civilians try to talk like cops. "What makes him a mook?"

"He's a total loser," Chandler says.

"Black?"

"No, she spared us that cliché, anyway," Chandler says. "Kyle's a white bridge-and-tunnel type who thinks he's the next Scorsese. Except instead of making *Mean Streets* he has to shoot a sex tape with Bryce Anderson's daughter."

"And now he's threatening to put it out," Malone says. "How much does he want?"

"A hundred K," Chandler says. "If that tape gets out, it will ruin this kid's life."

Not to mention her daddy's chance at getting elected, Malone thinks. A law-and-order candidate who wants to come down on street gangs but can't control his own kid. "This Kyle have a last name?"

"Havachek."

"You have an address?"

Chandler slides a piece of paper across the table. Havachek lives up in Washington Heights.

"Is she living with him?" Malone asks.

"She was," Chandler says. "Lyndsey moved back in with Mom and Dad and that's when the blackmail threat came."

"He lost his means of support and needs a new one," Malone says.

"That's my interpretation as well."

Malone puts the paper in his pocket. "I'll take care of it."

Now Chandler looks nervous, like he wants to say something but doesn't know how to do it politely. Malone would help him out, but he don't feel like it. Finally Chandler says, "Bill indicated that you could handle this without . . . getting carried away."

Malone wants to make him say it. Like a wiseguy making a similar request. I want the guy whacked. I don't want him whacked. I want him punished, taught a lesson . . .

If it took this loser getting murdered to stop that sex tape going out, he thinks, they'd want me to murder him. If not, they don't want the extra hassle, never mind something on their conscience.

Fuck, I hate these people. But he takes Chandler off the hook. "I'll be appropriate."

They love that word.

"So we're on the same page?" Chandler asks.

Malone nods.

"In regard to paying you for your time—"

Malone waves it off.

That ain't how it works.

Russo picks him up on Seventy-Ninth Street.

"What did the mayor's guy want?" Russo asks.

"A favor," Malone says. "You got a little time?"

"For you, sweetheart . . ."

They drive up to Washington Heights, find the address in a shitty building on 176th between St. Nicholas and Audubon. Russo parks on the street, Malone sees a kid on the corner, walks over and slips him a twenty. "This car—*all* of it—is here when we get back, yeah?"

"You cops?"

"We're undertakers if this car gets jacked."

Havachek lives on the fourth floor.

"Why is it," Russo asks as they go up the stairs, "mooks can never live on the first floor? Or in buildings that have elevators? I'm getting too old for this shit. The knees."

"The knees go first," Malone says.

"Thank Christ, huh?"

Malone knocks on Havachek's door and hears, "Who is it?"

"You want a hundred grand, you don't want a hundred grand?" Malone asks.

The door opens a chain's width. Malone kicks it in the rest of the way.

Havachek's tall, skinny, has a man bun and a nasty bruise already forming on his forehead where the door hit him. He's wearing a dirty jersey sweater and black skinny jeans over a pair of Chelsea boots. He steps back, puts his hand to his forehead to feel for blood.

"Get undressed," Malone says.

"Who the fuck are you?"

"I'm the guy who just told you to get undressed," Malone says. He pulls his gun out. "Don't make me tell you again, Kyle, because you're not going to like the alternate request."

"You're a porn star, right?" Russo asks. "So this shouldn't be a problem for you. Now get your fucking clothes off."

Kyle strips down to his shorts.

"Everything," Russo says, sliding his belt from its loops.

"What are you going to do?" Kyle asks. His legs are quivering.

"You want to be a porn star," Malone says. "You need to get used to this."

"All in a day's work," Russo says.

Kyle steps out of his shorts, covers his genitals.

"Now is that any way for a porn star to act?" Russo asks. "Come on, stud, show us what you got."

He gestures with his gun and Kyle puts his hands up.

"How does it feel?" Malone asks. "Naked in front of strangers. You think that's how Lyndsey Anderson might feel? She's a nice girl, not some ratchet you put in a porn film."

"She put me up to it," Kyle says. "Said it was a way to get money out of her folks."

"That's not going to happen, Kyle," Malone says. "You upload it yet?"

"No."

"Tell me the truth."

"It's the truth!"

"That's good," Malone says. "That's a good answer for you."

He grabs the laptop, sees they're above an alley, and opens the window.

"It cost twelve hundred dollars!" Kyle yells.

"Something is going out this window," Malone says. "You or your laptop. Choose."

Havachek chooses the laptop. Malone shoves it out the window and watches it shatter on the concrete below. "Lyndsey was in on this?"

"Yes."

"Smack him, tell him 'bullshit.'"

Russo swings the belt on the back of Kyle's thighs. "Bullshit."

"No, she was," Kyle says. "It was her idea."

"Smack him again."

Russo smacks him.

"I'm telling the truth!"

"I believe you," Malone says. "You just deserve some smacks. You deserve a lot more than that, but I'm going to be appropriate."

"He's very appropriate," Russo says.

"But I'll tell you this, Kyle," Malone says. "This tape shows up anywhere, or I hear you pull this stunt on or with any other girl, we're going to come back and you'll remember these slaps with a sense of nostalgia."

"As the good old days," Russo says.

"Now, when Lyndsey texts you asking what's up," Malone says, "you're not going to answer. You're not going to answer her phone calls, her Facebook messages, you're not going to call her or contact her, you're just going to disappear. And if you don't . . ."

Malone points the gun at his forehead.

"You're just going to *disappear*," Malone says. "Move back to Jersey, Kyle. You don't have what it takes to play the game in the city."

"Whole different game," Russo says.

Malone puts his hands on Kyle's shoulders. Fatherly, coachlike. "Now I want you to sit here naked for an hour and think about what a sleazy douchebag you really are." Then he brings his knee up—hard. Kyle goes down into a fetal position, groaning in pain, sucking for air. "We do *not treat women* that way. Even if they ask us to."

As they walk back down the stairs, Malone asks, "Was I inappropriate?"

"No, I don't think so," Russo says.

The car is waiting for them when they get there.

Intact.

Malone calls Chandler. "That thing is taken care of."

"We owe you," Chandler says.

Yeah, you do, Malone thinks.

Claudette just wants to bust balls tonight and that's all there is to it.

And when a woman—black, white, tan, aubergine, whatever, Malone thinks—wants to bust balls, balls are going to get busted.

Maybe it's the news on TV—footage of the cops rounding up black kids, the protesters, what-the-fuck-ever. Maybe it's the fact that the TV stations have cleverly blended the project raids into the Michael Bennett case and Cornelius Hampton is at his accustomed spot in front of the cameras saying, "There is no justice for young African American men. I guarantee you that if Sean Gillette was white, gunned down in broad daylight in the middle of a white neighborhood, the police would have a suspect in custody already. Just as I guarantee that if Michael Bennett was white, the case against his killer would have gone to a grand jury long before this."

With exquisite timing, the DA just brought the Bennett case to the grand jury, and now it will take weeks, if not months, to return a decision. Couple that with the killings in the Nickel, the community is seething.

"Is he right?" Claudette asks.

They're sitting in front of the TV, eating some Indian takeout he brought back—chicken tikka for her, lamb korma for him.

"About what?" Malone asks.

"Any of it?"

"You think we're not working hard to find out who killed those two people today?" Malone asks. "You think we lay back on it because they're black?"

"I'm asking."

"Yeah, well, fuck you."

He's not in the mood for this bullshit.

Claudette is, though. "Be honest, you going to tell me that, subconsciously at least, Gillette doesn't mean a little less to you because he's just another 'Jamaal'? That's what you call them, right? 'Jamaals'?"

"Yeah, we call them 'Jamaals,'" Malone says. "Also 'idiots,' 'mopes,' 'skels,' 'bangers,' 'corner boys'—"

"'Niggers'?" Claudette asks. "I've heard cops in the E-room, chuckling about banging some nigger 'longside the head. Tuning up some moolie. Do you talk that way, Denny, when I'm not around?"

"I don't want to fight," he says. "It's been a day."

"Poor you."

The korma tastes like shit now and he feels the evil coming over him. "The only kid I beat up today was white, it makes you feel better."

"Great, you're an equal opportunity thug."

"There were two people killed today," Malone says, because he can't seem to stop himself. "That kid and an old lady. And do you know why? 'Cuz a nigguh gots to sling his dope."

"Now fuck *you*."

"I'm working my ass off trying to close those cases."

"That's right," Claudette says. "They're 'cases' to you, not people."

"Jesus Christ, Claudette," he says, "are you trying to tell me that every patient who rolls in on a gurney is a fully realized human being to you and sometimes not just another job? Another piece of meat? That you try to save but at the same time, you don't hate them just a little bit for bleeding their fucked-up, drunk, stoned, stupid-ass violent shit all over you?"

"You're talking about yourself, not me."

"Yeah, and it wasn't all that pain, was it," Malone says, "all those other people's pain that made you shoot smack, was it?"

"Go fuck yourself, Denny." She gets up. "I have an early shift."

"Go to bed."

"I think I will."

She waits up long enough she thinks he's asleep when she slips into bed and it almost feels like he's back on Staten Island.

Malone has hellish dreams.

Billy O jerks on the floor like a downed power line.

Pena's mouth gapes, his dead eyes stare vacantly and yet with accusation. Snow falls from the ceiling, white bricks spill out of the wall, a dog lunges on its chain, puppies whine in fear.

Billy sucks for air, a fish flopping on the bottom of the boat.

Malone weeps and pounds on Billy's chest. More snow blows out Billy's mouth onto Malone's face.

It freezes on his skin.

Machine gun rounds explode in his head.

He opens his eyes.

Looks out Claudette's window.

It's jackhammers.

City workers in yellow helmets and orange vests fixing the street. A supervisor sits on a truck gate, smoking a cigarette, reading the *Post*.

Fuckin' New York, Malone thinks.

Motherfuckin' New York.

The sweet, juicy, rotten apple.

It wasn't just Billy in the dreams.

That was just last night.

Three nights before it was that DOA back when he was in the Tenth. He answered the call and went up to the sixth floor in the Chelsea-Elliott projects. The family was sitting at the table eating supper. When he asked them where the body was, the father jerked his thumb at the bedroom door.

Malone went in and saw a kid lying on the bed, facedown.

Seven-year-old boy.

But Malone didn't see any wounds, no signs of blunt trauma,

nothing. He turned the boy over and saw the needle still sticking out of the kid's arm.

Seven years old and he was shooting smack.

Swallowing his rage, Malone went back and asked the family what the hell had happened.

The father said the kid "had problems."

Then went back to eating.

So there's *that* dream.

There are others.

Eighteen years on the Job, you see things you wish you hadn't. What's he supposed to do, "share" that with some therapist? With Claudette? Sheila? Even if he did, they couldn't understand.

He goes into the bathroom and splashes cold water on his face. When he comes out, Claudette is in the kitchen making coffee. "Bad night?"

"I'm okay."

"Of course you are," she says. "You're always okay."

"That's right." Jesus, what's her fucking problem? He sits down at the table.

"Maybe you should go talk to someone," Claudette says.

"Career suicide," Malone says. She doesn't know what happens when a cop voluntarily goes to a shrink. Desk duty—the rest of his career—because no one wants to be on the street with a potential whack job. "Anyway, I don't see myself going to some shrink whining about I have bad dreams."

"Because you're not weak like other people."

"Jesus shit," Malone says, "if I wanted to hear what an asshole I am, I'd—"

"Go back to your wife?" she asks. "Why don't you?"

"Because I want to be with you."

She stands at the counter and puts together the salad she has for lunch, carefully arranging the ingredients in a plastic container. "I get you think that only other cops can understand what you go through. Y'all feel aggrieved because you're blamed for killing

Freddie Gray or Michael Bennett. But you don't know how it feels to be blamed because you *are* Freddie Gray or Michael Bennett. You think people hate you because of what you do, but you don't have to think that people hate you because of what you *are*. You can take that blue jacket off, I live twenty-four seven in this skin.

"Here's what *you* can't understand, Denny—what you can't understand, because you're a white man, is the sheer . . . *weight* . . . of being black in this country. The sheer exhausting weight that presses your shoulders down and tires your eyes and makes it hurt just to walk sometimes."

She presses the lid on. "And you were right last night—sometimes I do hate my patients and I'm *tired,* Denny, tired of cleaning up the things they do to each other, we do to each other, and sometimes I hate them because they're black like me and because it makes me wonder about myself."

She puts the container in her bag.

"So that's what we go through, baby," Claudette says. "Every damn day. Don't forget to lock up."

She kisses him on the cheek and goes out.

An early spring has come to the city like a gift.

Snow has turned to slush, water runs in the gutters like little brooks. A trace of sunshine promises warmth.

New York is coming out of winter. Not that it ever hibernated; the city had just pulled its collar up and put its head down against the winds that whipped through its canyons, freezing faces and numbing lips. New Yorkers push through winter like soldiers through gunfire.

Now the city uncovers itself.

And Da Force gets ready to hit the Nickel.

"Take it easy at first," Malone tells Levin. "Don't try to prove yourself. Just lay back, watch, get the hang of things. Don't worry, we'll get you on the sheet."

Get you an arrest, let you look good on the paperwork.

They're going into Building Six in north St. Nick's to do a vertical.

The gang already knows the cops are there, and in four other buildings. The ten-year-old wannabes sounded the alarms with shouts and whistles. People flee the lobby like Malone's crew has anthrax. The couple who stay just give them sullen eye-fucks, and Malone hears one of them mutter, "Michael Bennett." He ignores it.

Levin walks toward the stairwell door.

"Where you going?" Russo asks him.

"I thought we're going to check the stairs."

"You're going to walk up the stairs."

"Yeah . . ."

"Fucking moron," Russo says. "We take the elevator to the roof and then walk *down* the stairs. Save the legs and then we're coming in above any problems instead of below them."

"Oh."

"NYU, huh?"

An old lady sitting on a metal folding chair just shakes her head at Levin.

They ride up to the fourteenth floor and get out.

The walls are graffiti, gang tags.

The crew walks down to the metal door that leads to the stairs, opens it, and it's chaos as four Spades scatter like a covey of quail because one of them has a gun. They take off down the stairs.

More out of instinct than anything, Malone starts to chase them, but then Levin vaults the railing and drops ahead of him.

"Newbie, hold up!" Malone yells.

But Levin is gone, pounding down to thirteen, and then Malone hears the shot. Hears it, hell, it echoes through the stairway, bruising his eardrums, rendering him deaf, and as his ears ring he flies down the stairs expecting to see Levin bleeding out, except what he sees is Levin chasing the guy down the stairs, then leaping like a linebacker and tackling the shooter from behind. Slams him onto a landing just as Malone gets there.

The banger tries to throw the gun down the stairs but Russo has caught up and he grabs it.

Levin is hyped. "Secure that gun! The asshole shot at me!"

He's jacked on fear and adrenaline but wrestles the shooter into cuffs. Monty puts the shooter on the floor and kneels on his neck. Levin sits on the landing with his back up against the wall, breathing hard as the adrenaline drops.

"You okay?" Malone asks.

Levin just nods, too freaked out to talk.

Malone gets it, knows from experience that "I just almost got killed" feeling. "Catch your breath, then you take him to the Three-Two. I want you to get the collar."

When Malone gets to the precinct, Levin is waiting for him. "Odelle Jackson. He had a warrant on a ten-to-fifteen crack bust. Why he took a chance winging a shot at a cop."

"Where is he now?"

"Squad room."

Malone goes up to the detective squad and sees Jackson in the cage.

Levin is sitting in the locker room.

"What the fuck, Levin?" Malone asks. "Jackson looks like he just got out of church."

"What should he look like?" Levin asks.

"Like he caught a serious beating."

"I don't do that," Levin says.

"He tried to kill you," Monty says.

Levin says, "And he'll go away for it."

"Look," Malone says, "I know you're concerned with 'social justice' and you want 'the minority community' to love you, but if

Jackson goes to Central Booking looking like he ain't been tuned up, every mook in New York will think it's okay to shoot at an NYPD officer."

"If you don't break out the gym set on this individual," Monty says, "you'll put us all in danger."

Levin looks stricken.

"We're not saying stick a plunger up his ass," Russo says. "But you don't fuck him up, no one in this house is going to respect you."

"Go do the right thing," Malone says, "or clean out your locker."

Twenty minutes later they come downstairs to put Jackson on the bus to Central Booking. His head looks like a pumpkin, his eyes are slits, he's limping and holding his ribs.

Levin did a job on him.

"You fell down the stairs when my guys busted you, right?" Malone asks Jackson. "You need medical attention?"

"I'm okay."

Yeah, you're okay *now*, Malone thinks. The jailers in Central Booking don't like cops, so they're going to leave you alone. Different story when you get to the joint, where the COs always feel their lives are threatened and take assaults on cops very seriously. You'll be a hero in the population, but the guards are going to give you a ride down another set of stairs.

Levin, he looks sick.

Malone gets it—he felt the same way when an old-timer made him tune up his first perp.

If memory serves.

It was a long time ago.

Monty comes into the room and hands Malone a sheet of paper. "Mr. Jackson here is having a very bad day."

Malone looks at the sheet. The bullet Jackson winged at Levin matches the bullet that ended up in Mookie Gillette's chest.

Same gun.

"Hey, Sarge?" Malone says. "Unhook this guy, huh. We'll be

in Interview One. And call Minelli up in Homicide. He's going to want in on this."

Jackson's hooked to a bolt on the table.

Malone and Minelli sit across from him.

Malone says, "You may be having the worst day in the history of days. You shoot at a cop and miss, and now you're down for a double homicide."

"Double? I didn't shoot Mrs. Williams."

"Well now, here's an interesting theory," Minelli says. "According to the law, your shooting of Mookie led directly to his shooting of Mrs. Williams. So you're down for both."

"I didn't shoot Mookie," Jackson says. "I was there, but I didn't shoot him. I was just the walkaway."

The shooter passes the weapon to a junior member, who walks away.

"You still have the murder weapon," Minelli says. "And you used it again."

"They gave it to me," Jackson says, "told me to get rid of it."

"And you didn't," Malone says. "Dumb shit."

"Who gave you the gun?" Minelli asks. "Who was the shooter?"

Jackson looks down at the table.

"Look, you know how this works," Minelli says. "You can go for the murders or someone else can. I don't give a shit which. It clears my sheet either way."

"I get it," Malone says. "Killing Mookie gives you street cred. But do you really want to go down for Mrs. Williams?"

"I'm still going for the cop."

"New York law," Malone says. "Forty to life for shooting at a police officer. With two previous convictions, bet on life."

"So I'm fucked anyway."

"You give us the shooter," Malone says, "maybe we can help you on the cop shooting. We can't get you a walk, but we can have the

ADA tell the judge you cooperated on a double homicide. Forty, you do fifteen, you still have a life. The other way, you die in there."

"I give them up," Jackson says, "they kill me inside anyway."

Malone sees it in his eyes—the kid knows his life is over.

Once the machine has you, it doesn't let you go until it's chewed you up.

"You have a grandma?" Malone asks.

"'Course I got a grandma," Jackson says. It's at least ten seconds before he says, "Jamichael Leonard."

"Where do we find him?" Minelli asks.

"His cousin's." He gives them the address.

Malone takes him back to get on the bus to Central Booking. "We'll get in touch with your PD."

"Whatever."

They put him on the chain and load him on the bus.

"You want in on this collar?" Minelli asks Malone.

"No," he says. "Too much ink makes us targets. Do me a solid, though. Give Levin an assist and bring Sykes in on it before you go pick him up."

"Yeah?"

"Yeah, why not?"

As any good wiseguy knows, you want to eat, you don't eat alone. You kick up, and there's all kinds of coin.

He goes down to the locker room and finds Russo, Montague and Levin.

"If it makes you feel any better, newbie," Malone says, "Jackson gave up the Williams shooter. You get an assist."

It helps but it doesn't fix it. He sees it in Levin's eyes—the first time you give up a little bit of yourself to the street, it hurts. The scar tissue hasn't formed yet, and you feel it.

"I think," Malone says, "we've earned a Bowling Night."

CHAPTER 8

Bowling Night is a Task Force institution.

A mandatory attendance, no-excuses-accepted night when the men tell their wives and girlfriends that they're going bowling with the guys.

It's the team leader's privilege—some would call it his duty—to call Bowling Nights as a way of letting off steam, and when a cop gets shot at, that's a lot of steam.

A brother cop gets killed, you don't talk about it; a cop has a near miss, you *have* to talk about it—get it out, laugh about it, because tomorrow or the next day you're going to have to go down another stairwell.

They do 10-13s frequently—the name comes from the radio code for "officer needs assistance"—where they coop up somewhere and party, but Bowling Night is something different: dress sharp, no wives, girlfriends, or even *gumars,* none of the usual cop bars.

Bowling Night is strictly first class, all the way.

Sheila, with the perspicacity of a Staten Island cop wife, once said, "You don't go bowling. That's just a cover to pig out, get drunk and fuck cheap whores."

That isn't true, Malone thought as he walked out the door that night. It's a cover to *dine* out, get drunk and fuck *expensive* whores.

Levin doesn't want to come.

"I'm beat," he says. "I think I'll just go home and chill."

"This is not an invitation," Malone says, "it's a summons."

"You're coming," Russo says.

"You're part of the team," Monty said, "you make Bowling Night."

"What do I tell Amy?"

"You tell her you're going out with your crew, don't wait up," Malone says. "Now go home, clean up, dress nice. Meet us at Gallaghers at seven."

Corner table at Gallaghers on Fifty-Second.

Russo looks extra sharp tonight—slate-gray suit, custom-tailored white shirt, French cuffs, pearl cuff links.

"You hear the shot?" Russo asks.

"Not until later," Levin says. "That's the funny thing. I didn't hear it until later."

"Man, you fucking tackled that asshole," Russo says. "Sign this guy up for the Jets."

"The Jets *tackle*?" Malone asks.

It goes on like that, making Levin talk, making him take some credit for being brave, for surviving.

"Thing is," Malone says, "you're probably good for life now."

"What do you mean?" Levin asks.

Montague explains, "Most cops don't get shot at their entire careers. You did, and it missed. Odds are you never take another shot, you walk away unscathed after twenty, pull your pension."

Malone fills their glasses. "Here's to that!"

Russo asks, "Remember Harry Lemlin?"

Malone and Monty start to laugh.

"Who was Harry Lemlin?" Levin asks. He loves these old stories, and he's not even pissed that they fined him a hundred bucks for wearing a shirt with buttons on the cuffs.

"French cuffs," Malone told him. "When the team goes out, we go out in style. We make an impression. French cuffs, cuff links."

"I don't own any cuff links."

"Buy some," Malone says, taking a hundred out of Levin's wallet.

Now Levin asks again, "Who was Harry Lemlin? Tell me the story."

"Harry Lemlin—"

"Never Say Die Harry," Monty says.

"Never Say Die Harry," Russo says, "was a comptroller in the mayor's office in charge of making the budget look somewhat legit. And he was *hung*. Those stallions they put out to stud? They look at Harry, they hang their heads in shame. Harry's dick arrived at meetings two minutes before the rest of him did. Okay, so Harry is a regular at Madeleine's, this is back in the day she does most of her business at the house."

Malone smiles. Russo is going into storytelling mode.

"Anyway, back then it was, what, Sixty-Fourth and Park. So Harry, he starts taking Viagra. Best thing that ever happened according to him. Penicillin, polio vaccine, fuck that—Harry is in love with the blue pill."

"How old was he?" Levin asks.

"You gonna let me tell the story?" Russo asks, "or keep interrupting me? Kids these days."

"I blame the parents," Monty says.

"That's another hundred," Malone says.

"Harry was sixtysomething, I dunno," Russo says, "but fucking like he's nineteen. Two girls at a time, three, he's a steam engine. Girls are tag-teaming, he's wearing them out. Madeleine, she doesn't care, she's making money, and the girls, they love him, he's a big tipper."

"Tipped by the inch," Monty says.

"How come Monty doesn't get fined?" Levin asks.

"That's *another* hundred."

"So this one night," Russo says, warming up to the story, "the three of us are out doing a stakeout on this coke dealer's place, and we get a call on Malone's private phone from Madeleine. All upset, crying, 'Harry's dead.' We go running over there and sure enough, there's Harry, in the sack, hookers standing around him weeping like he's Jesus or something, and Madeleine says, 'You have to get him out of here.'

"No shit, we think, because this is going to be a major embarrassment, the comptroller found naked at one in the morning in the rack with a brace of call girls. We gotta move the body. First problem is getting Harry dressed, because he had to go two eighty and there is, shall we say, an obstacle in the way."

"An obstacle?" Levin asks.

"Harry's soldier is still standing at attention," Russo says, "ready for duty. We're trying to get his boxers on, never mind his trousers, which are a little tight to begin with, and there's this flagpole to contend with . . . and it *ain't going down,* whether it's the pill or *rigor mortis,* we don't know, but . . ."

Russo starts laughing.

Malone and Monty start laughing, too, and Levin, he's having a great time. "So what did you do?"

"The fuck *could* we do?" Russo asks. "We keep wrestling, we get clothes back on him—his pants, his shirt, his jacket and tie, everything, except he has major wood poking out, I swear it's getting bigger, like his dick is Pinocchio and just told a lie.

"I go down, twenty the doorman to go for a smoke and I guard the lobby. Monty and Malone heft this guy into the elevator and we drag him out the side door into our car, which is no easy task.

"So Harry's propped up in the front seat like he's drunk or something and we drive all the way downtown to his office. A hundred for the security guard, back in the elevator, we set him down in his chair behind his desk like he's this dedicated employee burning the midnight oil."

Russo takes a sip of his martini, signals for another. "But now what? What we should do is just get the fuck out of there, let them find him in the morning, but we all like Harry. Very fond of the guy, and we don't have the heart to just let him sit there rotting, so . . .

"Malone here calls the desk sergeant at the Five. Makes up this bullshit about walking past the building, seeing lights on, thought he'd go up to see his old friend Harry, blah, send a unit.

"The uniforms come up, then the duty ME. Takes one look at Harry, says, 'The guy's heart exploded.' We nod, like yeah, isn't it sad, he was overworked, then the ME says, 'But it didn't do it here.' We're all like, 'What do you fucking mean?' and he goes into some long explanation about lividity and morbidity and that he didn't shit his pants and what's more, the deceased has a hard-on like a battering ram, and he's looking at us like 'what's going on,' so we take him aside and tell him.

"'Look,' I say. 'Harry tapped out in the saddle and we want to spare the widow and the kids the embarrassment. Can you work with us on this?'

"'You moved the body,' he says.

"We confess.

"'That's a crime,' he says.

"We agree. Malone here, he tells the guy we'll owe him a solid, do the right thing, and the doc he says, 'Okay.' Writes it up like Harry died at his desk, a faithful servant of the city."

"Which he was," Monty says.

"Absolutely," Russo says. "Except now we have to go to Rosemary, tell her her husband has passed. We drive over to their place on East Forty-First, ring the bell, Rosemary, she's in a robe and curlers, we tell her. She cries a little, she makes us all some tea, then . . ."

Russo's martini arrives.

"She wants to see him. We tell her why don't she wait until tomorrow, we made the ID, it's not necessary, but no. She wants to see her husband."

Malone shakes his head.

"So, okay," Russo says. "We go to the morgue, show our shields, they slide Harry out of the drawer, and I have to say they did their best. They had him covered with sheets, blankets, but no . . ."

"Tent pole. Like you could hold a revival meeting under there.

The circus, I don't know—elephants, clowns, acrobats, the whole nine yards—and Rosemary, she looks and she says . . ."

They all start laughing again.

"Rosemary, she says, 'Look at Little Harry—never say die.'

"She was proud of it. Proud that he died in the saddle, doing what he loved to do. We're getting hernias lugging this horny bastard around, and she knew all about it all the time.

"Calling hours? You know sometimes the wiseguys, they have to have closed caskets? They had to close Harry's casket from the waist down. Rosemary said send him to heaven ready."

Monty lifts a glass. "Here's to Harry."

"Never say die," Malone says.

They clink their glasses.

Then Russo looks over Levin's shoulder. "Oh, shit."

"What?"

"Don't turn around," Russo says. "At the bar. It's Lou Savino."

Malone looks alarmed. "Are you sure?"

"It's Savino and three of his crew," Russo says.

"Who's Lou Savino?" Levin asks.

"'Who's Lou Savino?'" Russo says. "Are you kidding me right now? He's a capo in the Cimino family."

"Runs the Pleasant Avenue crew," Malone says. "He has an open warrant out. We gotta take him."

"Here?" Levin asks.

"What the fuck," Russo says, "do you think IAB would think, it got word we were in the same place as a mobster with an open warrant and we let him walk away?"

"Jesus," Levin says.

"It has to be you," Malone says. "He hasn't made us yet, but if one of us gets up, he'll bolt like a rabbit."

"We'll back you, kid," Russo says.

Monty says, "Be polite."

"But firm," says Russo.

Levin gets up. He looks nervous as hell, but he walks to the bar where Savino is having drinks with three of his guys and their *gumars*. If they're sitting in the main room of any restaurant, they always want to be seen with beautiful women; if it's just the men, they'd be in a private room.

Whether or not to have women at dinner on Bowling Night has long been a topic of discussion in Malone's team. He could argue it either way—on the one hand, it's always nice to have a lovely woman by your side at dinner. On the other hand, it's too showy. A group of well-known detectives out to an expensive dinner is borderline as it is; to be more ostentatious with call girls is another thing.

So Malone has vetoed it. He doesn't want to rub it in IAB's faces, and besides, it's a good chance for the men to talk. The restaurant is noisy, the chance of getting a wire in remote, and even if IAB did, the sound would be so murky and confused that you could deny it was even you. The tape would never make it through the evidentiary hearing.

Now he and his team watch Levin approach Savino. "Excuse me, sir?"

"Yeah, what?" Savino doesn't look too happy to be interrupted, especially by someone he doesn't know.

Levin shows his badge. "You have a warrant. I'm afraid I'll have to place you under arrest, sir."

Savino looks around at his crew and shrugs, like *What the fuck is this bullshit?* He turns back to Levin and says, "I don't have no warrant."

"I'm afraid you do, sir."

"Don't be *afraid,* kid," Savino says. "Either I have a warrant or I don't, and I don't, so you don't got to be afraid of nothing."

He turns his back on Levin and signals the bartender for another round.

"This is a thing of beauty," Monty says. "A beautiful thing."

Levin reaches behind him for his cuffs. "Sir, we can do this like gentlemen, or—"

Savino whirls on him. "If we were gonna do this like gentlemen, you wouldn't be interrupting my social evening in front of my associates and my lady friends, you . . . what are you, Italian? Jewish?"

"I'm Jewish, but I don't see what—"

"—you kike, hebe, Christ killer motherfucker, you—" Savino looks over his shoulder, sees Malone and yells, "Ball *buster*! You ballbuster!"

Levin turns around to see Malone and Russo practically falling out of their chairs and Monty's shoulders heaving up and down in laughter.

Savino slaps Levin on the shoulder. "They're *goofing* you, kid! What is this, fucking Bowling Night, right? You got some *coglioni* on you, though, coming up on me like that. 'Excuse me, sir' . . ."

Levin walks back to the table. "Okay, that was embarrassing."

Malone notices he takes it well, though, he's laughing at himself. And the kid went—three mob guys in front of their women, and the kid went. It says something.

Russo raises his glass. "Here's to you, Levin."

"Was that really Lou Savino?" Levin asks.

"What, you think we hired actors?" Russo says. "No, that's him."

"You know him?"

"We know him," Malone says. "He knows us. We're in the same business, only on different sides of the counter."

The steaks arrive.

Another rule of Bowling Night—you order steak.

A big red juicy New York Strip, a Delmonico, a Chateaubriand. Because it's good, it's what you should have, and if you're in the same restaurant as wiseguys you want to be seen eating meat.

Cops fall into two categories—grass eaters and meat eaters. The grass eaters are the small-timers—they take a cut from the car-towing companies, they get a free coffee, a sandwich. They take what comes, they're not aggressive. The meat eaters are the predators, they go after what they want—the drug rips, the mob payoffs, the cash. They go out and hunt and bring it down, so it's important that when the unit is out as the Unit, it dresses tight and eats steak.

It sends a message.

You think it's a joke, but it's not—they're literally looking to see what's on your plate. If it's a cheeseburger, guys are talking about it the next day. "I saw Denny Malone at Gallaghers the other night and he was eating, are you ready for this? Hamburger."

The wiseguys will think you're cheap or broke or both, and either one sends a message to their reptilian brains that you're weak, and the next thing you know, they're trying to take advantage of that. They're predators, too; they cut the weak out of the herd and go after him.

Malone's steak is great, though, a beautiful New York Strip cooked rare with a cold red center. Instead of the baked potato, he went with big cottage fries and a pile of green beans.

It feels good to cut into the steak, to chew it.

Substantial.

Solid.

Real.

It was the right decision to call Bowling Night.

Big Montague digs into a sixteen-ounce Delmonico, his concentration thorough. In a rare revelation, he once told Malone that he grew up in a household where meat was a rare treat; as a kid he ate his breakfast cereal with water instead of milk. And he was a big kid, always hungry. Monty should have been a street thug; his size made him the perfect bodyguard and enforcer for some mid- to high-level dealer. But he was too smart for that, Malone thinks. Monty's always had the ability to see around the next corner, know what's coming, and even as a young teenager he saw that the dope-slinging life led to a cell or a coffin, that only the guys at the top of the pyramid made the real money.

But he observed that police always ate.

He never saw a hungry cop.

So he went the other way with it.

Those days, the Job sucked down black candidates like salt peanuts. You were AA, had two legs and could see beyond your thumbs, you were in. They didn't expect a black candidate to have an IQ of 126, though, which is what Monty tested. Big, brilliant, black, he had "detective" written all over him from day one.

Even the cops who hate blacks give him his props.

He's one of the most highly respected cops on the Job.

Now he looks tight in a midnight-blue tailored Joseph Abboud suit, powder-blue shirt, his red tie obscured by the linen napkin tucked in at his neck. Monty ain't gonna take a chance on staining a hundred-dollar shirt, he don't care what it looks like.

"What you looking at?" he asks Malone.

"You."

"What about me?"

"Love you, man."

Monty knows this. He and Malone don't do that jive brothers-from-another-mother, ebony-and-ivory bullshit, but they are brothers. He has a brother who's an accountant in Albany, another doing a fifteen-to-thirty in Elmira, but he's closest to Malone.

Only makes sense—they spend at least twelve hours a day together, five or six days a week, and they depend on each other for their lives. It's no cliché—you go through that door, you never know. You want your brothers with you.

Just as there's no question that being a black cop is different, it just is, that's all. Other cops, except his brothers here, look at him a little different, and the "community"—as the social activists, big-mouthed ministers and local politicians laughably call the ghetto— see him either as a potential ally who should help them out, or as a traitor. An Uncle Tom, an Oreo.

Monty don't care.

He knows who he is: he's a man trying to raise a family and get his kids the fuck out of the "community"—that community who'll rob each other, cheat each other and kill each other for a nickel bag.

While his brothers at this table would die for each other.

Malone once said that you should never partner with anyone you wouldn't leave alone with your family and all your money. You did that with any of these men, when you came back, your family would be laughing and there'd be more money.

They order dessert—mud pie, apple pie with big wedges of cheddar cheese, cheesecake with cherries.

After that, coffee with brandy or sambuca, and Malone, he decides he needs to even things up a little for Levin, so he says, "Never Say Die Harry was great, but you want to talk dead bodies, though . . ."

"Don't do it," Russo says. But he starts laughing.

"What?" Levin asks.

Monty's laughing, too, so he knows the story.

"No," Malone says.

"Come on."

Malone looks at Russo, who nods, and then says, "This was back when Russo and me were still in bags down in the Six. We had this sergeant—"

"Brady."

"Brady, who liked me," Malone says, "but for some reason *hated* Russo. Anyway, this Brady, he liked to drink, and he used to have me drop him off at the White Horse so he could get a load on and then pick him up later, bring him back to the house, he could sleep it off.

"So this one night, we get a DOA call, and in those days, a uniform had to stay with the body until the ME came in to call it. It's a bitter cold night, subzero, and Brady he asks me, 'Where's Russo?' I says, 'On his post.' He says, 'Get him over there on the DOA.' It sounds nice, right? Get Russo out of the cold, indoors, but Brady knows that Phil here . . ."

Malone starts laughing again. "Back then, Russo was *terrified* of dead bodies."

"Scared stiff, so to speak," Monty says.

"Fuck the both of you."

"So I try to talk Brady out of it," Malone says, "because I know Russo's a total pussy about this and might faint or something, but

Brady ain't havin' it. Has to be Russo. 'You tell him to get his fuckin' ass over there and stay with the body.'

"It's a brownstone over off Washington Square, the body's in bed on the second floor and it's clearly natural causes."

"This old gay guy," Russo says. "Owned the whole brownstone, lived alone, had a heart attack in bed."

Malone says, "I leave Russo there and go back to sit outside the White Horse. Brady comes out, he's half in the bag, he tells me drive him over to the DOA's house. He's been out of the bar, what, five seconds, and he's in the car hitting a flute—"

"What's a flute?" Levin asks.

"A Coke bottle filled with booze," Monty says.

"We drive by," Malone says, "Russo's standing on the stoop, freezing his balls off. Brady goes ape-shit, screaming at Phil, 'I told you to stay with the body, asshole! You march your ass inside, up-stairs and stay there, or I'll write you up.' Russo goes back in, we go back to the bar.

"I'm sitting out there, a call comes over the radio, a 10-10, shots fired, and I hear the address. It's the same address as the DOA residence!"

"What the fuck," Levin says, delighted.

"What *I'm* thinking," Malone says. "I run into the bar, find Brady and say, 'We got a problem.' We go racing over there, run up the freakin' stairs, and there's Russo, with his gun drawn, the DOA is sitting bolt upright in the bed, and Phil here has put two rounds into his chest."

Malone's laughing so hard now he can barely get the words out. "What happened is . . . gas starts moving around inside the body . . . and they do weird things . . . this one sat straight up . . . scared Russo . . . so bad . . . he puts two in the guy's chest . . ."

"I'm looking at the freaking undead!" Russo says. "The fuck am I supposed to do?!"

"So now we got a *real* problem," Malone says, "because if that guy wasn't dead, Russo has not only discharged his firearm, he's looking at a homicide charge."

"I'm scared shitless," Russo says.

Monty's shoulders are shaking as he chuckles, tears running down his cheeks.

Malone says, "Brady asks me, 'You sure this guy was dead?' 'Pretty sure,' I say. He says, '*Pretty* sure? What the fuck is that?!' I say, 'I dunno, he had no pulse.' And he sure as shit didn't have a pulse after Russo put two in his heart."

"So what did you do?" Levin asks.

Malone says, "The duty ME is Brennan, the laziest fuck ever to occupy the position. I mean, they gave him the job so he couldn't work on *live* people. He comes over, takes in the situation, looks at Russo and says, 'You shot a dead guy?'

"Phil's shaking. He says, 'So the guy was dead?' 'You kidding me?' Brennan says. 'He croaked three hours before you shot him, but how the fuck am I going to explain two rounds in his chest?'"

Monty dabs at his cheek with his napkin.

"This is where, I have to say, Brady earns his stripes," Malone says. "He says to Brennan, 'That's going to involve a lot of work on your part. Reports, an investigation, you might have to testify . . .'

"Brennan says, 'How about we just call it even?' The wagon comes, we bag the guy up, I deem it natural causes, Russo here gets new underwear."

"Amazing," Levin says.

Lou Savino and his party get up to leave. Savino nods to Malone, who nods back.

Fuck IAB.

If the mobsters don't know who we are, don't show us respect, we're not doing our jobs.

The bill comes to over five bills, or would if they were charged.

The waitress, she delivers the check, it comes to zero. But she delivers a check in case they're being watched. Malone lays a credit card down, she takes it back, he pretends to sign it.

They leave two hundred in cash on the table.

You never, ever stiff a server.

For one thing, it's not right. For the other, once again, the word gets around that you're cheap. What you want, you walk into a place, a server sees you and says, "Give me *that* party."

That way you always get a table.

And if you're not with your wife, no one is going to notice or remember.

You never stiff a server or take change for a twenty whether you're at a bar or a bodega.

That's for grass eaters, not Force detectives.

It's just the cost of doing business.

You can't deal with it, go back on patrol.

Malone calls for the car.

Bowling Night they always get a town car and a driver.

Because they know they're going to get shit-faced and no one wants to blow their gig on a DUI if some rookie patrolman writes it up or calls it in before knowing what's what.

Half the wiseguys in New York own car services because it's easy to launder money through them, so they have no problem getting one comped. Of course the driver is going to tell his boss every place they went and what they did, but they don't care. That's as far as it's going to go—no driver is ever going to rat them to IAB or even admit they were in his car. And who gives a shit some mobster knows they get drunk and laid—they know that already.

And the car service knows better than to send them some Russian or Ukrainian or Ethiopian—it's always a goombah who knows the score, knows to keep his ears open and his mouth shut.

Tonight's driver is Dominic, a fiftysomething mob "associate" who's had them before and knows he's going to get tipped out big, likes having guys in Armani, Boss and Abboud get in and out of his car. Is going to get right next to the curb so his clients' Guccis, Ferragamos and Maglis don't get wet. Gentlemen who treat his car with respect, aren't going to puke in it, eat smelly fast food, fill it with dope smoke, get into fights with their women.

He drives them up to Madeleine's on Ninety-Eighth and Riverside.

"We're going to be a couple of hours at least," Malone tells him, slipping him a fifty, "you want to get dinner."

"Just call me," Dominic says.

"What is this place?" Levin asks.

"You heard us talk about Madeleine's," Malone says. "This is Madeleine's."

"A brothel?"

"You could call it that," Malone says.

"I don't know," Levin says. "Amy and I are, you know, exclusive."

"You put a ring on her finger?" Russo asks.

"No."

"So?" Russo says.

"Look, I think I'll just go home," Levin says.

"It's called Bowling Night," Monty says. "Not Bowling Dinner. You're coming in."

"Come upstairs," Malone says. "And hang out. You don't want to get laid, okay, you don't want to get laid. But you're coming with us."

Madeleine owns the whole brownstone but is very discreet about what goes on in there so the neighbors don't get their noses out of joint. Most of her business these days is off-location anyway; the house is just for small parties and special guests. She doesn't do the old "lineup" anymore; the men preselect online.

She greets Malone personally at the door with a kiss on the cheek.

They came up together; she was still taking dates when he was in uniform. She was walking home through Straus Park one night, some asshole decided to hassle her and this uniformed cop shall we say, "intervened," brought his nightstick down on the jerk's head and then gave him a few shots to the kidneys to emphasize his point.

"Do you want to press charges?" Malone asked her.

"I think you just did," Madeleine answered.

They've been friends and business associates ever since. He protects her and sends business her way; in return she comps him and his team and lets him look at her black book to see if she has any clients who might be useful. Madeleine Howe's house is never raided, her girls never threatened or harassed—at least not for long and never twice—and never stiffed.

And on the rare occasion when a girl goes rogue and tries to blackmail one or more of the clients, Malone takes care of that, too. He pays her a visit, explains the legal ramifications of what she's trying to do, and then describes what the women's jail is like for a very attractive, spoiled girl like herself and explains that if he has to handcuff her it is likely the last bracelet she will ever receive from a man. She usually takes the proffered airline ticket instead.

So the men in Madeleine's black book—the high-roller businessmen, the politicians, the judges—whether they're aware of it or not, also get protection from Da Force. They don't see their names splashed across the front page of the *Daily News* and they also don't get stupid. More than once, Malone and Russo have had to go talk to some hedge fund manager or rising political star who's fallen in love with one of Madeleine's escorts and tell him that's just not the way it works.

"But I love her," one would-be gubernatorial candidate told them. "And she loves me."

He was going to leave his wife and kids—and career—to start a coffee roasting business in Costa Rica with a woman whose name he thought was Brooke.

"She's paid to make you feel that way," Russo told the guy. "That's her job."

"No, this is different," the guy insisted. "It's the real thing."

"Don't embarrass yourself," Malone said. "Man up here—you have a wife and kids. You have a family."

Don't make me put her on the phone and tell you you have a dick like a golf pencil and bad breath, and that she tried to get Madeleine to send someone else the last time.

Now Madeleine welcomes them in and they take the little elevator upstairs to a tastefully furnished apartment.

The women are gorgeous.

Which they should be, at two thousand dollars a date.

Levin, his eyes bug out of his head.

"Easy there, College," Russo says.

"I've selected your dates," Madeleine says, "based on your previous preferences. But for the new guy, I had to guess. I hope Tara will make you happy. If not, we can go back to the book."

"She's beautiful," Levin says, "but I'm not . . . partaking."

"We can just have a couple of drinks and a good conversation," Tara says to Levin.

"That sounds great."

She leads him over to the bar.

Malone's date calls herself Niki. She's tall and leggy with a throwback Veronica Lake hairstyle and ice-blue eyes. He sits with her, has a scotch alongside her dirty martini, talks for a few minutes and then she takes him into one of the bedrooms.

Niki wears a tight black dress with a deep décolletage. She peels the dress down and off, revealing the black lingerie that Madeleine knows he likes without him asking for it.

"You want anything special?" she asks.

"You're already special."

"Maddy said you were a charmer."

She starts to take off her stiletto heels but Malone says, "Keep them on."

"You want me to undress you, or—"

"I'll do it myself." He gets out of his clothes and puts them on the hangers that Madeleine has provided so her married clients don't go home with wrinkled suits. He takes his pistol and puts it under the pillow.

Niki gives him a look.

"You never know who's going to come through the door," Malone says. "It's not a kink. If it bothers you, I'll ask for someone else."

"No, I like it."

She gives him a two-thousand-dollar fuck.

Around the world in eighty minutes.

Afterward, Malone gets dressed, puts the gun back into its holster, and leaves five one-hundred-dollar bills on the side table. Niki puts her dress back on, takes the money and asks, "Buy you a drink?"

"Sure."

They go back out into the living room. Monty is there with his date, an impossibly tall black woman. Russo isn't finished yet, but that's Russo.

"I eat slow, I drink slow and I make love slow," he's said. "Savor."

Levin isn't at the bar.

"Did the newbie bail on us?" Malone asks.

"He went to a room with Tara," Monty says. "In the words of Oscar Wilde, 'I can resist everything but temptation.'"

Russo finally comes in with a brunette named Tawny who reminds Malone of Donna. Classic, Malone thinks, the guy cheats on his wife with a woman who looks like his wife.

A few minutes later Levin comes in looking a little drunk, a lot sheepish and totally fucked out.

"Don't tell Amy, okay?" he says.

They crack up.

"'Don't tell Amy'!" Russo says, wrapping his arm around Levin's shoulder. "This kid, this fucking kid, he goes Batman on a Jamaal in a vertical and misses a bullet. Then he breaks the gym set out on him. *Then* he goes to cuff Lou Savino in front of his women and his crew in the middle of Gallaghers, then he wets his dick in thousand-dollar pussy, comes out and says, 'Don't tell Amy'!"

They all crack up again.

Russo kisses Levin on the cheek. "This kid! I love this fucking kid!"

"Welcome to the team," Malone says.

They have another drink and then it's time to go.

The women come with them up to 127th and Lenox.

A club called the Cove Lounge.

"Why do you listen to that moolie music?" Russo asks Malone on the way up there.

"Because we work with moolies," Malone says. "Anyway, I like it."

"Monty," Russo asks, "you like this hip-hop shit?"

"Hate it," Monty says. "Give me some Buddy Guy, BB, Evelyn 'Champagne' King."

"How old *are* you guys?" Levin asks.

"Yeah, who do you listen to?" Malone asks. "Matisyahu?"

They pull up outside the Cove. The line outside sees the limo and looks for who gets out, expecting a hip-hop star. They see two white guys get out and they don't like it.

Then one of them recognizes Malone.

"It's the cops!" he yells. "Hey, Malone! Motherfucker!"

The doormen let them right in. The Cove is done in blue and purple light pulsing in beat with the music.

The other color is black.

Counting Malone, Russo, Levin and their dates, there are exactly eight people in the club who aren't black.

They get stares.

But they get a table.

The hostess, a beyond beautiful black woman, leads them straight to the raised VIP section and sits them down.

Four bottles of Cristal come a minute later.

"Compliments of Tre," the hostess says. "He said to tell you your money doesn't spend here."

"Tell him thank you," Malone says.

Tre doesn't officially own the club. The twice-convicted rapper/ record producer couldn't get a liquor license with a rocket launcher, but he owns the club. Now he literally looks down at Malone from a raised platform in the VIP section and raises his glass.

Malone raises his back.

People see it.

It chills things out.

If the white cops are good with Tre, they're good.

"You know Tre?" Niki asks, impressed.

"Yeah, a little bit."

The last time the Job wanted to talk with Tre, Malone brought him in personally. No handcuffs, no perp walk, no cameras.

Tre appreciated the respect.

Started to throw some security work to Malone, who does it himself or with Monty if it's important. The more routine stuff he passes to other cops in Manhattan North, who are grateful for the money.

And Tre gets off on having racist cops as employees. Was sending them out for coffees and cheesecake and shit until Malone got wind of it and put a stop to it. "They are *New York City police officers,* there to protect your ass. You want a snack, send one of your flunkies."

Now Tre comes down and slides in next to Malone.

"Welcome to the jungle," he says.

"I *live* here," Malone says. "You live in the fucking Hamptons."

"You should come out sometime."

"I will, I will."

"Party with us," Tre says. "The missus likes you."

His black leather jacket has to go a couple of grand, the Piaget watch a lot more.

There's money in the music, in the clubs.

"Black or white," Tre says, "all money spends green."

Now he asks Malone, "Who's going to protect me from the police? Young black man can't walk the streets anymore without getting shot by a cop, usually in the back."

"Michael Bennett got shot in the chest."

Tre says, "I hear different."

"You want to play Jesse Jackson," Malone says, "have a ball. You have some evidence, bring it on in."

"To the NYPD?" Tre asks. "That's what we would call a white-wash."

"What do you want me to do, Tre?"

"Nothin'," Tre says. "I'm just giving you a heads-up, is all."

"You know where to find me."

"I do." Tre goes into his pocket, comes out with a cigar-sized blunt. "In the meantime, let this make you well."

Gives him the blunt and leaves.

Malone takes a sniff. "Jesus fuck."

"Light up," Niki says.

Malone lights up, takes a hit and passes it to Niki. It's primo shit, Malone thinks. Then again, coming from Tre, what else would it be? A sweet, mellow high—energizing—more sativa than indica. The blunt gets passed around the table until it hits Levin.

He looks at Malone.

"What," Malone says. "You never smoked weed?"

"Not since I came on the Job."

"Well, we're not telling anyone."

"What if I get tested?"

They laugh at him.

"No one told you about the Designated Pisser?" Russo asks.

"What's that?"

"Not *what*," Monty says. "*Who*. Officer Brian Mulholland."

"That guy who sweeps up the locker room?" Levin asks. "The House Mouse?"

Most precincts have one—a cop who's not fit for street duty but shy of retirement. They keep him inside, cleaning up, running errands. Mulholland was a good cop until he answered a call and found a baby who'd been "dipped"—held in a bathtub of scalding water. After that, he hit the bottle but it hit him back harder. Malone persuaded the captain at the Three-Two to keep him on the Job, hide him as the House Mouse.

184 / DON WINSLOW

"He's not just the House Mouse," Russo says, "he's also the Designated Pisser. You get notice of a Doyle, Mulholland pisses into a baggie for you. Your piss is a hundred proof, but you test clean for dope."

Levin takes a hit and passes it.

"Brings up another story," Malone says, looking at Monty.

"Fuck all of you," Monty says.

"Montague here," Malone says, "had his PT coming up. And he isn't exactly, shall we say, 'undernourished.'"

"*And* your mamas," Monty says.

"I mean, Monty can't *walk* a mile," Malone says, "never mind run one in the required time. So what he does is, he—"

Monty holds up a hand. "There was a rookie, a handsome and distinguished young African American gentleman, who shall go nameless—"

"Grant Davis," Russo says.

"—who had been a track-and-field standout at Syracuse University," Monty says.

"He had a tryout with the Dolphins," Malone says.

"This was a double opportunity," Monty says. "One, for me to pass the PT, and two, to prove that the Job cannot tell one black man from another, and furthermore, doesn't care to."

Malone says, "So Monty uses his big-dick gold-shield swag to convince this rookie to take Monty's ID and run the test for him. The kid was scared shitless, which apparently made him run faster because . . . he broke the departmental record for the mile."

"I didn't think I needed to tell him to slack off a little," Monty says.

"But no one catches on," Malone says.

"Proving my point," says Monty.

"Until," Malone says, "some genius at One P decides he's going to improve the relationship between the Fire Department and the Job by holding a friendly little . . . track meet."

Levin looks at Monty and grins.

Monty nods.

"This commander has the records pulled and sees that Detective William Montague has a time in the mile akin to an Olympic athlete and figures he has his man," Malone says. "The brass at One P start laying down money with their brethren of the Fire Department."

"Those knuckle draggers take the bets," Russo says, "because a few of them know the real William J. Montague and figure they have a sure thing."

"Which they do," Malone says. "Because there's no way we can sub the fake Monty for the real Monty in front of all those cops and firemen who know him. Monty goes into training—which means one less cigar a day and easy on the barbecue sauce, and the big day rolls around. We show up in Central Park and the Fire Department has a ringer—a probie from Iowa who was the Big Ten champion in the mile. I mean, this kid—"

"White boy," Monty says.

"—looks like a freakin' god," Malone says. "He looks like a Greek sculpture, and Monty, he shows up in plaid Bermuda shorts, a T-shirt hanging over his gut and a cigar in his mouth. The commander takes one look at him and about shits himself. He's all, like, 'What the fuck did you do? How much could you fucking eat in one month?' The brass have thousands on this race, and they are pissed.

"They go to the starting line. The pistol goes off and for a second I think the commander shot Monty. Monty, he takes off—"

"If you can call it that," Russo says.

"—gets five strides," Malone says, "and topples over."

"Hamstring," Monty says.

"The Fire baboons start jumping up and down," Malone says, "cops are cursing, handing their money over. Monty's on the ground holding his leg, we're laughing our asses off."

"But didn't you guys lose a lot of money?" Levin asks.

"Are you fucking kidding me?" Russo asks. "I got my cousin Ralphie on the Fire Department to lay our money down against Usain Bolt-Down-His-Food over here, so we cleaned up. And the commander walks away totally disgusted, I hear him say, 'One slow nigger in Harlem, and he's mine.'"

Levin looks at Monty to see how he takes "nigger."

"What?" Monty asks him.

"You know, the N-word," Levin says.

"No, I don't know the 'N-word,'" Monty says. "I know 'nigger.'"

"And you're okay with it?"

"I'm okay with Russo saying it," Monty says. "I'm okay with Malone saying it. Someday I might be okay with you saying it."

"How does it feel to be a black cop?" Levin asks Monty.

Malone winces. This could go either way. Monty could blow, or he could get professorial.

"How does it 'feel'?" Monty asks. "I don't know, how does it feel to be a Jewish cop?"

"Different," Levin says. "But when I show up, Jews don't hate me."

"You think blacks hate me?" Monty asks. "Some do. Some call me a Tom, a house nigger. But the truth is, whether they say it or not, most black people think that I'm trying to protect them."

"How about inside the Job?" Levin asks, not letting it go.

"There are haters on the Job," Monty says. "Haters are everywhere. At the end of the day, though, most cops don't see black and white, they see blue and everyone else."

"But by 'everyone else,'" Levin says, "most people think we mean 'black.'"

It gets quiet, then they all get that stupid high smile you get from powerful weed. That blunt gets them fucking *blasted*. Then they're up and dancing. Which is a surprise to Malone, because he doesn't dance. But he is now, bopping with Niki in the thick crowd of clubgoers, the music throbbing through the veins in his arms, swirling around in his head, Monty ultracool, black man cool beside him, even Russo up and dancing, they are all *fucked up*.

Dancing in the jungle with the rest of the animals.

Or the angels.

Or who could tell the fucking difference.

They drive Levin home, down to West Eighty-Seventh off West End. His girl, Amy, doesn't look too thrilled when they carry her semiconscious boyfriend to the door.

"He got a little over-refreshed," Malone says.

"I guess so," Amy says.

Cute-looking girl.

Dark, curly hair, dark eyes.

Smart looking.

"We were celebrating his first collar," Russo says.

"I wish he'd called me," Amy says. "I like to celebrate."

Good luck, smart Amy, Malone thinks. Cops celebrate with other cops. No one else understands what you're celebrating.

Being alive.

Taking down bad guys.

Having the best job in the world.

Being alive.

They toss Levin on the sofa.

He's out.

"Nice to meet you, Amy," Malone says. "I've heard a lot of nice things."

"Same," Amy says.

They dispatch Dominic to take the women back and then roll down Lenox Avenue in Russo's car, with the stereo blasting and the windows open, singing along with N.W.A. at the tops of their lungs.

Searching my car, looking for the product
Thinking every nigga is selling narcotics.

Driving down this old street, this cold street, past the tenements, past the projects.

Malone hangs out the front window.

I don't know if they fags or what
Search a nigga down and grabbing his nuts.

Russo lets out a demonic laugh and they all shout—

Fuck tha police
Fuck tha police
Fuck tha police
Fuck tha police!

Rolling through the jungle.
Stoned, drunk, high.
Through the hard gray of early dawn.
Yelling to the few startled people on the sidewalks—

Fuck tha police
Fuck tha police
Fuck tha police
Fuck tha police!
I want justice!
I want justice!

All together now—

Fuck you, you black motherfuckersssssssss!!!!!

CHAPTER 9

They take him as he walks toward his apartment.

A black car pulls over and three guys in suits get out.

Fucked up as he is, at first Malone thinks it's the dope. Can't really focus on them, doesn't really care. Sounds like a bad joke, right, "Three guys in suits get out of a car and—"

Then a jolt—they're hitters.

Pena's people?

Savino?

He starts to reach for his gun when the lead guy shows his badge, identifies himself as "Special Agent O'Dell—FBI."

He looks like a fed, Malone thinks. Short blond hair, blue eyes. Blue suit, black shoes, white shirt, red tie, Church Street Gestapo motherfucker.

"Please get in the car, Sergeant Malone," O'Dell says.

Malone holds up his shield. His words come out like mud. "I'm on the Job, you fuckface Church Street fuck. NYPD, *real* police. North Manhattan—"

"You want us to cuff you right here on the street, Sergeant Malone?" O'Dell asks. "In your neighborhood?"

"Cuff me for what?" Malone asks. "Public intox? That's a federal crime now? I showed you my shield, for Chrissakes, a little professional courtesy, huh?"

"I'm not going to ask you again."

Malone gets in the car.

Fear spins around his fucked-up head.

Fear?

Shit, *terror.*

Because it hits him—they have him on the Pena rip.

Thirty to life tilting heavy toward life.

John grows up without a father, Caitlin walks down the aisle without you, you die in a federal lockup.

The terror of that blasts through the booze and the weed and the blow and shoots electric jolts through his heart. He feels like he could throw up.

He takes a breath and says, "If this is about inspectors and chiefs taking cash and prizes, that's above my pay grade. I don't know anything about that."

Sounds like Fat Teddy to himself. *I ain't know nothin'.*

"Don't say another word," O'Dell says, "until we get there."

"Get where? Church Street?"

New York FBI headquarters.

The Waldorf, it turns out. They take a side door, go up a service elevator to the sixth floor and then into a suite at the end of the hall.

"The Waldorf?" Malone asks. "What, I get red velvet cake?"

"You want red velvet cake?" O'Dell asks. "I'll call room service. Jesus Christ, you're a mess. What the hell have you been doing? If we piss-test you now, what's going to come up? Weed? Coke? Dexedrine? That's your shield and your gun right there."

A laptop computer is open on the coffee table. O'Dell points at the sofa in front of it and says, "Sit down. You want a drink?"

"No."

O'Dell says, "Yes, you do. Trust me, you're going to need it. Jameson's, right? A good mick like you isn't going to drink Protestant whiskey. No Bushmills for a guy named Malone."

"Quit jerking me off and tell me what this is about," Malone says. It ain't the cool he wants to play but he can't help himself. Can't stand to wait another second to hear the death sentence—

Pena.

Pena.

Pena.

O'Dell pours a whiskey and hands it to him. "Sergeant Dennis Malone. Manhattan North Special Task Force. Hero cop. Your father was a cop, your brother was a fireman, gave his life on nine/eleven—"

"Keep my family out of your mouth."

"They'd be so proud of you," O'Dell says.

"I don't have time for this bullshit." He heads for the door. More like staggers, his feet feel like wood, his legs like Jell-O.

"Sit down, Malone. Take some weight off, watch a little TV." This comes from a squat middle-aged guy sitting in an easy chair in the corner.

"The fuck are *you*?" Malone asks.

Stretch it out. Stall. Get your motherfucking head together. This ain't no dream, this is your life. One wrong play and the rest of your fucking life is down the shitter. Clear your dumb donkey cop head.

"Stan Weintraub," the guy says. "I'm an investigator with the U.S. Attorney's Office, Southern District of New York."

FBI and Southern District, Malone thinks.

All federal.

No state or IAB.

"You make me come into work this time of the morning," O'Dell says, "the least you could do is sit down and watch a little television with me."

He turns on the video on the computer screen.

Malone sits and watches.

Sees his own face on the screen as Mark Piccone hands him an envelope and says, *"Your finder's fee on Fat Teddy."*

"Thank you."

"Can you straighten it out?"

"Who's riding?"

"Justin Michaels."

"Yeah, I can probably straighten that out."

They have him cold.

He hears Piccone ask, *"How much?"*

"Are we talking a reduction or a nol pros*?"*

"A walk."

"Ten to twenty K."

"And that includes your cut, right?"

"Yeah, of course."

Dead to rights.

How could you be so fucking stupid, let your guard down because it's Christmas? The fuck is wrong with you? Did they have Piccone, and he set you up, or were they on you?

Shit, how long have they had you up? What do they know? Is it just Piccone or do they have more? If they know about Piccone, do they know about the Fat Teddy rip, too? That puts Russo and Monty in the jackpot with you.

But it's not Pena, he thinks.

Don't panic.

Be strong.

"What you got," Malone says, "is me taking a referral fee from a defense attorney. Go ahead, hang me. This isn't worth your rope."

"We'll decide that," Weintraub says.

"I was helping this guy Bailey out," Malone says. "He's a CI."

"So you have a CI file on him," O'Dell says. "We can pull that, look at it?"

"See, he's more useful to me alive."

"He's more useful to you as a source of income," Weintraub says.

"You're not in the driver's seat here," O'Dell says. "You're in the shit. We've got enough on that tape to take your badge, your gun, your job, your pension."

"Put you in a federal lockup," Weintraub says. "Five to ten."

"Federal time," O'Dell says. "You serve eighty-five percent of it."

"No shit? I didn't know that."

"Unless you want to go to a state facility with the guys you put in there," Weintraub says. "How would that work out for you?"

Malone stands up and gets right in Weintraub's face. "You gonna play Bobby Badass with me? You can't. You don't have the game. Threaten me like that again I'll put you through that wall."

"That's not the way to play this, Malone," O'Dell says.

Yeah, it is, Malone thinks. Play it tough, play it hard. These guys are just like the dopes in the street—you show weakness, they eat you alive.

"Are there ADAs other than Michaels selling cases?" Weintraub asks.

O'Dell don't look happy with him, so that's their first mistake. Weintraub tipped their hand—they're interested in lawyers, not cops.

So it was Piccone, not me, they had up.

Fuck, I dodge IAB for fifteen years and then walk into someone else's jackpot. Now I have to find out if Piccone knows or not. "Ask Piccone."

"We're asking you," Weintraub says.

"What do you want me to do, piss myself?"

"We want you to answer the question," O'Dell says.

"If Piccone is cooperating," Malone says, "you already know the answer."

Weintraub starts to lose his temper. "Are there ADAs in the district selling cases?!"

"The hell do you think?"

"I asked you what the hell *you* think!" Morally outraged.

So Piccone isn't cooperating. Probably doesn't know he's a recording artist yet.

"I think you *know*," Malone says. "But I think you don't *want* to know. You'll *say* you want it all, clean out the whole stable. End of the day you'll go after a few defense attorneys you got beefs with. Prosecutors, judges will skate. Next time you jam one of them up will be the first time."

"Did you say judges?" Weintraub asks.

"Grow up."

Weintraub doesn't answer.

"It doesn't have to go this way," O'Dell says.

Here it comes, Malone thinks. The deal.

How many skels have I offered the deal?

"Do you collect directly from the ADAs?" O'Dell asks. "Or do you get it through the defense lawyers?"

"Why?"

"If it's you, you wear a wire," O'Dell says. "Get them on tape. You bring the money to us, it's vouchered as evidence."

"I'm not a rat."

"Famous last words."

"I can do the time."

"I'm sure you can," O'Dell says. "But can your family?"

"I told you, keep my family out of it."

"No, *you* keep your family out of it," O'Dell says. "You put them into this. *You*. Not us. How are your kids going to feel knowing that their father is a crook? How is your wife going to feel? What are you going to tell them about college—they can't go because the savings went to defense lawyers, Dad doesn't have his pension, and the universities don't take food stamps?"

Malone doesn't say anything.

This O'Dell guy is good, for a fed. Knows the buttons to push. An Irish Catholic from Staten Island going on food stamps? You wouldn't live down the shame for three generations.

"Don't give me an answer now," O'Dell is saying. "Take twenty-four, think about it. We'll be here."

He hands Malone a slip of paper.

"That's a hello-phone," O'Dell says. "One hundred percent secure. You call it in the next twenty-four hours, we'll set up a meeting with our boss and see what we can work out."

"If you don't call," Weintraub says, "we'll put the cuffs on in your squad room, in front of all your brother officers."

Malone doesn't take the slip of paper.

O'Dell shoves it in his shirt pocket. "Think about it."

"I'm not a rat," Malone says again.

Malone walks uptown, hoping the fresh air will clear his head, let him think. He feels sick, nauseated from the stress and the fear, the drugs and the booze. They waited, the fucking assholes, he realizes. They picked their shot, waited to grab you at your weakest, when your head was already fucked up.

It was the right move, the move you would have made.

You go after a perp, you try to go in just at dawn, when the guy is asleep, make his dream a nightmare, get a confession out of him before he realizes the alarm clock isn't going to ring.

Except these fucks don't need to get a confession out of you, they got you on camera and now they're offering you the out you've offered a hundred skels—"Be my CI, my snitch. Climb out of the pit and throw someone else in instead, shit, you don't think they'd do the same to you, the tables were turned?"

He's heard himself say it a hundred fucking times.

And ninety times out of that hundred it worked.

Malone comes to Central Park South and turns west toward Broadway, past what used to be the Plaza Hotel. One of the best moonlighting security gigs he ever had—guarding some film equipment that arrived before the crew. They paid him to sit in a suite at the Plaza ordering room service, watching TV and looking out the window at the beautiful women.

Midmorning now, springtime, the tourists are out in force and he hears the babel of language—Asian, European, New Yawk— that's one of the sounds of the city to him. It feels weird, strange— his whole life has changed in the last two hours but the city goes on around him, people walk to where they're going, they have conversations, they sit at sidewalk cafés, take rides in the horse-drawn carriages, as if Denny Malone's world hadn't just come down around him.

He makes himself suck in some of the spring air.

Realizes that the feds made a mistake.

They let him go, let him out of the room, let him get into the

196 /   DON WINSLOW

world and get a little perspective. I would never let a skel out of the room unless he lawyered up, Malone thinks, and even then I'd try to keep him there and not let him see that there was any other world except my face, no other possibilities than what I was holding in my hand.

But they did, so take advantage of it.

Think.

Okay, they have you for a four-to-five federal time, but you don't know you're going away, he tells himself. You have money stashed just for this emergency.

One of the first things he learned, one of the first things he told his guys, is put the first $50K away—in cash where you can get to it—in case you get popped. That way you always have bail money and a down payment on a lawyer.

You might be able to beat this, you draw the right prosecutor, the right judge. It's a dogshit charge anyway. Half the judges in the system would want to shut this investigation down, they knew about it. Even if you don't beat it, you can probably plead it down to two.

But suppose you get the whole four, Malone thinks. Those are four critical years for John, the years he goes one way or the other. And Caitlin? Malone's heard all the stories about girls without fathers, how they go looking for that love with the first guy who comes along.

No. Sheila's a great mom, and there's always Uncle Phil, Uncle Monty and Aunt Donna.

They'll keep the kids straight.

They'll be hurt but they'll be all right. They're Malones, they're tough, and they come from a neighborhood where sometimes fathers "go away." The other kids won't pick on them for that.

And college, I've got that covered already.

A man handles his business.

The kids' tuition is in a trap under the shower.

The guys will take care of Sheila, she'll still get her envelope. So fuck your food stamps.

They took an oath. If the worst happens, Russo will be at his house with an envelope every month, will take his son to ball games, straighten him out if he has to, make sure he does the right thing.

Wiseguys take the same oath, but nowadays they rarely follow up past a few months. One of theirs is in prison or the dirt, his wife has to go to work, his kids look like ragamuffins. Didn't used to be that way—now it's a big reason wiseguys turn rat.

It's not that way with this crew—Monty and Russo know who to go see to get Malone's stashed money, and every penny of it would go to keep Sheila comfortable.

And he'd keep earning a full share in the joint.

So you don't have to worry about your family.

Claudette, you can always get money to her she needs it. But as long as she's off the shit, she's okay. She's been clean for almost a year now, has her job, her family, some friends. Maybe she waits for you, maybe not, but she'll be all right.

He reaches the southwest edge of the park and walks around Columbus Circle onto Broadway.

Malone loves walking Broadway, always has.

Lincoln Center is always beautiful, and now he's back on his beat, his turf, his territory.

His streets.

Manhattan North.

Goddamn, he loves this street. Has since his stint in the Two-Four. The old Astoria building, Sherman Square, which they used to call "Needle Park," Gray's Papaya. Then the old Beacon Theater, the Hotel Belleclaire and the spot where Nick's Burger Joint used to be. Zabar's, the old Thalia, the long gentle slope uptown.

He ain't afraid of doing the time. Sure, there'll be cons in there looking to even scores, and they're tough guys, but I'm a tougher guy. And I won't go in unprepared—the Ciminos will make sure there's a welcome committee at whatever prison they send me to. No one jacks with mobbed-up guys.

If I even do any time.

Any which way, you lose your job. If the criminal charges don't take you out, the Departmental Disciplinary Hearing will. It's a rigged court—the commissioner never loses. If he wants you out, you're out.

No gun, no badge, no pension, no job and no other department in the country will touch you.

What the hell am I going to do?

He doesn't know how to do anything else. Being a cop is the only job he's ever had, the only job he's ever wanted.

And now it's over.

It hits him like a punch in the face. I'm done being a cop.

Thanks to one stupid, careless, jackass moment on a Christmas afternoon, I'm done being a cop.

Maybe I can pick up with a security company or an investigative firm, he thinks. Then he rejects that. He don't want to be a fake cop, a has-been, and that kind of job would always put him in contact with real cops who'd pity him, or look down on him, or at least remind him of what he used to be and isn't anymore.

Better to have a clean break, do something totally different.

He has money in the bank, a lot more money when they flip the Pena rip.

I can start a business, he thinks. Not a bar—every retired cop does that—but something else.

Like what, Malone? he asks himself.

Like freakin' what?

Like nothin', he thinks.

All you know how to do is be a cop.

So he goes to work.

CHAPTER 10

Where you been?" Russo asks him.

Malone looks at his watch. "Noon tour, I'm on time."

He's on time, but his head is fucking reeling. Booze hangover, drug hangover, sex hangover, fear hangover.

They've got him by the fucking balls and he doesn't know what to do.

"That's not what I'm talking about," Russo says. "You haven't changed your clothes. You smell like booze, weed and pussy. Expensive pussy, but still . . ."

"I been at my girlfriend's," Malone says. "That okay with you?"

It's the first lie.

To his partner, his best friend, his brother.

Tell him, Malone thinks. Take him and Monty out into the alley and tell them. You got your dick caught in the Piccone thing, you're going to work it out, they got nothing to worry about.

But he doesn't.

"You went to your girlfriend's?" Russo laughs. "Looking like that? How'd that go?"

"Like it looks," Malone says. "It's okay with you, Mom, I thought I'd shower here, change."

If he looks like hell, Levin looks like hell lined with shit. He's hunched over on the bench, trying to tie his shoes, but it seems like too much for him. When he looks up and sees Malone, his face is white.

And guilty.

Like a perp in the room ready to go.

Levin will make a good cop, Malone thinks, but he'll never be an undercover. Can't keep the guilt off his face.

"Bowling Night isn't for pussies," Malone says.

"Just pussy," Russo says. "But you already know that, don't you?"

"I don't want to talk about it."

"Poor Emily," Russo says.

"Amy."

"As in 'Don't tell Amy,'" Monty says.

"The fuck's the difference?" Russo says. "Don't worry, Dave—what happens in Manhattan North stays in Manhattan North. No, wait, that's Vegas. What happens in Manhattan North, we tell everybody."

Malone goes in, takes a shower. Pops two go-pills, changes into a blue denim shirt and black jeans.

When he gets out, Russo says, "Sykes wants to see you."

Malone goes up to the captain's office.

"You look like hell," Sykes says. "Out celebrating?"

"You should be, too," Malone says. "You closed Gillette/Williams, the noose is off your neck, the *Post* and the *News* have woodies for you."

"The *Amsterdam News* is calling me an Oreo."

"You care?"

"Not really," Sykes says.

But Malone knows he does.

"I'm pleased about Gillette/Williams," Sykes says, "but it doesn't solve the bigger problem. In fact, it only makes it worse—if Carter gets those weapons, he'll hit back hard."

"I talked to him," Malone says.

"You did what?"

"I happened to bump into him," Malone says. "So I took the opportunity to ask him to stand down."

"And?"

"You're right. He won't."

More lies of omission. He doesn't tell Sykes that he knows for a fact one of his detectives is on Carter's pad, running interference, in fact, on the gun deal. Can't tell him, because Sykes would slap Torres in cuffs. So instead, he says, "We're on it."

"You want to be a little more specific?" Sykes asks.

"We're placing a visual surveillance on 3803 Broadway, where we believe Teddy Bailey is setting up the deal."

"Can that get us Carter?"

"Probably not," Malone says. "You want the guns or you want Carter?"

"First the one, then the other."

"We get the guns," Malone says, "Carter is going down anyway."

"I want him arrested," Sykes says, "not killed by Carlos Castillo."

"Does it matter?" Malone asks.

"I won't have the Task Force perceived as operating on behalf of one drug operation versus another," Sykes says. "This is New York, not Mexico."

"Jesus Christ, Captain," Malone says. "You want these guns or you don't? We both know DeVon Carter isn't going anywhere near them. Just like we both know these homicide clearances are going to buy you a little time, but not a lot before One P is up your ass again."

"Get the guns," Sykes says. "Just be aware that your team is serving as the point of the Task Force spear, not a loose cannon of your own."

"Don't worry," Malone says. "When the bust goes down, you'll be in on it."

You'll be there to spike the ball for the touchdown celebration.

But you don't want to know how I get you to the red zone.

He walks downstairs into a nasty freakin' ambush.

It's Claudette.

Two uniforms have her by the elbows and try to move her gently out of the lobby, but she ain't havin' it.

"Where is he?" she says. "Where's Denny?! I want to see Denny!"

Malone comes through the door to see this.

She's jonesing. She was high and now she's jangling, her nerves starting to jump ugly at her.

She sees him, too. "Where have you been? I looked for you last night. I called you. You didn't answer. I came to your place, you weren't there."

Most of the uniforms look appalled and scared. A couple smirk, until Monty turns his gaze on them.

"I got this," Malone says.

He takes Claudette from the officers. "Let's go outside."

But she has that strength that crazy gives a person and won't budge. "Who is she? You smell like pussy, you motherfucker. White pussy, some ratchet?"

The desk sergeant leans out from the counter. "Denny—"

"I know! I got it!"

He picks Claudette up by the waist and carries her to the door as she kicks and screams, "You don't want your friends to see me, asshole?! You're ashamed of me in front of your cops?! He fucks me, y'all! I let him fuck me in the ass when he wants! In my black ass!"

Sykes is standing on the stairs.

Watching this.

Malone wrestles Claudette out the door into the street. Plain-clothes guys coming in stare at them.

"Get in the car," Malone tells her.

"Fuck you."

"Get in the fucking car!"

He shoves her through the passenger door, slams it, walks around and gets in. Hits the lock button, rolls up her sleeves and sees the needle mark.

"Jesus, Claudette."

"Am I under arrest, Officer?" Claudette asks. "Gosh, Officer, is there something I can do to avoid going to jail?"

She unzips his fly and bends over.

He straightens her up. "Knock it off."

"Can't get it up? Your whore wear you out?"

He takes her chin between his left thumb and forefinger. "Listen to me. *Listen to me.* I cannot be having this. You cannot come here."

"Because you're ashamed of me."

"Because it is my place of work."

Claudette breaks down. "I'm sorry, Denny. I got so desperate. You left me alone. You left me all alone."

It's an explanation and an accusation.

He gets it.

A junkie goes into the alley alone with the disease, it's the disease that walks out.

"How much did you shoot?" he asks.

He's scared because it's a new world out there—the dealers are mixing fentanyl with the smack—it's forty times stronger and if she got a dose of that she could OD. Junkies are dropping out there, dying like gays back in the worst of the AIDS days.

"Enough, I guess," she says. And repeats, "You left me alone, baby, and I couldn't take it so I went out and scored."

"Who fixed you?"

She shakes her head. "You'll hurt him."

"I promise, I won't. Who?"

"What difference does it make?" she asks. "You think you can threaten every dealer in New York?"

"You think I can't find out?"

"Then find out," she says. "I'm hurting, baby."

He drives her home. Grabs a get-well bag from under the dashboard and brings it up with him.

"Go into the bedroom and shoot," he says. "I don't want to watch."

"It's my last, baby," she says. "They'll give me some come-down shit at the hospital, I know a doctor. I'll step it down, I promise."

He sits on the sofa.

If I go to jail, he thinks, she dies.

She'll never make it alone.

Claudette comes out a few minutes later. "Tired now. Sleepy."

Malone lays her on the sofa, goes into the bathroom, kneels down and pukes into the toilet. He's violently sick until there's nothing left to throw up and he dry heaves. Then he sits on the black-and-white tile floor, reaches up to the sink for a hand towel and wipes the sweat off his face. After a couple of minutes, he gets up, splashes cold water on his face and the back of his neck.

He brushes his teeth until the vomit smell is gone.

Then he takes his phone and punches in the number.

Hears "Hello."

O'Dell must have been sitting by the phone, the smug bastard, waiting. Knowing I was going to cave.

Malone says, "I'll give you lawyers. But no cops, you hear me?"

I will never give you brother cops.

CHAPTER 11

S ykes waves him upstairs the second he walks into the house.

He gets up to the office, Sykes asks, "Have you ever heard of 'rape under the color of authority'?"

"No."

"For example," Sykes says, "if a person in a position of power, say a police detective, has a sexual relationship with a person under that power, say a criminal informant, that is rape under the color of authority. It's a felony—ten years to life."

"She's not a CI."

"She was high."

"She's not a CI," Malone repeats.

"Then who is she?" Sykes asks.

"That's not your business," Malone says.

"When a woman causes a tawdry scene in the lobby of my station house," Sykes says, "it is very much my business. I cannot have one of my detectives' personal lives embarrassing the Job in public. You're married, aren't you, Sergeant Malone?"

"Separated."

"Does this woman reside in Manhattan North?"

"Yeah."

"So you carrying on with a woman who lives in your jurisdiction," Sykes says, "is conduct unbecoming an officer. At the very least."

"Bring charges."

"I will."

"No, you won't," Malone says. "Because I just cleared your big fucking case, your career is back on track and you're not going to do anything to put a negative light on your command."

Sykes stares at him and Malone knows he's right.

"Keep your personal messes out of my station house," Sykes says.

Malone and Russo cruise up Broadway north of 158th.

"You want to talk about it?" Russo asks.

"No," Malone says. "But you do, and you're going to, so go ahead."

"A black woman with a drug problem?" Russo asks. "It's not good, Denny, particularly given the current, shall we say, sensitive racial environment."

"I'll take care of it."

"By which you mean you'll end it?"

"By which I mean I'll take care of it," Malone says. "Subject closed."

Broadway up here is broken into north and south lanes with a strip of trees in the center, and the nail shop below Carter's safe house is on the west side.

"It's a second-floor walk-up," Russo says. "Fat Teddy can't be liking that."

Russo pulls over by an ATM on the east side of the street, they get out and pretend to take out money but instead watch Babyface walk into the liquor store next to the nail shop.

Five minutes later he comes out with a six-pack of Colt 45, which he passes to Montague.

Malone and Russo cross Broadway and go into a diner. Fifteen minutes later Montague comes in and sits down across from Malone.

"Go on," Malone says. "Say it."

"What am I going to say?" Monty asks. His eyes have mischief in them, but Malone sees the seriousness underneath. "I prefer black women, too."

"That was some scene," Russo says.

"I admire your taste in women," Monty says. "I truly do. But with all the heat on us right now, the last thing we need is more attention."

"I told Russo I'll take care of it."

"And I heard you," Monty says. "On more pressing matters, the Chaldean gentleman wants to keep his liquor license. I explained that he just sold alcohol to a minor. He doesn't seem to know Carter, and I told him we just wanted to use his back storeroom for a few weeks and all is forgiven."

Malone gets up. "We better get the fuck out of here."

They get back into the car and watch as Levin goes in. It takes him forty-five minutes, then he comes out, gets into the car, and Russo drives them out of there.

"We can punch a hole in the drywall," Levin says, "push a wire up to the second floor and we've got ears on Carter's little office."

"What about shifts?" Russo asks. "Teddy knows me, Malone and Monty, and you can't do twenty-four seven."

"You guys are techno Neanderthals," Levin says. "Once we get the wire in, I can monitor it on my laptop anywhere close with Wi-Fi. Which is, like, everywhere. And we don't do twenty-four seven, just when Teddy comes in."

"Nasty Ass can give us that," Malone says. "Levin, you sure you're good with this? No warrant, it's illegal as shit. We get caught, you lose your shield, maybe go to jail."

Levin smiles. "Just don't tell Amy."

"You coming back to the house?" Russo asks Malone.

"No, I have to go downtown," Malone says. "Prep for Fat Teddy's Mapp hearing."

"Good luck with that," Russo says.

"Yeah." It's the stupid fucking irony of this whole thing. To make the gun case, they have to keep Fat Teddy out of jail and on the street, and if they'd known that then, they could have gotten him a walk without buying the case.

And none of this federal bullshit would have happened.

Now he has to buy the case to keep his own ass out of jail.

He feels like he's going to puke.

Quit feeling sorry for yourself, Malone thinks.

Man up and do what you got to do.

Malone finds Nasty Ass junkie-bopping up Amsterdam at 133rd and pulls over. "Get in."

He'd forgotten how bad the snitch smells. "Jesus, Nasty."

"What?" Nasty is relaxed, happy. He must have scored.

"You ever use a toilet?"

"I don't have no toilet."

"Borrow one," Malone says. He rolls the windows down. "You know a nurse who used to score around here? Name is Claudette?"

"A sister? Real pretty?"

"Yeah."

"I seen her."

"Who does she score from?"

"Slinger named Frankie."

"White guy?" Malone asks. "Works Lincoln Playground?"

"That's him."

Malone gives him a twenty.

"White people are cheap."

"That's why we have the money," Malone says. "Get out."

"White people rude, too."

"Now I have to turn this car in, get a fresh one," Malone says.

"You hurtful, man. You a hurtful motherfucker."

"Call me."

"Cheap, rude and hurtful."

"Out."

Nasty Ass gets out of the car.

Frankie sits on the steel bench in the holding cell at the end of the hall.

Malone picked him up and took him to Three-Two, not Manhattan North. Then let him sit for a while to get him jacked up. The cell stinks of piss, shit, vomit, sweat, fear, desperation, hopelessness and a heavy dose of Axe cologne that Frankie probably lifted from Duane Reade.

Malone opens the door and walks in. "No, don't get up."

Frankie's in his early thirties, his head is shaved, he has tattoo sleeves and more tats on his neck.

Malone rolls up his own sleeves.

Frankie sees it. "You gonna beat me up?"

"You remember a woman named Claudette?" Malone asks. "You sold her some shit today?"

"I guess so."

"You guess," Malone says. "You knew she was clean, because you hadn't seen her for a while, right?"

"Or she went somewhere else," Frankie says.

"You a junkie, too?"

"I use."

"So you deal to pay for your own shit," Malone says.

"Pretty much." He's trembling.

"You know why they put you in this particular cell?" Malone asks. "The video camera doesn't reach. And you know how it is these days; if it's not on camera, it didn't happen."

"Oh, Jesus."

"Jesus isn't here," Malone says. "What you got is me. And the difference between him and me is that he's a forgiving kind of guy, and I don't have an ounce of forgiveness in my entire body."

"Oh, God, did she OD?"

"No," Malone says. "If she had, you'd have never made it to the house. Listen to me. Frankie, look up at me and listen—"

Frankie looks up at him.

Malone says, "I promised her I wouldn't hurt you. So they're going to cut you loose after I leave. But—listen to me, Frankie—next time you see her, you *run,* don't walk, in the other direction. If you ever sell her dope again, I will find you, and I will beat you to death. And now you know that I keep my promises."

He walks out of the cell.

sobel Paz, the U.S. attorney for the Southern District of New York, is a killer.

A fucking killer, Malone thinks.

Caramel skin, jet-black hair, red lipstick over a wide mouth and thin lips. Probably in her early forties but looks younger. Comes into the room in a black business jacket over a tight skirt and high heels.

Dressed to kill.

They're back at the fucking Waldorf.

Paz made sure to arrive last.

Same thing with mob guys, Malone thinks. The boss is always the last to arrive at a meeting. Make the other people wait, establish the pecking order. These fucks are no different.

Old school, Malone stands up.

Paz doesn't offer her hand. Just says, "Isobel Paz, U.S. attorney."

"Denny Malone. NYPD detective."

She doesn't smile, either. Just smooths her skirt and sits down across from him. "Have a seat, Sergeant Malone."

He sits down. Weintraub starts up a digital recorder. O'Dell presents her with a cup of coffee like it's his balls he's offering up, then he sits down.

So we're all at the fucking table, Malone thinks.

Now what?

Paz says, "Sergeant Malone, let me be clear. I don't think you're a hero. I think you're a criminal who takes bribes from other criminals. Just so we understand each other."

Malone doesn't answer.

"I would just as soon put you behind bars for betraying your oath, your badge and the public trust," Paz says, "but we have higher-value targets to go after. That being the case, I'm just going to hold my nose and work with you."

She opens a file. "Let's get down to business. You will have to make a proffer, during which you will admit to any and all crimes you committed up to this moment. If you lie, by omission or commission, any arrangement we make will be null and void. If you commit any further crimes that go beyond the scope of this investigation and do not have our specific approval, any arrangement we make will be null and void. If you perjure yourself in any sworn affidavit or in testimony, any arrangement we make will be null and void. Do you understand?"

Malone says, "I won't go after cops."

Paz looks over at O'Dell and Malone sees it—he didn't tell her about that part of the deal. O'Dell looks across the coffee table at him. "Let's cross that bridge when we come to it."

"No," Malone says. "There is no bridge that goes there."

"Then you go to jail," Paz says.

"Then I go to fucking jail."

And fuck you.

"Do you think this is a joke, Sergeant Malone?" Paz asks.

"You want me to bring you lawyers, I'll hold my nose and work with you," Malone says. "You ask me to work against cops, you can go fuck yourself."

"Turn off the tape," Paz snaps at Weintraub. She looks at Malone. "Maybe you have me confused with one of your usual Southern District, prep school Ivy League dickwads. I'm a PR from the South Bronx, tougher streets than you came from, *hijo de puta*. I'm the middle child of six kids, my father worked in a kitchen, my mother sewed knockoffs for the Chinese downtown. I went to Fordham. So if you fuck around with me, you donkey asshole, I'll send you to a federal supermax where you'll be drooling your oatmeal inside of six weeks. *Compréndeme, puñeto?* Turn the tape back on."

Weintraub turns the tape back on.

"This tape will be filed securely and only accessible to the people at this table," Paz says. "There will be no transcript. Agent O'Dell will summarize these proceedings in a report, which will be accessible only to authorized Southern District, New York State and FBI personnel."

"That 302 could get me killed," Malone says.

O'Dell says, "I guarantee its security."

"Right, because there are no crooked feds," Malone says. "No lawyer upside down on his house, no secretary whose husband is behind on the vig—"

Paz says, "If you know names—"

"I don't know any names," Malone says. "I only know 302s have a way of winding up in social clubs next to espresso cups, and that the reason there won't be a transcript is so the bureau can put its own spin on what I've said."

Paz sets down her pen. "Do you want to make a proffer or not?"

Malone sighs. "Yes."

No proffer, no deal.

She swears him in. Malone promises to tell the truth, the whole truth . . .

"You've seen evidence of yourself accepting a payment for referring a defendant to legal counsel," Paz says. "Do you acknowledge that?"

"Yes."

"You also appear to be entering a conspiracy to bribe a prosecutor to fix a case on behalf of that defendant. Is that accurate?"

"Yes."

"Is that called 'buying a case'?"

"That's what I call it."

"How many times," Paz asks, "have you 'bought a case' or facilitated in such?"

Malone shrugs.

Paz looks at him with disgust. "So many you've lost count?"

"You're mixing two things," Malone explains. "Sometimes I'd refer a suspect to a lawyer for a fee. Other times I would help approach a prosecutor to buy a case and get a kickback from the prosecutor for that, too."

"Thank you for the clarification," Paz says. "How many simple referral fees have you accepted from defense attorneys?"

"Over the years?" Malone asks. "Maybe hundreds."

"And from prosecutors who've been paid off?"

"Probably twenty or thirty," Malone says. "Over the years."

"Do you deliver the payment to the prosecutor?" Weintraub asks.

"Sometimes."

"How many times?" Paz asks.

"Twenty?"

"Are you asking me or telling me?" Paz says.

"I didn't keep records."

"I'm sure you didn't," Paz says. "So roughly twenty. I want names. I want dates. I want everything you can remember."

So this is crossing a line, Malone thought. If I start naming names, there's no going back.

I'm a rat.

He starts with the oldest cases, giving them people he knows are retired or have moved on to other jobs. Most prosecutors don't stay in the job for too long, but use it as an apprenticeship to get to the more lucrative defense bar. This will still jam them up, but not as bad as the guys still on the job.

"Mark Piccone?" O'Dell asks.

"I took money from Piccone," Malone says. Because what the fuck, they all heard it.

"Is that the first time?" Paz asks.

"Did it look like the first time?" Malone says. "I'd say I've referred Piccone probably a dozen times."

"How many times have you taken payoffs to prosecutors for him?"

"Three."

"Were they all with Justin Michaels?" Paz asks.

Michaels is small potatoes, Malone thinks, why all this for little routine shit? Michaels isn't a bad guy—he'll take money on lowball busts that aren't going anywhere anyway, but he's stand-up on the assaults, the robberies, the rapes.

Now they're going to jam him up.

No, Malone tells himself, now *you're* going to jam him up.

But fuck it, they know anyway.

He says, "Two of them were with Michaels."

"Which cases?" Weintraub asks. He's angry.

"One was a dope case, a quarter key of coke," Malone says. "Guy named Mario Silvestri."

"That mother*fucker*," Weintraub snaps.

It draws a wry smile from Paz.

"What was the other one?" Weintraub asks.

"It was a dogshit gun charge on a smack slinger named . . ." Malone says. "I don't remember his real name, his street name was 'Long Dog.' Clemmons, maybe."

"DeAndre Clemmons," Weintraub says.

"Yeah, that's it," Malone says. "Michaels jacked up the chain of evidence, the judge threw it out in the evidentiary. You want the name of the judge?"

"Later," O'Dell says.

"Yeah, later," Malone says. "And I'll bet that somehow won't make it into the 302."

"So Silvestri and Clemmons," Paz says. "And now Bailey."

"You weren't going to get convictions on those guys, anyway," Malone says, "so what difference does it make if someone other than drug dealers made a little money for a change?"

"Are you really trying to justify this?" Paz asks.

"I'm only saying that we fined these skels a few grand," Malone says, "which is more than you could have done."

"So you distribute justice," Paz says.

You're damn right I do, Malone thinks. More than the "system" does. I distribute it on the street when I beat some creep who's molested a child, I deliver it in the courts when I "testilie" about some heroin dealer you'd never convict if I didn't, and yeah, I deliver it when I fine these motherfuckers some money you'd never get out of them.

He says, "There's all kinds of justice."

"And I suppose you donate this money to charity?" Paz asks.

"Some of it."

Every now and then he takes an envelope of cash and mails it off to St. Jude's, but these motherfuckers don't need to know that. Malone doesn't want their dirty hands touching something clean.

"What else have you done?" Paz asks. "I need full disclosure."

Jesus shit, Malone thinks.

It's Pena.

This has all been a setup for Pena.

But do you think I'm going to volunteer it? Malone thinks. You think I'm some junkie skel in the interview room who's going to go for anything just to get well?

"If you ask questions, I'll answer them," Malone says.

"Have you ever robbed drug dealers?" Paz asks.

This is about Pena, Malone thinks. If they know anything, they'll press on it. So keep it short, don't give them an opening. "No."

"Have you ever taken drugs or money that you haven't vouchered?" Paz asks.

"No."

"Have you ever sold drugs?"

"No."

"You've never given drugs to an informant?" Paz asks. "Legally, that constitutes selling."

I have to give her something, Malone thinks. "Yes, I've done that."

"Is that a common practice?"

"For me, yes," Malone says. "That's one way I garner the information that gets me the arrests I bring to you."

And have you ever seen an addict suffer? he thinks. Seen one jones? Shake, cramp up, beg, cry? You'd fix them, too.

"Is it common practice among other cops?" Paz asks now.

"I'm speaking for myself," Malone says. "Not other cops."

"But you must know."

"Next question."

"Have you ever beaten a suspect to obtain information or a confession?" Paz asks.

Are you fucking kidding me? I've whaled the living shit out of them. Sometimes literally. "I wouldn't say 'beaten.'"

"What would you say?"

"Look," Malone says, "maybe I've slapped a guy. Shoved him into a wall. That's about it."

"That's all?" Paz asks.

"What did I just say?" You ask but you don't want to know. You want to live on the Upper East Side or in the Village or up in Westchester and you don't want the shit leaking into your nice neighborhoods. You don't want to know how that happens for you. You just want me to do it.

"What about other cops?" Paz asks. "What about your teammates? Are they in on selling cases?"

"I'm not talking about my teammates."

"Come on," Weintraub says, "you expect us to believe that Russo and Montague aren't in on this with you?"

"I don't have any expectations about what you believe or don't."

"You make all that money by yourself?" Weintraub says. "You don't cut them in? What kind of partner are you?"

Malone doesn't answer.

"It's unbelievable on the face of it," Weintraub mutters.

"The proffer requires full disclosure," Paz says.

"I already made it clear," Malone says, "I won't go after cops. Here's what you got now, *chica*. You got one defense attorney for capping, you got one cop for bragging he can buy a case. You can get Piccone disbarred, you can take my shield and maybe put me inside for a couple of years, but you and I both know your bosses are going to look at that and ask, *Is that all we get for our money?* You'll look like an asshole.

"So now let me tell *you* how it's going to go," he continues. "It's as simple as ABC. Anyone But Cops. I'll get you Michaels. I'll get you a few defense lawyers and a prosecutor or two. I'll even throw in a couple of judges if you have the balls. In exchange for that, I walk. No jail time, I keep my shield and gun."

Malone stands up, walks to the door and puts his fingers to his mouth and ear, like *Call me.*

He's waiting for the elevator when O'Dell comes out.

It must have been a quick meeting.

"All right," O'Dell says. "We have a deal."

Yeah we do, Malone thinks.

Because everyone can be bought.

It's just a matter of finding the right coin.

Claudette's sick.

Nose-running, body-shaking, bone-aching junkie sick.

Malone has to give her credit, though—at least she's trying to kick again.

But she quickly disabuses him of that notion. "I tried to score but I couldn't find my guy. Did you do something to him?"

"I didn't hurt him, if that's what you mean," Malone says. "You get a doctor to give you something? Because if not, I got a guy—"

"Trauma doctor gave me some Robaxin," she says.

"You're not afraid he'll dime you to admin?"

"After the shit I seen him do?"

"Is it helping?"

"Does it look like it's helping?"

He's heating up water to make some herbal tea. The herbs will do exactly shit, but the tea might warm her up a little.

"Let me take you to detox."

"No."

"I get worried, you know?"

"Don't," she says. "Alcoholics die in withdrawal, not heroin users. We just get sick. And go out and use again."

"That's what I'm worried about."

"If I was going to, I would have," she says.

She finishes the tea. He wraps a blanket around her and then holds her, rocks her like a baby.

It was another guy, he'd have told him to cut this woman loose. A junkie, what you do is you hold a funeral like she's dead, you grieve, and then you move on, because the person you knew ain't there anymore.

But he can't seem to do that with Claudette.

N ext morning, Malone goes into Rand's down the street from the courthouse with a copy of the *New York Post* under his arm. A few minutes later, Piccone slides into the booth across from him and sets the *Daily News* on the table. "Page Six is good today."

"How good?"

"Twenty thousand dollars good."

It costs more to buy some cases than others. Simple possession, a couple of grand. Possession with intent to sell, you're looking double digits. A heavyweight with intention could go six figures, easy, but then again, if the defendant has that kind of weight, he has that kind of money.

Weapons charges these days, it gets up there, especially if the defendant has a yellow sheet. Fat Teddy could be going for five to seven years, so this is a bargain.

Malone has to pin Piccone down, they told him. Pretend the conversation is being played for a jury. "If I get Michaels to sell the case for twenty, you good with that?"

Malone takes the *Daily News,* sets it down beside him.

"Only if you get him to drop, decline to prosecute."

"For twenty K I can get him to say it was *his* gun."

"What are you having?" Piccone asks. "The pancakes are sort of edible."

"No, I gotta move." He gets up with the *Daily News,* leaves the *Post* for Piccone. He goes into the men's room and cuts $5K from the envelope inside the paper, puts that in his pocket and goes on the street.

Malone's always thought that 100 Centre Street is one of the most depressing places on earth.

Nothing good ever happens in the Criminal Courts Building.

Even when the rare good, like a bad guy getting convicted, sneaks through the bad, it's always behind a tragedy. There's always a victim, at least one grieving family, or a bunch of kids whose daddy or mommy is going away.

Malone finds Michaels in the hallway. Hands him the paper. "You should read this."

"Yeah, why?"

"Fat Teddy Bailey."

"Bailey, he's fucked."

"Fifteen K get your dick out of his ass?"

"Did you take a finder's fee?" Michaels asks.

"You want this money or you don't?" Malone asks. "But it's for a pass, not a plea."

Michaels puts the paper in his canvas bag. Then he starts the show. "Goddamn it, Malone, this gets tossed on a Dunaway."

Probable cause.

A couple of people glance over as they pass by. Malone glances over to make sure they're watching and then for their benefit he yells, "Known felon, and I saw a gun bulge!"

"What kind of coat was Bailey wearing?"

"The hell am I, Ralph Lauren?" Malone says, playing it out.

"A *down* coat," Michaels says. "A North Face down coat. You gonna stand there and tell me—no, you gonna tell a *judge*—you could see a .25 under that? I'm supposed to go in there and look like an asshole? A racist asshole, to boot?"

"You're supposed to go in there and do your job!"

"You do yours!" Michaels yells. "Make a goddamn bust I can work with."

"You're going to put this mook back on the street."

"No, *you're* going to put him back on the street," Michaels says, walking away.

"Pussy," Malone says. "Jesus Christ."

People look at him standing in the hallway. But it's not unusual—cops and ADAs get into it all the time.

Malone goes up to the third floor of the old textile building in the Garment District where O'Dell has set up his operation.

A couple of desks and the hello-phone. Red boxes of files. Cheap metal cabinets, a coffeemaker. Malone hands him the five grand, shucks his jacket, rips off the wire and sets it on the desk.

"Did you get it?" O'Dell asks.

"Yeah, I got it."

Weintraub grabs the tape, fast-forwards it to the conversation with Michaels. Listens and then says, "God fucking damn it."

"This gonna do it?" Malone asks. "I put them both in the shit for you?"

"What, you feel bad?" Weintraub says. "You want to take their place?"

"Shut up, Stan," says O'Dell. "You did a good job, Denny."

"Yeah, I'm a good rat," Malone says, heading for the door and out of that sickening fucking place, literally a rat-hole. And what's this fucking "Denny"? he thinks. We friends now or something? It's all "Stan" and "Denny," like we're on the same team now? And patting me on the head, "You did a good job, Denny"? I'm your fucking dog now?

"Where are you going?" O'Dell asks.

"The fuck is it to you?" Malone asks. "Or what, I'm not free to leave, you're afraid I'm going to go warn the guy? Don't worry, I'd be too ashamed."

"You have nothing to be ashamed of," O'Dell says. "You're going to be ashamed, you should be ashamed of what you *were* doing, not what you're doing now."

"I didn't come here looking for your fucking absolution."

"No?" O'Dell asks. "I kind of think you did. I think some part of you wanted to get caught, Denny."

"Is that what you think?" Malone asks. "Then you're an even bigger asshole than I thought you were."

"You want to get coffee, a drink?" O'Dell asks.

Malone whirls on him.

"Don't *handle* me, O'Dell." You know how many informers I've handled, coddled, seduced, told them they were doing the right thing? I give them heroin, not coffee, and I know the cardinal rule of dealing with them—you can't think of them as people, they're snitches. You start falling in love with them, caring about them, thinking of them as anything but what they are, they'll end up killing you.

I'm your snitch, O'Dell.

Don't fuck up by trying to treat me like a person.

Claudette says pretty much the same thing to him when he goes to check in on her.

He walks in the door and the first words out of her mouth are "Are you ashamed to be seen with me?"

"The fuck did *that* come from?" he asks. He looks to see if her eyes are pinned but they aren't. She hasn't been using, she's been hanging in there, jonesing, and he knows it's tough as hell and she's angry and now she's going to take it out on him.

"I've been thinking about why I relapsed."

You relapsed because you're an addict, he thinks.

"Why haven't I ever met your partners?" she asks. "You've met their mistresses, haven't you?"

"You're not my mistress."

"What am I?"

Oh, fuck. "My girlfriend."

"You haven't introduced me because I'm black," she says.

"Claudette, one of my partners *is* black."

"And you don't want him to know you're doing a sister," she says.

Yeah, that's partially true, Malone thinks. He didn't know how Monty would react, whether he'd be okay with it or if he'd be pissed. "Why do you want to meet them?"

"Why *don't* you want me to meet them?" she asks back. "Is it because I'm black or because I'm an addict?"

"Nobody knew about that," Malone says.

"Because nobody knew about me."

"Well, they do now," Malone says. "Why are my partners so important to you?"

"They're your family," she says. "They know your wife, your children. You know theirs. They know everyone important in your life, except me. Which makes me think I'm *not*."

"I don't know what more I can do to—"

"I'm your shadow life," she says. "You hide me."

"That's bullshit."

"We almost never go out," she says.

That's true. Between her schedule and his it's a tough get and anyway, it's awkward, even in 2017—a white man with a black woman in Harlem. When they do go out together—to a coffee shop or the grocery store—they get looks, sideways glances and sometimes outright stares.

And he's not just a white man, he's a white *cop*.

That causes hostility, or something worse, maybe some of the locals figuring Malone will cut them a break because he's with a black woman.

"I'm not ashamed of you," Malone said. "It's just that . . ."

He goes on to explain his concern that the people in the neighborhood might think he'd slacken up. "But you wanna go out, we'll go out. Let's go out right now."

"Look at me, I'm a mess," she says. "I don't want to go *out*."

"Jesus Christ, you just said—"

"I mean, what is this, some kind of 'brown sugar' thing?" she asks. "Jungle fever? You just come over here and fuck me?"

"No."

You fuck me *back,* baby, he thought, but was just smart enough not to say.

"Denny, did you ever think you might be one of the reasons I use?"

Jesus fucking Christ, Claudette—you ever think you're one of the reasons I just turned fucking snitch, that I just turned fucking rat, that your fucking addiction, your fucking disease is what made me do that?!

"Fuck you," he says.

"Fuck you right back."

He gets up.

"Where are you going?" she asks.

"Somewhere that's not here."

"You mean somewhere away from me."

"Yeah, okay."

"Go," Claudette says. "Go away. You want to be with me, you treat me like a person. Not some junkie whore."

He slams the door on his way out.

CHAPTER 14

Malone and Russo take in a Rangers game, tickets on the blue line comped by a guy from the Garden who still likes cops.

Which is, like, fewer and fewer people, Malone thinks.

Just last month, two plainclothes in an unmarked vehicle out near Ozone Park in Queens saw a guy standing next to a double-parked car with an open bottle of booze.

A bullshit C-summons, but when they went to front the guy, he ran.

You run on cops, they're gonna chase, it's the golden retriever mentality. They cornered him, he pulled a gun, the cops shot him thirteen times.

The family hired a lawyer who started litigating the case in the media. "A father of five young children was hit with thirteen bullets, including shots to the back and head, all because of an open container."

First you had Garner killed over selling Luckys, then Michael Bennett, now you have a guy killed over a freakin' open container.

Gotta hand it to the commissioner, though, he stood up. "The best way to not get shot by a New York City police officer is not carry a gun and not raise that gun toward them."

Syntax and grammar aside, as Monty observed, it was a strong statement, especially when the commissioner added, "My cops go out there every day and put their lives at risk and the attorneys, the games they play."

The lawyer fired back. "We certainly have empathy for good cops who risk their lives to protect our communities—who doesn't?

But as for 'games' being played . . . one needs to simply open up a newspaper any day of the week to learn of the lying, cheating and stealing committed by members of the NYPD, so you'll excuse me if I don't immediately take their word for what occurred."

So the Job's taking it from all sides.

The protesters are out, the activists are calling for action and the tension between the police and the community is worse than ever.

And still no call from the Bennett grand jury.

So when black guys aren't shooting black people, the cops are shooting black people.

Either way, Malone thinks, black people die.

And he goes on being a cop.

New York goes on being New York.

The world goes on being the world.

Yeah, it does and it doesn't. His world has changed.

He's a rat.

The first time you do it, Malone thinks, it's life changing.

The second time, it's just life.

The third time, Malone thinks, it's *your* life.

It's who you are.

The first time he wore a wire he felt like everyone in the world could see it, like it was glued to his forehead. It felt like a thick scar on his skin, a cut that still stitched and pulled.

This last time it slipped on easier than his belt. He hardly noticed it was there.

O'Dell doesn't call him a rat.

The FBI agent calls him a "rock star."

Rock star.

By mid-May, Malone had given the feds four defense lawyers and three ADAs. Paz's office is busy typing up sealed indictments. They're not going to make arrests until they're ready to spring the entire trap.

The fucked-up thing is that when he's not trapping dirty lawyers, Malone just goes on being a cop.

Like none of this is really happening.

He goes to the Job, he works with his team, he monitors the surveillance on Carter, he deals with Sykes. He rides the streets, works his snitches, makes the busts that are there to be made.

He goes to the shooting scenes.

Two weeks after the Gillette/Williams killings a Trinitario up in Inwood was walking home from a club and took a round in the back of the head. Ten days later a Spade in north St. Nick's got laced with a shotgun blast from a drive-by. He's in Harlem Hospital but he ain't going to make it.

And as Malone predicted, the goodwill from the Williams arrest lasted about an hour and a half. Now Sykes is catching it at the CompStat meeting, the commissioner's catching it from the mayor, the mayor from the media.

Sykes is all up Malone's ass for progress on the guns.

He's up everyone's ass.

Got Malone working Carter, Torres on Castillo, has the plainclothes out trying to get guns off the street, the undercovers trying to buy them.

Yeah, shit flows downhill.

It's Levin that gets them the break.

Fuckin' Levin, he showed up one day with his iPad and sat in the liquor store closet banging away. Russo and Monty, they figured the kid was just screwing around online, watching Netflix, they didn't care, it's a monotonous gig and you gotta do something, but one day he came out looking prouder than a fourteen-year-old who just got his first tit and he opened up the iPad and said, "Look at this."

"The fuck you do?"

"I hacked his phones," Levin said. "I mean, not the voice, we can't hear the other half of the conversations, but every time he makes or receives a call, it comes on the screen."

"Levin," Monty said, "you may have actually justified your existence on this earth."

No shit.

Now they know who Fat Teddy's talking to, and he's talking to Mantell a lot.

"Volume analysis," Levin said. "As they get closer to a delivery, the traffic will pick up."

"But how do we know where they're going to exchange?" Malone asked.

"We don't yet," Levin said. "But we will."

"Carter won't go near the exchange," Monty said. "He's not even on the phone now, has Fat Teddy handling everything."

"We don't care about Carter," Malone said. "Just the guns."

Maybe stop a bloodbath.

So Malone's trying to be a real cop, do real police work, restore the peace in his kingdom.

Peace of mind, that he can't restore.

The shooting war going on inside his own head.

Monty wasn't interested in coming to the Rangers game. "Black folk don't go near ice."

"There are black hockey players," Malone said.

"Race traitors."

They'd have taken Levin, but you can't get him off the Fat Teddy surveillance with a crowbar and a hand grenade. So it's just Malone and Phil there to watch the Penguins wipe the Rangers out of the playoffs. They're sitting with beers and Russo says, "The fuck's going on with you?"

"What do you mean?"

"When's the last time you saw your kids?"

"Who are you, my priest right now?" Malone asks. "You want to fuck me in the ass, Father?"

"Drink your beer. Sorry I asked."

"I'll come out this weekend."

"Do what you want," Russo says. Then he asks, "What about the black woman, you deal with that?"

"Jesus fucking Christ, Phil."

"Okay, okay."

"Can we watch the fucking game?"

They watch the fucking game as the Rangers do what the Rangers do, blow a lead in the third period and then get beat in OT.

Malone and Russo go to the bar at Jack Doyle's after the game for a nightcap, the TV news is on and Reverend Cornelius is talking about the Ozone Park "police killing."

Fucking lawyer-looking fuck in a suit standing at the bar, his tie loosened around his neck, starts shooting his mouth off. "Cops executed that guy."

Russo sees the look in Malone's eyes.

Seen that look before, and now Malone's had a few beers and three Jamesons back to back to back.

"Take it easy."

"Fuck him."

"Let it slide, Denny."

But the loudmouth won't let it go, starts lecturing the whole bar about the "militarization of our police forces" and the funny thing is Malone don't even disagree with him, it's just he's not in the mood for this shit.

He's staring at the guy, the guy sees it and looks back at him and Malone says, "What are you looking at?"

The guy wants to back down. "Nothing."

Malone slides off the stool. "No, what the fuck you looking at, mouth?"

Russo gets behind him, puts his hand on his shoulder. "Come on, Denny. Chill."

Malone shoves his hand off. "*You* fucking chill."

The guy's buddies, they're trying to move him out of the bar and Russo is all in agreement with that, he says, "Why don't you take your friend home?"

"What are you, a lawyer?" Malone asks the guy.

"Yeah, as a matter of fact."

"Well, I'm a cop," Malone says. "I'm a New York City fucking police detective!"

"Enough, Denny."

"I'll have your badge," the guy says. "What's your name?"

"Denny Malone! Sergeant Dennis John Malone! Manhattan motherfucking North!"

Russo lays a couple of twenties on the bar. Says to the bartender, "It's okay, we're getting out of here."

"After I kick this pussy's ass," Malone says.

Russo gets between them, shoves Malone back and hands the guy his card. "Look, he's had a tough week, a few too many. Take this, you need a favor sometime, a ticket fixed, whatever, you call."

"Your buddy's an asshole."

"Tonight I can't argue," Russo says. He grabs Malone and hauls him out of the bar and shoves him onto Eighth Avenue.

"Denny, what the fuck?!"

"Guy pissed me off."

"You want to get IAB up our ass?!" Russo asks. "Give Sykes more of a hard-on for you than he already has? Jesus."

"Let's go get a drink."

"Let's put you to bed."

"I'm a New York City police detective."

"Yeah, I heard that," Russo says. "Everybody did."

"New York's finest."

"Okay, champ."

They walk to the parking lot and Russo drives him home. Takes him upstairs. "Denny, do yourself a favor. Stay here. Don't go out anymore tonight."

"I won't. I got court tomorrow."

"Yeah, you're going to look great," Russo says. "You going to set an alarm or should I call you?"

"Alarm."

"I'll call you. Get some sleep."

Drunk dreams are the worst dreams.

Maybe because your brain is already fucked over and ready to give up to the sickest shit you got running around in there.

Tonight he dreams about the Cleveland family.

Two adults, three kids dead in their apartment.

Executed.

The kids ask him for help but he can't help them.

He can't help them, he just stands there and cries and cries and cries.

Malone gets up in the morning and downs five glasses of water.

Head hurts like a motherfucker.

Whiskey with a beer chaser is good; beer with a whiskey chaser is a catastrophe. He pops three aspirin, two Dexies, showers and shaves and then gets dressed. His court costume today is a white shirt with a red tie, blue blazer, gray slacks and polished black shoes.

You don't wear a suit to court unless you're at least a lieutenant or above because you don't want to show up the lawyers and you want the jury to see you as an honest working stiff.

No cuff links today.

No Armani, no Boss.

Straight-up Jos. A. Banks.

Mary Hinman sees him and laughs. "That your schoolboy costume?"

Red hair, freckled pale skin, the special prosecutor for Narcotics could be out of the cast of *Riverdance* if she were taller.

But Hinman is small, a description she rejects.

"I'm not small," she says when the topic comes up. "I'm *concentrated.*"

Which is no-shit true, Malone thinks now, sitting across the table from her. Hinman is ferocious, a five-four little ball of rage who came up the traditional way—Catholic all-girls school, Fordham University, then NYU law. Hinman's feet can't touch the floor from the barstool but she can drink you under the table. Malone knows. He went shot for shot with her the night she got a verdict against a dealer named Corey Gaines for killing his girlfriend.

Malone lost.

Hinman put him in a cab.

She comes by it honest—her father was an alcoholic cop, her mother an alcoholic cop's wife.

Hinman knows cops—she knows how it works. Nevertheless, when she was a rookie ADA, Malone had to teach her a few things her father hadn't. It was her first major drug case—long before she'd elbowed past her male counterparts to become special prosecutor—and Malone was in plainclothes in Anti-Crime.

But it was a whole kilo of coke Malone and his then partner Billy Foster made in a tenement on 148th. They got a tip from a snitch, but not enough to get a warrant. Malone wasn't about to hand it over to Narcotics—he wanted the collar—so he and Foster went in on a gunshot warrant, arrested the dealer and then called it in.

It got him a chewing out from his sergeant and Narcotics, but it also got him attention. Normally he wouldn't care if it also got a conviction, but he wanted this scalp on his belt and was worried that a rookie ADA—a woman, to boot—would jack up his case.

When she called him in for witness preparation, Hinman said, "Just tell the truth and get the conviction."

"Which?" Malone asked.

"What do you mean?"

"I mean," Malone said, "I can tell the truth or I can get the conviction. Which do you want?"

"Both," Hinman said.

"You can't have both."

Because if he told the truth, they'd lose the case on a Mapp issue because Malone had no warrant and no probable cause to enter the apartment. The evidence would become the "fruit of a poisoned tree" and the dealer would walk.

She thought this over for a few seconds and then said, "I can't suborn or encourage perjury, Officer Malone. I can only advise you to do what you think you need to do."

Mary Hinman never advised Malone to just tell the truth again.

Because the real truth that they both know is that without cops "testilying," the DA's office would hardly get any convictions at all.

This doesn't bother Malone.

If the world played fair, he'd play fair. But the cards are stacked against the prosecutors and police. *Miranda, Mapp,* all the other Supreme Court decisions, give the advantage to the skels. It's like the NFL these days—the league wants touchdown passes, so a defensive back can't even touch a receiver. We're the poor defensive backs, Malone thinks, trying to keep the bad guys from scoring.

Truth, justice and the American way.

The American way is, truth and justice maybe say hello in the hallway, send each other a Christmas card, but that's about the extent of their relationship.

Hinman gets it.

Now she sits across the table in a courthouse meeting room and looks at Malone. "The hell did you do last night?"

"Rangers game."

"Uh-huh," she says. "You ready to testify? Give me a preview."

"My partner, Detective Sergeant Phillip Russo," Malone says, "and I received information from neighborhood residents that there was suspicious activity at 324 West 132nd Street. We had set up a visual surveillance of the address and observed a white Escalade pull up and the defendant, Mr. Rivera, get out. I didn't have a conclusive reason to believe that it contained drugs, certainly not sufficient visual evidence to indicate probable cause."

This was the cool part of their dance—take it the other way to convince the jury that you're telling the truth. Plus, they expect it from watching television.

Hinman asks, "If you didn't have probable cause, what gave you the right to force entry into the apartment?"

"Mr. Rivera was not alone," Malone says. "Two other men exited the vehicle with him. One was carrying a MAC-10 machine pistol with a suppressor," Malone says. "The other was carrying a TEC-9."

"And you saw these."

Malone says the magic words. "They were in plain sight."

If a weapon is in plain sight, you don't need probable cause. You have immediate cause. And the weapons *were* in plain sight—at Malone's feet.

"So you gained entry to the address," Hinman says. "Did you identify yourselves as police officers?"

"We did. I yelled, 'New York City police!' and our badges were clearly visible on lanyards over our protective vests."

"What happened next?" Hinman asks.

We planted the machine guns on those dumb mooks. "The suspects dropped their weapons."

"What did you find in the apartment?"

Malone says, "Four kilos of heroin and an amount of American currency in $100 bills that eventually turned out to be $550,000."

She goes over the boring shit about the voucher numbers and how he could be certain that the heroin he seized was the same heroin now in the courtroom, blah blah blah, and then she said, "I hope you bring a little more energy at trial than you did in this session."

"In the words of Allen Iverson," Malone says, "'We're talking about practice here. *Practice.*'"

Hinman says, "We're talking about Gerard Berger."

This is how Malone sums up his opinion of Gerard Berger—

"If he was on fire," Malone has said, "I'd piss gasoline on him to put it out."

Denny Malone hates three things in life, not necessarily in the following order:

1. Child molesters
2. Rats (the human variety)
3. Gerard Berger

The defense attorney doesn't pronounce his name like what you get at P.J. Clarke's, he pronounces it "Bur-jay" and insists that you do too. Which Malone steadfastly refuses to do, except in open court, so he doesn't look like a smart-ass in front of the judge.

Anywhere else, it's Gerry Burger.

Malone isn't alone in his hatred of Berger. Every prosecutor, cop, correctional officer and victim despises him. Even his own clients hate him, because by the time the case is concluded, Berger owns much of what they used to—their money, their houses, their cars, their boats, sometimes their women.

But, as he reminds them, "You can't spend money in prison."

Berger's clients usually don't go to prison. They go home, or they go on probation, or they go into drug rehab or anger management classes. They go back to doing what they were doing, which is usually something criminal.

He doesn't care.

Drug traffickers, murderers, wife beaters, rapists, child molesters—Berger will take any client who has a fat wallet or a story that can be sold to a publisher or the movies or preferably both, such as Diego Pena. He's seen versions of himself portrayed by A-list actors, some of whom have come to him for advice, which he sums up in the simple phrase "Be a total asshole."

It has been said that the only time any of Berger's clients confess is on *Oprah*—and then he has the confession tossed out.

Berger doesn't bother to hide his wealth—he flaunts it. Multithousand-dollar custom suits, custom shirts, designer ties, designer shoes, expensive watches. He comes to court in Ferraris or Maseratis, cars that were given to him, Malone figures, in lieu of payment. He has the penthouse on the Upper East Side, the summer place in the Hamptons, the ski condo in Aspen that was signed over to him by a grateful client who now resides in Colombia and whose deal doesn't allow him to come back to the United States anyway.

Malone has to admit that Berger is very good at what he does.

He's a great paper lawyer, a genius at motions (especially to exclude), a canny and vicious cross-examiner and a master of opening statements and closing arguments.

The biggest secret to his success is that he's dirty.

Of this, Malone is convinced.

He's never been able to prove it, but Malone would bet his left testicle that Berger has judges on the arm.

The other filthy secret of the so-called justice system.

Most people don't realize it, but judges don't make a lot of money. And they usually have to spend a lot to get the robe. The mathematics of that means that a lot of them can be bought.

It doesn't take a lot to swing a case—a motion granted or denied, evidence excluded or admitted, testimony allowed or stricken. Little things, small things, arcane details that can spring a guilty defendant.

The defense bar knows—shit, everyone knows—which cases they can buy. One of the most lucrative judicial posts is on the scheduling docket; for the right money you can pay to have a case assigned to the judge you've already purchased.

Or rented, anyway.

.

Malone and Hinman do their dance on direct examination and then they adjourn for a few minutes before Berger starts his cross. Malone goes to take a shit. When he comes out of the stall to wash his hands, Berger is at the next sink.

They look at each other in the mirror.

"Detective Sergeant Malone," Berger says. "What a pleasure."

"Hey, Gerry Burger, how's it hanging?"

"Oh, it's hanging just fine," Berger says. "I can't wait to get you on the stand. I'm going to eviscerate you, humiliate you, and show you to be the lying, corrupt police officer that you are."

"You buy the judge, Gerry?"

"The corrupt see only corruption," Berger says. He dries his hands. "See you on the stand, Sergeant."

"Hey, Gerry," Malone calls after him. "Your office still smell like dog shit?"

Malone and Berger, they go way back.

He takes the stand and the bailiff reminds him that he's still sworn in.

Berger smiles at him and says, "Sergeant Malone, does the phrase 'testilying' mean anything to you?"

"Generally."

"Well, generally, what does it mean, around police circles?"

"Objection," Hinman says. "Relevance."

"He may answer."

"I've heard it in reference to police not telling the exact truth on the stand," Malone says.

"The exact truth," Berger says. "Is there an *in*exact truth?"

"Same objection."

"Where is this going, Counselor?" the judge asks.

"I'll develop, Your Honor."

"All right, but do so."

"There are different points of view," Malone says.

"Ah." Berger looks to the jury. "And isn't it true that officers' point of view is that they 'testilie' in order to convict a defendant that they feel is guilty, regardless of the admissible evidence?"

"I've heard it used in that context."

"But you've never done it."

"No, I have not," Malone says. If you don't count a few hundred exceptions.

"Not even on your last answer?" Berger asks.

"Argumentative!"

"Sustained," the judge says. "Move on, Counselor."

"Now," Berger says, "it's your testimony that you did not have probable cause to enter the apartment on suspicion of drugs, is that correct?"

"Yes."

"And it's your sworn testimony that you did have probable cause based on your seeing my clients' associates carrying weapons. Is that correct?"

"Yes."

"You saw the weapons."

"They were in plain sight," Malone says.

"Is that a yes?"

"Yes."

"And absent your seeing those weapons 'in plain sight,'" Berger says, "you had no probable cause to enter that domicile, is that correct?"

"That is correct."

"And when you saw those weapons," Berger says, "they were in the suspects' possession, is that correct?"

"Yes."

"I'd like to enter into evidence this document," Berger says.

"What is it?" Hinman asks. "We haven't been notified of this."

"It just came into our possession, Your Honor."

"Both counsel approach the bench."

Malone watches Hinman go up. She flashes him a WTF look, but he doesn't know what the fuck, either.

"Your Honor," Berger says, "this is an evidence voucher dated 5/22/2013. You'll note it logs in a MAC-10 pistol with the serial number B-7842A14."

"Yes."

"It was vouchered into the evidence room of the Thirty-Second Precinct on the date recorded. The Thirty-Second is, of course, in Manhattan North."

"What's the relevance of this?"

"If the court admits," Berger says, "I will demonstrate relevance."

"Admitted."

"I object," Hinman says. "We were not given access to this document—"

"Your objection is preserved for appeal, Ms. Hinman."

Berger goes back to the cross-examination. He hands Malone a document. "Do you recognize this?"

"Yes, it's an evidence voucher for the MAC-10 pistol removed from one of the suspects."

"Is that your signature?"

"Yes."

"Will you read for us the serial number of that weapon?" Berger asks.

"B-7842A14."

Berger hands him another document. "Do you recognize this?"

"It appears to be another evidence voucher."

"Well, it doesn't 'appear' to be," Berger says. "That's what it is, isn't it?"

"Yes."

"And it vouchers in a MAC-10 pistol, isn't that right?"

"That's correct."

"Please read us the date of that voucher."

"May 22, 2013."

Goddamn it, Malone thinks. Goddamn it, they assured me the weapons were squeaky clean.

Berger is walking him toward a cliff and there's no stopping.

"Now please read us the serial number," Berger says, "of the MAC-10 pistol seized on May 22, 2013."

I'm totally fucked, Malone thinks.

"B-7842A14."

Malone hears the jury react. He doesn't look over, but he knows they're staring daggers at him now.

"It's the same weapon, isn't it?" Berger asks.

How the fuck did he get this voucher? Malone wonders.

Like everything else, dummy. He bought it.

"It seems to be."

"So," Berger says, "as an experienced police officer, could you tell us how the same weapon could be locked away in the Thirty-

Second Precinct evidence room and then magically appear 'in plain sight' in the suspects' hands on the night of February 13, 2015?"

"Argumentative. Calls for speculation."

"I'm going to allow it." The judge is *pissed.*

"I don't know," Malone says.

"Well, there are only so many possibilities," Berger says. "Is it possible it was stolen from the evidence locker and sold to alleged drug traffickers? Is that a possibility?"

"I suppose that's possible."

"Or is it more possible," Berger says, "that you took this weapon in order to plant it on the suspects and cook up a pretext for probable cause?"

"No."

"Not even possible, Sergeant?" Berger asks, enjoying himself immensely. "Not even possible that you burst into that domicile, shot two suspects, *killed* one of them, planted weapons on them, and then lied about it?"

Hinman jumped up. "Argumentative, speculative. Calls for a hypothetical. Your Honor, defense counsel is—"

"Approach the bench."

"Your Honor," Hinman says, "we do not know the provenance of this document, we were not allowed sufficient time to investigate its legitimacy, its accuracy—"

"Goddamn it, Mary," the judge says, "if you cooked up this case—"

"I wouldn't for one moment impugn Ms. Hinman's ethics," Berger says. "But the fact remains that if Sergeant Malone did not see the weapons as he claims that he did, there was no probable cause, and any evidence found in the domicile is fruit of a poisoned tree. I'll move to dismiss, Your Honor."

"Not so fast," Hinman says. "Defense counsel himself brought up the possibility that the weapon was stolen from the locker, and—"

"You bring me one big headache here," the judge says. He sighs, then adds, "I'm going to exclude the MAC-10."

"That still leaves the TEC-9."

"Right," Berger says, "the jury is going to believe that one weapon is dirty but the other is clean. Please."

Malone knows that Hinman is considering her options, all of them shitty.

One of them is that NYPD officers are selling automatic weapons out of their evidence rooms to drug dealers. Another is that a highly decorated NYPD detective perjured himself on the stand.

If she goes with that it could open up a flood of headlines, the shooting becomes wrong, and IAB launches an investigation on one Sergeant Denny Malone, including all his previous testimony. Hinman could lose not only this case, but have twenty others reversed. Twenty guilty skels will walk out of prison and she'll walk the plank.

There's one other option.

He hears Hinman ask Berger, "Would your client be open to a plea offer?"

"It depends on the offer."

Malone feels the bile rise in his mouth as Hinman says, "One count of simple possession. A twenty-five-thousand-dollar fine, two years with time served deducted, and deportation."

"Twenty thousand, time served and deportation."

"Your Honor?" Hinman asks.

The judge is disgusted. "If the defendant agrees, I will accept that plea and issue the negotiated sentence."

"One more thing," Hinman says. "The record is sealed."

"I have no problem with that," Berger says with a smirk.

There was no media in the room, Hinman thinks. There's a good chance of keeping this off the radar.

"The record is sealed," the judge says. "Mary, the court is not happy about this. Go do the paperwork. Send Malone into my chambers."

The judge gets up.

Hinman walks over and tells Malone, "I'm going to fucking kill you."

Berger just smiles at him.

Malone goes into chambers. The judge doesn't offer him a seat.

"Sergeant Malone," the judge says, "you were about three syllables away from losing your shield, your gun, and being indicted for perjury."

"I stand by my testimony, Your Honor."

"As will Russo and Montague," the judge says. "The Blue Wall."

Goddamn right, Malone thinks.

But he keeps his mouth shut.

"Thanks to you," the judge says, "I have to release an almost certainly guilty defendant. To protect the NYPD, who are supposed to be protecting us."

It's thanks to Berger, asshole, Malone thinks. And some careless assholes at the Three-Two too lazy to shit-can an old evidence voucher. Or who are on Berger's pad. Either way, I'll find out.

"Do you have anything to say, Sergeant?"

"The system is screwed up, Your Honor."

"Get out, Sergeant Malone. You make me sick."

I make you sick, Malone thinks as he walks out. You make me sick, you hypocrite. You just participated in a cover-up of this thing, you know what's going on. You didn't protect cops out of the goodness of your heart, you protected us because you have to. You're part of the system, too.

Hinman is waiting for him in the hallway.

"Both our careers were swirling around the bowl in there," she says. "I had to cut that bastard a deal to save us."

Poor you, Malone thinks. I cut deals every damn day, a lot worse than this one. "You knew the score, so cut the Joan of Arc routine."

"I never told you to commit perjury."

"You don't care what we do when you get convictions," Malone says. "'Do what you have to do.' But let something go south, then you say, 'Play by the rules.' I'll play by the rules when everyone else does."

After all, he thinks as he walks out, they don't call it the Criminal Courts for nothing.

alone meets his team up at Montefiore Square, which isn't a square but a triangle formed by Broadway, Hamilton Place and 138th.

"What do we got?" Malone asks.

"Fat Teddy's made thirty-seven calls to Georgia area codes in the past three days," Levin says. "The shipment's definitely coming."

"Yeah, but coming where?" Malone asks.

"Teddy won't give them an address until the last minute," Levin says. "If he does it from the office, we might pick it up, but if he does it from the street, we'll know when he makes the call, but not what he says."

"Can we get a warrant on Teddy's phones?" Monty asks.

"Based off what he heard off an illegal tap?" Malone says. "Not these days."

Levin grins.

"What's funny?" Russo asks.

"What if we take Teddy?" Levin asks.

"He's not going to tell us shit," Russo says, "I don't care how many Ding Dongs we have."

"No," Levin says. "I have a better idea."

He lays it out.

The three older cops look at one another.

Then Russo says, "See, this is the difference between City College and NYU."

"Sit on it," Malone tells Levin. "Let us know when it's on."

Malone sits down with Sykes in the captain's office.

"I need buy money," Malone says.

"For what?"

"Carter's guns coming up on the Pipeline," Malone says. "Mantell's not going to sell them to Carter, he's going to sell them to us."

Sykes gives him a long look. "Mapp issues?"

"There won't be any. We're going to do it on the street."

"Behind what?"

"A CI's going to give us the meet," Malone says. "We'll take the CI's place."

"Did you file this CI?"

"Right after I leave your office."

"How much?"

"Fifty thousand," Malone says.

Sykes laughs. "You want me to go to McGivern for fifty thousand dollars based on something you heard that you shouldn't have?"

"I'll have a typed and sworn CI statement."

"As soon as you leave my office."

"McGivern will get it for you," Malone says. It's a risk but he has to take it. "If you tell him it's me."

That's a turd for Sykes to swallow.

"When is this going down?" Sykes asks.

Malone shrugs. "Soon."

"I'll talk to the inspector," Sykes says. "But this travels down the straight and narrow. You communicate, you keep me in touch every step of the way."

"You got it."

"And I want you to bring in another team when it goes down," Sykes says. "Use Torres and his people."

"Captain Sykes . . ."

"What?"

"Not Torres."

"What's wrong with Torres?"

"I need you to trust me on this one," Malone says.

Sykes looks at him for several long seconds. "What are you trying to tell me, Sergeant?"

"Let my team handle the buy," Malone says. "Bring the plain-clothes and the uniforms in on the seller. You distribute the collars any way you want—the whole Task Force dines out."

"Only not Torres."

"Only not Torres."

More silence.

More of a look.

Then Sykes says, "If you fuck me on this, Malone, I will set a fire up your ass that will never go out."

"I love it when you talk dirty to me, boss."

"Did you perjure yourself in the Rivera case?" Paz asks him.

"Who'd you have lunch with," Malone asks, "Gerry Berger?"

She tosses a file on the table. "Answer my question."

"This file was sealed," Malone says. "How did Berger get it to give it to you?"

She doesn't answer.

"You think that piece of shit wins all his cases because he's so smart?" Malone asks. "Because all his clients are innocent? You don't think he ever bought a ruling, got some evidence tossed with an envelope?"

"He didn't need that to get your evidence tossed, did he?" Paz asks. "You manufactured probable cause and then committed per-jury."

"If you say so."

"The record says so," Paz says. "Does Mary Hinman normally countenance this kind of thing to make her cases?"

"You going after her now?"

"If she's dirty."

"She's not," Malone says. "Leave her alone."

"Why? You fucking her?"

"Jesus Christ."

"If you perjured yourself," Paz says, "our deal is invalid."

"Do it," Malone says. He holds his hands out to be cuffed. "No, come on, right now. Do it."

She keeps glaring at him.

"Yeah, that's what I thought." He lowers his hands. "You know why you won't? *Brady versus Maryland*—you have to notify defense attorneys if a cop involved in their cases ever knowingly lied under oath. Because if I told you I had, it would open up forty or fifty old cases of guys who are locked up and are going to want new trials. And it will open up questions of whether your buddy prosecutors knew I was lying and tolerated it to get those convictions. So don't give me your sanctimonious, condescending bullshit because I'll bet to get to where you are you did the same goddamn thing."

Silence in the room.

"You fuckin' feds," Malone says. "You'd lie, cheat, sell your mother's eyes to get a conviction. It's only wrong when a cop does it."

"Shut up, Denny," O'Dell says.

"I've got you, what, six indictments now? Seven?" Malone asks. "When is this over? When is it enough?"

"It's over when we tell you it's over," Paz says.

"When is that?" Malone asks. "How high up you want to go? You got balls, Paz, you got big enough balls to go after judges? How much you think they clear after taxes? Enough for the condo down in West Palm? How about when they go to Vegas, get comped? Lose a bundle and it gets written off, too? You interested in how *that* happens?"

"What are you," Weintraub asks, "a crusader all of a sudden?"

Paz says, "If you know something—"

"*Everybody* knows it!" Malone says. "The fuckin' Hindu at the newspaper stand knows it! A ten-year-old black kid on the corner knows it! What I'm asking is how come *you* don't know it?"

Silence.

"Yeah, it gets real quiet now," Malone says.

"We have to work from the bottom up," O'Dell says.

"Well, that's convenient, isn't it," Malone says. "That works out nice for you. You never have to lay *your* asses on the line."

"I'm not going to sit here and be lectured by a crooked cop," Paz says.

"You know what, you don't have to," Malone says.

He gets up.

"Sit down, Denny," O'Dell says.

"You got your money's worth from me," Malone says. "I gave you all the lawyers I worked with. I'm done."

"Then we charge you," Paz says.

"Yeah, put me on the stand," Malone says. "See what names I name, see what happens to your careers then."

"Any professional aspirations I may harbor," Paz says, "have nothing to do with this."

"And I'm the Easter Bunny."

He walks toward the door.

"You know, you're right, Malone," Paz says. "You've taken us as far as you can with lawyers. Now I want cops."

You dumb mick motherfucker, Malone thinks, the lawyers were just the come-along, to get you in. How many times have you used the same game on snitches? Once you get their cherry, they're yours, you put them on the street and use them up.

But you thought you were different, dumb shit.

"I told you from the jump," Malone says. "No cops."

"You're going to give me cops. Or when we unseal these indictments against the lawyers, I'll put it out that it was you." Paz lets that sit and then smiles at him. "Run, Denny, run."

This bitch has you by the balls, Malone thinks. You're trapped. If she puts out the word that you're a rat, they'll all come after you— the Job, the Ciminos, the motherfuckers in City Hall.

You're dead.

Malone says, "You spic cunt."

Paz smiles at him. "Spic cunt is famously good. That's why everyone wants them some. Get me cops. On tape."

She walks out.

For Malone the room is spinning. He controls himself enough to say to O'Dell, "We had a deal."

"We're not asking for your partners," O'Dell says. "Just get us one or two other guys. There have to be cops even you think are over the line, Denny. Brutal cops. Cops we need to get off the street."

"I won't hurt my partners," Malone says.

"This is you *saving* your partners," O'Dell says. "Do you think we're stupid? That we think you could pull off shit like Rivera by yourself? If we charge you with that, they go too—Russo and Montague."

"They're in your hands, Malone," Weintraub says. "Don't fumble."

"Denny," O'Dell says, "I like you. I don't think you're a bad guy. I think you're a good guy who's done some bad things. There's a way out of this, for you and your partners. Work with us and we'll work with you."

"What about Paz?"

"You know she can't be privy to a deal like that," O'Dell says.

Weintraub asks, "Why do you think she left?"

"We have an understanding," O'Dell says.

"If I give you one or two others," Malone says, "I have your sacred word—on the eyes of your children—you don't hurt my partners."

"You have my word," O'Dell says.

How do you cross the line?

Step by step.

CHAPTER 16

F at Teddy is on the move.

Fast as Fat Teddy can move, anyway.

From across Broadway, in the liquor delivery truck, Malone watches him come down from the nail shop and hit the street and he's still on the phone.

"It's on," Levin says, looking at his iPad screen.

Teddy has used three phones to call the same Georgia cell phone and now he's walking downtown on Broadway.

"He just dialed a 212," Levin says.

"That's him telling Carter it's going," says Monty.

"Where do you want to take him?" Russo asks.

"Wait," Malone says.

They stay parallel as Teddy crosses 158th. Then he turns right onto 157th and right again up Edward Morgan Place.

"If he's going into Kennedy's Chicken," Monty says, "it's too much of a stereotype for me."

They turn behind him.

"Did he make us?" Russo asks.

"No," Malone says. "Too much on his mind."

"That's his car," Russo says. "Outside the coffee shop."

"Let's do it." He dials Nasty Ass. "Do your thing."

Nasty hadn't wanted to be involved in this at all. Flat-ass balked at it. "Man, I could've got caught last time. I don't want to have to go back to Baltimore again."

"You won't."

Nasty tried another. "Ain't Carter protected by Torres?"

Yeah, that's the fucking idea, Nasty.

"*You* run the Task Force now?" Malone asked. "They replaced Sykes with an Ichabod Crane–looking black junkie motherfucker, no one sent me the memo? I'll decide where I work, asshole."

"I'm just sayin' . . ."

"Don't be sayin' anything except you gonna do what I ask you to do."

So now Nasty's out on the street and he calls 911. "I see a man with a gun."

Gives the address.

It hits the radio and Russo answers it. "Manhattan North Unit there. We got it."

They jump out of the truck, walk up behind Teddy and mug him just before he gets to his car.

Teddy ain't joking around this time, he got no mouth to give.

This is serious business.

Monty puts him against the car.

Levin takes his phone.

Malone says to Teddy, "I swear to God, one fuckin' word . . ."

They hustle him back into the truck.

"You have some shitkicker friends coming up from the South?" Malone asks him.

Teddy doesn't say anything.

Monty climbs into the truck with a briefcase. "Look what I found."

He opens the case. Stacks of hundreds, fifties, twenties. "Save me the trouble, Teddy. How much?"

"Sixty-five," Teddy says.

Malone laughs. "Did you tell Carter sixty-five? What's the real number?"

"Fifty, motherfucker."

Russo takes fifteen out of the case. "It's a sad, corrupt world."

"Have you ever met Mantell," Malone asks, "or just talked to him over the phone?"

"Why you wanna know?"

"Here's how it's going to go," Malone says. He holds up a sheaf of papers, the CI file he placed for Teddy. "Either you become my CI *right now,* or this paperwork gets leaked to Raf Torres, who sells it to Carter."

"You'd do that to me, Malone?"

"Oh *hell* yes," Malone says. "I'm doing it to you *now,* dumbfuck. Now what are you gonna do, because I don't want your cracker friends getting hinky."

"I ain't never met Mantell."

"Sign here, here and here," Malone says, offering him a pen.

Teddy signs.

"Where were you going to make the exchange?" Malone asks.

"Up by Highbridge Park."

"The crackers know that?"

"Not yet."

Teddy's phone rings.

Levin looks at Malone. "Georgia."

"You have a shutdown code?" Malone asks.

"No."

Malone gestures to Levin, who holds the phone up to Teddy.

"Where are you?" Teddy asks.

"Harlem River Drive. Where am I going?"

Teddy looks to Malone, who holds up a pad.

"Dyckman east of Broadway," Teddy says. "There's a car service garage on the uptown side. Pull into the alley."

"You got our money?"

"The fuck you think?" Teddy asks.

Levin clicks off.

"Very good, Teddy," Malone says. "Now call Carter, tell him everything is copacetic."

"What?"

"Good," Monty says.

Teddy dials as Malone holds the CI statement up to remind him of the stakes.

"Yeah, it's me," Teddy says into the phone. "S'all good. . . . Twenty minutes, half hour maybe. . . . All right."

He clicks off.

"An Oscar-winning performance," says Russo.

"You got boys waiting at Highbridge Park?" Malone asks.

"What you think?"

"So you're gonna drive your fat ass up there," Malone says. "You're gonna wait for these hillbillies, except they're not going to show up."

"You don't need me to make the buy?"

"Nah," Malone says. "We have our own fat black man. I can hear you thinking, Teddy, so you think about this—if your new white friends don't show up at Dyckman, I file your paperwork with Carter."

"What I tell him?"

"Tell him to watch the news," Malone says. "And then tell him he shouldn't be doing business on my turf."

Teddy gets out of the truck.

Russo cuts up Teddy's $15K, hands Levin his share.

Levin puts his hand up. "You guys do what you want. I didn't see anything. It's just . . . I don't do that."

"It doesn't work that way," Russo says. "You're either in or you're out."

"If you don't take it," Montague says, "we don't know that we can trust you to keep your mouth shut."

"I'm not a rat," Levin says.

Malone feels a twinge in his gut.

"No one said you were," Montague says. "It's just that you got to have skin in the game, you feel me?"

"Take the money," Russo says.

"Give it to charity if you want," Montague says. "Drop it in the poor box."

"Send it to St. Jude's," Malone says.

"Is that what you do?" Levin asks.

"Sometimes."

Levin asks, "What happens if I don't take the money?"

Russo grabs him by the shirt. "You with IAB, Levin? You a 'field associate'?"

"Get your hands off me."

Russo does, but he says, "Take your shirt off."

"What?"

"Take your shirt off," Montague says.

Levin looks to Malone.

Malone nods.

"Jesus Christ." Levin unbuttons his shirt, opens it for them. "Happy now?"

"Maybe it's under his balls," Russo says. "Remember Leuci?"

"If you have anything under your balls but your taint," Montague says, "you'd better tell us now."

"Peel them," Malone says.

Levin shakes his head, unbuckles his belt and slides his jeans down to his knees. "Would you like to look up my asshole, too?"

"Would you like us to?" Russo asks.

Levin pulls his jeans back up. "This is demeaning."

"Nothing personal," Malone says. "But you don't take money, we have to wonder what you're about."

"I just want to be a cop."

"Be one, then," Malone says. "You just fined DeVon Carter three grand."

"That's the way it works?"

"That's the way it works."

Levin picks the money up and counts it. "It's short."

"The hell you mean?" Russo asks.

"Fifteen thousand divided by four is three thousand seventy and change," Levin says. "This is three thousand flat."

They laugh. Russo says, "Well, we got us a real Jew on the team now."

"One share goes to expenses," Malone says.

"What expenses?" Levin asks.

"What," Russo asks, "you want a line-item account?"

"Take Amy out to dinner," Malone says, "don't worry about it."

"Buy her something nice," Montague says.

"Not *too* nice," says Malone.

Russo takes out a thick manila envelope and a pen. "Address this to yourself, mail it. That way you don't have it on you."

They get back in the car, swing by a post office, then drive up to Dyckman.

"What if Teddy warns them?" Levin asks.

"Then we're fucked," Malone says. But he gets on the horn to Sykes and advises him to get some backup units over to Highbridge Park. Gives him the make, model and registration of Fat Teddy's car.

Levin is nervous as a whore in church.

Malone doesn't blame the kid—it's a huge score, a huge bust, the kind that makes careers, gets you a gold shield. And it was his motherfucking genius idea that put it together.

Teddy's phone rings.

Monty answers. "Where you at?"

"Coming west on Dyckman."

"I see you," Monty says. "Yellow Penske truck?"

"That's us."

"Bring it on in."

The rental truck pulls into the alley.

A biker type—long hair, beard, leather cut with an ECMF rocker—gets out the passenger side with a pump shotgun. Swastika tat on his neck and an 88—numeric code for the Nazi salute Heil Hitler.

Win-win for this motherfucker, Malone thinks—make some cash and hand the "mud people" tools to kill each other.

Monty gets out of the liquor truck with his left hand raised and a briefcase in his right hand. Malone and Russo come out behind him, standing in back and to the side for open shooting lanes.

Malone sees the biker get hinky. "I didn't expect white."

"We just wanted to make you comfortable," Monty says.

"I don't know about this."

"Oh, there's a lot of black around you," Monty says. "You just don't see them because it's night."

"Hold up." The biker calls Teddy's number. Hears it ring in Monty's pocket and relaxes a little. "Okay."

"Okay," Monty says. "What you got for me?"

The driver gets out, walks around and opens the back of the truck. Malone follows Monty and looks inside as the biker starts to open crates. There are enough guns in there to keep Homicide busy for two years—revolvers, automatics, pump shotguns and automatic rifles—an AK, three AR-15s, including a Bushmaster.

"It's all there," the biker says.

Monty swings the briefcase onto the tailgate and opens it. "Fifty large. You want to count it?"

Yeah, he does—he counts the stacks of marked, registered bills. "On the money."

Malone and Russo start to off-load the guns and carry them back to the liquor truck.

"Let Mantell know," Monty says, "we'll buy as much as he can send."

The biker smiles. "As long as you're using them on other 'people of color.'"

Monty can't help himself. "And maybe cops."

"Works for me."

Yeah, does that work for you? Malone thinks. We'll see how it works for you when some CO is beating your kidneys into Jell-O, you meth-smoking, jerky-eating, cousin-fucking shitkicker. I'd do it right now for you if I didn't want to hand this bust to Sykes and Da Force.

They finish off-loading.

"You need directions?" Monty asks the driver.

Monty thinks of everything. Sykes has the location covered from all compass points, but this will give him a heads-up on which way the truck is likely to head.

"Back the way we came, I guess," the driver says.

"Or just go straight up Dyckman here to the Henry Hudson, south to the GW Bridge, then 95 back to Dixie."

"We'll find our own way," the biker says.

"Motherfucker," Monty says, shaking his head, "if we was going to rip you, we'd do it right here, not chasing you down the highway."

"Mantell will be in touch."

"Heil Hitler."

The Penske truck backs out and true to paranoid form, turns right onto Dyckman to drive all the way across the city before it can get back on a highway.

Malone gets on the horn.

"Suspect is coming east on Dyckman."

"We have a visual," Sykes says.

Levin's grinning.

"Wait for it," Malone says.

Then it goes off—sirens, yelling. Malone and Levin walk out on the street and see the red flashers as the sector cars move in.

"Well," Malone says, "there are two mothers, at least, who won't be getting fucked tonight. Levin, that was some real police work you did."

"Thanks."

"Seriously," Malone says. "You saved some lives tonight."

A sector car comes down and Sykes gets out of the backseat. Full uniform, freshly shaved, camera-ready. "What do we have, Sergeant?"

"Come on." He leads Sykes back to the truck.

Sykes looks at the weapons. "Jesus Christ."

"You call McGivern?" Malone asks. Sykes doesn't bring McGivern in on this from the jump, the inspector will cockblock his career until he pulls the pin.

"No, Sergeant, I'm an idiot," Sykes says. "He's on his way."

He's still looking at the guns.

Malone knows what it means to him. Sure, it's great for his career, but it's more than that. Like the rest of them, Sykes has seen the bodies, the blood, the families, the funerals.

For a few seconds, Malone almost likes the man.

And for himself, he feels like a cop again.

Instead of a rat.

A cop taking care of his business, taking care of his people. Because of tonight, there'll be less death and suffering in the Kingdom of Malone.

Another car rolls up and McGivern gets out.

"This is fine work, gentlemen!" he hollers. "Fine work, Captain! It's a great night to be a New York City police officer, isn't it?!"

He walks up closer to Sykes. "You seized the buy money, didn't you?"

"Yes, sir," Sykes says.

More cars roll in. Crime Scene people, Task Force guys. They start taking photographs and vouchering the seized weapons before they take them into the house, where they'll be laid out for a morning press conference.

After the paperwork is done, Sykes surprises everyone by announcing that the first round down at the Dublin House is on him.

First implies second, which implies third and after that, who's counting?

Somewhere between five and six Malone finds himself sitting next to Sykes at the bar.

"If someone asked me," Sykes says, "to name the best and the worst cops I've ever worked with, I would answer Denny Malone."

Malone lifts his glass to him.

Sykes lifts his and they toss them back.

"Never seen you out of uniform before," Malone says.

260 / DON WINSLOW

"I did three years UC in the Seven-Eight," Sykes says. "Would you believe that?"

"No. Can't see it."

"I had dreads."

"Get the fuck out of here."

"Hand to God," Sykes says. "That was good work tonight, Malone. I hate to think what would happen if those guns hit the street."

"DeVon Carter ain't gonna be happy."

"Fuck Carter."

Malone starts to laugh.

"What?" Sykes asks.

"I was just thinking about this time," Malone says, "Monty and Russo and Billy O and me and about six other off-duty detectives are sitting at this bar and this black kid . . . no offense . . . walks through the door with a gun, yells it's a holdup. World's dumbest stickup guy, right? Must have been a first-timer because he looked about nineteen and he's scared to death. So he points the gun and Mike, behind the bar, just looks at him, and all of a sudden this poor kid has probably twelve guns pointed back at him and all these cops are laughing and yelling 'Get the fuck outta here' and the kid spins like he's in a cartoon and runs out the door, we don't even follow him. We just go back to our drinks."

"But you didn't shoot."

"He was a kid," Malone says. "I mean, what kind of dumbass sticks up a cop bar?"

"A desperate one."

"I guess."

"Difference between you and me?" Sykes says. "I'd have gone after him."

A *party* is going on around them. Monty is dancing to the music all on his own, Russo and Emma Flynn are trading shots, Levin is table-surfing, Babyface is trashing a bunch of plainclothes at beer pong.

Malone's heart is breaking.

He's going to betray these people.

He's going to give them cops.

Laying a twenty on the bar, Malone says, "I'd better go."

"Denny 'Last Call' Malone?" Sykes asks.

"Yeah."

I'd better go before I get any drunker, start talking, spilling my guilty guts, slobbering all over the bar and telling everyone what a piece of shit I am.

Levin sees him get up. "Malone! You can't leave yet!"

Malone waves to him.

"Malone!" Levin yells. He raises his beer mug. "Everyone. Everybody. Hey, y'all motherfuckers! Listen up!"

"He's going to feel this tomorrow," Sykes says.

"Jews can't drink," Malone says.

Levin looks like the freakin' Statue of Liberty with his mug raised above his head like a torch. "Ladies and gentlemen of Da Force! I give you Sergeant Denny Malone! The best motherfucking, ball-breaking, perp-busting badass on the streets of our fair city! The King of Manhattan North! Long Live the King!"

The cops take up the chanting, yell, "Long Live the King! Long Live the King! Long Live the King!"

Sykes smiles at Malone.

"You're an all right guy, Captain," Malone says. "I don't like you very much, but you're an all right guy. Take care of these people, okay?"

"That's my job," Sykes says, looking around the bar. "I love these fucking people."

Me too, Malone thinks.

He walks out.

He doesn't belong there anymore.

Doesn't belong at Claudette's either.

He goes back to his apartment, polishes off what's left of a bottle of Jameson's by himself.

CHAPTER 17

The press conference looks like Open Mike Night at the Chuckle Hut.

Classic, Malone thinks.

The weapons are laid out on tables, carefully labeled, looking lethal and beautiful. A line of suits and brass stand on the dais waiting their turn at the microphone. In addition to Sykes, who doesn't even look hungover, and McGivern, you got Neely, the chief of detectives; Isadore, the chief of patrol; Police Commissioner Brady; the deputy commissioner; the mayor; and for reasons that passeth Malone's understanding, the Reverend Cornelius.

McGivern says a few words of departmental self-congratulations and then introduces Sykes, who speaks in technical terms about the operation, the weapons seized and how proud he is of the many Task Force personnel who worked together to achieve this outcome.

He yields the mike to the commissioner, who broadens the congratulations to include the entire department and makes a point of going on for a while just to make the mayor wait.

When Hizzoner finally gets the mike, he stretches the credit out to include every suit in or around City Hall, especially and including himself, and talks about how the department and the administration working together makes this a safer city for everybody, and then he introduces the good reverend.

Malone already felt like throwing up, but now he really feels like throwing up as Cornelius preaches about the community, non-violence and the root economic causes of said violence and how the community needs "programs not pogroms" (and nobody knows what the fuck that means) and then dances a tightrope as he tries to urge the police to do more while warning them not to do too much.

All in all, Malone thinks, it's a great performance.

Even U.S. Attorney Isobel Paz, representing the Southern District of New York, which has done so much to combat interstate weapons trafficking, seems to enjoy the show.

When Malone's phone rings, it's Paz, and he can see her across the crowded lobby. "Don't think this is going to help you, shitbird. I still want cops."

"Now more than ever, right?" Malone asks, looking at her. "The commissioner was looking very mayoral, I thought."

"Cops. On tape. Now."

Click.

Torres confronts him in the locker room at Manhattan North.

"You and me need to talk," Torres says.

"Okay," says Malone.

"Not here."

They walk outside and across the street, into the treed courtyard outside St. Mary's.

"You *motherfucker*," Torres says.

Good, Malone thinks, the angrier the better. Anger makes Torres careless, he makes mistakes. He gets right up on Malone.

"Get out of my face," Malone says.

"I should kick your fucking ass."

"I'm not one of your girls."

Torres's voice goes to a rasp. "The fuck you doing, hitting that shipment? On Dyckman? That's my turf. You were supposed to stay out of the Heights."

"Carter made the deal from *my* turf."

"You just gave your turf to Castillo, asshole," Torres says. "What's Carter supposed to do without guns?"

264 / DON WINSLOW

"Die?"

"I had a piece of that deal, Malone. A finder's fee."

"What, we give refunds now?"

"You don't fuck with my money, Malone."

"Okay, okay," Malone says. Then, feeling like a piece of shit, he makes his pitch. Get Paz what she wants. "What's it going to take to make this right? What was your piece?"

Torres calms down a little. Then he sticks his neck in the noose. "Fifteen. Plus the three Carter's not paying me this month now that we fucked him."

"You want the sweat off my dick, too?"

"No, you can keep that," Torres says. "When do I get my money?"

"Meet me in the parking lot," Malone says.

Malone goes back there, takes $18K out of the console and puts it in an envelope. Torres shows up a few minutes later and slides into the passenger seat. In the closeness of the car, Malone can smell the man—the stale coffee breath, the cigarette smoke on his clothes, the too-strong cologne.

Torres says, "So?"

It's not too late, Malone thinks. Not too late to back off from hurting a brother cop, even a low motherfucker like Torres. Until he takes the money, they got nothing on Raf, just him talking some bullshit.

You cross this line, there's no going back.

"Yo, Malone?" Torres is asking. "You got something for me, or what?"

Yeah, I got something for you, Malone thinks. He slides him the envelope. "Here's your money."

Torres puts the envelope in his pocket. "Do me a favor? Jerk yourself off, lose this hard-on you got for Carter. Believe me, Castillo is worse."

"Carter is history," Malone says. "He just don't know it yet."

"Don't cross me again, Denny."

"Kiss my skinny Irish ass."

Torres gets out of the car.

Malone opens his shirt and checks the recording device. It's on, it got the exchange, Torres is a walking dead man.

And so are you, Malone thinks.

The man you used to be doesn't exist anymore.

Then he drives downtown to deliver the tape to O'Dell. Fifteen, twenty times on the way he thinks about just dumping the tape and driving away. But if I do, he thinks, I just drop Russo and Monty into my shit. So if it's a choice between them and Torres . . .

Weintraub pops it into the machine right away and Malone listens to—

"The fuck you doing, hitting that shipment? On Dyckman? That's my turf. You were supposed to stay out of the Heights."

"Carter made the deal from my turf."

"You just gave your turf to Castillo, asshole. What's Carter supposed to do without guns?"

"Die?"

"I had a piece of that deal, Malone. A finder's fee."

"What, we give refunds now?"

"You don't fuck with my money, Malone."

"Okay, okay. What's it going to take to make this right? What was your piece?"

"Way to be, Malone," Weintraub says. "You're getting the hang of this."

"Fifteen. Plus the three Carter's not paying me this month now that we fucked him."

"You want the sweat off my dick, too?"

"Nice touch," Weintraub says.

"No, you can keep that. When do I get my money?"

"Did you give him the designated bills?" Weintraub asks.

"Yeah."

"We got him," Weintraub says.

O'Dell says, "Good job, Malone."

"Fuck you."

"Our boy's feeling all guilty because he flipped on a drug-dealing cop," Weintraub says. "Torres deserves everything he gets."

"Which is what?" Malone asks.

"We're going to take him to a nice farm in the country where he'll be happy playing with all the other crooked cops," Weintraub says. "The hell you think is going to happen?"

"That's enough," O'Dell says. "Denny—"

"Don't open your mouth to me."

"I know how you're feeling."

"No, you don't."

Malone walks out of the room. His footsteps echo in the empty hallway.

Jesus Christ, he thinks, you just did it.

You hurt a brother cop.

You can tell yourself you didn't have a choice. You had to do it, right? For your family, for Claudette, for your partners. Yeah, you can tell yourself that and it's all true, but none of it changes the fact that you just hurt a brother cop.

Then the hallway starts tilting, his legs feel unsteady and all of a sudden he's leaning against the wall, grabbing at it as if it can keep him from falling. Then he bends over and puts his face in his hands.

For the first time since his brother died, he sobs.

CHAPTER 18

Claudette looks lovely.

White on black.

A tight sheath of a white dress shows off her figure and her dark skin. Gold hoop earrings, red lipstick, her hair up in a 1940s retro do with her white flower.

Stunning.

Heart-cracking, blood-heating, eye-popping beautiful.

Malone falls in love with her anew.

They're having a real date.

She was right, he decided. For whatever fucked-up reason, he'd been hiding her. Leaving her alone with her doubt and her addiction.

Fuck everyone.

If the rednecks on the Job don't like it, fuck them. And if the brothuhs think it means he's going to cut them some slack, they'll learn quickly enough they're wrong.

And there's something else.

He needs her.

After setting up a brother cop, even an asshole like Torres, he needs her.

So he picked up the phone and called. Was a little surprised she didn't just hang up on him when he said, "This is Sergeant Malone of Manhattan North."

There was a little pause before she said, "What can I do for you, Detective?"

He could tell from her voice she was clean.

"I know this is last minute," he said, "but I have reservations tonight at Jean-Georges and no one merciful enough to have dinner with an insensitive, neglectful jerk like myself, and while I'm pretty sure a woman such as yourself already has plans, I thought I'd take a chance and ask if there's any possibility you would have dinner with me."

He endured a long silence before she said, "A table at Jean-Georges is hard to get."

Fuckin' A, he thought. He'd had to remind the maître d' of a certain incident he'd quieted down before it made Page Six. "I just told them there was a chance—just a chance—that the most beautiful and charming lady in New York might grace their establishment, and they fell all over themselves."

"You're laying it on thick."

"Subtlety is not my strong suit," Malone said. "How about it?"

Another long silence before she said, "I'd be delighted."

He takes her to Jean-Georges because she likes French things.

Zagat rated, three Michelin stars, expensive, impossible to get a reservation unless you're a celebrity detective. But it's Malone, even though he's dressed in a nice suit, who's a little nervous in the fancy place, not Claudette.

She looks like she was born there.

The waiter thinks so, too, addresses most of his questions and comments to her, and she handles it like she's been doing it her whole life. She quietly suggests wines and dishes and Malone goes with them.

"How do you know all this?" he asks her, picking his way through the toasted egg yolk with caviar and herbs, which is actually a lot better than he'd thought it would be.

"Believe it or not," she says, "you're not the first man I ever dated. I've been south of 110th, gosh, five or six times, maybe even seven."

He feels like a fucking idiot. "Go ahead, squeeze my shoes. I deserve it."

"Yes, you do," she says. "But I'm having a wonderful time, baby. Thank you for bringing me here. It's beautiful."

"*You're* beautiful."

"See, you're doing better already."

Malone picks the Maine lobster, Claudette the smoked squab.

"Isn't that a pigeon?" Malone asks.

"It is a pigeon," she says. "Didn't you ever want revenge?"

They don't talk about the smack, her "slip," her jonesing. She's feeling better now, looking better. He thinks maybe she's over it. For dessert they take a sampling of chocolate "tastings," during which Claudette says, "So this is our first real date in a long time."

"The key word there is 'first.'"

"With our schedules," Claudette says, "it's hard to find time."

"I might start working a little less," Malone says. "Take a little more time off."

"I'd like that."

"Yeah?"

"Very much," she says. "But we don't have to always do, you know, *this.*"

"It's nice, doing this."

"I just want time with you, baby," Claudette says.

Malone gets up to use the men's, but instead he goes to the woman at the hostess stand and tells her he wants a real bill, bust-out retail because there are some things you get comped for, other things you pay for.

You take your girl out, you pay for it.

The hostess says, "The manager said—"

"I know," Malone says, "and I appreciate it, but I'd like a real bill."

The real bill arrives. He pays it, leaves a nice tip and pulls the chair out for Claudette. "I thought you might like to go to Smoke. Lea DeLaria is there tonight."

Malone doesn't know who that is, just that she's a singer. He went to the website and looked it up.

"I'd love that," Claudette says. "I love *her*. But you don't like jazz."

"This is your night."

The Smoke Jazz and Supper Club is up on 106th and Broadway, back on Malone's turf. It's small, only about fifty seats, but Malone already called to reserve a spot in case she wanted to go.

They get a table for two.

DeLaria sings standards in front of a bass, drums, piano and saxophone quartet. Claudette feigns astonishment. "A white woman who can sing. My, my."

"Racist."

"Just keeping it real, baby."

Between songs, DeLaria looks down at Claudette and asks, "Is he nice to you, darlin'?"

Claudette nods. "Very nice."

DeLaria looks at Malone. "You'd better be. She's so beautiful. I might just take her away from you."

Then she launches into "Come Rain or Come Shine."

I'm gonna love you, like nobody's loved you,
Come rain or come shine
Happy together, unhappy together
Come rain or come shine . . .

There's a little stir in the crowd as Tre comes in with a posse. DeLaria gives him a nod of acknowledgment as Tre goes to his table, then the hip-hop mogul spots Malone and then Claudette and gives Malone a nod of respect.

Malone nods back.

"Do you know him?" Claudette asks.

"I do some work for him from time to time," Malone says. And now the word will be out everywhere that badass Denny Malone is dating a sister.

"Do you want to meet him?" Malone asks.

"Not really," Claudette says. "I'm not so much into hip-hop."

Malone knows what's going to happen next and it does. A bottle of Cristal arrives at the table courtesy of Tre.

"What kind of work do you *do* for him?" Claudette asks.

"Security."

DeLaria changes over to "You Don't Know What Love Is."

"Billie Holiday," Claudette says.

She gets lost in it.

Malone looks over at Tre, who's looking back at him, reevaluating him, trying to figure out who the guy is that he's seeing now.

I get it, Malone thinks. I'm trying to do the same thing.

The white dress slides off her like rain flowing down obsidian.

Her lips are full and warm, her neck musky.

After they make love and she falls asleep, he lies awake and looks out her window and remembers the words of the song—

Until you've faced each dawn with sleepless eyes,
You don't know what love is . . .

CHAPTER 19

is cell phone rings again.

He ignores it again, turns back into Claudette and tries to go back to sleep with his face in the sweet crook of her neck. Then his conscience gets the better of him and he looks at his phone.

It's Russo. "Did you hear?"

"Hear what?" Malone asks.

"About Torres," Russo says.

It sends a jolt through Malone. "What?"

"He ate his gun."

Right out in the Manhattan North parking lot, Russo tells him. Two uniforms heard the shot, ran out and found him in his car. Motor running, AC on high, radio blasting salsa music and Torres's brains sprayed over the back windshield.

No note.

No message.

No skid marks, the man just did it.

"Why the fuck would he do that?" Russo asks.

Malone knows why.

The feds pressed him. Become a rat or go to jail.

And Torres had an answer for them.

Brutal, mean, racist, lying, vicious motherfucker Raf Torres had an answer for them.

Fuck you. I go out like a man.

Malone gets out of bed.

"What's up?" Claudette asks sleepily.

"I gotta go."

"Already?"

"A cop killed himself."

Malone bursts through the door, grabs O'Dell by the lapels, lifts him out of his chair and walks him into the wall.

"I've been trying to call you," O'Dell says.

"Motherfuckers."

Weintraub gets up and comes over to break it up but Malone turns and gives him the death stare, like if you really want in on this you're going to get in on this, and Weintraub backs off. Says weakly, "Settle down, Malone."

"What did you do?" Malone asks. "Try to flip him? Get him to wear a wire? Or else you were going to cuff him at the precinct house in front of his brother officers, make him do the perp walk out the door in front of the television cameras and a crowd of locals hooting 'Pig!' Talked to him about going to prison, what would happen to his family?"

"We did our job."

"You killed a cop," Malone says to O'Dell, his spit flicking into his face. "You're a cop killer."

"I tried to call you, the second I heard," O'Dell says. "This is not on us, it's not on you, it's on him. He made his own choices, including this last one."

"Maybe he made the right choice," Malone says.

"No, he didn't," O'Dell says. "He didn't have the guts to face up to what he's done. You did, Malone. You're making it right."

"By killing a brother cop."

"Torres took the coward's way out," Weintraub says.

Malone explodes off the chair, gets in his face. "Don't you say that. Don't you fucking ever say that. I saw that man go down the stairwells, I saw him go through the doors. Where were you, huh? Having a two-martini lunch? Safe in bed with your girlfriend?"

274 | DON WINSLOW

"You didn't even like the guy."

"That's right, but he was a cop," Malone says. "He was no coward."

"All right."

"Sit down, Denny," O'Dell says.

"*You* sit down."

"What are you, high?" O'Dell asks. "Are you jacked up on something?"

Just a half-dozen go-pills and a couple of lines of blow. "Test me. I piss hot, you can add it to the charges, how's that?"

"Calm down."

"How the fuck am I supposed to calm down?!" Malone yells. "You think it's going to end here? You don't think there aren't going to be rumors? People aren't going to start asking questions? Fucking IAB will be all over this!"

"We'll take care of it."

"Like you took care of Torres?"

"Torres was not my fault!" O'Dell says. "And if you call me a cop killer again, I'll—"

"You'll fucking what?!"

"You're not innocent in this, Malone!"

Paz walks in. Looks at them and says, "When you girls are through with your hissy fits, maybe we can get down to work."

Malone and O'Dell are glaring at each other, ready to go.

"Okay, neither of you has the biggest dick," Paz says. "*I* do. So sit down, gentlemen."

They sit down.

"A crooked cop took his own life," Paz says. "Boo-fucking-hoo. Get over it. The issue now is damage control. Did Torres talk to anyone before he canceled his reservation? Tell anyone about the investigation? Find out what people are saying, Malone."

"No."

"'No'?" Paz asks. "Are you filled with remorse now, *papi*? Irish Catholic guilt? You want to climb up on the cross and nail yourself to it? Fight off the impulse, Malone. I have you down more for the survivor type, anyway."

"You mean the Judas type."

"Don't do it to yourself, Malone," Paz says. "Hang in there. All I want to know is what your brother officers are saying about Torres. They're going to talk about it anyway. They talk to you, you talk to us. It's that simple. Is there a problem with this I'm not aware of?"

There are so many problems you're not aware of, Malone thinks.

"And let's look for alternative explanations for Torres's suicide," Paz says. She looks to Malone. "Was he a drinker? A druggie? Marital difficulties? Financial problems?"

"Not that I know of."

Torres was making good money. He had a wife, three kids and at least three women he kept up in the Heights.

"Even if rumors start about the investigation," Paz says, "this could work out for you, Malone. Your brother officers will think the rat is dead. He couldn't stand the guilt and offed himself. It clears the way for you."

"To do what?" Malone asks. "I gave you what you wanted."

"We need a wider base under him," Paz says. "We don't want to show that he was only taking from one cop, but a whole stable. We want multiple charges. Was Torres kicking up?"

"Did you ask Torres?"

"He said he'd get back to us," Weintraub says.

"I guess he did, huh?" Malone says.

The house is in turmoil.

When Malone gets to Manhattan North, the news trucks are already there. He pushes his way through the reporters with a curt "No comment" and goes in. The place is a bedlam of rumor, anger and fear. He makes his way through the knots of uniformed officers talking by the desk and feels eyes on his back as he goes upstairs to the Task Force.

He knows what they're thinking—*Malone knows something. Malone always knows something.*

Everyone's at his desk—Russo, Montague, Levin. They look up as he comes in.

"Where you been?" Russo asks.

Malone ignores the question. "Anyone get to the ME?"

"McGivern's on it," Russo says. He juts his chin at Sykes's office, where the inspector stands watching Sykes on the phone.

"IAB?" Malone asks.

"They want to talk to every detective on the Task Force," Montague says.

"We all got called in," Levin says.

"Here's what you say," Malone says. "You don't know shit. You don't know about alcohol, drugs, money problems, troubles at home, nothing. Let his team talk about that if they want."

He walks over, knocks on Sykes's door and walks in without waiting for an answer.

McGivern puts a hand on his shoulder. "Jesus, Denny."

"I know."

"What the hell happened?"

Malone shrugs.

"It's a shame," McGivern says.

"You talk to the ME?"

"He's leaving the door open as to accidental," McGivern says.

"That's the best thing you could have done for Torres, Inspector," Malone says. "But it's out in the media as a suicide?"

"It's a shame," McGivern repeats.

Sykes gets off the phone and looks at Malone. "Where have you been, Sergeant?"

"Asleep," Malone says. "I guess I didn't hear the phone."

Sykes looks shaken. Malone doesn't blame him—his smooth flight path of a career just hit major turmoil.

"What can you tell me about this?" Sykes asks.

"I just got here, Captain."

THE FORCE / 277

"You didn't see any signs of this?" Sykes asks. "Torres didn't confide anything to you?"

"We weren't exactly close, sir," Malone says. "What does his team say? Gallina, Ortiz, Tenelli . . ."

"Nothing," Sykes says.

Of course not, Malone thinks. And good.

"They're still in shock," McGivern says. "It's bad enough when a brother officer falls to a felon's bullet, but something like this . . ."

Christ, Malone thinks, he's already writing his speech.

Sykes is staring at Malone. "There are rumors that IAB had Torres up. Do you know anything about that?"

Malone meets his stare. "No."

"So you don't know of any reason," Sykes asks, "that IAB might have been investigating Torres?"

"No."

"Or any detective on the Task Force?" Sykes asks.

"It's your command, sir," Malone says. The threat is clear—dig into this, you dig your own grave.

McGivern steps in. "We're getting ahead of ourselves, gentlemen. Let's allow Internal Affairs to do its job."

"I expect you to give IAB your full cooperation," Sykes says to Malone. "And that of your entire team."

"That goes without saying."

Sykes says, "Let's get real, Malone. As you go, so goes the Task Force. The men will follow your lead. You set the tone."

It's a remarkable admission, no less for being true.

"We're not going to cover up," Sykes says. "We're not going to put up the barricades, huddle behind them and pull in on ourselves."

That's exactly what we're going to do, Malone thinks.

"We will be open and transparent," Sykes says, "and let the investigation go where it goes."

You do that, Malone thinks, it will go right up your ass. "Is that all, sir?"

"Set the tone, Sergeant."

You got it, Malone thinks as he walks out. He signals Russo and Montague to come with him, goes back downstairs and walks up to the desk. "Sarge, can you get their attention for me?"

"Yo, listen up!"

It gets quiet.

"All right," Malone says, "we're all hurting about Torres. Thoughts and prayers to his family. But right now we have to *handle our business*. If you talk to the media, here's what you say: 'Sergeant Torres was a beloved and respected officer and he will be missed.' That's it. Be polite but keep moving. I don't believe there's anyone here like this, but if one of you thinks you're going to become a TV or social media star behind this—I will have your ass."

He pauses to let that set in and for Russo and Montague to back him up with their eyes. Then he says, "Look, there are going to be citizens on your beats celebrating. Do not respond. They're going to try to goad you into getting stupid, but do not do it. I don't want to see any of you get jammed up with a brutality beef. Stay cool, remember faces, and we'll settle with them later—you have my word on that.

"If IAB questions you, cooperate. Tell them the truth—that you don't know anything. And that is the truth. Thinking you know something and actually knowing it are two very different things. You give rats any cheese, they just keep coming back. We keep our house clean, they go away. Questions."

There aren't any.

"All right," Malone says. "We're the freaking N-Y-P-D. Let's go out and do our jobs."

It's the talk the captain should have given but he didn't. Malone goes back upstairs and sees Gallina, Torres's partner, standing by his desk.

"Let's take a walk," Malone says.

They go out the back to avoid the media.

"What the fuck happened?" Malone asks. If Torres talked to anyone, it was Jorge Gallina. Him and Torres were tight.

"I don't know," Gallina says. He's clearly shaken, afraid. "He was quiet yesterday. Something was wrong."

"But he didn't say what?"

"He phoned me from his car," Gallina says, "and just said he wanted to say good-bye. I asked him, you know, 'What the fuck, Raf?,' and he said, 'Nothing,' and hung up."

Guy's going to end his life, Malone thinks, and he calls his partner, not his wife, to say good-bye.

Cops.

"Did IAB have him up?" Malone asks, feeling like a fucking creep.

"No," Gallina says. "We'd have known. What are we going to do now, Malone?"

"Shut it down," Malone says. "I mean not as much as a fixed parking ticket. Stonewall IAB and keep our noses clean. The Rat Squad starts to paint Raf dirty, we'll get the media all over them."

"Okay," Gallina says.

"Where's Torres's money?"

"All over the place," Gallina says. "I have about a hundred in a fund."

"Gloria know that?" Last thing you want is a widow worrying about money on top of everything else.

"Yeah, but I'll remind her."

"How's she doing?"

"She's a mess," Gallina says. "I mean, she was talking divorce, but she still loves him."

"Get to his *gumars*," Malone says. "Lay some cash on them, tell them to shut their mouths. And for Chrissakes make sure they know that coming to the funeral is not a smart idea."

"Okay. Good."

"You need to chill out, Jorge," Malone says. "The rats smell fear like sharks smell blood."

"I know. What if they want me to take a polygraph?"

"You call your delegate, he tells them to go fuck themselves,"

Malone says. "You're in grief, you're in shock, you're in no condition for that."

But Gallina is scared. "You think IAB was on him, Malone? Jesus, you don't think Raf was wearing a wire?"

"Torres?" Malone asks. "No fucking way."

"Then why did he do it?" Gallina asks.

Because I gave him up, Malone thinks. Because I dropped him in the jackpot, put the gun in his hand.

"Who the fuck knows?" Malone says.

He goes back into the house. McGivern is waiting for him.

"This is bad, Denny," McGivern says.

No shit, this is bad, Malone thinks. Worse maybe than he thought, because Bill McGivern, an NYPD police *inspector* with more connections than an alderman, looks scared.

Old, all of a sudden.

His pale skin looks like paper, his white hair like the top of an aspirin bottle, the ruddiness of his cheeks now looks like just broken veins.

McGivern says, "If IAB had Torres—"

"They didn't."

"But what if they did?" McGivern asks. "What did he tell them? What did he know? Did he know about me?"

"I'm the only one who brought you envelopes," Malone says. For all Manhattan North.

But shit yes, Torres knew.

Everyone knows how it works.

"Do you think Torres was wearing a wire?" McGivern asks.

"Even if he was, you have nothing to worry about," Malone says. "You didn't talk business with him, did you?"

"No, that's right."

"Has IAB called you in?" Malone asks.

"They don't have the nerve," McGivern says. "But if someone talks . . ."

"They won't."

"The Task Force is solid, Denny? Stand-up guys?"

"Totally," Malone says. At least I fuckin' hope so.

"I hear rumors," McGivern says, "that it isn't IAB, it's the feds."

"Which feds?"

"Southern District," McGivern says. "That Spanish bitch. She has ambitions, Denny."

McGivern makes it sound dirty. *Ambitions,* like she has crabs. Like being ambitious makes her a whore.

Malone hates the *buchiach,* too, but not for that.

"She wants to hurt the Job," McGivern says. "We can't let her do that."

"We don't even know it's her," Malone says.

McGivern ain't listening. He says, "I'm two years away from pulling the pin. Jeannie and I have a cabin up in Vermont."

And a condo on Sanibel Island, Malone thinks.

"I want to spend time in that cabin," McGivern says. "Not behind bars. Jeannie isn't well, you know."

"I'm sorry to hear that."

"She needs me," McGivern says. "Whatever time we have left . . . I'm counting on you, Denny. I'm counting on you to shut this down. Do what you have to do."

"Yes, sir."

"I trust you, Denny," McGivern says, putting his hand on Malone's shoulder. "You're a good man."

Yeah, Malone thinks, walking away.

I'm a king.

It's going to be brutal, Malone thinks, to keep this tied down.

For one thing, the street is going to be talking. Every half-ass low-level dope slinger Torres ever ripped or beat on is going to come forward to tell the story now that they don't have to be afraid of him.

Then the guys he put away are going to start to chirp from their cells. *Hey, Torres was a dirty cop. He lied on the stand. I want a retrial, no, I want my conviction tossed out.*

282 / DON WINSLOW

It comes out that Torres was dirty, it's full-employment act for the criminal defense bar. Those assholes will reopen every case Torres ever touched; shit, that the whole Task Force ever touched.

And it could come out. It takes only one guy to break. Gallina's already shaken. If he goes, he's not only going to flip on his own team, but on everyone.

The dominos tumble.

We have to shut it down.

Not *we*, motherfucker. *You*.

You started the ball rolling.

Malone's the last on his team to go talk with IAB.

His guys did what they needed to do and Russo told him, "They got nothing. They know shit."

"Who is it?"

"Buliosi and Henderson."

Henderson, Malone thinks. We finally catch a break.

He goes into the room.

"Have a seat, Sergeant Malone," Buliosi says.

Lieutenant Richard Buliosi is a typical IAB prick. Maybe it's the acne scars that made him a rat, Malone thinks, but the guy definitely has a beef with the world to work out.

Malone sits down.

"What can you tell us," Buliosi asks, "about the apparent suicide of Sergeant Torres?"

"Not much," Malone says. "I didn't know him all that well."

Buliosi looks at him with a show of incredulity. "You were in the same unit."

"Torres mostly worked the Heights and Inwood," Malone says. "My team is mostly in Harlem."

"Hardly worlds apart."

"You'd be surprised," Malone says. "That is, if you worked the streets."

He regrets the dig instantly but Buliosi lets it go. "Was Torres depressed?"

"I guess so, huh."

"I mean," Buliosi says, starting to get irritated, "did he show signs of depression?"

"I'm not a shrink," Malone answers, "but as far as I observed, Torres was his usual prick self."

"You didn't get along?"

"We got along fine," Malone says. "One prick to another."

You gonna get in on this, Henderson? Malone wonders, looking at him. I need to remind you you got skin in this game? Henderson gets the message. "My understanding is that Torres had a reputation as a hard-ass up here. Is that accurate, Malone?"

"If you don't have a rep as a hard-ass 'up here,'" Malone says, "you're not going to last long 'up here.'"

"Is it accurate to say," Henderson asks, "that detectives were selected for the Task Force somewhat based on that quality?"

"I'd say that's accurate, yes."

"That's the problem with the Task Force," Buliosi says. "It's almost designed for trouble."

"Was that a question, sir?"

"I'll tell you what the questions are, Sergeant," Buliosi says.

You think so, Malone thinks, but right now we're talking about what I want to talk about, aren't we?

Buliosi asks, "Do you know if Torres was doing anything that might have caused him concern for his job or his future?"

"That's more your business, isn't it?"

"We're asking you."

"Like I said," Malone says, "I don't know what Torres was doing or what he wasn't doing."

"You haven't heard rumors," Buliosi asks, "around the house?"

"No."

"Was he taking money?"

"I don't know."

"Ripping drug dealers?"

"I don't know."

Buliosi asks, "Are you?"

"No."

"You sure about that?"

"I think I'd know," Malone says, meeting his stare.

"You're aware," Buliosi says, "of the consequences of lying to IAB in the course of an investigation."

Malone says, "That would involve intradepartmental discipline, potential dismissal from the job as well as possible criminal charges for obstructing justice."

"That's right," Buliosi says. "Sadly, Torres is dead. You don't have to protect him."

Malone feels his temper coming up out of his gut. Like he wants to smash this motherfucker's face in for him, shut his smarmy fucking mouth. "Are you sad about it, Lieutenant? Because I don't read that on your face."

"As you said, you're not a shrink."

"Yeah, but reading assholes' faces is kind of my job."

Henderson jumps in. "That's enough, Malone. I know you're hurting about the loss of a brother officer, but—"

"The next time I see an IAB guy eat his gun will be the first time," Malone says. "You don't do that, lawyers don't, wiseguys don't. You know who does? Cops. Only cops. *Real* cops, that is."

Henderson says, "I think that will be all for now, Sergeant. Why don't you take a little personal time, get yourself together."

"We reserve the right to reinterview," Buliosi says.

Malone gets up. "Let me tell you both something. I don't know why Torres did what he did. I didn't even like the guy. But he was a cop. The Job takes a toll. Sometimes it's sudden, a skel tosses a lucky shot at you and that's it. Other times it's slow, builds so slow you don't even notice it, but then one day you wake up and you can't take it anymore. Torres didn't kill himself—one way or the other, the Job killed him."

"Do you need to see a departmental shrink?" Buliosi asks. "I can arrange an appointment for you."

"No," Malone says. "What I need is to go back to work."

He meets Henderson in Riverside Park by the softball fields.

"Thanks for all your help in the room," Malone says.

"You didn't help with your attitude," Henderson says. "Now Buliosi has a hard-on for you."

"Like IAB didn't before," Malone says. "You guys have wood for *every* real cop."

"Gee, thanks, Denny."

Malone looks across the river at Jersey. Only good thing about living there, he thinks, is you have a view of New York. "Did you guys have Torres up?"

"No."

"You sure?"

"To quote the immortal Denny Malone," Henderson says, "'I think I would have known.' It wasn't us. Maybe it was the feds. Southern District has it out for the commissioner."

Jesus, Malone thinks. Fucking radar. "Well, IAB's on it now. How much is it going to cost?"

"It's headline news, Denny," Henderson says. "The *News,* the *Post,* even the *Times.* On top of this fucking Bennett thing—"

"All the more reason for shutting it down," Malone says. "You really think the commissioner wants you digging up skeletons in Torres's closet? Scandals don't last, but the boys at One P do. And they have long memories. They'll wait for this to die down and then they'll fuck you. You'll retire the same rank you are now, if you even make it that far."

"You're right."

"I already know that," Malone says. "What I want to know is how much?"

"I'll have to take it to Buliosi."

"Then why are you still standing here?" Malone asks.

"Jesus, Malone, if I swing and miss, I go to jail."

"Where do you think you'll go if Gallina flips?" Malone asks. "Larry, I'm telling you—we go, you go with us."

He walks away and leaves Henderson standing there looking at New Jersey.

"Oh, this is beautiful," Paz says. "Are you seriously telling us that IAB is on the pad? You were tossing bones to the watchdogs?"

"Not all of them," Malone says.

"What do they do for you?" O'Dell asks.

"Tip us off," Malone says. Then he adds, "You wanted cops."

"A thing of beauty," Paz says. "On a certain sick level, it's almost admirable—he's going to rat out the Rat Squad."

"How high up in IAB does it go?" Weintraub asks.

"I pay a lieutenant," Malone says. "What he does with the money after that, I have no idea."

"You can get this on camera?" Weintraub asks. "An IAB lieutenant taking a bribe."

"What did I just say?"

They all look at Paz.

She nods.

"No," Malone says. "I want to hear you say it, boss lady. 'Sergeant Malone, go after Internal Affairs.'"

"You have my authorization."

Good, Malone thinks.

Turn the rats against each other, let them chew each other's rat faces off.

Weintraub asks him, "Do you think your guy can move Buliosi?"

"He's not my guy."

"Sure he is," Weintraub says. "You own him."

"I don't know."

"We need to shut down IAB," Paz says. "A premature disclosure would threaten our investigation."

"You mean steal your thunder," Malone says.

"I *mean*," Paz says, "that if IAB is dirty, it will suppress the evidence and seal its leaks. We'll be left with just Henderson."

Right, Malone thinks. What they're really afraid of is the commissioner will beat the mayor to the punch, announce the corruption, own it, and come out a hero.

"This fucking Torres," Paz says. "Who knew he was such a pussy?"

"So you're not going to move on IAB?" Malone asks.

"The hell we're not, just not *yet*," Paz says. She walks over to Malone, her perfume reaching him before she does. "Sergeant Malone, you beautiful dirty cop, you may have single-handedly brought down corruption in the defense bar, the prosecutor's office, IAB and the entire NYPD."

"It's bigger than Serpico," Weintraub says, "Bob Leuci, Michael Dowd, Eppolito, any of those guys."

Malone's phone rings.

O'Dell nods for him to take it.

It's Henderson.

He has an answer.

A hundred thousand dollars buys Buliosi.

"It could be a countersting," O'Dell says.

"The fuck do I have to lose?" Malone asks.

"Our entire investigation," Weintraub says. "If you pay Buliosi and he's playing you, IAB will take down the Task Force and then we're fucked."

"And you'll give us up, won't you?" Paz asks.

"In a heartbeat."

"Maybe it's time," O'Dell says, "we coordinated with IAB. If they *are* clean, our investigations are going to start tripping over each other, anyway."

"Are you out of your fucking mind?" Paz asks. "They're about to sell the Torres investigation."

"Or not," O'Dell says.

"If we bring them in now," Weintraub says, "they just throw Henderson under the bus and shut it down. They're not going to do anything beyond that to embarrass the commissioner."

"They'll just circle the wagons," Paz says. "Shut us down."

"And then the mayor doesn't get to be governor," Malone says, "and you don't get to be mayor. That's what this is about. Spare me the song-and-dance about stopping the corruption. You *are* the corruption."

"And you're white as snow," Paz says.

"New York snow," Malone says.

Dirty, gritty, hard.

Paz turns back to O'Dell. "We pay Buliosi."

O'Dell asks, "Do we even have a hundred thousand? In cash?"

No one answers.

"It's okay," Malone says. "I got it."

And I got you.

I might even have a way out of this.

"You're famous, Sergeant Malone," Rubenstein says.

They're sitting upstairs at the Landmark Tavern.

"Nah," Malone says.

Malone can't tell if Rubenstein's gay or not, like Russo thought, but Russo thinks all journalists are gay, even the women. One thing Malone *can* tell about Rubenstein is that he's dangerous. A predator always recognizes another predator.

"No, come on," Rubenstein says. "The biggest drug bust in history—you're as close to a celebrity cop as this city has."

"Don't tell my captain that, okay?" Malone says.

"The word on the street is that *you* run Manhattan North," Rubenstein says, smiling.

Dangerous.

"Don't write that or we're done," Malone says. "Look, all this needs to be on . . . what do you guys call it . . ."

Malone knows full well what they call it.

"Deep background," Rubenstein says.

"That's it," Malone says. "No one can know I'm giving you information. I'm trusting you here."

"You can."

Yeah, right I can. You trust a reporter like you trust a dog. You got a bone in your hand, you're feeding him, you're good. Your hand's empty, don't turn your back. You either feed the media or it eats you.

"You had a case against Pena before, didn't you?" Rubenstein asks.

Jesus fuck, who's this guy been talking to? "That's right."

"Did that affect the way you handled it?" Rubenstein asks.

"Do you know about Irish Alzheimer's?" Malone asks.

"No."

"You forget everything but the grudges," Malone says. "Look, we didn't know what we were going to come up against when we went into that building. As it happened, bad guys with guns wanted to slug it out. One of them was Pena. Am I glad that we won and they didn't? Yes. Do I enjoy killing people? No."

"But it must have an effect on you."

"'The tortured cop,'" Malone says. "That's a stereotype. I sleep fine, thanks for your concern."

"How do you think the inner-city community views police these days?" Rubenstein asks.

"With mistrust," Malone says. "Look, there has been a long history of racism and brutality in the NYPD. No serious person could deny that. But things have changed. People don't want to believe that, but it's true."

"The Michael Bennett shooting would seem to indicate otherwise."

290 / DON WINSLOW

"Why don't we wait until the facts are in?" Malone says.

"Why does it take so long to complete an investigation?"

"Ask the grand jury."

"I'm asking you," Rubenstein says. "You've been involved in a number of shooting incidents."

"And each one has been determined to have been justified," Malone says.

"Maybe that's my point."

"I didn't come here to debate," Malone says.

"What did you come here for?" Rubenstein asks.

"Rafael Torres," Malone says. "There's been a lot of speculation in the media . . ."

"That he was a crooked cop," Rubenstein says. "Protecting drug dealers."

"It's bullshit."

"You have to agree," Rubenstein says, "that it's not an outrageous idea. I mean, there's ample precedent."

"The 'Dirty Thirty,' Michael Dowd," Malone says. "Ancient history."

"Is it?"

"No one wants heroin off the streets more than cops do," Malone says. "We deal with the violence, the crime, the suffering, the overdoses, the bodies. We go to the morgues. *We* go tell the families. Not the *New York Times*."

"This seems to make you angry, Sergeant."

"Goddamn right it makes me angry," Malone says, pissed for letting himself get taunted. "People throwing around careless accusations. Who have you guys been talking to?"

"Do you give up *your* sources, Sergeant?" Rubenstein asks.

"All right, that's fair," Malone says. "Look, I came here to tell you the real reason Torres killed himself."

He slides an envelope across the table, material that his tame doctor on the West Side provided after complaining that it was medical malpractice.

Rubenstein opens it and looks at the X-ray and doctor's report. "Pancreatic cancer?"

"He didn't want to go out that way."

"Why didn't he leave a note?" Rubenstein asks.

"Raf wasn't that kind of guy."

"And he wasn't the dirty cop kind of guy either?"

Fuck you, Rubenstein. "Look, would Torres take a free cup of coffee, a sandwich? Okay, sure. But that's as far as it went."

"I heard on the street he was practically DeVon Carter's bodyguard."

"I hear all kinds of shit on the street," Malone says. "Did you know Jack Kennedy is managing an Applebee's on Mars? Trump is the love child of reptilians who live under Madison Square Garden? In the current environment, the 'community' will believe anything bad about cops, and repeat it, and it becomes 'truth.'"

"Here's the funny thing," Rubenstein says. "People in 'the community' *were* talking to me about Torres, and then they stopped. They don't return my calls, they walk away from me. It's almost like someone put some pressure on them."

"You guys are fuckin' unbelievable," Malone says. "I just gave you the real reason Torres took Exit 38, but you want to get on the grassy knoll anyway. I guess it makes a better story, huh?"

"The truth makes the best story, Sergeant."

"And now you have it."

"Did your bosses send you?"

"You see me on a bicycle?" Malone says. "I came here on my own to protect a brother officer's reputation."

"And the Task Force's."

"Yeah, that too."

"Why'd you come to me?" Rubenstein asks. "The *Post* will usually whore for the department."

"I read your heroin articles," Malone says. "They were good, you got it right. And you're the fuckin' *Times*."

Rubenstein thinks for a few seconds and then says, "What if I write that a confidential but reliable source revealed that Torres was suffering from a painful and terminal illness."

"You'd have my gratitude."

"What does that get me?"

Malone gets up. "I don't fuck on the first date. Dinner, maybe a movie, we'll see what happens."

"You have my number."

Yeah, I do, Malone thinks, walking out onto the street.

I got your number.

He meets Russo and Monty at the co-op.

Where they usually go to relax, chill out, but nothing's chill in there now. The air is close and tight, and Russo and Monty, two tough sons of bitches, are rattled. Russo doesn't have that smile on his face, Monty looks positively grim, the cigar in his mouth cold and out.

And Levin's not even there.

"Where's the newbie?" Malone asks.

"He went home," Russo says.

"He okay?"

"He's shook, but he's okay," Russo says. He gets up from the sofa and paces around the room. Looks out the window and then back to Malone. "Jesus Christ. You think Torres gave us up?"

"If he did, we'd be in cuffs already," Monty says. "Raf Torres was a lot of things, but he wasn't a rat."

It goes into Malone like a blade.

Because Big Monty's right. Raf Torres was a drug slinger, a whoremonger and a woman beater, Malone thinks, but he wasn't me. He wasn't a rat and he didn't look his partners in the eye and lie to them, like I'm about to do.

"Still, the fucking heat's coming down," Russo says.

"It wasn't IAB," Malone says, feeling like shit. "At least not as far as Henderson knows. He's moving to shut them down on it. It's going to cost us a hundred K from the slush fund."

"The cost of doing business," Monty says.

"So it's who, the feds?" Russo asks.

"We don't know," Malone says. "Could be nobody. For all we know, Torres just got tired of being a worthless piece of shit and put an end to it. I put out a cover story he was sick."

A silence as Monty and Russo look at each other. They'd been talking to each other before he got there, and Malone wants to know what they have on their minds. Fuck, are they wondering about me?

"What?" Malone asks, his fucking heart stopped.

Russo starts, "Denny, we've been talking . . ."

"Jesus Christ, just say it," Malone says. "You got something on your mind, let it come out your fucking mouth."

Russo says, "We think it's time to move the Pena smack."

"*Now?*" Malone asks. "With all this heat?"

"*Because* of all this heat," Russo says. "What if we need to take off, or money for lawyers? If we wait, we might be in a situation we *can't* lay it off."

Malone looks to Monty. "Where are you with this?"

Monty rolls his cigar, carefully lighting it. "I'm just not getting any younger, and Yolanda's been on me to spend more time with the family."

"You talking about leaving Da Force?" Malone asks.

"The *Job*," Monty says. "I have my twenty coming up in a few months. I'm not so sure I don't want to finish out at some desk in the outer boroughs, pull the pin, take my pension and move the family to North Carolina."

"If that's what you want to do, Monty," Malone says, "you should do it."

"North Carolina," Russo says. "You don't want to stay in the city?"

"The boys," Monty says, "especially the two older ones, are getting to that mouthy age. They don't want to do what they're told, they want to talk back. The truth of it is, I don't want them talking smack to the wrong cop and getting shot."

"The fuck, Monty?" Russo says.

So this is what it's come to, Malone thinks—a black cop is afraid another cop is going to shoot his kid.

"It's not something the two of you have to think about," Monty says. "Your kids are white, but it's something Yo and I have to think about. Scares her half to death; if it isn't a cop, it's some banger."

"Black kids get shot in the South," Malone says.

"Not like up here," Monty says. "Do you think I want to leave? Shit, I don't even like getting a *meal* outside of New York. But Yo has family down near Durham, there are good schools, I can get a good position at one of the colleges . . . Look, we've had a good run. But everything comes to an end. Maybe this whole Torres thing is trying to tell us to walk away with the house money. So, yes, I think I want to cash out."

"Yeah, okay," Malone says. "I'm thinking Savino. He'll take it up to New England somewhere. Keep it off our turf."

Russo says, "So we'll meet with him."

"Not us," Malone says. "Me."

"The fuck?"

So if it comes to it, I can swear into a polygraph you weren't there, Malone thinks. "The fewer of us the better."

"He's right," Monty says.

"All right, let's get Raf in the dirt, and then I'll set it up," Malone says. "In the meantime, let's all chill, let this blow over."

etective Sergeant Rafael Torres receives an inspector's funeral.
The Job's way of letting the world know it has nothing to
hide, Malone thinks, nothing to be ashamed of.

The *Times* helped.

Rubenstein's article was "wood"—a top-of-the-fold front-page
story with his sole byline under HERO COP SUCCUMBS.

And artistic, Malone thinks.

"No one really knows why Rafael Torres did what he did.
Whether it was accidental or intentional, whether it was the terminal
agonizing illness or the decades of waging the interminable war
on drugs. All we know is that he pulled the trigger on a life full of
pain . . ."

Well, that much is true. Torres did inflict a lot of pain.

His wife, his family, his whores, his *gumars,* his arrestees, pretty
much anyone he ever came into contact with. Yeah, maybe himself,
although Malone doubts it. Raf Torres was a sociopath, incapable of
feeling anyone else's pain.

But he did pull the trigger, Malone thinks.

You have to give him credit for that.

The funeral is at Woodlawn Cemetery, in the Bronx. Malone
had forgotten Torres was from up here. The place is huge, hundreds
of acres, with enormous cedar and pine trees, full of ornate mau-
soleums. Malone has only been here once before, when Claudette
dragged him out to lay flowers on Miles Davis's grave.

Like all the other cops at the funeral, Malone is in full dress. His blue jacket, white gloves, a black band over his gold shield, his other medals. Malone doesn't have a lot—he don't like medals because you have to put yourself up for them, and that strikes him as pussy.

He knows what he's done.

So does everyone who matters.

The funeral is a painful reminder of Billy's.

The formation, the bagpipes, the gun salute, the color guard . . .

Except Billy didn't have kids, and Torres does, two girls and a boy standing bravely beside their mother, and Malone feels an icy stab of guilt—you did this to them, you left them without a father.

The wives are there too, not just from Torres's team but from the whole force. It's expected, and they're lined up in their black funeral dresses that they wear too often. Like crows on a phone line, Malone thinks unkindly, and he knows what they're feeling, too—sad for Gloria Torres and guilty they're relieved it's not them.

Sheila's lost a few pounds, no question.

She looks good.

Even looks a little tearful, although she despised Torres and hated when they had to socialize with him.

The mayor is saying a few words, but Malone don't know what they are because he ain't listening and what the fuck difference does it make? Most of the cops are making at least a subtle show of not paying attention because they hate his guts, think he's betrayed them every chance he's had and is going to do it again with the Michael Bennett shooting.

Hizzoner is smart enough to keep it short and turn it over to the commissioner, and Malone figures the only reason they don't just gut each other right there and save everyone the trouble of coming out for another funeral is that they're afraid of a standing ovation.

The cops do listen to the commissioner, who, although a total dick, does have their backs on the Bennett shooting and the rest of the brutality shit. Also, they're afraid not to, because the chief of patrol and chief of D's are watching and taking names. Mayors and PCs come and go, but those guys stay in their jobs forever.

Next comes the priest, another guy Malone don't listen to. Hears the fuckin' parasite say something about Torres being in heaven, which only shows he never knew Torres.

The Job had to jack the Church into doing a full funeral anyway and burying him in consecrated ground, seeing as how Torres was a suicide, which is a mortal sin, and he didn't get Last Rites.

Fuckin' clowns.

Do the right thing, see the man off in front of his family and let him go to hell. He was goin' anyway, if there even is such a place. But the Job is a repeat customer and donates a lot of money, so the Church yielded, and Malone can't help but observe that the priest is Asian.

The fuck, they couldn't sober up an Irish priest long enough to do a cop funeral? Or a PR who wasn't too busy diddling a little boy? They had to get some, what is he, Filipino, or whatever the fuck he is? He'd heard the Church was running out of white priests and now he guesses that's true. The Flip pygmy finally shuts up, the bagpipes start in, and Malone thinks about Liam.

Him and all those other funerals back then.

Those goddamn bagpipes.

The music stops, the rifles crack, the folded flag is delivered, the formation breaks.

Malone walks over to Sheila. "Hell of a thing, huh?"

"It's the kids I feel for."

"They'll be okay."

Gloria is a good-looking woman, still young and attractive. Lustrous black hair, good figure, she'll have no problem replacing Raf, she wants to.

And truth is, Gloria Torres might just have won the fucking lottery. She was about to divorce her husband when he canceled his reservation, and now she gets both his official and unofficial pensions.

Malone made sure Gloria got her fat envelope and that the system's in place for monthly payments.

Torres will keep earning.

"What about the hookers?" Gallina had asked him.

"You're out of the whore business."

"Who the fuck are you to—"

"I'm the guy pulled IAB off your ass," Malone said. "That's who the fuck I am. Your team wants to go off the reservation, see what happens."

"Is that a threat?"

"It's reality, Jorge," Malone said. "The reality is you're not smart enough to handle your own shit. Those girls are on buses back to where they came from and that's an end to it."

Malone walks over to give his respects to Gloria Torres.

Assholes are too dumb to know what I did for them, Malone thinks. I got the feds and IAB locked into mutually assured destruction, I got the whispers about Torres silenced. With any luck, this thing gets buried with him and we all go back to living our lives.

Malone gets into the line to speak with the widow and when he gets up to her, he says, "I'm so sorry, Gloria, for your loss."

He's shocked when she whispers, "Get the fuck away from me."

He just looks at her.

"Cancer, Denny?" she asks. "He had *cancer*?"

"I was protecting his reputation," Malone says.

Gloria laughs. "Raf's reputation?"

"For you, for the kids."

"Don't you talk about his kids."

She stares at him, pure fucking hatred in her eyes.

"What—"

"It was you, you son of a bitch," Gloria hisses.

Malone feels like he's been hit in the face. Can't believe he heard what he's hearing. He forces himself to look at her.

She says, "Raffy told me."

It was you.

Russo launches an overhand right at Ortiz and it connects.

Ortiz steps back, holding a hand up to his bloody mouth, but Russo isn't through, he steps in about to follow with the left, but Malone hauls him off.

"You crazy?" Malone asks. "*Here?*"

With half the NYPD brass looking on?

"You hear what he said about you?" Russo asks, his face red and twisted in rage. "He called you a fucking rat!"

Russo tries to twist out of Malone's hold, but now Monty has stepped in too, and walks them backward. Levin moves into the space between them and Gallina's people. Monty keeps walking Russo back and away from the funeral, where cops are turning and staring.

"He called Malone a rat," Russo says. "Says Torres told his wife."

"If he did," Monty says, "that's Torres's last gift of malevolence from the grave. Let the haters hate."

Russo twists out of Malone's grasp and holds his hands up. "I'm okay. I'm okay."

He leans his hand on a headstone and catches his breath.

Levin comes over. "What's going on?"

Russo shakes his head.

"Torres's people are claiming that Malone was working with the feds," Monty says, "and set him up."

"That's not true, is it?" Levin asks.

Malone lunges at him. "The fuck—"

Monty gets between them and grabs Malone. "We're going to fight each other, too?"

"It's bullshit!" Malone yells, almost believing himself.

"Of course it's bullshit," Monty says. "They put it out as a test, see how we'd react."

"If it's a test," Levin says, "why say it was the feds, not IAB?"

It has the stench of truth, Malone thinks.

"Because we have IAB on the pad and they know it," Russo says. "What the fuck you think you know about anything, newbie?"

"I don't," Levin says.

"You calmed down?" Monty asks Malone.

"Yeah."

Monty lets go of him.

It's happened in one minute, Malone thinks. *One minute* after the accusation and Monty's become the leader and I'm damaged goods. He don't blame Monty, he's doing what he needs to do, but Malone can't let that happen.

He says to Monty and Russo, "Go tell them—Charles Young Park, ten o'clock tonight. Everyone comes."

Monty walks away through the headstones.

"That's good," Levin says. "We'll get this straightened out."

"You sit this one out," Malone says.

"Why?"

"There's shit you don't need to know," Malone says.

"Look, either I'm on the team or I'm—"

"I'm looking out for you," Malone says. "One day you might have to take a polygraph and it would be good for you to say 'I don't know' without ringing the bells."

Levin stares at him. "Jesus Christ, what are you guys into?"

"Shit I'm trying to keep you out of."

"I already took money," Levin says. "Am I jammed up here?"

"You have a career in front of you," Malone says. "I'm trying to protect that. None of this concerns you—be somewhere else tonight."

Russo and Monty come back.

The meeting is set up.

"This is over!" Malone yells. "This is fucking over!"

"Calm down," Paz says.

"*You* calm the fuck down!" Malone yells. "This rumor will be all over the Task Force—shit, all over the Job—by this afternoon! I'm a marked man! I have a bull's-eye on my fucking back!"

"Deny it," Paz says.

She leans back in her chair and looks at him calmly.

They're up in the "safe house" on Thirty-Sixth Street, which Malone don't think is so safe anymore.

"'Deny it'?" Malone asks. "Torres told his wife."

"That's what she told you," Paz says. "They might be just trying to flush you out."

"And they recruited Gloria to do it?" Malone asks.

Paz shrugs. "Gloria Torres is hardly the grieving widow. And she has a rooting interest in making sure the flow of dirty money keeps coming in."

Malone looks at O'Dell. "Did you give me up to Torres?"

"We played him the tape of the two of you," O'Dell says. "But we told him we had the entire Task Force up."

"So they know you fucking have me!" Malone says. "You goddamn fucking idiots! You goddamn fucking Southern District empty-suit morons! Jesus Christ . . ."

"Sit down, Malone," Paz says. "I said sit down."

Malone sits heavily on one of the metal chairs.

"We always knew," Paz says, "that at some point in time you'd be exposed. But I'm not sure we're there yet. As far as Torres's people know, it could be anyone on the Task Force or no one. So, yes, deny it."

"They won't believe me."

"Convince them," Paz says. "And stop the whining. We didn't put you in this situation—you did it to yourself. I advise you to re-member that."

"Save your advice for your girlfriends."

"I don't have any," Paz says. "I'm too busy dealing with dirtbags like you and the late Rafael Torres. He was dirty—his team is dirty. You're dirty and your whole team is dirty."

"I will not—"

"Yeah, yeah, I know," Paz says. "You won't do anything to hurt your partners. We heard you the fifteenth time. You want to protect your partners, Malone? You suck it up, you stay on the Job, you keep bringing us indictments."

"We're going to get him killed," O'Dell says.

Paz shrugs again. "People die."

"Nice," says Weintraub.

Paz asks Malone, "What's your play?"

"We have a meet tonight," Malone says. "My team and Torres's."

"One-stop shopping," Paz says. "You're going wired."

"Fuck that," Malone says. "You don't think the first thing they're going to do is pat me down?"

"Don't let them."

"Then they'll know for sure."

"You know what I don't like about, you, Malone?" Paz asks. "In addition to everything? You think I'm stupid. The real reason you don't want to wear a wire to this meeting is that it will incriminate your partners. I have already assured you, I have put it on the record—if your precious partners have committed no other crimes than we already know about or can reasonably infer from your personal involvement, they get a walk, courtesy of your cooperation."

O'Dell steps up. "If he goes to this meeting wired, and they pat him down, we *will* have succeeded in getting him killed. If that doesn't matter to you, Isobel, it will also mean that he won't be available to corroborate any of the recordings."

"There's always that," Weintraub says.

Paz says, "I want a full, truthful, signed affidavit from Malone detailing the meeting."

"Do you want backup?" O'Dell asks Malone.

"What?"

"In case you get in trouble," O'Dell says. "We can have people there to pull you out."

Malone laughs. "Yeah—some feds are going to go into that hood and not get made by cops or the community. Fuck, you'd *get* me killed."

"If you get yourself killed," Paz says, "the deal is off."

Malone can't tell if she's kidding.

Malone sticks the SOG knife in his boot.

The Sig Sauer is in a holster at his waist, the Beretta at the small of his back, and he's taped extra clips to his ankles.

To meet with other cops, Malone thinks.

To meet with other cops.

Yeah, but they're cops who want to kill me.

The Colonel Charles Young Playground is four baseball diamonds scraped out of the dirt between 143rd and 145th, east of Malcolm X and west of Harlem River Drive where the 145th Street Bridge comes off the Deegan. The 145th Street subway station is across Malcolm X, giving Malone another way out if he needs it.

As arranged, he meets the team on the southwest corner of 143rd and Malcolm and they walk into the playground together.

Russo's wearing his leather overcoat and Malone knows he's carrying the shotgun underneath. Monty has a Harris tweed jacket—the .38 bulge visible at his hip.

"It's Runnymede," Monty says as they cross 143rd toward the baseball diamonds.

"Runny who?"

"Runnymede," Monty says. "The barons are challenging the king."

Malone don't know what Monty's talking about—he only knows that Monty knows what he's talking about, and that's good enough. Anyway, he gets the gist—knows who the king is and who the barons are.

A couple of kids and a few junkies get the fuck out of the park when they see the cops coming.

Malone's phone buzzes and he looks at the number.

It's Claudette.

He should take it but he can't, not right now. He feels a twinge of guilt—he should have gone over there or called her, but with everything that's been happening he hasn't had the time.

Fuck, he thinks, maybe I should take a second and call back.

Then he sees the Torres people come from the uptown side of the playground. They've been waiting, Malone knows, to see if we came alone.

Can't blame them.

Malone watches them walk toward him at the middle of the diamonds. Knows they'll be heavy, too.

It's more like some shoot-out in an old western, Malone thinks, than freakin' barons and kings. The two sides—fuck, we're sides now—step up to each other.

"I'm patting you down," Gallina says to Malone.

"Why don't we *all* get naked?" Malone asks.

"Because we're not rats."

"Neither am I."

"That's not what we heard," says Tenelli.

"The fuck *did* you hear?" Russo asks.

"Let's make sure we're not making a recording first," Gallina says.

Malone stretches his arms out. It's humiliating, but he lets Gallina pat him down for a wire.

"Now the rest of your team," Gallina says.

"Everyone pats each other down," Malone says. "We don't know it ain't one of you."

It looks ridiculous, cops frisking each other, but they get it done.

"Okay," Malone says, "can we talk now?"

"Haven't you talked enough already?" Tenelli asks.

"I don't know what Gloria told you," Malone says, "but I didn't give Torres up."

"She said the feds played Torres a recording of him and you," Gallina says. "He wasn't wired, so it had to be you."

"Bullshit," Malone says. "They could have had a listening device from a parked car, or a rooftop, anywhere."

"Then why haven't they come for you?" Gallina asks.

"Or have they?" asks Tenelli.

"No."

"Why is that?" Tenelli asks.

"They will," Gallina says. "And then what are you going to do?"

"Tell them to go fuck themselves," Malone says. "They don't have shit on anyone else here, and they won't."

"Unless you give it up," Gallina says.

"I won't hurt a brother officer."

Tenelli asks, "How do we know you haven't already?"

"I've never hit a woman," Malone says, "but you're pushing me to it."

"Come on."

Gallina stops it again. "What's that going to prove? If it wasn't you, Malone, how did the feds get on us in the first place?"

"I don't know," Malone says. "You assholes were on Carter's pad—maybe he flipped. You were running hookers, maybe that brought them on us."

"What about the newbie, Levin?" Ortiz asks.

"What about him?"

"Maybe he's the rat," Ortiz says. "Maybe he's working with the feds?"

"Get the fuck out of my face."

"Or what?"

"I'll *get* you out of my face."

Ortiz backs off. "What now?"

"We stay clean," Malone says.

"What about the Carter pad?"

"I'll deal with Carter from now on."

Tenelli says, "First you get Torres killed, then you take food off our tables?"

"Listen to me," Malone says. "Raf put *me* in the jackpot, not the other way around, but I will deal with it. If I have to fall on the sword, I will. But we can all walk away with this if we're smart. We have IAB in our pocket, they can't hurt us without blowing themselves up. The Job has had too much bad publicity already, they'll let this lie if nothing else comes up."

"What about the feds?" Gallina asks.

"The long, hot summer's just around the corner," Malone says. "The Bennett report is going to come out, and if it exonerates that stupid shit, this city is going to blow up. The feds know that, they know they're going to need us to keep this city from burning. Keep your noses clean, do your fucking jobs. I'll get us through this."

They don't look happy, but none of them say anything.

The king is still the king.

Then Monty speaks up. "Police work is a dangerous job. We all know that. But if anything happens to Malone—if he catches a bullet, a concrete block falls on him, he gets hit by lightning, I'm going to come looking for the people on this playground. And I'll kill you."

Both sides walk away.

They go back to the co-op.

"Don't discuss business with anyone outside us," Malone says. "And don't talk about anything in the house, in cars, anywhere we're not one hundred percent certain is secure."

"The feds have you and Torres on tape?" Monty asks.

"Sounds like it."

"What have they got?"

"I only had two conversations with Torres that are incriminating," Malone says. "One on Christmas, he came to see me about Teddy. The other was after the gun bust, he came to me about Carter. I don't remember exactly what got said, but it isn't good."

Russo asks, "What if the feds do come after you?"

"I don't give them anything," Malone says.

Monty says, "That means jail."

"Then it means jail."

"Jesus, Denny."

"I'm all right," Malone says. "You'll take care of my family."

"Goes without saying." This from Russo.

"Let's hope it don't come to that," Malone says. "I ain't out of the game yet. But if it does . . ."

"We got your back," Russo says. "What about Levin?"

"Jesus, you too?"

"All this shit happens when he came on the team," Russo says.

"*Post hoc, ergo propter hoc,*" Monty says.

"What?"

"'After this, therefore because of this,'" Monty says. "It's a fallacy of logic. Just because this shit started after Levin came on doesn't mean it started *because* Levin came on."

"He took his cut of Teddy's money," Malone says.

"Yeah, but took it where?" Russo asks. "Maybe it's vouchered with the feds."

"Okay," Malone says, "go to his place two or three in the morning, see if he has the money stashed."

"If he doesn't . . ."

"Then we have questions," Malone says.

Malone goes out and walks to his car.

It's time to move the smack.

It's the worst fucking time to do anything risky, but he has to move the Pena smack.

CHAPTER 21

They meet in St. John Cemetery.

"The fuck we have to come all the way out to Queens for?" Lou Savino asks.

"You want to meet on Pleasant Avenue?" Malone says. "It's a federal movie set. Here you can always say you were just paying respects to old friends."

Half the major bosses from the Five Families are buried out here. Luciano himself, Vito Genovese, John Gotti, Carlo Gambino, Joe Colombo, even old Salvatore Maranzano, who started it all.

St. John is sort of the Gangster Hall of Fame.

And then there's Rafael Ramos.

It doesn't seem like two years have gone by since he and another cop, Wenjian Liu, were shot as they sat in their radio car in Bed-Stuy. The whack job who did it said it was revenge for Eric Garner and Michael Brown. Said he was putting "Wings on Pigs." Had the sense to blow his own brains out before the NYPD got to him.

The gun he used came through the Iron Pipeline.

Where were the fucking demonstrations then? Malone wonders. Where were the signs that said "Blue Lives Matter"?

Malone was at Ramos's funeral here—the largest in police history, over a hundred thousand people. A lot of cops turned their backs on the mayor when he delivered the eulogy.

Hizzoner turned his back on them over the Eric Garner thing.

"Give Pigs Wings," Malone thinks.

Kiss my pig ass.

THE FORCE / 309

Anyway, it's a nice June morning, good day to be outside.

Malone says, "You sure about this? Your bosses hear you're dealing, they'll take you out."

Cimino family rule: you deal, you die.

It's not because they have moral compunctions, it's that the heavy sentences induce guys to flip. So if you get busted with dope, you're too big a risk and you have to go.

"That's not for dealing," Savino says. "That's for getting *caught* dealing. As long as the bosses get their beaks wet, they don't give a shit. And how else am I going to eat, right?"

Yeah, right, Malone thinks.

Louie crying poor is pretty funny. Like he needs to sling smack to put a little bread on the table. He just knows there's a fucking killing to be made here. A fucking windfall, if he can pull it off.

"You let me worry about me," Savino is saying. "What do you want for it?"

"A hundred grand a kilo," Malone says.

"What the fuck world you live in?" Savino asks. "I can get smack for sixty-five, seventy."

"Not Dark Horse," Malone says. "Not sixty percent pure. The market price is a hundred."

"That's if you can go straight to the retailer," Savino says. "Which you can't. Which is why you called me. I can go seventy-five."

"You can go fuck yourself, too."

"Think about it," Savino says. "You can do business with family, white people instead of niggers and spics."

"Seventy-five's not enough," Malone says.

"Make a counter."

"We got *Shark Tank* going on here," Malone says. "Okay, Mister Wonderful, we'll do ninety a kilo."

"You just want me to bend over a headstone here, you can fuck me in the ass?" Savino asks. "Maybe I could go eighty."

"Eighty-seven."

"The fuck, are we Jews?" Savino says. "Can we do this like

gentlemen, say eighty-five? Eighty-five thousand a kilo times fifty. Four million, two hundred fifty thousand dollars. That's a lot of chocolate-glazed."

"Do you have it?"

"I'll get it," Savino says.

That means he's going to have to go to other people, Malone thinks. More people means more talk, more risk. But it can't be helped. "Another thing, you don't put this out in Manhattan North. Take it upstate, New England, just not here."

"You're a piece of work," Savino says. "You don't care there are addicts, just as long as they're not *your* addicts."

"Yes or no?"

"Deal," Savino says. "Only because I don't feel like standing out in a graveyard any longer. Gives me the creeps."

Yeah, Malone thinks. Nothing like a graveyard to bring it home someday you'll have to pay, answer for what you've done.

Fuckin' nuns.

"When do we do this?" Savino asks.

"I'll give you a time and a place," Malone says. "And *cash*, Lou. Don't show up with hot jewelry and some paper on a bad loan."

"Cops." Savino smirks. "So suspicious."

Before he leaves, Malone goes to pay his respects at Billy's grave.

"This is for you, Billy," Malone says. "It's for your son."

Malone opens the trap under the shower.

What do the PRs call it? *La caja.*

The fifty kilos of horse are each wrapped in blue plastic with stickers indicating that they're Dark Horse. Malone rips off the stickers and flushes them down the drain. Then he puts the kilos in two North Face duffel bags he bought for the occasion, replaces the trap in the shower, hefts the bags one at a time down the elevator and puts them in the back of his car.

Normally he'd have Russo or Monty or both with him, but he

wants to keep them out of this, just present them with their cut of the cash like it's Christmas all over again. It's tricky, though, flying solo with no backup.

But that's your world now, he tells himself as he turns north on Broadway and drives uptown. You're on your own until you can get out from under Paz and the feds, and until that happens you have to protect your guys.

It would be good to have them along, though, in case Savino tries to rip him. He doubts that will happen, because they have so many ties with the Cimino *borgata,* but you're talking a lot of money and a lot of dope here, and you never know what that's gonna do to a guy.

Savino might just take the big home-run swing.

Which he wouldn't do if Russo or Monty was there.

But now it's just me, with a Sig, a Beretta, and a knife. Yeah, okay, and the MP5 in a sling under my jacket. I have a lot of firepower but only one trigger finger, so what I'm mostly counting on here is Savino's honor.

Used to be you could count on that with mob guys.

Used to be a lot of things, though.

He turns onto the West Side Highway and drives up past the GW Bridge, then into Fort Tryon Park below the Cloisters. One o'clock in the morning, the park is pretty empty, and if someone is there, it isn't for a good reason. You're a transient building an illegal fire, or you've brought a hooker there, or you're looking for a blow job—although a lot of that shit stopped since the gays came out of the closets.

Or you're looking to make a dope deal.

Which is what I'm looking to do, Malone thinks, just like any other skel.

If it wasn't me, it would just be someone else, Malone thinks, knowing it's an age-old rationalization even as he thinks it. But it's age-old because it's true. Right now in some lab in Mexico they're cranking out more of this shit, so if it wasn't these fifty keys, it would be their replacements. And if it wasn't me, it would be someone else.

So why should the bad guys make all the money all the time? The guys who torture and kill. Why shouldn't me and Russo and Monty make a little something, build a future for our families?

You spend your whole fucking life trying to keep this shit out of people's arms and no matter how much you seize, how many dealers you bust, it just keeps coming anyway, right up the line from the opium fields, to the labs, to the trailer trucks, to the needles and into the veins.

One smooth, ever-flowing river.

No, he gets his own hypocrisy.

Knows he might as well be shooting this directly into Claudette's arm.

But if it ain't me, it's just someone else.

And the irony of it is, I use it to send her to rehab. Send my kids to college. Instead of it goes to some Mexican or Colombian to buy another Ferrari, some more gold chains, a pet tiger, a country estate, a harem.

Anyway, you tell yourself what you gotta tell yourself to do what you gotta do.

And sometimes you even fuckin' believe it.

He pulls off where Fort Tryon Place meets Corbin Drive. He wants to still be on his Manhattan North turf, something goes wrong here, but he also knows what every skel knows—you want to move around precincts. Start in the Two-Eight, do the deal in the Three-Four, all of it also covered by Manhattan North.

That way if the shit comes down and you get popped, you got a shot at paperwork getting fucked up between precincts and jurisdictions. Rivalries and jealousies can get in the way and maybe even spring you.

It's why, for instance, hookers stroll the streets that border precincts, because no cop wants to make a bust across the line. Too much paperwork. Same with low-level dealers—nickel- and dime-bag guys. They see a cop coming they just cross the street and most of the time the cop won't follow. If there's a chase now, Malone will drive down through Manhattan but Savino will cross into the Bronx, get a whole other borough involved.

The Bronx and Manhattan hate each other.

Unless the feds get involved, then they hate the feds.

What the public doesn't know is just how tribal cops are. It starts with ethnicity—you got the biggest tribe, the Irish; then you got the Italian Tribe and the Every Other Kind of White Guy Tribe. Then you got the Black Tribe, the Hispanic Tribe.

They each have their clubs—the Irish have the Emerald Society, the Italians the Columbia Association. The Germans are the Steuben Society, the Polacks the Pulaski Association, the other white guys have a catchall called the St. George's Society. The blacks are the Guardians, the Puerto Ricans have the Hispanic Society, the twelve Jews got the Shomrim Society.

Then it gets complicated, because you got the Uniform Tribe, the Plainclothes Tribe and the Detective Tribe that cut across all the ethnic tribes. Most of all you got the Street Cop Tribe versus the Administration Tribe, a subclan of which is the Internal Affairs Tribe.

Then you got the boroughs, the precincts and the working units.

So Malone is in the Irish Detective Street Cop Manhattan North Special Task Force Tribe.

And another tribe, he thinks—the Dirty Cop Tribe.

Savino is already at the pull-off.

Blinks the lights of his black Navigator twice. Malone pulls up to the front of the Navigator so it will have to reverse to get out fast. He can't see into the SUV. Then Savino gets out.

The capo is wearing, honest to God, a tracksuit, because some of these guys just can't help themselves. The gun bulge is at his waist by his right hand and he's got a big shit-eating grin on his face.

It occurs to Malone that he doesn't like Savino very much. Especially when the back doors open and three Dominicans get out.

One of them is Carlos Castillo.

Clearly the *jefe,* he's wearing a black suit, white shirt, no tie, and he looks like money. Black hair slicked back, a thin mustache. The other two are gunmen—black jackets, jeans, freakin' cowboy boots and AKs.

Malone takes out the MP5 and holds it at his hip.

"Easy," Savino says. "It's not what it looks like."

The fuck it ain't, Malone thinks. You set me up. All that shuck-and-jive in the cemetery, you don't have the money. It was a *fugazy*—a front, a façade to get me whacked.

Castillo smiles at him. "What, do you think we didn't know how many kilos were in that room? How much money?"

"What do you want?"

"Diego Pena was my cousin."

Don't back down, Malone tells himself. Backing down gets you killed. Looking weak gets you killed. "Murder a New York Police Department detective in New York City? The world will come down on your head."

If I don't blow it off first.

"We're the cartel," Castillo says.

"No, *we're* the cartel," Malone says. "I got thirty-eight thousand in my gang. How many you got?"

Castillo takes it in. This is no stupid guy. "It's unfortunate. So for the time being I'll have to settle for recovering our property."

One of the Malone Rules: Never take a step back.

"You can *buy* it," he says.

"It's generous of you," Castillo says, "offering to sell us back our own product."

"You're getting a deal that this guinea motherfucker cut for you," Malone says. "Otherwise it would be bust-out retail."

"You stole it."

"I *took* it," Malone says. "There's a difference."

Castillo smiles. "So *I* could just take it."

"Your *guys* could," Malone says. "I'll send *you* where I sent your cousin."

"Diego would never have drawn a gun on you," Castillo says. "He was too smart. Why fight what you can buy?"

Malone says, "Diego got what he deserved."

"No, he didn't," Castillo says calmly. "You didn't have to kill him. You wanted to."

It's fucking true, Malone thinks. "We going to do this or not?"

One of the Domos goes back to the car, comes back with two briefcases. He starts to hand them to Castillo, but the man stares at Malone and shakes his head, so his gunman hands them to Savino instead.

Nice Halliburtons.

Savino walks up, sets them on the hood of Malone's car and opens both of them, showing him the stacks of hundreds.

"It's all there," Castillo says. "Four million, two hundred and fifty thousand dollars."

"You want to count it?" Savino asks.

"I'm good." He doesn't want to be out here any longer than he has to and he doesn't want to take his eyes off the Domos for the time it would take to count the money. Anyway, if they were going to short him, they might as well just rip him.

Malone puts the cases on the floor of the car by the front passenger seat, walks around, grabs the duffel bags and sets them on the hood.

Savino carries the bags over to Castillo, who opens them and looks inside. "The labels are missing."

"I took them off," Malone says.

"But it's the Dark Horse."

"Yeah," Malone says. "You want to test it?"

"I trust you," Castillo says.

Malone has his finger on the MP5 trigger. If they're going to shoot him, this is the moment, when they know they got the heroin and they can still grab their money back. The *jefe* nods to one of his guys, who grabs the duffel bags and takes them back to Savino's car.

Savino smiles. "Always a pleasure doing business with you, Denny."

Yeah, Malone thinks, and Castillo here would have killed me if he didn't want to do business with the Cimino family. And you and me are going to have a serious conversation, Louie.

Castillo stares at Malone. "You know you're just on a reprieve."

"Aren't we all?" Malone asks.

He gets back in his car and pulls out. Four and a quarter mil sits on the car floor next to him. His adrenaline is shrieking as he drives, then the fear and anger hit him like a double shot with a hammer and he starts to shake.

Sees his hands quiver on the steering wheel and grips it hard to try to stop it. He snorts air through his nose to slow his heartbeat down.

I thought I was dead, he thinks.

Thought I was fucking dead.

I got through that one, he tells himself, but Pena's cousin isn't going to let it go. He's just going to wait for an opening and then he'll take it. Or maybe contract it out through the Ciminos. Louie will ask me to a sit-down and I'll never come back. A lot of it is going to be a matter of who's more valuable to the Ciminos—me or the cartel.

I'd put my money on the Domos.

And the other thing.

The fucking Domos will put this out on the street in Manhattan North, to put DeVon Carter out of business.

Junkies on my turf will die.

Something else I get to live with.

He drives south along the Hudson and the black water shines silver from the lights of the bridge.

alone puts the cases with the money back in *la caja* and then goes and pours himself a drink.

His hands have stopped shaking, at least, and he uses the whiskey to wash down a couple of Dexies. It's already after 3 A.M. and John has a baseball game at 8:30 he don't want to miss. He sits and waits for the go-pills to hit and then he leaves the apartment and gets into his car and drives out to Staten Island so he can watch the sun come up over the ocean.

So there he is, Malone walking alone along the beach with the sun a fiery red and the sea a reflected rose, and the Verrazano-Narrows Bridge an amber arc. A flock of gulls at the water's edge stubbornly hold their position as he walks past them. He's the interloper here; they're waiting for the tide to bring in the seaweed and with it their breakfast, but Malone, the speed stops him from being hungry even though he hasn't eaten since lunch yesterday, and he thinks, Good for you, gulls. Don't let anyone move you out of your place. You got the numbers.

Sometimes when he was a kid his dad would take them down to this beach and he loved to chase the gulls. Then if the water was warm enough, his dad would take him in bodysurfing and that was the best thing in the world. He'd like to go in now even though the water is still freezing, but he doesn't want to get the salt on his skin because there's no place to shower and anyway he doesn't have a towel.

But it would be good to get into the cold water, and then he realizes that he forgot to shower and he hopes he doesn't stink. Sniffs his armpit and it don't smell so bad.

He hasn't shaved, either, and that might upset John, so when he gets back to the car he takes out the Dopp kit he keeps under the front seat and dry-shaves in the visor mirror. It scrapes and isn't as smooth as he wants but at least he looks decent.

Then Malone drives to the baseball park.

Sheila is already there and John's team is warming up, the kids looking unhappy early on a Saturday morning that would otherwise be a day to sleep in.

Malone walks over to her. "Good morning."

"Rough night?"

He ignores the gibe. "Caitlin here?"

"She stayed over at Jordan's last night."

Malone is disappointed and can't help but suspect that was part of the plan, him being disappointed. He looks over and waves to John, who gives him a sleepy wave back. But smiles. That's John, always has a smile.

"You want to sit together?" Malone asks Sheila.

"Later, maybe," she says. "I got the first shift, concession stand duty."

"You got any coffee?"

"Come on, I'll make some."

Malone follows her to the little shack where they do the concessions. Sheila looks good in a green fleece jacket and jeans. She makes the coffee, pours him a cup and he also takes a glazed doughnut because he knows he should eat. He lays down a ten and tells her put the change in the jar.

"Big spender."

He takes an envelope out of his jacket pocket and slips it to her. Sheila takes it and puts it in her bag.

"Sheel," Malone says, "anything should happen, you know where to go, right?"

"Phil."

"And if something happened to him?" Those two cops, Ramos and Liu, partners, just sitting in their car and they both got it.

"Then Monty," Sheila says. "Something going to happen, Denny?"

"No," Malone says. "I just wanted to check you know what to do."

"Okay." But she looks at him, worried.

"I said I'm just checking, Sheila."

"And I said okay." She starts laying out candy bars, packages of cookies and granola bars. Then apples and bananas and juice boxes. "Some of the mothers want us to have kale. How the hell we supposed to put out kale?"

"What's kale?"

"Exactly, huh?"

I guess, Malone thinks. He really doesn't know what kale is. "So how is Caitlin?"

"I dunno, what time is it?" Sheila says. She focuses on laying out her counter as she adds, "She might be by here later, depending on when they get up."

"That would be nice."

"Yeah, depending on when they get up."

Malone feels lost for conversation but doesn't think he should walk away yet. "Everything good with the house?"

"Do you care, Denny?"

"Yeah, that was me who just asked." It takes nothing, freakin' nothing for them to get into a fight.

"You could have the guy come over and check the water heater," Sheila says. "It's making those funny noises again. I've called him like three times."

Goddamn Palumbo, he'll jack the wives around, like the noises are just in their heads. "I'll take care of that."

"Thank you."

It annoys her, though, he can tell, that she still needs the "husband" to get the attention she should get just being her. If I were a woman, Malone thinks, I'd probably be out there with a machine gun, spraying the streets and screaming.

"Sheila, you got any lids?"

She tosses him one.

After a suitable silence, Malone wanders off to the bleachers across the fence from the first-base line. A few parents are already seated, some of the women with blankets over their laps. A few of them have thermoses and doughnut boxes from Dunkin'. The fuck, Malone thinks, they can't spend a buck at the stand, support the kids?

He knows most of the parents, nods hellos, but sits by himself.

He used to be at PTA meetings and talent shows and shit with these people. Pizza Hut after games, backyard barbecues, pool parties. He still goes to the school events but isn't invited to the extracurriculars. I guess I tore up my suburban dad card, Malone thinks, or they did. It's not like they're hostile or anything, it's just different.

They're playing the national anthem from a tape. Malone stands up, puts his hand over his heart and looks out at John in line with his teammates.

I'm sorry, John.

Maybe someday you'll understand.

Your fucked-up father.

The game starts. John's team is the home team so they start in the field and Malone watches John trot out to left. He's big for his age so they put him in the outfield. Profiling, Malone thinks. Actually, he's got a pretty good glove, but not a lot of bat. Will swing at anything, and the opposing pitchers know it so they throw him garbage. But Malone ain't gonna be one of those jerk-off dads who screams at his kid from the stands. The fuck difference does it make? No one here is going to the Yankees.

Russo sits down next to him. "You look like shit."

"That good?"

"We went to Levin's last night," Russo said. "Two in the morning, I thought the kid was going to piss his pants. The girlfriend wasn't too thrilled either."

"And?"

"Money was in a suitcase in the back of the closet," Russo says. "I told him, kid, you have to do better than that."

"So he checked out," Malone says.

"I wouldn't go that far," Russo says. "Maybe they have him playing a longer game. Maybe they're after the Pena rip. Denny, we have to move that shit."

"I did," Malone says. "You're a million and change richer than you were last night."

"Jesus. On your own?" Russo don't like that.

Malone tells him about selling the smack to Savino, and about Carlos Castillo and the Dominicans.

"You sold them back their own smack?" Russo asks. "Denny freaking Malone."

"It ain't over," Malone says. "This Castillo wants to get us back for Pena."

"Shit, Denny, half North Manhattan wants to whack us," Russo says. "This is no different."

"I dunno. The Ciminos, the Domos . . ."

"We have to have a talk with Lou," Russo says. "That's not right, springing them on you like that."

"I'll handle it."

"The fuck, you the Lone Ranger lately?" Russo asks. "I feel like you're keeping me out of things."

A kid hits a ball to deep left and they watch as John tracks it down, snags it and holds it up for the umpire to see.

"Way to be, John!" Malone yells.

They're quiet for a while, then Russo asks, "You okay, Denny?"

"Yeah. Why?"

"I don't know," Russo says. "If there was something bothering you, you'd tell me, right?"

The words are there but they're caught in his throat.

Everything changes at that moment.

His old priests might have told him that there are sins of commission and sins of omission, that it's not always the things you do, but the things you don't that cost you your soul. That sometimes it's not the spoken lie but the unspoken truth that opens the door to betrayal.

"What do you mean?" Malone feels like shit. This is the one guy he should be able to talk to, to tell. But he can't do it. Can't bring himself to tell Russo that he's become a rat. Unless Phil is trying to feel him out; maybe he's starting to believe what Gloria Torres said.

Because it's true.

Trust your partner, Malone tells himself.

You can always trust your partner.

Yeah, but can Russo?

Some motion in the parking lot catches Malone's attention. He glances over and sees Caitlin get out of a Honda CR-V. She leans back in to wave good-bye, and then Malone watches her walk to the concession stand, get up on her toes and kiss her mom on the cheek.

Russo notices, but Russo notices everything. "You miss that?"

"Every damn day."

"There's a fix for that, you know."

"Jesus, you too?" Malone asks.

"I'm just saying."

"It's too late," Malone says. "Anyway, I don't want it."

"Bullshit, you don't," Russo says. "Look, you can still do what you want on the side, but keep the center the center."

"Bless me, Father, for I have sinned."

"*Va fangul.*"

"Watch your language, my kid's coming over."

Caitlin climbs up the bleachers. Malone reaches his hand down to steady her and pull her up. She snuggles up against him. "Hi, Daddy."

"Hi, sweetheart." Malone kisses her on the cheek. "Say hi to your uncle Phil."

"Hi, Uncle Phil."

"Is that Caitlin?" Russo asks. "I thought it was Ariana Grande."

Caitlin smiles.

"What's new, honey?" Malone asks.

"I had a sleepover. At Jordan's."

"Did you have fun?"

"Yes."

She jabbers on about all the fun little-girl stuff they did and then asks when he's coming to visit them again and when can they come stay with him and then she sees a couple of friends down by the fence in back of home plate and Malone says, "It's okay, Cait. You can go be with your friends."

"But you'll say good-bye, right?"

"Of course."

He watches her go to her friends, then picks up his phone and finds Palumbo on the speed dial.

"Let me speak to Joe, please," Malone asks.

"He's on a call."

"He's in the men's room jerking off," Malone says. "Put him on the phone."

Palumbo gets on. "Hey, Denny!"

"'Hey, Denny,' my ass," Malone says. "The fuck, Joe? My wife has to call you three times, you still don't show up? What's that?"

"I've been busy."

"Is that right?" Malone asks. "So maybe next time you get a truck impounded for fistfuls of tickets, *I'm* busy."

"Denny, how can I make this right?"

"When my wife calls, you get over there." He clicks off. "Fuckin' mook."

"Do you love how when these guys *do* show up," Russo says, "they never got the right tools? Whole truck in your driveway, they ain't got the one tool they need to do the job. Donna, she don't play. One time she told Palumbo, 'I'd give you your check, but I don't have the right pen.' He got the message."

"Yeah, that ain't Sheila."

"Italian women," Russo says. "You want money from them, you get the job done."

"We still talking plumbing here?"

"Sort of."

"How are your kids?"

"The two boys are assholes," Russo says.

"Anyway, you got their college taken care of now."

"Pretty much."

"So, that's good, huh?" Malone asks.

"You kiddin' me?"

They know what they've done and why.

If I go down, Malone thinks, my kids can feel bad about their criminal father, but they'll feel bad from college.

But I ain't goin' down.

The game goes on for what feels like forever. A real low-scoring defensive battle, Malone thinks sarcastically, like 15–13, and John's team wins. Malone goes down to talk to him. "You played good."

"I struck out."

"You struck out swinging," Malone says. "Which is the important thing. And how many outs did you make in the field? Those are as good as runs, John."

His kid smiles at him. "Thanks for coming."

"Are you kidding?" Malone asks. "I wouldn't miss it. The team going to Pizza Hut?"

"Pinkberry," John says. "It's healthier."

"Well, I guess that's good."

"I guess so," John says. "You want to come?"

"I gotta get back to the city."

"Catch the bad guys."

"There you go."

Malone hugs him but doesn't kiss him so as not to embarrass him. He says good-bye to Caitlin and then goes over to Sheila. "You didn't come sit."

"Marjorie never showed," Sheila says. "Probably too hungover."

Russo's waiting for him in the parking lot. "Do we need to talk some more?"

"About what?"

"You," Russo says. "I'm not an idiot. You haven't been yourself lately . . . distracted . . . a real moody fuck. You been off the radar odd times. Couple that with this stuff behind Torres offing himself . . ."

"You got something you want to say, Phil?"

"You got something *you* want to say, Denny?"

"Like what?"

"Like it's true," Russo says. He's quiet for a minute, then he says, "Look, maybe you got jammed up. It happens. Maybe you saw a way out. I can understand that, you got a wife, kids . . ."

Malone's heart hurts.

Cracking like a stone in fire.

"It wasn't me," Malone says.

"Okay."

"It wasn't me."

"Yeah, I heard you."

But he looks at him like he don't know if he believes him. But he says, "Thanks, huh? For handling that thing."

"Go fuck yourself."

On Staten Island, it's an expression of affection.

CHAPTER 23

L ate on a Saturday afternoon, Malone has a pretty good idea where to find Lou Savino.

The old Italian coffee shops where Lou would like to hang out on the sidewalk sipping espresso like Tony Soprano don't exist anymore, so Savino likes to go into Starbucks, get an espresso and sit outside in the little fenced-in patio off 117th Street.

It's pathetic, Malone thinks. There's Lou sitting out there in his dumbass tracksuit with one of his soldiers, an unmade wannabe named Mike Sciollo, holding forth and checking out the ass strolling by.

Don't underestimate him, though, Malone tells himself. You did that last night and it could have gotten you killed. Lou Savino didn't become a capo by being stupid. He's a smart, ruthless motherfucker, Malone thinks as he goes in.

Even smart ruthless motherfuckers have to piss. Savino lives all the way up in Yonkers, so he's going to use the john before he gets back in the car. Sure enough, Malone sees Lou get up and come inside and times his approach just as Savino steps into the john and starts to close the door.

Malone sticks his foot inside, pushes it open and shuts it behind him.

"Denny," Savino says, "I was going to give you a call."

It's tight in there, close.

"You were going to give me a call?" Malone asks. "Did you think about maybe giving me a freakin' call *before* you turned me over to Castillo?"

"It was business, Denny."

"Don't give me that Sollozzo bullshit," Malone says. "You and I have business, too. You should have told me, Lou. You gave me your word you'd take that smack away from my turf."

"You're right. You are," Savino says. "But *you* were wrong, doing Pena like that. You know that, Denny. You should have let him walk away."

"Where do I find Castillo?"

"You don't want to find him," Savino says. "He wants to cut off your fucking head."

"I'm going to shrink his and put it in my pocket," Malone says, "so his smart mouth is always sucking my balls. Where is he, Lou?"

Savino laughs. "What are you going to do? Pistol-whip me like I'm one of your moolies? Come *on*."

Savino looks over Malone's shoulder, like he's expecting Sciollo to bang on the door, ask if he's okay. "We're hearing things about you. Some people are very concerned."

Malone knows "some people" means Stevie Bruno. And he's "concerned" that I'm a rat because I have a lot to give up on the Cimino *borgata*.

"Tell those people they got nothing to worry about," Malone says.

"I vouched for you," Savino says. "I'm responsible for what you do. They'll kill me, too. I've been invited to a sit-down, you know what that means."

"I wouldn't go if I were you."

"Yeah, well, you've been invited too, asshole," Savino says. "Half past twelve tomorrow. La Luna. Attendance is not optional. Come alone."

"And get a bullet in the back of the head?" Or something worse, Malone thinks. A knife in the spine, a wire around the throat, my dick stuffed in my mouth. "Pass."

"Look," Savino says, "I'll vouch for you if you keep me covered on the heroin."

"You didn't tell Bruno about that?"

"It must have slipped my mind," Savino says. "The greedy fuck would want twenty points. You and me, we take each other's backs, we can both walk out of this meeting, Denny."

"Yeah, okay."

"See you tomorrow."

Sciollo knocks on the door. "What, Lou, you drown in there?"

"Get the fuck outta here!" He looks at Malone. "You think you can take on the whole world?"

Yeah, I do, Malone thinks.

The whole fucking world, it comes to that.

He's driving back downtown, all of a sudden he feels like he can't breathe.

Like the car is closing in on him.

Fuck, like the whole world is closing in on him—Castillo and the Dominicans, the Ciminos, the feds, IAB, the Job, the mayor's office, God only knows who else. He feels this tightening in his chest and wonders if he's having a heart attack. He pulls the car over, reaches into the glove compartment, takes out a Xanax and pops it down.

This ain't you, he thinks.

A fucking, what, a *panic attack*?

It ain't you.

You're Denny freakin' Malone.

Malone puts the car back in drive and heads down Broadway. But he knows there are eyes on him. From the sidewalks, the windows, the buildings, the cars. Eyes in black faces, brown faces. Old eyes, young eyes, sad eyes, angry eyes, accusing eyes, junkie eyes, skel eyes, the eyes of children.

There are eyes on him.

He drives to Claudette's.

She's high.

Not neck-drooping, head-lolling high, but grooving to the music high. Cécile McLorin Salvant, someone like that. Claudette opens the door and dances away from it, waving him in with her fingers.

Smiling like the world is a bowl of cream.

"Come on, baby, don't be a drag. Dance with me."

"You're high."

"You're right," Claudette says, turning around to look at him. "I'm high. You want to climb up here where I am, baby?"

"I'm good."

And it's never going to be any better, he thinks. She's never going to get any better. But you can't always be there and the smack can.

The smack you just put on the street.

She moves back across the room and wraps her arms around him. "C'mon, baby, I want you to dance with me. Don't you want to dance with me?"

The trouble is he does.

He starts to sway with her.

She feels warm against him.

He could stay like this forever but they don't dance for long because the heroin starts to take hold and she starts to nod. But as she does, she murmurs, "You didn't answer when I called."

There's that old saying about being "crazy about" someone. And I am, he thinks, I'm crazy about this woman. It's crazy to love her, crazy to stay with her, but I do and I will.

Crazy love.

He carries her to bed.

CHAPTER 24

Sunday comes like it always does for Malone, with a vague child-hood unease at not going to Mass.

Malone dozed more than slept, his waking thoughts about Claudette.

Now he makes two coffees, goes back into the bedroom and wakes her up. She opens her eyes and he sees it takes a second or two for her to recognize him. "Good morning, baby."

Claudette smiles.

A tranquil, Sunday-morning we-can-lay-around-in-bed smile.

He says, "Last night—"

"Was beautiful, baby," she says. "Thank you again."

She doesn't remember a fucking thing. She will, he thinks, when she really comes to and the jones start to kick in.

He should stay with her, he knows it.

But—

"I have to go to work," he says.

"It's Sunday."

"So go back to sleep."

"I think I will," she says.

La Luna is old school, Malone thinks.

Kind of place Savino sees in his wet dreams. All the way down in the Village, they want me away from my turf.

And the Ciminos have a crew down here.

What he should have done was call Russo, maybe Monty, too. Have them back him up.

Except the meeting is about him being a rat.

Maybe O'Dell.

That's what he should have done, but he decided fuck that.

Sciollo meets him at the door. "I have to pat you down, Denny."

"There's a nine at my waist," Malone says. "A Beretta at my back."

"Thanks." Sciollo takes the weapons from him. "I'll give them back on your way out."

Yeah, Malone thinks. If I'm coming out.

Sciollo pats him down for a wire. Doesn't find one and takes him to a booth in the back. The place is almost empty, a few guys at the bar, one couple making out.

Savino sits in a booth with Stevie Bruno, who looks out of place in his all-L.L.Bean wardrobe—checked shirt, vest, tan corduroy slacks and Dockers. He even has a canvas man-bag on the seat beside him. He don't look happy behind his cup of tea, the suburban god-father forced to come into the dirty city.

He has four guys with him, within sight and out of earshot.

Bruno nods to Malone to sit down in the booth. Malone does and Sciollo sits in a chair near the edge of the booth.

They have him blocked in.

"Denny Malone, Stevie Bruno," Savino says. He has this nervous, edgy smile on his face.

"The couple starting a family at the bar," Malone says. "Which one's the hitter, the boy or the girl?"

"You seen too many movies," Bruno says.

"I just want to see a few more."

"You want a drink, Denny?" Savino asks.

"No thanks."

"First for an Irish guy," Savino says. "I never seen it before."

"You bring me down here to do jokes?"

"It's no joke," Bruno says. "Word all over is you're a CW for the feds."

Wiseguys don't mind cops so much but they hate feds, viewing them as fascists and persecutors who pick on anyone with a vowel at the end of his name. They particularly hate Italian feds and rats who inform for the feds.

Malone knows the distinction—an undercover cop playing a role isn't a rat. A dirty cop who's been in business with them and then flips is.

"You believe that?" he asks.

"I don't want to believe it," Savino says. "Tell us it isn't true."

"It isn't true."

"The dying words of a man to his wife," Bruno says. "I tend to believe that."

"The feds had *both* me and Torres up," Malone says. "I don't know how. I can only tell you I wasn't wearing a wire."

"Then why did they bring Torres in and not you?" Bruno asks.

"I don't know."

"That's even worse."

"Torres didn't know about my relationship with your family," Malone says. "I never discussed it with him, so you can't be on any tape they have of me and him."

"But if the feds bring you in," Bruno says, "they'll flip you about everything."

Savino looks at Malone anxiously. Malone knows what he's thinking, what he don't want him to say: *If I was a CW for the feds, Savino here would have already been busted on a thirty-to-life heroin beef and he'd be trading up for you as we speak.*

Instead Malone says, "How much money have I made for the Cimino *borgata*? How many bags of cash have I taken to prosecutors, judges, city officials for contract bids? Over how many years with no problems?"

"I don't know," Bruno says. "I was in Lewisburg."

Jesus fuck, Savino, say something.

But Savino don't.

Malone says, "Fifteen years don't mean anything?"

"It means a lot," Bruno says. "But I don't know you at all, because I was away most of that time."

Malone stares at Savino, who finally says, "He's good people, Stevie."

"You'd bet your life on that?" Bruno asks, giving Savino the death stare. "Because that's what you're doing."

Savino takes a second to answer.

It's a long goddamn second.

"I would, Stevie," he says. "I vouch for him."

Bruno takes this in and then asks, "What are you going to tell the feds?"

"Nothing."

"You can do four to eight?"

"It'll be closer to four," Malone says. "Your guys will keep the brothers from making me their bitch, right?"

"Stand-up guys," Bruno says, "don't get bent over."

"I'm a stand-up guy," Malone says.

"Here's the problem," Bruno says. "You're looking at four, but I get popped for as much as littering, I die in the joint. So the big question for me right now is, can I take the risk? If you're a rat, tell the truth now, we'll make it quick and painless, I'll make sure your wife gets her envelope. Otherwise . . . if I have to drag the truth out of you . . . it's going to be ugly, and your missus is on her own."

Malone feels anger rising inside him like boiling water and he can't turn the flame off under it. And he knows they're testing him, giving him the out just like a pair of cops in the room would do.

Any sign of weakness, he's dead.

So he goes the other way with it.

"Never threaten me," Malone says. "Never threaten my money. Never threaten my wife."

"Take it easy, Denny," Savino says.

Bruno says, "We just want the truth."

"I told you the truth," Malone says.

"Okay," Bruno says. He reaches into his man-bag and comes out with a stack of paper and lays it on the table. "What's the truth about *this,* stand-up guy?"

Malone sees his 302.

He grabs Sciollo by the hair, slams his face into the table and kicks the chair out from under him. Then Malone reaches into his boot, comes out with the SOG knife, grabs Savino by the head and puts the blade to his neck.

Two guys, one of them the guy who was kissing the girl, pull guns.

"I'll cut his guinea throat," Malone says.

"Get out of his way," Savino groans.

They look to Bruno, who nods.

He'd do a clean hit in the place, but he ain't gonna allow a bloodbath that ends up on the front page of the *Post.*

Malone drags Savino out of the booth and backs toward the door, holding Savino as a shield, the blade along his throat. He says to Bruno, "You want me to go O.J. on him, threaten my wife again. Go on, open your mouth to me about her again."

"He's a dead man anyway," Bruno says. "So are you. Enjoy your last day on earth, rat motherfucker."

Malone reaches backward for the door handle, pushes Savino down and goes out the door.

Trots to his car down the block.

"He had my 302!" Malone yells.

"All right," O'Dell says. But he's shook.

"'It's *secure,*' you told me," Malone yells, pacing around the room. "In a safe . . . only the people in this room—"

"Settle down," Paz says. "You're alive."

"No thanks to you!" Malone says. "They have my 302! They have proof! You're so busy trying to hurt dirty cops, and you don't see them in your own operation!"

"We don't know that," O'Dell says.

"Then how did they get it?!" Malone says. "They didn't get it from me!"

"We have a problem," Weintraub says.

"No shit!" Malone punches the wall.

Weintraub is looking through the 302. "Where in here is anything about you and the Ciminos?"

"It isn't," Malone says.

"Full disclosure," Paz says. "That was our agreement."

Then it hits him. "God . . . Sheila . . ."

"We have agents on the way," O'Dell says.

"Fuck that," Malone says. "I'm going myself."

He starts for the door.

"Stay where you are," Paz says.

"You gonna fuckin' stop me?!"

"If I have to," Paz says. "There are two federal marshals in the hallway. You aren't going anywhere. Use your head. Stevie Bruno is not going to send someone out to Staten Island to do anything to your wife in the middle of the afternoon. He's trying to stay out of jail, not throw himself in it. We have some time here."

"I want to see my family."

"If you had told us about this," Paz says, "you'd have been wired in that meeting and we'd have Bruno behind bars now. All right, blood under the bridge, you're forgiven. But now you need to tell us—what did you do with the Ciminos?"

Malone doesn't answer. He sits down and puts his head in his hands.

"The only way," Paz says, "you can protect yourself and your family is to put Bruno away. Give me something I can get a warrant on."

"I never met with him before."

"Yes, you did," Paz says.

Malone looks up, sees in her eyes that she's perfectly willing—no, insistent—that he perjure himself.

O'Dell won't meet his gaze. He looks away.

Weintraub shuffles more papers.

"We'll put you and your family in the program," she says. "You come out to testify—"

"Fuck that."

"There is no choice here," Paz says. "You have no choice."

"Let me out of here," Malone says. "I'll take care of Bruno myself."

"You know what?" Paz says. "Bring the marshals in, cuff him. I'm done with this dumb donkey."

"What about my family?!" Malone asks.

"They're on their own!" Paz yells. "What do you think I am, Social Services?! *You* put your loved ones in jeopardy! It's on *you,* not me! Buy them a Rottweiler, an alarm system, I don't know."

"You fucking bitch," Malone says.

"Why aren't the marshals in here?" Paz asks.

Malone says, "You guys are dirtier than I ever thought of being."

It's quiet. There's no answer to that.

"Okay," Malone says. "Turn on the recorder."

He started with the mob the way that most cops who go there do, taking a slim envelope to look the other way on gambling shops.

Nothing big, a hundred here or there.

He knew Lou Savino when the capo was a street guy who just got his button. One day Savino approached him up in Harlem, asked him if he wanted to earn.

Yeah, Malone wanted to earn.

One of Savino's guys had a bullshit beef, shit, the guy was just protecting his sister, who this fucking dirtbag had beat up, but there was one fucking witness didn't understand that. Maybe Malone could get a look at the 5, get the witness's name and address, save the city the cost of a trial, everyone a lot of trouble.

No, Malone didn't want no part of a witness getting beat up, maybe killed.

Savino laughed. No one was talking about anything like that, come on. They're talking about sending the witness on a nice vacation, maybe even buying the guy a car.

A car? Malone asked. Must have been a hell of a beating.

No, it was just that Savino's guy was on parole, so the assault conviction puts him back upstate for ten years. You call that justice? That isn't justice. Shit, it makes you feel better about it, you can deliver the envelope yourself, make sure no one gets hurt. You take a taste for yourself, everyone comes out happy.

Malone was nervous about approaching the arresting officer but it turned out he had no reason to be. It was easy, a hundred to look at the 5, come back anytime. And the witness, he was delighted to drive down to Orlando, take the kids to Disneyworld. Win, win, win, everyone did come out happy except for the guy who got his jaw broke, but he had it coming anyway, hitting a woman.

Justice was served.

Malone served some more justice for the Ciminos, then Savino approached him about something else. He works in Harlem, right? Right. Knows the hood, knows the people. Sure. So he knows a *ditzune* preacher has a church on 137th and Lenox.

The Reverend Cornelius Hampton?

Everyone knew him.

He was leading a protest at a construction site for not hiring minority workers.

Savino handed Malone an envelope and asked him to bring it to Hampton. The reverend didn't want to be seen around no guineas.

This to stop the protest? Malone asked.

No, you dumb fucking mick, it's to keep the protest going. We got a double play here—the reverend starts a protest, shuts the site down. The contractor comes to us for protection. We take a share of the project, the protest ends.

We make, the reverend makes, the contractor makes.

So Malone went up to the church, found the reverend, who took the envelope like it was UPS.

Didn't say a word.

That time, the next time or the time after that.

"The Reverend Cornelius Hampton," Weintraub says now. "Human rights activist, man of the people."

"Did you meet with Steven Bruno about any of this?" Paz asks. "Did he ever approach you?"

"I believe he was in your custody at the time," Malone says.

"But your understanding was that Savino was working under his instructions," Paz says.

"Hearsay," says Weintraub.

"We're not in court, Counselor," Paz says.

"Yes," Malone says, "it was definitely my understanding that Savino was acting as an agent of Bruno's."

"Did Savino tell you that?"

"Yes. Several times."

Which we all know is a lie, Malone thinks.

But it's the lie they want to hear.

He goes on.

The next payoffs he made for the Ciminos were a couple of years later, after Bruno got out of Lewisburg.

Who are they, Malone wanted to know.

More laughs from Savino.

City officials—the kind who award contract bids.

"Shut the recorder off," Paz says.

Weintraub shuts it off.

"Did you say city officials?" Paz asks. "Did you mean City Hall?"

"The mayor's office," Malone says. "The comptroller's, the Office of Operations . . . You want to turn the tape back on, I'll repeat it."

He stares at her.

"This just came home for you, huh?" Malone asks. "Maybe this is something you don't want to know about."

"*I* want to know about it," O'Dell says.

"Shut up, John."

"Don't tell me to shut up," O'Dell says. "You have a credible witness here who says that city officials are on the Cimino family pad. Maybe Southern District doesn't want to know, but the bureau is very interested."

"Ditto," Weintraub says.

"'Ditto'?"

"You opened this door, Isobel," Weintraub says. "I have a right to walk through it."

"Be my guest," Paz says. She leans over, turns the recorder back on and looks at Malone, like *go ahead*. "Name names."

She's trapped, Malone knows.

He names names.

"Jesus Christ," Weintraub says. "To coin a phrase."

"Yeah," Malone says. "I built a lot of houses in Westchester. Nantucket cottages, vacations in the Bahamas . . ."

He looks at Paz.

They both know this is enough to bring down the administration, ruin careers and aspirations, including hers. But she's got no choice now, and she guts it out. "Who in the Cimino family did you meet with to arrange these payoffs?"

"Lou Savino," he says, staring at her. He waits a second, and then adds, "And Steven Bruno."

"You met with Mr. Bruno personally."

"On several occasions."

He makes up some likely dates and locations.

"Let's be clear," Paz says. "Are you saying that on several occasions, as noted, Steven Bruno gave you money and instructed you to deliver it to city officials for the purpose of rigging construction bids?"

"That's exactly what I'm saying."

"This is unbelievable," Weintraub says.

"Perhaps literally," Paz says.

She's a slick piece of shit, Malone thinks. She's trying to have it both ways, preserving her options until she figures out her play, sees how the chips fall.

Weintraub sees it, tries to pin her down. "Are you saying you don't find him credible?"

"I'm saying I don't know," Paz says. "Malone is a demonstrated liar."

"You really want to open *that* door?" Weintraub asks.

"I want to see my family," Malone says.

"Not yet," Paz says. "Is that it, Sergeant Malone? Obstructing justice? Bribing public officials?"

"That's it," Malone says.

I'm not going to tell you about the drug connection.

Or Pena.

Right now it's four to eight.

Pena's the death penalty.

Paz says, "You just confessed to a handful of felonies not included in our original agreement, which is now, of course, voided."

Malone can almost smell her brain burning, she's working so hard. He presses, "You going to arrest me or not?"

"Not now," she says. "Not *yet*. I want to confer with my colleagues."

"Confer," Malone says. "Maybe you can confer about the rat in your operation."

"It's not safe for you on the street," O'Dell says.

Malone laughs. "Now you worry about that? I've been shot, stabbed—I've been down a hundred stairways and alleys, through a thousand doors with God knows what on the other side, and *now* you're worried about me? After you just almost got me killed? Fuck you all."

He walks out.

"We whack them all now," Russo says. "Bruno, Savino, Sciollo, all the fucking Ciminos if we have to."

"We can't do that," Malone says.

They're in the co-op.

"It's out on the street already," Monty says. "Denny Malone had

an armed confrontation with three wiseguys in a known mob hang-
out. It's only a matter of time before IAB comes asking what you
were doing there."

"You don't think I fucking know that?"

Monty asks, "Why did they want to meet?"

"They heard Torres's bullshit," Malone said. "I guess they believed it, I dunno."

"Why didn't you call us for backup?" Russo asks.

"I thought I could handle it," Malone says. "I did handle it."

"If we had been there," Monty says, "there would have been no
confrontation. No noise on the street, no IAB. Then you go off the
radar for three hours. That, considered with what Torres's people
have been saying—"

"What are *you* saying, Monty?"

"Simply this," Monty says. "In less than sixty days now I'm
leaving the Job. I'm taking my family and leaving the city. And I
am not going to let anything, or anyone, get in the way of that.
So if there's something we need to take care of, Denny, then let's
take care of it."

Malone walks down to his car and gets in.

A wire loop comes over his neck.

The wire pulls back and tightens.

Reflexively, Malone grabs at the cord but it's too tight against his
throat and he can't rip it off or even dig his fingers in to create any
breathing space. He reaches for the gun he set on the passenger seat
but his hand can't grip the handle and then drops it.

Malone flings his elbows back, trying to strike his assailant, but
he can't twist enough to get any leverage. His lungs ache for air, he
feels himself blacking out, his legs start to kick out spasmodically,
what awareness he has left tells him he's dying and in his mind his
voice starts to chant a childhood prayer—

Oh my God, I am heartily sorry for having offended Thee.

And I detest all my sins . . .

He hears his throat croaking.

The pain is awful.

And I detest all my sins . . .

And I detest all my sins . . .

all my sins . . .

my sins . . .

sins . . .

And then he's dead and there is no blinding white light only darkness and there's no music just shouting and he sees Russo and wonders if Phil is dead, too; they say you see everyone you love in heaven but he doesn't see Liam or his dad only Russo grabbing him by the shoulder, grabbing him and throwing him onto the hard asphalt of the street and then he's coughing and gagging and spitting as Russo picks him up and walks him toward another car and then Malone is in the passenger seat with Russo behind the wheel where he belongs in this land of the living and not of the dead and the car pulls out.

"My car," Malone croaks.

"Monty has it," Russo says. "He's behind us."

"Where are we going?"

"Somewhere we can have a private chat with the backseat driver."

They go up the West Side Highway and pull off into Fort Washington Park, near the GW Bridge.

Malone gets out. His legs feel unsteady under him as he sees Monty drag the guy out of the car onto an island of grass between two branches of the Hudson River Greenway.

Staggering over, Malone looks down at him.

The guy is already beat up, half-conscious. His head looks like the butt of a .38 smashed into it—hair mixed with caked blood. He's maybe in his midthirties, black hair, olive skin. He could be Italian or Puerto Rican or, shit, Dominican.

Malone kicks him in the ribs. "Who are you?"

The guy shakes his head.

"Who sent you?" Malone asks.

Guy shakes his head again.

Monty grabs the guy's arm and lays his hand in the car door. "The man asked you a question."

He kicks the door shut.

The guy screams.

Monty opens the door and pulls him out.

The guy's fingers are shattered, pointing off in all directions, bones poking through the skin. He holds his wrist with his other hand and stares, then howls again and looks up at Monty.

"Now we do the other hand," Monty says. "Or you can tell us who you are and who sent you."

"*Los Trinitarios.*"

"Why?"

"I don't know," the guy says. "They just told me . . . be in the car . . . if you came out . . ."

"What?" Malone asks.

"Do you. Bring them your head. For Castillo."

Russo asks, "Where's Castillo now?"

"I don't know," the guy says. "I didn't meet with him. I just got orders."

"Put your other hand in the door," Monty says.

"Please . . ."

Monty pulls his .38 and points it at his head. "Put your other hand in the door."

Crying, the guy sets his hand in the door.

He's shaking from head to toe.

"Where's Castillo?" Monty asks.

"I have a family."

"I *don't?*" Malone asks. "Where is he?"

Monty starts to kick the door.

"Park Terrace! The penthouse!"

"What do we do with this guy?" Monty asks.

"The Hudson's right there," says Russo.

"No, please."

Russo leans over him. "You tried to kill a *New York police detective.*

Take his head off. What the fuck do you *think* we're going to do with you?"

The man whimpers, holds his hand. He curls into a fetal position, giving up, and starts to chant. "Baron Samedi . . ."

"What's he gibbering about?" Russo asks.

"He's praying to Baron Samedi," Monty says. "The god of death in Dominican voodoo."

"Good choice," Russo says, pulling his off-duty weapon. "Finish up. You need a chicken or something, you're SOL."

"No," Malone says.

"'No'?"

"We already have Pena on our score sheet," Malone says. "We don't need another homicide beef to worry about."

"He's right," Monty says. "It's not like our friend here is going to be handling any more garrotes."

"If we leave him alive," Russo says, "it sends the wrong message."

"I'm kind of losing my interest in messages," Malone says. He squats beside his would-be killer. "Go back to the DR. If I see you in New York again, I will kill you."

They get in the cars and drive up to Inwood.

Park Terrace Gardens is a castle.

The condo buildings sit on a hill near the tip of the peninsula that is the northern end of Manhattan, the far outer reaches of the Kingdom of Malone.

The peninsula is defined by the Hudson River to the west and Spuyten Duyvil Creek to the north and east, which separates Manhattan from the Bronx. Three bridges span the Spuyten Duyvil—a railway bridge that edges the river, then the Henry Hudson Bridge, and farther to the east, where the creek bends south, the Broadway Bridge.

"The Gardens," as the residents call it, is a complex of five eight-story gray stone buildings constructed in 1940, now all co-ops, set in a wooded block between West 215th and West 217th.

To the south is Northeastern Academy and the small Isham Park; to the west, the much larger Inwood Hill Park buffers the Gardens from Route 9 and the river. North of the Gardens, one residential block yields to public buildings—Columbia University's athletic complex, a soccer stadium and a branch of New York Presbyterian Hospital—between it and the creek.

The Muscota Marsh lies to the northwest.

The views from the top floors of the Gardens' units are spectacular—the Manhattan skyline, the Hudson, the oak slopes of Inwood Hill, the Broadway Bridge. You can see a long way.

You can see someone coming.

The team drives in two cars up Broadway, Inwood's central artery. A small side street runs west onto Park Terrace East and they take this north to 217th, pull over and look at the building where Castillo lives in the penthouse on the north side.

It just confirms what Malone already knew.

They can't get to Castillo here.

The heroin dealer, the man who ordered a New York detective to be decapitated, is protected not so much by the stone towers or the moat around them as by the law. This isn't a project, a tenement or a ghetto. It has a co-op board, a homeowners' association, its own website. Most of all, it has rich white people, so you can't just storm in there and haul Castillo out. The law-and-order residents of the Gardens would be on the phone to the mayor, the city council, the commissioner in five seconds, protesting "storm trooper" tactics.

They need a warrant to go in there, which they're not going to get.

And be honest, Malone tells himself, you can't go get a warrant because you're dirty. The last thing in the world you can do is arrest

Carlos Castillo and he knows it. So he can sit up in his castle and move his heroin and arrange to kill you.

Suck it up.

What's your play?

Sooner or later, Castillo is going to put the Dark Horse out on the street. He'll supervise it personally, that's his job.

When he does, you can take him there.

So what you have to be is patient.

Back off now, put Castillo under surveillance and wait for him to move. Contact Carter, give him Castillo's whereabouts.

Play the cards you have, don't worry about the ones you don't. A pair of jacks is as good as a straight flush if you know how to manage them. And you have better than jacks.

Russo has his binoculars out and is looking at the penthouse terrace.

"What are we looking at?" Levin asks. He's still pissy about the 2 A.M. roust at his place.

"Don't take it personal," Russo told him. "We had to check you out, see if you're clean."

"See if I'm dirty, you mean."

"The fuck did you just say?" Malone asked.

Levin was smart enough to keep his mouth shut about that. He just said, "Amy was pretty mad."

"She ask you about the money?" Russo asked.

"Sure."

"What did you tell her?" Monty asked.

"To mind her own business."

"Our boy is growing up," Russo said. "Now you *have* to marry her. So she can't testify."

"I'm giving that money to charity," Levin said.

Now Malone says to him, "This is Carlos Castillo's safe house. We're going to put it up."

"A wire?"

"Not yet," Malone says. "Right now just a visual."

"Hey," Russo says, handing Malone the binoculars.

Malone sees Castillo himself come out with a morning cup of coffee to enjoy the sunrise.

The king surveying his kingdom.

Not yet, Malone thinks.

It ain't your kingdom yet, motherfucker.

messed up," Claudette says.

Part of him hadn't even wanted to walk through the door, afraid of what he'd find.

But he decided he had to check up on her.

He owes her that.

And he loves her.

Now she's in that remorseful phase he's seen a hundred times. She's sorry (they both know she is), she won't do it again (they both know she will). But he's motherfucking exhausted. "Claudette, I can't do this right now, I'm sorry, but I just can't."

She sees the mark on his neck. "What happened to you?"

"Someone tried to kill me."

"That's not funny."

"Look, I need a shower. I need to clear my head."

He goes into the bathroom, strips and steps into the shower.

His body aches.

Malone scrubs his skin until it hurts. Can't scrub off the welt, can't scrub off the filth he feels on his skin, in his soul. His old man used to come home from the Job and step right into the shower— now he knows why.

The street stays with you.

It sinks into your pores and then your blood.

And your soul? Malone asks himself. You gonna blame that on the street, too?

Some of it, yeah.

You've been breathing corruption since you put on the shield, Malone thinks. Like you breathed in death that day in September. Corruption isn't just in the city's air, it's in its DNA, yours, too.

Yeah, blame it on the city, blame it on New York.

Blame it on the Job.

It's too easy, it stops you from asking yourself the hard question.

How did you get here?

Like anyplace else.

A step at a time.

Thought it was a joke when they warned you at the Academy about the slippery slope. *A cup of coffee, a sandwich, it leads to other things.* No, you thought, a cup of coffee was a cup of coffee and a sandwich was a sandwich. The deli owners were grateful for your service, appreciative of your presence.

What was the harm?

There wasn't really.

There still isn't.

Then there was 9/11.

Jesus, don't blame it on that. You haven't sunk so low you'd blame it on that, have you? A dead brother, twenty-seven dead brothers, a shattered mother, a broken heart, the stench of burned corpses, ashes and dust.

Don't blame it on that, ace.

You blame it on that you can never visit Liam's grave again.

Plainclothes is where it really started.

You and Russo walked into a stash house, the skels took off and there it is—money on the fucking floor. Not a lot, a couple of grand, but still, you had a mortgage, diapers, maybe you wanted to take your wife out someplace that had tablecloths.

Russo and you looked at each other and you scooped it up.

Never said anything about it.

But a line was crossed.

You didn't know there were other lines.

At first it was targets of opportunity—money left by fleeing dealers, cash or freebies offered by a madam in exchange for looking the other way or looking out, an envelope from a bookie. You didn't seek it—you didn't hunt, you gathered, but if it was there, you took.

Because what harm did it do? People are going to gamble, they're going to get laid.

And okay, maybe then you went to a burglary or a store break-in and maybe you took something the thief didn't. Nobody got hurt except the insurance company and they're bigger crooks than anybody.

You're in court all the time—you see how incompetence, inefficiency, and shit yes, corruption, turn loose guys you risked your life to put on trial. You watch them walk away and grin at you, grin in your face, and then one day a defense lawyer comes up to you outside the courthouse and says we work in the same system anyway, maybe we can make it work for both of us, and he gives you a card and says there's a taste in it for you if you send me referrals.

And why the hell not? The accused is going to get a lawyer anyway and everyone in the system is getting paid but you so why shouldn't you take a piece if it's offered? And then if he wants you to bring an envelope to a willing prosecutor to let a guy walk who's probably going to walk anyway—shit, you're just taking more of the dealer's money.

You took advantage of crimes, you didn't set crimes up to take advantage, and then . . .

It was a crack mill on 123rd off Adam Clayton Powell. You hit it by the book, a warrant and everything, and the dealer didn't run—he just sat there calmly and said, "Take it. I walk away and you walk away and we're both better off."

And now you're not talking one, two grand, you're talking fifty, you're talking serious money, the kind of money you put it away, it puts your kids through college. Like the dealer ain't going to get himself a Gerry Burger and walk anyway? Shit, at least you punished him, cost him some money, issued a fine—why should it go to the state instead of in your pocket, where it can do some good?

So you let him walk.

You don't feel good about it but you don't feel as bad as you thought you would because you got there step by step. Why should the lawyers make the money? The court system? The prisons?

You shortcut the whole process and issue justice on the spot.

What kings do.

But there was still a line you hadn't crossed. You didn't even realize you were walking toward it.

You told yourself you were different, but you knew you were lying. And you knew you were lying when you told yourself that was the last line you'd cross, because you knew it wasn't.

Used to be you'd cheat on the warrants to make righteous busts—take dope and criminals off the street. Then came the time when you cheated on the warrants to make busts so that you could make rips.

You knew you'd make the transition from scavenger to hunter.

You became a predator.

An out-and-out criminal.

Told yourself it was different because you were robbing drug dealers instead of banks.

Told yourself you'd never kill anyone to make a rip.

The last lie, the last line.

Because what the fuck were you supposed to do when you went into a mill and they wanted to slug it out? Let yourself get killed or gun them down. And then were you supposed to not take the money, not take the drugs, just because some dirtbags had been taken off the count?

You took money with blood literally on it.

And you took the dope.

And let them call you a hero cop.

And half believed it.

And now you're a drug dealer.

No different from the dirtbags you came on the Job to fight.

Now you're naked and you can't wash the mark of Judas off

your body or out of your soul and you know that Diego Pena wasn't drawing his gun to shoot you, you know that you flat-out murdered him.

You're a criminal.

A skel.

The shower door slides open and Claudette gets in. She stands under the water with him and traces her finger down the fading scar on his leg, then the livid scar across his throat.

"You're really hurt," she says.

"I'm indestructible," he says, wrapping his arms around her. The spray of the shower mingles with tears on her soft brown skin.

"Life is trying to kill us," she says.

Life, Malone thinks, is trying to kill everyone.

And it always succeeds.

Sometimes before you die.

He gets out of the shower and dresses. When she comes out, he says, "I can't come back here for a while."

"Because I'm using again?"

"No, that ain't it."

"You're going back to your wife, aren't you?" she says. "The red-headed Irish Staten Island mother of your children. No, that's good, baby, that's where you belong."

"I'll decide where I belong, 'Dette."

"I think you have."

"It's not safe for you to have me here," Malone says. "Some people are coming after me."

"I'm willing to risk it."

"I'm not." He clips the Sig Sauer at his hip.

The Beretta 8000D in an ankle holster.

A 9 mm Glock in a shoulder holster.

Then he slides an extra-large black T-shirt over all of it and slips the SOG knife into his boot.

Claudette stares at him. "Jesus Christ, who's coming after you?"

"The City of New York," Malone says.

CHAPTER 26

N ed Chandler lives on Barrow Street west of Bedford.

He opens the door a crack and sees the badge. Then he doesn't see anything because the door comes in and Denny Malone shoves him onto the sofa and sticks a gun into the side of his head.

"Mother*fucker,*" Malone says.

"What? What? Take it easy."

"Paz is the mayor's girl, right?" Malone asks. "Spearheading his charge against the Job?"

"If you want to put it that way," Chandler says. "Jesus, Malone, can you put the gun down?"

"No, I can't," Malone says. "Because people are trying to kill me. One hour after I tell Paz about payoffs to City Hall, someone wraps a wire around my throat. It was one of Castillo's people, but Castillo is partnered up with the Ciminos and the Ciminos are partnered up with City Hall—"

"I wouldn't say 'partnered'—"

"I delivered the fucking envelopes!" Malone says, shoving the barrel harder into Chandler's temple. "Who leaked my 302?"

"I don't know."

"You believe in God, Ned?"

"No. I don't know . . ."

"You don't know the answers, right?"

"Right."

"You want to learn all the answers," Malone says, "tell me you don't know again. Who leaked the 302?"

"Paz."

Malone takes the gun from Chandler's head. "Talk."

"We weren't tracking her investigation," Chandler says. "If you'd come to us earlier, Malone, we could have shut it down or at least redirected it. When we found out it was you, we knew it was going to be a . . . problem."

"A problem you thought the Ciminos would take care of for you."

Chandler doesn't answer. He doesn't need to.

"And when they missed," Malone says, "Castillo took a shot."

Chandler says, "That was on him. You killed someone in his family, right?"

"And you were all there to applaud when I did." But they don't know, Malone thinks. They don't know about the rip. They don't know their asshole buddies in the Cimino family handed fifty keys of smack to the Dominicans.

There's still a way out of this.

"You made the payoff allegations in front of the feds," Chandler says. "Not just Paz, but the FBI, Weintraub. You've put certain people in a very difficult position."

"Not if I'm dead and can't testify."

Chandler shrugs. It's true.

"Which certain people?" Malone asks. "Who's coming after me?"

"Everyone," Chandler says.

Right, Malone thinks—Castillo, the Ciminos, Torres's team, Sykes, IAB, the feds . . . City Hall.

Yeah, that's about everyone.

"It doesn't have to go down this way," Malone says. "I'll take care of Castillo. I'll deal with the Ciminos. You get me a sit-down with 'certain people.'"

"I don't know if I can do that," Chandler says. "No offense, Malone, but you're poison."

"Oh, I know you can do that," Malone says. "See, I have nothing to lose, Neddy, and I will put two right through your fucking head."

Chandler picks up the phone.

They call Fifty-Seventh Street "Billionaires' Row."

A doorman takes Malone up the private elevator to the penthouse at One57 and Bryce Anderson opens the door personally.

"Sergeant Malone," Anderson says, "please come in."

He ushers Malone into a living room with floor-to-ceiling windows, the view from which justifies the hundred-million-dollar price tag. All of Central Park stretches out beneath them, all of the West Side to the left, the East Side to the right. This is what rich people get to look at, Malone thinks, the city stretched out at their feet.

The entire back wall of the room is a saltwater aquarium with its own coral reef.

"Thanks for meeting me so early," Malone says.

"I don't like the sun to find me sleeping," Anderson says. He looks the part of a real estate mogul—tall, blond hair, hawk nose, piercing eyes. "Chandler indicated this wasn't exactly a social call. Would you like coffee?"

"No."

He stands by the window with dawn over New York as a backdrop.

It's deliberate.

He's showing Malone *his* kingdom.

"Should we 'pat each other down,' Sergeant," Anderson asks, "or can we do this like gentlemen?"

"I'm not wired."

"Neither am I," Anderson says. "So . . ."

"I delivered a lot of envelopes for the Cimino family," Malone says, "not a few of which found their way here."

"Maybe," Anderson says. "Listen, Detective, if I took envelopes, they were chump change. I took them to get things done, to get things built, and that was the way to do it. Look out there . . . that building . . . that building . . . that one. Do you know how many jobs that meant? How much business? Tourism? You're not naive, you know what it takes to rebuild a city. Do you want to go back to the bad old days? Unemployment? Crack vials like seashells under your feet?"

"I just want to survive."

"And what's that going to take, do you think?" Anderson says. "You still have a problem with at least two crime organizations that want you dead. You seem to make enemies, Malone, like Lay's makes chips."

"Comes with the Job," Malone says. "I can take care of the narcos and the wiseguys. The federal government's too big for me. So is City Hall. When they're lined up together . . . You're going after the commissioner and the Job. I'm just one cop."

"You're one cop who got in the way," Anderson says. "And now you've put City Hall and other very powerful people, including me, in the crosshairs."

"You don't need to be."

"How so?"

"Shutting down a federal investigation," Malone says, "would be a lot easier than killing me."

"Apparently," Anderson says. "And if that investigation were to be shut down, would the people who rebuilt this city have a reason to worry about you?"

"You think I give a shit," Malone says, "who lines their pockets downtown? Who's going to be mayor, who's going to be governor? You're all the same cat to me."

"All cats are gray in the dark?" Anderson asks. "But why should we trust you, Malone?"

"How's your daughter?"

"What does that mean?" Anderson asks. But he's a smart man, and it comes to him quickly. "Of course, that was you. She's doing well now, thank you. And I mean, literally, thanks to you. She's back at Bennington. Dean's list."

"I'm glad to hear it."

"So this is blackmail," Anderson says. "You have a copy of her sex tape and you'll release it unless I get the investigation shut down?"

"I'm not you," Malone says. "I never even looked at the tape, much less kept a copy. Maybe that's why I don't have a place like this. Maybe that's why I'm just a working donkey in the city you rebuilt. There's no blackmail—you're smart enough to do the smart thing. But I'm telling you—if anyone comes after me, my family, my partners, I will come back and the next time I will kill you."

Malone walks over to the window. "It is a beautiful fucking city, isn't it? I used to love it like my life."

Isobel Paz takes her early-morning jog in Central Park up by the reservoir.

Malone falls in behind her.

Her hair is tied back in a long ponytail.

"Isobel," Malone says, "I don't suppose you've ever been shot in the back. Neither have I, but I've seen it a few times and it isn't pretty. Looks like it hurts, too. A lot. So if you turn around, or yell for help, or do anything, I'm going to put one in your kidney. Do you believe me?"

"Yes."

"You leaked my 302 to the Ciminos," Malone says. "Don't bother to deny it, I already know it, I don't even much care anymore."

"So now you're going to kill me?" She's trying to sound tough, but she's scared, her voice is quivering.

"Only a few lunch bucket lawyers and cops get it in the neck, right?" Malone says. "The trust fund babies get a walk. A cop takes a bribe, he's a criminal; a city official does it and it's just business as usual."

"What do you want?"

"I already got what I want," Malone says. "The guy with the

view of the park agreed to it. I just came to tell you how it's going to work. I walk. All charges. No jail time. I resign from the force, I go away."

"We can't put you in the program unless you testify," Paz says.

"I don't want the program," Malone says. "I can take care of myself, my family."

"How?"

Malone says, "You don't need to worry about how. You're right—it isn't your problem."

"What else?"

"My partners," Malone says, "keep their jobs, their badges, their pensions."

"Are you telling me that your partners are complicit?" Paz asks.

"I'm telling you that if you try to hurt them," Malone says, "I'll pull this whole city down on top of you. But I don't see certain people letting that happen."

Paz stops running and turns to look at him. "I underestimated you."

"Yeah, you did," Malone says. "But no hard feelings."

He peels off and goes to kill Lou Savino.

Savino's car isn't in his driveway up in Scarsdale.

Malone watches the house for a few minutes, then drives back to the city, to Savino's *gumar*'s apartment on 113th, a second-floor walk-up.

Putting his 9 mm behind his back, Malone rings the bell.

He hears footsteps inside, then a woman's voice saying, "Lou, what, did you lose your key again?"

Malone holds his badge up to the peephole. "Ms. Grinelli? NYPD. I'd like to talk with you."

She opens the door a chain width. "Is it Lou? Is he okay?"

"When did you last see him?"

"Oh my God." Then she remembers who she is, where she lives. "I don't talk to cops."

"Is he inside, Ms. Grinelli?"

"No."

"May I come in and look?" Malone asks.

"Do you have a warrant?"

He kicks the door open and goes in. Savino's *gumar* holds her face. "I'm bleeding, you asshole!"

His gun ready, Malone walks through the living room, then checks the bathroom and the bedroom, the bedroom closet, the kitchen. The bedroom window is closed. He walks back into the living room.

"When did you last see Lou?" Malone asks.

"Fuck you."

Malone sticks the gun in her face. "I'm not playing with you. When did you last see him?"

She's trembling. "Couple of days ago. He came over for a booty call and left. He was supposed to come over last night but he didn't show. Didn't even call, the asshole. Now this. Please . . . don't shoot me . . . please . . ."

Mike Sciollo is just getting home.

He's taking the keys out of his jeans pocket and opening the door to his building when Malone hits him in the back of the head with the pistol butt and pushes him inside, into the little foyer.

Malone shoves him against the mailboxes and sticks the pistol barrel behind his ear. "Where's your boss?"

"I don't know."

"Say good night, Mike."

"I haven't seen him!"

"Since when?"

"This morning," Sciollo says. "We had coffee, checked in, I haven't seen him since."

"You call him?"

"He don't pick up."

"You tellin' me the truth, Mike?" Malone asks. "Or are you helping Lou fly under the radar? If you're lying to me, your neighbors are going to find pieces of you on their electric bills."

"I don't know where he is."

"Then what are you still doing out on the street?" Malone asks. "If Bruno had Lou whacked, you're next on the endangered species list."

"I was just picking up a few things," Sciollo says. "Then I'm headed out."

"I fucking see you again, Mikey," Malone says, "I'm going to assume hostile intent and act accordingly. *Capisce?*"

He shoves Sciollo into the wall and walks back to his car.

Lou Savino ain't comin' back, Malone thinks as he drives uptown. Savino is in the river, or a landfill. They'll find his car out at Kennedy as if he took off somewhere, but he never left New York and never will.

Bruno will bury the 302.

Paz will bury the rest.

Anderson will see to it.

I'll take care of Castillo.

He goes home to get some sleep.

It's over.

You beat them.

CHAPTER 27

He's sound asleep when the door comes in.

Hands push his face against the wall.

More hands take his weapons.

His arms are twisted behind him, his wrists cuffed.

"You're under arrest," O'Dell says. "Malfeasance of duty, bribery, extortion, obstruction of justice—"

He's confused, disoriented. "You got this wrong, O'Dell! Talk to Paz."

"She's not in charge anymore," O'Dell says. "In fact, she's under indictment. So is Anderson. It was a nice play, Malone. Nice try. You're also under arrest for possession of narcotics with intent to sell, conspiracy to sell and/or distribute narcotics, and armed robbery."

"The fuck you talking about?" Malone asks.

O'Dell grabs him and turns him around.

"Savino turned himself in, Denny," O'Dell says. "He flipped. He told us all about Pena, about the smack you ripped and sold to him."

"I want a lawyer," Malone says.

"We'll even call him for you," O'Dell says. "What's his name?"

"Gerard Berger," Malone says.

Maybe there is a God, Malone thinks.

And maybe there's a hell.

But there's sure as shit no Easter Bunny.

PART 3

FOURTH OF JULY, THE FIRE THIS TIME

But I will send a fire on the wall of Tyrus, which shall devour the palaces thereof.

—AMOS 1:10

Let freedom ring, let the white dove sing,
Let the whole world know that today
Is a day of reckoning.

—GRETCHEN PETERS, "INDEPENDENCE DAY"

erard Berger interlocks his fingers, lays his hands on the table and says, "Of all the many thousands of phone calls that might have awoken me from sleep this morning, I must say that the last I expected was from you."

They're sitting in an interview room at the FBI offices at 26 Federal Plaza.

"So why did you come?" Malone asks.

"Given the source, I'll accept that as an expression of gratitude," Berger says. "And to answer the question, I suppose that I was intrigued. Not surprised, mind you; I knew that your more unfortunate dispositions would eventually land you in deep, scalding water, but I *am* surprised that it was me you would call to throw you a life preserver."

"I need the best," Malone says.

"My God, what it must have cost you to say that," Berger says, smiling. "Which brings up our first and most important topic of substance—do you have the funds to pay my fees? That is a threshold question—without a satisfactory answer we do not walk through the door together."

"How much do you charge?" Malone asks.

"A thousand dollars an hour," Berger says.

A thousand an hour, Malone thinks. An average patrol officer makes thirty.

"If you can let me walk out of here today," Malone says, "I can get your first fifty hours in cash."

"And after that?"

"I can buy another two hundred," Malone says.

"It's a start," Berger says. "You have a house, a car, perhaps a story sufficiently interesting to attract a book or film purchase. All right, Sergeant Malone, you have a lawyer."

"You want me to tell you what I did?" Malone asks.

"Oh my God, no," Berger says. "I have no interest at all in what you did. It's totally irrelevant. All that matters is what they can *prove* that you did, or think they can, anyway. What are the charges?"

Malone lays out what O'Dell told him—a slew of corruption charges, multiple counts of perjury and now grand theft and narcotics trafficking.

"This is in regard to the Diego Pena matter?"

"Is that a conflict for you?"

"Not at all," Berger says. "Mr. Pena is no longer my client. In fact, he's dead, as you know."

"You think I killed him."

"You did kill him," Berger says. "The issue is whether you *murdered* him, and it doesn't matter what I think. It doesn't matter if you *did* murder him, and I'm not asking if you did, by the way, so please shut your mouth. So far, they're not charging you with homicide. In fact, they haven't charged you with anything, they've simply arrested you. So shall we invite these fellows in and see what they do have?"

O'Dell comes in with Weintraub and they sit down.

"I thought you were a decent man," Weintraub says to Malone. "A good cop who got caught up in something and didn't know how to get out. Now I know you're just another drug dealer."

"If you've now gotten your personal disappointments and the excoriation of my client off your chest," Berger says, "may we proceed to substantive matters?"

"Sure," O'Dell says. "Your client sold fifty kilos of heroin to Carlos Castillo."

"And you know this how?"

THE FORCE / 367

"A confidential witness," Weintraub says. "Louis Savino."

"Lou Savino?" Berger says. "The convicted felon, known Mafi-oso, *that* Lou Savino?"

"We believe him," O'Dell says.

"Who cares what you believe?" Berger asks. "It only matters what a jury will believe, and when I get Savino on the stand and cross-examine him about his past and the deal that you will have doubtless offered him to testify, I would say that it's at least an even bet that the jury will not believe the word of a mobster against that of a hero police detective.

"If all you have is some fantastic tale spun to you by a drug dealer looking to avoid life in prison and whose multiple mug shots I will make wallpaper of in the courtroom, I suggest you release my client immediately, and with an apology."

Weintraub leans over, presses a button on a tape player and Malone hears Savino say, *"You let me worry about me. What do you want for it?"*

"A hundred grand a kilo," Malone says.

Weintraub pauses the tape and looks at Berger. "I believe that's your client."

He hits the tape again.

"What the fuck world you live in?" Savino asks. *"I can get smack for sixty-five, seventy."*

"Not Dark Horse," Malone says. *"Not sixty percent pure. The market price is a hundred."*

"That's if you can go straight to the retailer. Which you can't. Which is why you called me. I can go seventy-five."

"Let's fast-forward, shall we?" Weintraub says.

Malone hears himself say, *"We got* Shark Tank *going on here. Okay, Mister Wonderful, we'll do ninety a kilo."*

"You just want me to bend over a headstone here, you can fuck me in the ass? Maybe I could go eighty."

"Eighty-seven."

"The fuck, are we Jews?" Savino says. *"Can we do this like gentlemen,*

say eighty-five? Eighty-five thousand a kilo times fifty. Four million, two hundred fifty thousand dollars. That's a lot of chocolate-glazed."

The motherfucker was wired, laying pipe the whole time, maybe even since Christmas Eve when he was bitching about his bosses, how thin his envelope was. He was digging an escape tunnel in case he needed it.

Then he hears himself say, *"Another thing, you don't put this out in Manhattan North. Take it upstate, New England, just not here."*

Weintraub stops the tape. "Was that your attempt at civic virtue, Malone? Are we expected to be grateful?"

He hits the tape.

"You're a piece of work. You don't care there are addicts, just as long as they're not your addicts."

"Yes or no?"

"Deal."

"It's inadmissible," Berger says, sounding bored.

"That's debatable," Weintraub says. He looks at Malone. "Do you want to bet your life on a Mapp hearing?"

"Don't answer that," Berger says. He smiles at Weintraub and O'Dell. "What I heard, and what I believe a jury will hear, is a police detective setting up an undercover drug sale to a mobster."

"Really?" O'Dell asks. "If that were the case, Malone would have been wearing a wire. Where is the copy of that tape? Where is the warrant? Where is the approval from his supervisors? Will you be able to produce any of that?"

"It's well established that Sergeant Malone is something of a maverick," Berger says. "A jury will conclude that this was just another example of his going off on his own."

Weintraub smirks and Malone knows why.

If Savino taped the meeting at St. John's, he also taped the actual sale. Sure enough, Weintraub inserts another micro-disc into the machine and sits back. On the tape, Carlos Castillo says, *"What, do you think we didn't know how many kilos were in that room? How much money?"*

"What do you want?"

"Diego Pena was my cousin."

"Murder a New York Police Department detective in New York City? The world will come down on your head."

"We're the cartel."

"No, we're the cartel. I got thirty-eight thousand in my gang. How many you got?"

"How is a jury going to like a police officer bragging that the NYPD is the world's largest cartel?" O'Dell asks.

"You can buy it," Malone says on the tape.

"It's generous of you, offering to sell us back our own product."

"You're getting a deal that this guinea motherfucker cut for you. Otherwise it would be bust-out retail."

"You stole it."

"I took it. There's a difference."

"I think we've heard enough," Berger says.

"Please," Weintraub says, "let's don't do the 'This was an under-cover operation' thing. Where is the subsequent arrest of Castillo? Where is the impounded heroin? I'm sure it's vouchered into an evidence locker. But I don't think we *have* heard enough."

"We going to do this or not?"

"It's all there. Four million, two hundred and fifty thousand dollars."

"You want to count it?"

"I'm good."

Malone listens to the rest of his conversation with Castillo, then hears Savino say, *"Always a pleasure doing business with you, Denny."*

The room goes silent.

Malone knows that he's 100 percent fucked.

Berger asks, "Where is the U.S. attorney for the Southern District on this? It's her signature on Detective Malone's witness agreement."

"Ms. Paz has been removed from the case," Weintraub says.

"By whom?"

"Her boss," Weintraub says. "That would be the attorney general of the United States."

"May I ask why?"

"You may, but we have no obligation to answer," Weintraub says.

"I'm aware of that."

"Let's say she had a conflict of interest," Weintraub says, "and leave it at that. Ms. Paz is facing her own indictment, as might a number of people in and around City Hall."

"I'd like a moment with my client."

O'Dell says, "This isn't your office, Counselor. We're not going to be sent in and out like associates."

"I believe that my conversation with my client would move our discussion forward," Berger says. "I ask for your indulgence."

When O'Dell and Weintraub step out, Berger says, "What do you know about Paz?"

Malone tells him about his conversations with Chandler, Anderson and Paz.

"Paz tried to sell your deal," Berger says, "and they didn't buy. She miscalculated."

What Paz didn't figure on, Berger explains, is that the administration in Washington wants the mayor's political ambitions smothered in the crib and would relish a corruption scandal in New York. So when Paz pitched the deal to cover that up, Weintraub and O'Dell went Acela on her. She underestimated them.

"You played a strong card," Berger says. "I must say I'm impressed. But it wasn't strong enough."

"Can you keep Savino's tapes out on a Mapp hearing?" Malone asks.

"No," Berger says.

"So I'm fucked."

"Yes," Berger says, "but there are relative degrees of fucked. They want your cooperation in bringing down the mayor's administration, but it isn't as valuable as it was now that they have Savino. Shall we find out what your potential testimony is worth on the market?"

He goes out and gets the two feds.

They sit down.

Berger begins, "My client is already a cooperating witness."

"He *was,*" O'Dell says. "He subsequently confessed to crimes he didn't disclose in the original agreement, so his violation of the full disclosure clause nullifies the agreement."

"So what?" Berger asks. "He is now willing to testify to those previously undisclosed crimes. That's what you really want, isn't it? We're entertaining offers, gentlemen."

"Fuck you," Weintraub says. "We have Savino for that."

"We could make a deal on the other things," O'Dell says. "The bribery, the case fixing. We can't make a deal on a dirty cop putting fifty kilos of heroin out on the street."

"You knew I was doing drug rips," Malone says.

"Shut up, Dennis," Berger says.

"No, fuck these sanctimonious assholes," Malone says. "Fuck all of you. You want to talk about my crimes, what I've done? Let's talk about what *you've* done. You're as dirty as I am."

O'Dell explodes. Stands up and slams the table. "This shit has to end! I will not allow—do you hear me, I will not allow police officers to become gangs of bandits robbing drug dealers and then slinging dope on the streets! I'm ending it! And if that means I have to fall on my own sword, then that's what it means."

"Concur," Weintraub says. "Sit down, O'Dell, before you have a coronary."

O'Dell sits down. His face is red and his hands are shaking. "We have one deal to offer you."

"We're listening," Berger says.

"The days of you dictating who you give up, who you won't, who you hurt, who you protect are *over,*" O'Dell says. "We want it all now. Everything on every cop. McGivern, the Task Force and, yes, Malone, I want your partners—Russo and Montague."

"They don't have—"

"Don't give me that shit," O'Dell says. "Your partners were there on the Pena bust. They won medals for it. They were in on it, and don't tell me that they didn't know you took those fifty keys and don't try to tell me they didn't take money from the sale."

"That's right," Weintraub says. "Keep your mouth shut. Get thirty to life."

"That's up to a judge and a jury," Berger says. "We will take this to trial and we will win."

No, Malone thinks.

O'Dell's right. It's over. This has to end.

I go to prison.

Russo takes care of my family.

It ain't a great deal, but it ain't such a bad one either.

Anyway, it's the deal I have.

He says, "I'm done. No more talking, no more negotiating, no more deals. Do what you're going to do."

"Did you call me so you could be your own attorney?" Berger asks. "I wouldn't recommend it."

Malone leans across the table at O'Dell. "I told you, day one, I would never hurt my partners. I can do time."

"You probably can," Weintraub says. "But can Sheila?"

"What?"

"Can your wife do the time?" Weintraub asks. "She could get ten to twelve years."

"For what?!" Malone says.

"Can Sheila justify her income?" Weintraub asks. "When we turn the IRS auditors on her, can she justify her spending? Credit card payments she couldn't make unless she had a hidden source of income? We go in your house, are we going to find envelopes of cash?"

Malone looks at Berger. "Can they do this?"

"I'm afraid they can, yes."

"Think about your kids," O'Dell says. "They're going to have both parents in jail. And no home, Denny, because you have as much as a rain gutter you can't justify from your salary we'll take the house from you in civil forfeiture. The house, the cars, your savings account and Denny, look me in the eye, I'll take your kids' toys."

Weintraub says, "You have the dope money stashed away somewhere for your family, forget about it. What we don't take, your lawyer here will. You'll spend every penny on defense costs and fines. When you come out, *if* you come out, you'll be an old man without a penny to his name and adult children who don't know who he is except he's the guy that got their mother sent to the joint."

"I'll kill you."

"From Lompoc?" Weintraub asks. "Victorville? Florence? Because that's where you'll be, in a federal max on the other side of the country. You'll never see your kids, and your wife will be in Danbury with the diesels and the bull dykes."

"Who's going to raise your kids?" O'Dell asks. "I know the Russos are their guardians, but how's Uncle Phil going to feel about bringing up a rat's kids? Especially when you have no money to contribute. Is he going to put nice clothes on their backs, send them to college? Spend money taking them to visit their mom in prison?"

Weintraub says, "Russo's a cheap prick. Won't even buy a new overcoat."

"How can I do that to *their* families?" Malone asks.

"Are you telling us you love their kids more than your own?" O'Dell asks. "You love their wives more than yours?"

"Dennis, let's take this to trial," Berger says.

"That could work out," Weintraub says. "Maybe Sheila's trial will be in the same department, you can take lunch breaks together."

"You motherfucker."

"We're going to step out for ten minutes," O'Dell says. "Let you think about it, confer with your attorney. Ten minutes, Denny, and then that's it. You choose what happens after that."

They walk out, and Malone and Berger sit in silence. Then Malone gets up and walks over to the window, looks out at Midtown. It's New York busy—people scrambling, hustling a buck, trying to make it.

"This is hell," Malone says.

Berger says, "You've always hated defense attorneys. Thought we were the scum of the earth, helping guilty people to escape justice. Now you know, Denny, why we exist. When the small guy gets caught in the system—if he has a vowel at the end of his name, or God help him he's black or Hispanic, or even a cop—the machine just grinds him down. It's not a fair fight. Lady Justice has a blindfold over her eyes because she just can't bear to watch what happens."

"Do you believe in karma?" Malone asks.

"No."

"Neither do I," Malone says, "but now I have to wonder . . . the lies I told, the phony warrants . . . the beatings . . . the wiseguys, the Jamaals, the spics I put behind bars. Now I'm one of them. I'm their nigger now."

"You don't have to be," Berger says. "You have me."

Yeah, Malone knows all too well how good Berger is in court. He knows what else the lawyer has in mind, but if this gets past a grand jury—and it will—no prosecutor or judge is going to take a chance selling it.

"I can't risk my family," Malone says.

He didn't need the ten minutes. Malone knew as soon as they started talking that he wasn't going to let Sheila go to prison.

A man takes care of his family, end of story. "I'll take the deal."

"You'll have to do time," Berger says.

"I know."

"So will your partners."

"I know that, too."

Hell isn't having no choice.

It's having to make a choice between horrific things.

Berger says, "I can't represent Russo or Montague. That *would* be a conflict of interest."

"Let's get this done."

Berger goes out and gets O'Dell and Weintraub. When they sit down he says, "Detective Malone will make a full proffer of his

THE FORCE / 375

crimes and plead guilty to heroin trafficking. He will cooperate fully and serve as a cooperating witness against other serving police that he knows to be implicated in crimes."

O'Dell says, "That's not good enough. He has to wear a wire and get incriminating evidence against them."

"He'll wear a wire," Berger says. "In exchange, he wants a memorandum of cooperation from the sentencing judge recommending a sentence of no more than twelve years, to be served concurrently on any multiple charges, fines amounting to no more than one hundred thousand dollars and forfeiture of any funds gained through the illegal activities."

"Accept in principle," Weintraub says. "We can work out the details later. Final adjudication of the charges will be suspended pending the satisfactory completion of the defendant's cooperation."

"On the understanding that Malone's new 302 contains no lies or omissions," O'Dell says, "and that he commits no additional crimes."

Berger says, "Our other condition—"

"You're in no position to make demands," O'Dell says.

"If we weren't," Berger says, "we wouldn't be here. We'd be in a holding cell at the Metropolitan Correctional Center. May I go on? Detective Malone's cooperation as to Detectives Russo and Montague is contingent on a guarantee that no jurisdiction files charges against *any* of the spouses. That is nonnegotiable, must be placed in a separate memorandum countersigned by both of you and the U.S. attorney general."

"You don't trust us, Gerry?" Weintraub asks.

"I just want to make sure that everyone has skin in the game," Berger says, "and that if either or both of you leave your current positions, my client is still protected."

"Agreed," Weintraub says. "We have no desire to hurt families."

"Nevertheless you manage to do it on a daily basis," Berger says.

"Do we have a deal?" O'Dell asks.

Malone nods.

"Is that a yes?" Weintraub asks.

"My client agrees," Berger says. "What do you want, his blood?"

"I want him to say it."

"I speak for my client," Berger says.

"Well, let your client know," Weintraub says, "that if he decides to go Rafael Torres on himself to get out of this, the deal is off—his wife doesn't leave flowers on his grave for five to eight."

"We'll need his proffer now," O'Dell says.

Malone tells them all about the Pena bust, the theft of the cash and the heroin, and the subsequent sale of the heroin.

He doesn't tell them that the killing of Diego Pena was, in fact, an execution.

Malone and Berger walk out of the building together.

"This is why you called me," Berger says, "so that you walk out."

"Will you be there to walk me in?" Malone says. "When I surrender myself at the federal lockup?"

"We'll work on getting you Allenwood," Berger says. "It's a three-hour drive, your family could come visit."

Malone shakes his head. "They'll put me in seg, for 'my protection.' I won't get visitation for years. Anyway, I don't want my kids seeing me in prison. Going through all that, sitting around with skels' families in the waiting room. When the frequent fliers find out that they're visiting a cop, they'll be harassed, maybe threatened."

"It won't be for months, maybe years," Berger says. "A lot can happen in that time."

"I'll go get your money."

"We need to arrange a drop," Berger says. "It would hardly do to have you seen going into my office."

Malone almost laughs. "What do your rat clients usually do?"

Berger hands him a card. "It's a dry cleaner's. I have my little jokes."

"What about the rest of your fees?" Malone asks. "These forfeitures . . . I was counting on that money to pay you."

"Let me be very clear," Berger says. "I am first in line. The federal government is last. What can they do, collect money you don't have?"

"They can take my house."

"They're going to take that anyway," Berger says.

"Great."

"What do you care?" Berger says. "You'll testify for several years, so you'll be living on a military base. Your family will be in the program. When you get out, you'll join them. You can buy a lot more house for your money in Utah, I've heard."

"You have a condo on Fifth Avenue."

"And a house in the Hamptons," Berger says, "a cabin in Jackson Hole, and I'm looking at a *casita* on St. Thomas."

"You need someplace to dock your boat."

"Yes, that's right," Berger says. "This is a business, Detective. Justice is a *business*. I just happen to have done very well at it."

"Nice work if you can get it."

"Would you like to know what the downside is?" Berger asks.

"Sure."

"Nobody ever calls me when things are good," Berger says.

CHAPTER 29

There's heat and there's New York City heat.

Sweltering, simmering, steaming, filthy, fetid heat baking off the concrete and the asphalt, turning the city into an open-air sauna.

Hot time, summer in the city.

Malone woke up sweaty and was sweaty again thirty seconds after he stepped out of the shower.

It's better down here in Staten Island as he sits in Russo's backyard and sips from a bottle of Coors. His denim shirt is loose over his jeans and he wears a pair of black Nikes.

Wearing a ridiculous Hawaiian shirt, Bermuda shorts, and sandals over white socks, Russo flips the burgers on the grill. "Fourth of July. I love this country."

Monty's wearing a white guayabera shirt, khaki slacks and a blue trilby. Puffs on a big Montecristo.

The Russos' Fourth of July cookout, always held the weekend shift they have off nearest the Fourth.

A team tradition.

Attendance mandatory, a family day.

Wives, significant girlfriends—kids.

John is in the pool playing Marco Polo with Monty's boys and the Russo brothers. Caitlin sits with Sophia getting her makeup done, a major case of hero worship. Yolanda, Donna and Sheila are at the patio table, sipping sangria, their heads together in girl talk.

The announcement of Monty's impending retirement has been the talk of the barbecue. Yolanda is thrilled out of her mind to get her husband away from the risks of the Job and her kids away from the city. Seeing her happiness breaks Malone's heart.

"See those little idiots in the pool?" Monty says. "They're smart. College smart."

"They're black," Russo says, "they'll get a scholarship."

"They have a scholarship," Monty says. He chuckles. "The Pena Scholarship."

He touches his beer bottle to Russo's.

"The Pena Scholarship," Russo says. "I like that."

Malone feels his soul shrink inside him. Here at his best friend's house, with the man's family, making a tape that will take it all away from him.

But he does it anyway. Looking around to make sure none of the wives or kids are eavesdropping, he says, "We have to move on Castillo. If he gets busted before we get to him, he's going to say there was fifty kilos of heroin missing from the Pena voucher."

"You think they'd believe him?" Russo asks.

"You want to take the chance?" Malone asks. "Fifteen to thirty, federal time? We have to take him out."

He looks pointedly at Russo, who takes a sausage off the grill and puts it on a plate. "In the words of the immortal Tony Soprano, 'Some people gotta go.'"

Monty's busy rolling his cigar to get an even flame. "I have no problem putting two in Castillo's head."

"You ever feel bad about it?" Malone asks.

"Pena?" Russo says. "I took that baby killer's money and made something good out of it? My kids have a future? They're not going to carry loans around on their backs their whole lives. They get out of college free and clear. Fuck Pena, I'm glad what we did."

"Concur," Monty says.

The boys come to the edge of the pool and yell for their dads to come in and play. "In a few minutes!"

"You always say that!"

"You don't worry about their bone density in the water?" Russo asks.

"I worry about their *brain* density," Monty says. "So much young pussy around these days and they give it away for an iTunes download. I'm retiring down in North Carolina. I don't want any grandkids for a long time."

"Carolina's expensive," Malone says. "I'm looking at, fuck, Rhode Island. Where does the money go? The Pena money, the lawyer money, the other rips. I mean we have to have made, I dunno, a couple of million each over the years?"

"The hell are you today, Merrill Lynch?" Russo asks.

Malone says, "We don't know when we're gonna get another real payday. All we might get is our salary, maybe a little overtime."

"Monty," Russo says, "Malone wants to sell you some municipal bonds."

"We always knew it wouldn't last forever," Monty says. "Every good thing comes to an end."

"Maybe it's time I pull the pin, too," Malone says. "I mean, why take the chance some junkie skel throws a lucky shot. Maybe it's time to pick up my chips, step away from the table while I'm still a winner."

Russo says, "Jesus, you guys going to leave me alone with Levin?"

Malone says, "The beer, I gotta piss."

Donna collars him in the kitchen, puts her arm around his shoulders. She juts her chin at Sheila sitting outside and says, "This is nice, the two of you together, the family. Sheila told me she took a few days away to think—you getting back together again?"

"Looks like it, huh."

"I'm proud of you, Denny," she says. "Coming to your senses. Your life is here with them, with us."

Malone goes into the bathroom, turns on the tap to hide the sound, and cries.

The fourth beer slides down smoother than the third, the fifth easier than the fourth.

"You want to slow down a little?" Sheila asks him.

"You wanna not tell me what to do?" Malone asks. He walks away from her, over to the pool, where the annual "kids versus dads" game of water polo is going on.

John is having a great time and yells, "Dad! Come in and play!"

"Not right now, Johnny."

"Come on, Dad!"

"Get in here," Russo says. "They're kicking our butts."

"I'm good," Malone says.

Russo's had a few beers himself. Starts to get a little hostile. "Get your ass in here, Malone."

"No thanks."

It gets quiet at the party. Everyone's watching; the women pick up this is a little more tense than something about getting in the pool.

"Why not?" Monty asks. He's managed to play the game without getting his cigar wet.

"Because I don't feel like it," Malone says.

Because I'm wearing a wire.

"You shy now?" Russo asks.

"Yeah, that's it," Malone says.

"Ain't nothing we haven't seen before," Russo says. "Get in the goddamn pool."

He and Malone are glaring at each other now.

"I didn't bring a suit," Malone says.

"To a pool party," Monty says. "You didn't bring a suit."

Russo says, "I'll lend you one. Donna, go get Denny a suit."

But he don't take his eyes off Malone.

"Jesus, Phil," Donna says. "The man said he doesn't—"

"I heard what the man said," Russo says. "Did you hear what *I* said? Go in the goddamn house and get the man a goddamn bathing suit."

Donna storms into the house.

"Is there a reason you don't want to get undressed, Denny?" Monty asks.

"What's it to you?"

"You're coming in the pool," Monty says.

"*You* gonna make me?"

"If that's what it takes."

Malone explodes. "Fuck you, Monty! Fuck you, Phil!"

Sheila says, "Jesus, Denny!"

"Fuck you, too!" Malone yells.

"*Denny!*"

"Fuck *all* this!" Malone yells. "I'm out of here."

"You're not going anywhere," Russo says.

Sheila grabs him by the arm. "You shouldn't be driving."

He wrenches his arm away. "I'm fine."

"Yeah, you're fine!" she yells after him. "You're an asshole, Denny! You're a real asshole!"

He raises his middle finger as he walks away.

If Pirus and Crips all got along
They'd probably gun me down by the end of this song
Seem like the whole city go against me . . .

Malone has the sound system *pounding* Kendrick Lamar as he takes 95 back up to the city.

They know, he thinks.

Russo and Monty, they fucking *know.*

Jesus Christ.

He's doing ninety now.

Thinks about just steering into a light pole. It would be so easy. Drunk driving fatality, no skid marks. No one could ever prove it wasn't. Out fast and hard, the tape of your friends goes up in flames with the car.

With you.

Viking funeral right at the crash.

One-stop shopping.

Scatter my ashes over Manhattan North.

That would piss 'em off, I'm still there. Denny Malone, blowing around with the garbage.

Getting in people's eyes, their noses.

Snort me like coke, like smack.

Black Irish tar.

Do it, ace, don't be a pussy. Hit the gas pedal, not the brake. Jerk the wheel to the right and this is over.

For everyone.

Like Eminem says:

So while you're in it, try to get as much shit as you can
And when your run is over just admit when it's at its end.

Malone tightens his grip on the wheel.

Do it, bitch.

Do it, rat motherfucker.

Judas.

He jerks the wheel.

The Camaro goes flying across four lanes. Horns blare, brakes shriek, the steel posts of the sign come large in the windshield.

At the last second he swerves back.

The Camaro goes into spins, crazy 360s that whip his head around, the Manhattan skyline flashing off and on in his face.

Then the car slows and steadies, Malone hits the gas, steers back into a lane and heads into the city.

YAWK, YAWK, YAWK, YAWK

Malone rips the medical tape off his stomach and slams the recorder on the table. "Here it is. Fuck you. Here's my partners' blood."

"Are you drunk?" O'Dell asks.

"I'm high on Dex and beer," Malone says. "Add it to the charges. Pile the fuck on."

Weintraub says, "I have to leave the Hamptons to come in and listen to *this* shit?"

Malone yells, "My partners know!"

"Know what?" O'Dell asks.

"That I'm the rat!"

He tells them about the swimming pool incident.

"That's it?" Weintraub asks. "You wouldn't get in a fucking pool?"

"They're cops," Malone says. "They were born suspicious. They can smell guilt. They know."

O'Dell says, "It doesn't matter. If you have them cold on this tape, we take them tomorrow, anyway."

They listen to the tape.

"They're black, they'll get a scholarship."

"They have a scholarship. The Pena Scholarship."

"The Pena Scholarship. I like that."

"We have to move on Castillo. If he gets busted before we get to him, he's going to say there was fifty kilos of heroin missing from the Pena voucher."

"You think they'd believe him?"

"You want to take the chance? Fifteen to thirty, federal time? We have to take him out."

"In the words of the immortal Tony Soprano, 'Some people gotta go.' "

"I have no problem putting two in Castillo's head."

"You'll have to testify to corroborate," Weintraub says.

"I know."

"But it's good," Weintraub says. "You did a good job, Malone."

He turns the tape back on.

"You ever feel bad about it?"

"Pena? I took that baby killer's money and made something good out of it? My kids have a future? They're not going to carry loans around on their backs their whole lives. They get out of college free and clear. Fuck Pena, I'm glad what we did."

"Concur."

"Well, that's that," O'Dell says.

"I'll get indictments started on Russo and Montague," Weintraub says.

"You can't wait, can you," Malone says.

"Who the hell do you think you are?" Weintraub says. "You're not Serpico, Malone! You were taking with both hands, everything you could grab. Fuck you."

"Fuck you, too, asshole!"

"Let's go for a walk," O'Dell says. "Get some air."

They go down in the service elevator and walk out onto Fifth Avenue.

"You want to know what I think, Denny? I think you're feeling guilty. I think you feel guilty about everything that you've done, and I think now you're feeling guilty about betraying other cops. But you can't go both ways—if you're truly sorry for what you've done, then you'll help us put a stop to it."

"The fuck are you, my priest?"

"Sort of," O'Dell says. "I'm just trying to help you get past your own emotions and see this thing clearly."

"I've got a rat tag on me," Malone says. "I'm done. I'm no good to you anymore, anyway—you think any cop is going to talk with me now? Any lawyer?"

Malone stops walking. Leans against a wall.

"You've done a great thing," O'Dell says. "You're helping to clean up this city—the court system, the police department . . . we're grateful. You've quit protecting the 'brotherhood' that's out there shielding dope dealers, selling drugs themselves but who won't do anything to protect the people out there dying from overdoses, kids getting killed in drive-bys, babies dying from—"

"Shut the fuck up."

"This city's about to explode," O'Dell says, "and half the reason is dirty cops, brutal cops, racist cops. There aren't many of them, but they cover all the good ones with their shit."

"I can't stand it!"

"What you can't stand is the shame, Denny," O'Dell says. "It's not informing on other cops—what you can't bear is that you betrayed yourself. I get it, we both come from the same church, the catechism classes. You're not a bad person, but you've done bad things and the only way, the *only way* you're going to feel all right is if you come clean."

"I can't."

"Because of your partners?" O'Dell asks. "Do you think if they were in this jam, they wouldn't give you up?"

"You don't know those guys," Malone says. "They won't talk to you."

"Maybe you don't know them as well as you think."

"I don't *know* them?" Malone says. "I put my lives in their hands every damn day. I sit for hours with them on stakeouts, I eat shitty food with them, I sleep on cots next to them in the locker room. I'm the godfather of their children, they're the godfathers of mine, you think I don't *know* them?!

"Here's what I know about them—they're the best people I've ever known. They're better than me."

He walks away.

His phone rings.

It's Russo.

He wants to meet.

CHAPTER 30

Morningside Park.

The tension like barbed wire across Malone's chest.

At least he isn't wearing a wire. O'Dell wanted him to, but Malone told him to go fuck himself.

O'Dell didn't want him to go at all. "If you're right about their suspicions, they could kill you."

"They won't."

"Why go at all?" Weintraub asked. "We have enough to pick them up right now, you go into the program."

"You can't arrest them at home," Malone said, "not in front of their families."

"He could make the meeting," Weintraub said, "and we could pick them up then."

"Then he'd have to wear a wire."

"Fuck that," Malone said.

"If you don't wear a wire," O'Dell said, "we can't provide backup."

"Good. I don't want backup."

"Don't be an asshole," Weintraub said.

But that's what I am, Malone thought. I'm an asshole.

"What are you going to tell them?" O'Dell asked.

"The truth," Malone said. "I'm going to tell them the truth, what I did. At least give them a chance to prepare their families. You can arrest them tomorrow."

"What if they run?" Weintraub asked.

388 / DON WINSLOW

"They won't," Malone said. "They won't leave their wives and kids in the wind."

"If they do run," O'Dell says, "it's on you."

Now he stands in the park and watches Russo and Monty walk up from Morningside Avenue.

Russo's face is twisted with anger; Monty's is flat, unreadable. Cop faces.

And they're carrying heavy. Malone can see the extra weight on Russo's hip, can see it in Monty's walk.

"We're going to pat you down, Denny," Monty says.

Malone raises his arms. Russo steps in and searches for a wire.

Doesn't find one.

"You sobered up?" Russo asks.

"Sober enough."

"You have something you want to tell us?" Monty asks.

They know—they're cops, they're his brothers, they see it on his face, the guilt. But he can't bring himself to say it. "Like what?"

"Like they flipped you," Monty says. "They caught you and they flipped you and you gave us up."

Malone doesn't answer.

"Jesus, Denny," Russo says. "At my home? With our families? You wore a fucking wire at my *home*? While our wives talked and our kids played in the pool together."

"How did they get to you?" Monty asks.

Malone doesn't answer.

He can't.

"It doesn't matter," Monty says.

He pulls his .38 and aims it at Malone's face.

Malone don't go for his gun, just looks at Monty. "If you think I'm a rat, do it."

"I will."

"We have to be sure," Russo says. He's almost crying. "We have to be one hundred percent sure."

"What do you *need*?" Monty asks.

"I need to hear him say it," Russo says. He grabs Malone's arms. "Denny, you look me in the eye and tell me it isn't true, I'll believe you. Please, shit, man, tell me it isn't true."

Malone looks him in the eye.

The words won't come out.

"Denny, please," Russo says. "I can understand if . . . it could happen to any of us . . . just tell us the fucking truth, we can still fix this."

"How are we going to fix it?" Monty asks.

"He's my kids' godfather!"

"He's going to put your kids' father in jail," Monty says. "Mine too. Unless he's not around to corroborate the tape and testify. I'm sorry, Denny, but—"

"Denny, tell him we got it wrong!"

"He's going to think what he's going think," Malone says.

Russo pulls his piece. "I'm not letting you do it."

"What, we're all going to shoot each other?" Malone asks. "That's who we are now?"

His phone rings.

Monty says, "Go ahead. Slow."

Malone pulls his phone from his jeans pocket.

"Put it on speaker," Monty says.

Malone does.

It's Henderson from IAB.

"*Denny, I thought you should know,*" he says, "*I just got my head handed to me by the feds.*"

"The fuck you mean?"

"*Fed named O'Dell told me to lay off the Task Force, they got a guy in there,*" Henderson says. "*Denny, it's Levin.*"

Malone feels sick.

O'Dell, what did you do?

"You told me Levin was clean," Malone says.

"*He showed me the 302,*" Henderson says. "*It had Levin's name on it.*"

"Okay." Malone clicks off.

Russo sits down on the grass. "Jesus Christ. We were going to shoot each other. Jesus fucking Christ, I'm sorry, Denny."

Monty holsters his .38.

But slow.

Malone can see the big man thinking, playing chess in his head, going through the moves—Henderson is Denny's guy, feds only show documents to city cops when they're forced to . . .

He ain't sold.

Now it's Russo's phone that rings. He listens for a minute, clicks off and says, "Speak of the fucking devil."

"What?"

"Levin," Russo says. "He's got a visual on Castillo."

They walk to the work car.

Monty's eyes boring into him.

Malone can feel a .38 round going through the back of his head.

Old school.

And I'd deserve it, he thinks. I fucking deserve it.

I almost want it.

He slows down, gets beside Monty. "Were you really going to shoot me, Big Man?"

"I don't know," Monty says. "Let me ask you this—if the shoe were on the other foot, what would you have done?"

"I don't know I could shoot you."

"None of us know, do we," Monty says, "until we get there."

"What are we going to do about Levin?" Russo asks. "If Levin is with the feds, we're *fucked*, he puts us all in jail."

"What are you saying?" Malone asks.

"That if we bust Castillo," Russo says, "there are two people who can't come out of that raid alive."

Monty says, "Drug busts are dangerous work."

"You have a problem with that?" Russo asks.

Malone feels sick. What the fuck was O'Dell doing, covering for me? Tell them, tell them now. Three syllables—I'm a rat.

He can't say it.

Thought he could.

Instead, he says, "Let's move."

Maybe, he thinks, I'll get lucky.

And I'll get killed.

The building is on Payson Avenue, across the street from Inwood Hill Park.

"You're sure about this," Malone says.

"I saw the van pull up," Levin says. His voice is tense, excited. "All Trinis. They brought out duffel bags."

"And you *saw* Castillo," Malone says.

"They dropped him off and left," Levin says. "He went to the fourth floor. I saw him there before they pulled the shades."

"You're sure," Malone says. "You're sure it was him."

"One hundred percent," Levin says.

"Anyone else come or go?" Malone asks.

Levin says, "No one."

So we don't know how many people Castillo has in there, Malone thinks. Could be the ten Levin saw, could be twenty more already inside. Castillo's in there checking and counting before he puts the smack out, making sure none of his own people skimmed.

What we should do, Malone knows, is keep it under surveillance, call Manhattan North, let Sykes bring in an Emergency Services squad, the SWAT guys. Except we can't do that because this isn't a bust, it's an execution.

They all know the risk. And they all, with the exception of Levin, know why they're taking it.

No one says anything.

A silent assent.

392 / DON WINSLOW

"Gear up," Malone says. "Vests. Automatic weapons, we're going in heavy."

"What about a warrant?" Levin asks.

Malone catches Russo's glance. He says, "Gunshot warrant. We saw known gang members on the prowl, followed them and then heard gunshots. We didn't have time to call for backup. Anyone have a problem with that?"

"We still owe these people for Billy," Russo says, passing out the HKs.

Levin looks at Malone.

Malone says, "Arrests might not be our priority here."

Levin meets his look. "I'm good with that."

"You still good if there's a shooting board?" Malone says. "IAB?"

"I'm good."

Russo says, "We're mixing it up a little on this one. I'll breach, Levin goes in first. Malone sloppy seconds. Monty guards door."

He stares at Malone, like *don't go against me on this.* Levin looks at Malone, too—Malone always goes in first.

Malone asks, "Levin, you okay with this?"

"It's my turn," Levin says.

"Let's go," Malone says.

He fires two shots in the air.

Monty trots to the door and sticks the Rabbit in. Levin slides up beside him, presses himself against the wall and holds his HK at high port, ready to go.

The lock pops.

The door swings open.

Russo tosses in the flashbang.

The interior lights up.

Levin counts to three, yells, "Moving!," pivots and goes through the door. Rounds hit him instantly, from low to high—into his legs, his belly, his chest, his neck, his head.

He's dead before his body hits the floor.

Malone drops behind him and sees Trinis in green bandannas

crouching behind the stairwell railing. They have Kevlar body armor and combat helmets with heavy visors and night-vision goggles.

They run up the stairs.

Malone flattens himself on his back behind Levin's body. Hits the button on his radio and yells, "10-13! Officer down! Officer down!," then stretches his HK out over Levin's chest and squeezes the trigger.

Rounds come back, stitching into Levin.

Russo stands at the edge of the door, firing shotgun blasts. "Get the fuck out of there, Denny!"

Malone rolls over Levin's body and fires.

Then he gets up and moves.

Up the stairs.

"Denny! Back out!"

But Russo comes in.

So does Monty.

Malone hears them pounding up the stairs behind him.

He never used to worry about his back because Monty was behind him.

Now he's worried about his back. Because Monty's behind him, worried about *his* back, too, wondering if Malone stuck a knife in it.

Malone hears the Trinis running above him. Fuckin' kids are a lot faster than him. Racing to the fourth floor, protect the smack and the *jefe*. But it don't matter if they win the race, they got no place to go except the roof and that's a death trap.

But they stop and fire.

Rounds bounce around the stairway like it's a pinball machine. Off the walls, off the railing.

Malone hears Russo scream, "My eye!"

Malone turns to see him drop, curl into a ball and grab his face. A rust fragment from the railing. Monty presses him down, steps over him, squeezing his heft along the wall as he comes up.

"I'm okay!" Russo yells. "Just come down!"

Malone don't come down. Instead he runs up to the fourth-floor door, Monty behind him, gun lowered.

Malone steps aside.

Monty kicks in the door.

Malone goes in shooting.

Hears one Trini scream as a round hits him. Bullets come stitching across the concrete floor, throwing up sparks and fragments.

Malone drops to the floor and rolls to the side.

Looks back to see Monty raise his .38.

At him.

Malone crabs back to the wall next to the door. Pushes his back into the wall. Nowhere else to go.

Raises the HK at Monty.

They look at each other.

Monty fires into the doorway.

A Trini twirls out, hit in the groin below the vest. His AK fires into the ceiling. Monty takes him down with two shots to the legs. The Trini jackknifes and falls backward.

The Trinis aren't gonna give it up; they know they've killed a cop and they're not going out of there in cuffs. Their only options are the back door or killing the surviving police.

Malone swings his gun through the open door and fires, then ducks back as Monty uses the cover fire to move to the other side of the door. Looks at Malone like, *we're in it now.* Then he juts his chin at the doorway—go.

Malone launches up and through the door. Feels heavy punches in his ribs as rounds smack into his vest and he goes down.

A Trini walks toward him, a Glock aimed in front of him.

Malone lunges, tackles him around the legs and drives him to the floor. Wrests the gun out of his hand and beats him in the head with it, again and again, until the Trini's body goes limp.

Then he hears another burst and a body falls hard on top of him. He looks out from under and sees Monty lower his gun.

Monty looks at him.

Thinking about shooting again.

Friendly fire—it happens.

Sirens scream through the night. Flashers pulse outside the door. Malone pushes the body off him.

A body bolts off the fire escape landing.

Monty goes out the window after him.

No heroin in the room. No money counters.

No Castillo.

It was an ambush.

Castillo must have gone out the back before we got here, Malone thinks. He sussed out the surveillance and set me up, knowing I'm the one who always goes through the door.

That first blast was meant for me.

Levin took it instead.

Russo staggers into the room.

Footsteps pound up the stairs and Malone hears "NYPD!" They come down the hallway, firing.

"NYPD!" Malone screams. "We're police!"

Tries to remember the color of the day.

Russo yells, "Red! Red!"

Malone hears more shots from outside.

Bullets smack into the walls above them. It's Task Force—Gallina and Tenelli—coming up the hallway, firing in front of them. Russo hits the floor, crawls under a table. Malone squeezes himself into a corner. Takes off his lanyard, throws his shield out onto the floor where they can see it. "NYPD! It's Malone!"

Tenelli sees him, pretends not to.

She fires twice.

Malone throws his arms across his face. The rounds hit left of his head.

Russo yells, "Fuck! Stop! It's Russo!"

More feet, more voices.

Uniforms from the Three-Two, yelling, "Cease fire! Cease fire! It's cops! Russo and Malone!"

396 / DON WINSLOW

Tenelli lowers her weapon.

Malone gets up, goes for her. "You fucking cunt!"

"I didn't see you!"

"The fuck you didn't!"

A uniform gets between them.

Russo asks, "The fuck's Monty?"

"He went down the fire escape."

They go after him.

Fucking chaos in the streets. Sector cars rolling up, brakes screeching. Shouts, people running.

Monty lies on his back on the sidewalk.

Blood pumps out of his carotid artery.

Malone kneels and presses hard against the neck, trying to stop the bleeding. "Don't you go out on me, don't you go out on me, brother. Please, Big Man, don't you go out on me."

Russo spins around like a drunk, holding his head, crying.

A radio car from the Three-Two squeals in, the uniforms jump out with guns drawn and aimed. Malone screams, "We're on the job! Task Force! Officer down! Get medics here!"

He hears one of the uniforms say, "Is that fuckin' Malone? Maybe we got here too soon."

"Call a bus!" Russo yells. "One officer dead, two wounded, one critical!"

More cars are coming in, then an ambulance. The EMTs take over from Malone.

"Is he going to make it?" Malone asks, standing up. Monty's blood is all over him.

"Too soon to tell."

One of the EMTs goes over to Russo. "Let's get you help."

Russo shakes him off.

"Take care of Montague first," Russo says. "Go!"

The ambulance takes off.

A uniform sergeant walks up to Malone. "What the fuck happened here?"

"One dead officer inside," Malone says. "Five dead suspects down."

"Any of the perps alive?"

"I dunno. Maybe."

A uniform walks out of the warehouse. "Three DOA. Two bleeding out. One's shot in the femoral, the other's skull is bashed in."

"You want to talk to any of these fuckers?" the sergeant asks Malone.

Malone shakes his head.

"Wait ten," the sergeant tells the uniform. "Then call in five perps DOA. And get another bus here, let's recover that officer's body."

Malone sits down and leans against the wall. Suddenly he's exhausted, the adrenaline dump dropping him into the black hole. Then Sykes is there, bending over him. "What the fuck, Malone? What the fuck did you do?"

Malone shakes his head.

Russo stumbles over. "Denny?"

"Yeah?"

"This is *fucked up.*"

Malone gets up, lifts Russo by the elbow and walks him to a car.

A cop's doorbell rings at four in the morning there's only one reason.

Yolanda knows it.

Malone sees it on her face the second she opens the door. "Oh, no."

"Yolanda—"

"Oh, God no, Denny. Is he—"

"He's hurt," Malone says. "It's serious."

Yolanda looks down at his shirt—he'd forgotten that it has Monty's blood all over it. She stifles a cry, swallows it down and then straightens her neck. "Let me throw some clothes on."

"There's a sector car waiting for you," Malone says. "I have to go notify Levin's girlfriend."

"Levin?"

"He's gone."

Monty's oldest boy appears behind her.

Looks like a skinny version of his father.

Malone sees the fear in his eyes.

Yolanda turns to him. "Daddy's been hurt. I'm going to the hospital and you need to look after your brothers until Grandma Janet gets here. I'll call her on my way to the hospital."

"Is Dad going to be all right?" the boy asks, his voice trembling.

"We don't know yet," Yolanda says. "We need to be strong for him now. We need to pray and be strong, baby."

She turns back to Malone.

"Thank you for coming, Denny."

All he can do is nod.

He starts speaking, he'll start crying, and that's not what she needs.

Amy thinks it's another Bowling Night.

Comes to the door annoyed as shit, then sees that Malone's by himself. "Where's Dave?"

"Amy—"

"Where is he? Malone, where the fuck is he?"

"He's gone, Amy."

She doesn't get it at first. "Gone? Where?"

"There was a shooting," Malone says. "Dave got shot . . . He didn't make it, Amy. I'm sorry."

"Oh."

How many people has he had to tell that their loved ones aren't coming home. Some scream, or faint, others take it like this.

Stunned.

She repeats, "Oh."

"I'll drive you to the hospital," Malone says.

"Why?" Amy asks. "He's dead."

"The ME has to do an autopsy," Malone says, "in a homicide."

"Got it."

"You want to change real quick?"

"Right. Sure. Okay."

"I'll wait."

"You have blood on you," Amy says. "Is it—"

"No."

Maybe some of it, but he ain't going to tell her that. She changes quickly. Comes out in jeans and a light blue hoodie.

In the car she says, "You know why David transferred into your unit?"

"He wanted action."

"He wanted to work with you," Amy says. "You were his hero. You were all he talked about—Denny Malone this, Denny Malone that. I got sick of hearing about you. He'd come home talking about all the things he learned, all the things you taught him."

"I didn't teach him enough."

"It was a macho thing," Amy says. "He didn't want anyone thinking he was just another college-educated jewboy."

"Nobody thought that."

"Sure they did," Amy says. "He wanted so much to be one of you. A real cop. And now he's dead. And it's such a waste. I was perfectly happy with the college-educated jewboy."

"Amy, you and Levin weren't married," Malone says, "so you don't get his pension."

"I work," she says. "I'm good."

"The Job will bury him."

"Letting the irony of that statement slide for the time being," she says. "I'll tell his parents."

"I'll reach out to them," Malone says.

"No, don't. They'll blame you."

"So do I."

Amy says, "Don't look to me for sympathy. I blame you, too."

She stares out the window.

At the life she knew passing by her.

The hospital is chaos.

Usually is this time of the morning in Harlem.

A young Puerto Rican mother holds a coughing baby. An old homeless man with bandaged swollen feet rocks back and forth. A psychotic man, young, holds an intense conversation with the people in his head. Then there are the broken arms, the cuts, the stomach pains, the sinus infections, the flu, the DTs.

Donna Russo sits with Yolanda Montague, holding her hand.

McGivern and Sykes stand in the corner of the room, by the door, quietly conferring. They got a lot to talk about, Malone knows. One detective dead, another on the fence. Just days after a third detective from the same unit killed himself.

Less than a year after another one, Billy O, was killed in a similar raid.

Two uniforms from the Three-Two stand behind them, blocking the door from the horde of media outside.

More cops wait out there.

McGivern breaks away from Sykes and walks over to Malone. "A word with you, Sergeant?"

Malone follows McGivern down the hall.

Sykes walks after them. "One officer killed, another possibly dying. Five suspects, all minorities, dead. No backup, no support from Emergency Services, no operational plan, you don't bother to notify or inform your captain—"

"Now?" Malone asks. "You're going to start this *now*, with Monty lying in there—"

"You put him in there, Malone! And Levin—"

Malone goes for him.

McGivern gets between them. "Enough! This is a disgrace!"

Malone backs off.

"What happened, Denny?" McGivern asks. "There were no drugs in that warehouse. Just shooters geared out for combat."

"The Dominicans wanted revenge for Pena," Malone says. "They made threats on the Task Force. We followed them, it was a setup. I didn't see it, it was my fault, this is on me."

"The media are all over this," Sykes says. "They're already talking about out-of-control, trigger-happy cowboy cops. They're already asking if the Task Force should be shut down. I have to give them some answers."

McGivern stands up. "You think you can throw them Malone and they'll stop at that? If you give the press any opening at all, they will eat us *all* alive. Here are the answers you're going to give them: Four New York cops—hero cops—engaged a gang of killers in a desperate gun battle. One of those heroes was killed—he gave his life for this city—and another is fighting for his life. Those are the answers, and the only answers, that you will give. Do you understand me, Captain Sykes?"

Sykes walks away.

McGivern starts to say something and then hears a commotion in the lobby. The commissioner, the chief of detectives and the mayor are coming in through the crowd.

Cameras chatter.

Malone sees that Chief Neely is in full dress uniform. He must have taken time to climb into the costume before he came rushing over.

He beats the mayor over to Yolanda.

Bends over and says comforting things, Malone supposes. We're all behind you. Keep a good thought. Thirty-eight thousand of us will be out looking for the men who did this to your husband, and we'll get them.

Neely spots Malone and walks over.

Looks at McGivern, who finds somewhere else to be.

"Sergeant Malone," Neely says.

"Sir."

"Through this ordeal," Neely says, "I will support you, praise you to the press and back you up one hundred and ten percent. But you're finished on the Job. There's no place for your cowboy bullshit anymore. You got one and maybe two good officers killed. Do yourself a favor, take a disability buyout. I'll sign it."

He pats Malone on the shoulder and walks away.

A doctor in scrubs comes in, Claudette behind him. He looks around the room and spots Yolanda. Donna helps her up and they walk over to him. Malone and Russo stand at the edge within earshot.

"Your husband is out of surgery," the doctor says.

"Thank God," Yolanda says.

The doctor says, "We've taken him to ICU. The flow of blood to his brain was cut off for a considerable period of time. Also, another bullet nicked the cervical vertebrae and the spinal cord. At this point in time, we might have to consider lowering our expectations."

Yolanda breaks down in Donna's arms.

Donna walks her away.

The doctor goes back to the OR.

Malone approaches Claudette. "Translation?"

"It doesn't look good," Claudette says. "He has severe brain damage. Even if he makes it, you need to prepare yourself."

"For what?"

"The man you knew is gone," Claudette says. "If he lives, it will be at the most basic level."

"Christ."

"I'm sorry," Claudette says. "And guilty. When the 10-13 came in, I was afraid it was you. Then I was relieved it wasn't."

He sees she's clean.

Or at least not high on heroin.

Maybe her tame doc's got her propped up so she can work.

She looks over his shoulder and sees Sheila, walking in straight for Malone. She knows this has to be the wife.

"You'd better go," Claudette says.

Malone turns around, sees Sheila and walks over to her. She puts her arms around him.

"I have blood all over me," Malone says.

"I don't care," she says. "Are you all right?"

"I'm fine," Malone says. "Levin's dead, Monty's in bad shape."

"Is he going to make it?"

"Maybe he shouldn't," Malone says.

She sees Claudette and knows right the fuck away. "Is that her? She's pretty, Denny. I can see what you see in her."

"Not here, Sheila."

"Don't worry," Sheila says. "I'm not going to cause a scene, not in front of Yolanda, what she's going through."

She walks over to Claudette. "I'm Sheila Malone."

"I figured. I'm sorry about your friend."

"I just came over to tell you," Sheila says, "you want my husband, you can have him. Good luck with him, honey."

Sheila goes over to Yolanda and throws her arms around her.

There's nothing an Irish Catholic police inspector loves more than death and tragedy. McGivern's worse than an old lady for that stuff; several times Malone has walked into his office and caught him reading the obituaries.

Now he finds McGivern in the hospital chapel, clutching his rosary beads.

"Denny . . . I was just saying a prayer."

Malone lowers his voice. "If Homicide starts looking into motive, if they pick up Castillo, it might all come out."

"What all might come out?"

Don't you fucking play the innocent with me, Malone thinks. "The Pena thing."

"Oh, I don't know anything about that."

"Where do you think your fat envelopes came from?" Malone

asks. "We went in together on a lottery ticket, that was your share? It was just coincidence after the Pena bust your monthly went up like an insider stock?"

"You never told me anything about the Pena bust," McGivern says, his voice getting tight, "except what was in your report."

"You didn't want to know."

"And I still don't." McGivern gets up. "Excuse me, Sergeant. I have a gravely wounded officer to look in on."

Malone doesn't get out of the pew. "If they get Castillo, he might start telling stories about how many kilos were really in that room. If he does, that goes on me and on my partners, including the gravely wounded officer you're so concerned about."

"But you're going to stand up, aren't you?" McGivern says. "I know you, Denny. I know the man your father raised would never inform on a brother officer."

"I could go to prison."

"Your family will be taken care of," McGivern says.

"That's what mob guys say."

"We're different," McGivern says. "We mean it."

"You and my old man," Malone says, "were you on the pad together way back in the day?"

"We took care of our families," McGivern says. "You and your brother never went without. Your father saw to that."

"Like father like son."

"You're like a son to *me*, Denny," McGivern says. "Your father, may our Lord bless and keep him, made me promise that I'd look after you. Help you in your career, make sure you did the right thing. You're going to do the right thing now, aren't you? Tell me you're going to do the right thing."

"Which is to keep my mouth shut."

"That is the right thing to do."

Malone looks at his face. Sees the fear. "Then I'm going to do the right thing, Inspector."

He gets up and edges out of the pew.

McGivern steps into the aisle, faces the altar and crosses himself. Then he turns to Malone. "You're a good boy, Denny."

Yeah, Malone thinks.

I'm your good boy.

He don't cross himself.

What's the point?

They've moved Monty to Intensive Care.

When Malone goes up to ICU, a nurse blocks him in the hall outside Monty's room. "Immediate family only, sir."

"I'm immediate family," Malone says, showing her his badge as he moves around her. "But I appreciate you looking out."

Monty is still in a coma and unresponsive. He had a "coronary incident" but they managed to stabilize him. What the fuck for, Malone thinks, feeling guilty as he thinks it, that it would have been better if they'd just let him go.

Yolanda is slumped in a chair, dozing. Machines hum and beep, their tubes running into Monty's mouth, nose and arms. His eyes are closed; what Malone can see of his face where it isn't bandaged is purple and swollen.

He puts his hand on Monty's.

Leans over and whispers, "Big Man, I'm so sorry. I'm so god-damn sorry for everything."

This time he can't stop the tears. They pour down his face, drip onto Monty's hand.

"Don't blame yourself, Denny." Yolanda has woken up. "It's not your fault."

"I was in command. It was my fault."

"Monty's a grown man," Yolanda says. "He knew the risks."

"He's strong. He's going to make it."

"Even if he does," Yolanda says, "he's going to be a vegetable.

I'm going to have my husband in my apartment drooling in a wheel-chair. His disability insurance isn't going to pay for all he needs, not to mention three sons. I don't know what we're going to do."

Malone looks at her. "Yolanda, did Monty ever talk to you about the money?"

She looks confused.

"The extra money."

"From the moonlighting jobs? Sure, but—"

Shit, Malone thinks.

She doesn't know.

Malone bends down, puts his arms around her, says quietly, "Monty has over a million dollars stored away. Some in cash, some in investments. He didn't tell you?"

"I always thought we lived off his salary."

"You did," Malone says. "I guess he was saving the rest."

"Where—"

"You don't need to know," Malone says. "Phil knows where it is, how to access it. But talk to him tonight, Yo. *Tonight.*"

She looks into his eyes. "The Job, it doesn't leave you anything, does it?"

He squeezes her hand and walks out.

Russo sits in the little lounge outside ICU, leafing through an old copy of *Sports Illustrated*.

"We gotta talk," Malone says.

"Okay."

"Not here. Outside."

They walk through the hospital to a back door out by the service entrance. Dumpsters overflow with garbage, cigarette butts are grouped on the asphalt in little arcs where the chain smokers stood.

Malone sits on the stoop, puts his head in his hands.

Russo leans against a Dumpster. "Jesus Christ, who knew something like this would happen?"

"We did," Malone says.

"We didn't kill that kid, and we didn't shoot Monty," Russo says. "The Domos did."

"The hell we didn't," Malone says. "Let's at least be honest with each other. This thing has been no good since Billy died. Sometimes I think that was God punishing us for what we did. This ends tonight."

"The fuck it does," Russo said. "Our partner's dying in there. We have to respond."

"It's over," Malone says.

"You think this is just going to go away now?" Russo asks. "A shooting board? IAB? Homicide will be all over this and they'll be looking for a motive. It could open up the whole Pena thing."

"We're finished," Malone says.

"The only people who can give up anything about Pena are right here," Russo says. "As long as we stick with each other, they can't touch us. It's just you and me now, that's it."

Malone starts to sob.

Russo steps over, puts his hands on Malone's shoulders. "It's okay, Denny, it's okay."

"It's not okay." Red-faced, his cheeks streaked with tears, he looks up at Russo. "It was me, Phil."

"It's not your fault. It could have happened—"

"Phil, it wasn't Levin. It was *me*."

Russo stares at him for a second, then he understands.

"Oh, fuck, Denny." He sits down beside him. Sits quiet for a long time, like he's stunned, like he got hit with something. Then he asks, "How did they get to you?"

"It was stupid shit," Malone says. "Piccone."

"Jesus Christ, Denny," Russo says, "you couldn't do four years?"

"I would have. I kept you out of it," Malone says. "Then Savino flipped. The feds threatened Sheila. Said they'd put her away for tax evasion, receiving stolen property. I couldn't . . ."

"What about *our* wives?" Russo asks. "*Our* families?"

"They promised to keep all our families out of it if I gave you up," Malone says.

Russo arches his back. Looks up at the sky. Then he asks, "What did you give them?"

"Everything," Malone says. "Except killing Pena. It would go down as a felony murder for the three of us. And I got you on tape, talking about the bust, the money . . ."

"So I'm looking at what, twenty to life?" Russo says. "What's *your* deal? What did you get for flipping on us?"

"Twelve years," Malone says. "Confiscation. Fines."

"Fuck you, Denny," Russo says. Then he asks, "When are they taking me?"

"Tomorrow," Malone says. "I wasn't supposed to tell you until a few minutes before."

"That's fucking big of you."

"You can run," Malone says.

"How am I gonna run?" Russo asks. "I have a family. Christ, when my kids see me . . ."

"I'm sorry," Malone says.

"It's not all on you," Russo says. "We're grown men. We knew what we were doing. We knew where it could go. But how the fuck did we get here?"

"A step at a time," Malone says. "We were good cops, once. Then . . . I dunno . . . but we just put fifty kilos of smack out on our own streets. That's not what we started out to do. It's the exact opposite of what we started out to do. It's like you light a match, you don't think it's going to do any harm. Then the wind comes up and changes and it becomes a fire that burns down everything you love."

"I loved you, Denny," Russo says, getting up. "Like a brother, I loved you."

Russo walks away and leaves him sitting there.

alone walks through the front door of what used to be his home on Staten Island to find O'Dell standing there waiting for him.

"What are you doing in my house?" Malone asks.

"Keeping your family safe," O'Dell says. "The better question is, why aren't you?"

"Maybe you heard," Malone says. "I had a couple of brothers shot. One's dead, the other might as well be."

"I'm sorry."

"Yeah?" Malone asks. "You have a piece of that, laying a rat tag on Levin."

"I was trying to save your ass."

"You were trying to save your investigation."

"I didn't send him through the door," O'Dell says. "You did."

"Keep telling yourself that." He pushes past O'Dell and walks into the kitchen.

Sheila sits at the breakfast bar with her head down.

Two feds in suits stand against the wall, one looks out the kitchen-door window onto the backyard.

Sheila's been crying, he can see the red puffiness under her eyes.

"You guys want to give us a minute?" Malone asks.

The two agents look at each other.

"Let me rephrase that," Malone says. "Give us a fucking minute. Go help your boss guard the living room."

They leave the kitchen.

Sheila looks up at him. "You got something you want to tell me, Denny?"

"What have you heard?"

"Don't play me!" she yells. "I'm not some skel! I'm not IAB! I'm your wife! I deserve to know!"

"Where are the kids?" Malone asks.

"Oh, shit, it's true," Sheila says. "They're at my mother's. What happened, Denny? Are you in trouble?"

A part of him wants to lie to her, keep playing it out. But he can't do it—even if he wants to, she knows him too well, has always known when he's lying. Part of which crashed their marriage—she always knew when he was trying to lie.

So he tells her.

All of it.

"Jesus, Denny."

"I know."

"Are you going to jail?"

"Yeah."

"What about us?" she asks. "Me and the kids? What have you done to us?!"

"I didn't hear you complaining about the envelopes," Malone says. "The new living room furniture, your restaurant tabs—"

"Don't put this on me!" she yells. "Don't you dare put this on me!"

No, it's on me, Malone thinks.

No one put us here but me.

"I have cash put away," Malone says, "where the feds can't get to it. Whatever happens, you'll be taken care of . . . the kids' college . . ."

She's reeling. He can't blame her.

"Did you give them Phil?" she asks. "Monty?"

He nods.

"Jesus," she says. "How am I ever going to face Donna again?"

"It's okay, Sheel."

"It's okay?!" she asks. "We have federal agents in our house! Why are they here?"

He puts his arm around her shoulder. "Listen. Don't freak out on me. But we might have to go into the program."

"Witness protection?"

"Maybe."

"What the *fuck,* Denny?!" Sheila says. "We're supposed to take the kids out of school, away from their friends, family? Move to what, Arizona or someplace, we're going to be cowboys or something?"

"I don't know, it might be a fresh start."

"I don't want a fresh start," Sheila says. "I have family here. My parents, my sister, my brothers . . ."

"I know."

"The kids, they're never supposed to see their cousins again?"

"Let's take this one step at a time, okay?"

"What's the next step?"

"You and the kids," he says, "you take a little vacation."

"We can't pull them out of summer camp."

"Yeah, we can," Malone says. "We're going to. Soon as they come home. Go to, I don't know, the Poconos, you've always wanted to go there, right? Or that place up in New Hampshire."

"For how long?"

"I don't know."

"Oh my God."

"I need you to be strong, Sheel," Malone says. "I really need you to be strong right now. You have to trust me on this. To get this thing straightened out, take care of this for our family. Pack a few things. I'll get the kids' things together."

"That's all you have to say."

"What do you want me to say?"

"I don't know," Sheila says. "'I'm sorry'?"

"I'm sorry, Sheila." You don't know how sorry I am. "A couple of days, the feds will bring me to where you are and—"

"No, Denny."

"What do you mean, no?"

"I don't want to be with you anymore," Sheila says. "I don't want you around our kids."

"Sheel—"

"No, Denny," she says. "You talk a great game—family, brotherhood, loyalty. Honesty. Honesty, Denny? You want honesty? You're empty. You're an empty person. I knew you took money, I knew you were a crooked cop. But I didn't know you were a killer. And I didn't know you were a rat. But that's who you are, and I don't want my son growing up to be his father."

"You'd take my kids from me?"

"You already threw them away," Sheila says. "Like you threw everything else in your life away. Why wasn't I enough for you, Denny? Why weren't we enough for you? I knew the deal, shit, I grew up with the deal. You marry a cop, he's distant, he's removed, maybe he drinks too much, okay, maybe he fucks around a little. But he comes home. He comes home and he stays. I took that deal. I thought you did, too. Say good-bye to the kids. You owe them that. And then you owe it to them to stay away from them, let them forget about you."

It goes tough with the kids.

Harder even than Malone thought.

Shit, when he was a kid his old man said he was going to take him out of school he'd have pissed his pants with joy, but John and Caitlin were all about they had dance class, Little League, day camp.

And the feds frightened them.

Now they stand in the living room, looking out the window at the feds Malone told to wait out in the street, for Chrissakes.

"Who are they, Daddy?" Caitlin asks.

"Cop friends."

"How come we've never met them before?"

"They're new."

"How come they're driving us?"

"Because I have to go back to work," Malone says.

"Catching bad guys," John says, although this time he doesn't sound so sure.

"Why can't Uncle Phil take us?" Caitlin asks.

He puts his arms around both of them, draws them close. "Listen, I need you two to keep a big secret. Can you?"

They both nod, pleased.

"Me and Uncle Phil are working on a very big case," Malone says. "Top secret."

"I saw that on TV," John says.

"Well, that's what we're doing," Malone says. "We're pretending to be bad guys, do you understand? So if you hear someone say that we *are,* you have to pretend to go along with it. Don't say anything."

"Is that why we have to hide?" Caitlin asks.

"That's right," says Malone. "We're fooling the bad guys."

"Are the bad guys going to try to find us?" John asks.

"Nooooo, no."

"Then why are the new police going with us?"

"It's just part of the game," Malone says. "Now give me a big hug and promise me you're going to be good and take care of Mommy, okay?"

They hug him so tight he wants to cry. He whispers into John's ear. "Johnny."

"Yeah, Dad."

"You gotta promise me something."

"Okay."

"You gotta know," Malone says, choking back tears. "You're a good kid. And you're gonna be a good man. Okay?"

"Okay."

"Okay."

Then O'Dell comes in and tells them they have to get going.

Malone kisses Sheila on the cheek.

It's a show for the kids.

She doesn't say anything to him.

She already had her say.

He opens the car door and helps her in.

Watches his family drive away.

Donna Russo answers the door.

She's been crying. "Go away, Denny. You're not welcome."

"I'm sorry, Donna."

"You're *sorry*?" she asks. "You sat at our table, on Christmas Day. With my family. Did you know then? Did you sit there with us knowing you were going to destroy my family?"

"No."

"What did you come here for?" Donna asks. "So I could tell you I understand? I forgive you? So you could feel better about yourself?"

No, Malone thinks. So I could feel worse.

He hears Russo yell, "Is that Denny? Let him in!"

"No," Donna says. "Not in this house. He doesn't set foot in this house ever again."

Russo comes to the door. Looks like he's been crying, too. "Sheila and the kids, they're pretty busted up?"

"Yeah."

"Yeah," Russo says, "They don't know they're the lucky ones yet. This is my last night with my family, so unless you got something to say . . ."

"I just wanted to make sure—"

"I didn't eat my gun?" Russo asks. "Irish do that, not Italians. Us guineas think about living, not dying. We just think about doing what we have to do."

"I wish Monty *had* put one in my head."

"Suicide by cop?" Russo asks. "Too easy, Denny. Way too easy. If you don't have the balls to do it yourself, you live with what you

did. You live with being a rat. Now, you don't mind, I'm going to
go hug my kids while I can."

Donna closes the door.

Claudette stands in the doorway of her apartment, not letting him in.

She's clean, newly clean, her sobriety delicate, fragile, a porcelain
cup that would shatter at a harsh sound.

"Go back to your wife," she says, not unkindly.

Malone says, "She doesn't want me."

"So you come back to me?" Claudette asks.

"No," Malone says. "I came to say good-bye."

Claudette looks surprised, but says, "That's probably for the
best. We're no good for each other, Denny. I've been hitting the
meetings."

"That's good."

"I have to get clean," she says. "I'm *going* to get clean, and I can't
do that and love you at the same time."

She's right.

He knows that she's right.

They're two drowning people who grab on to each other, won't
let go, and sink together into the cold darkness of their shared sorrow.

"I just wanted you to know," Malone says. "You were never
'some whore I fucked.' I loved you. I still do."

"I love you, too."

"I'm dirty," Malone says.

"A lot of cops—"

"No, I'm *dirty*," Malone says. He has to tell her—it's time to
come clean. "I put heroin on the street."

"Oh," she says.

Just that, "Oh," but it says everything.

"I'm sorry," Malone says.

"What happens now?" she asks. "Are you going to jail?"

"I made a deal."

"What kind of a deal?"

The kind that puts me on the other side forever. The kind I couldn't look at you in the morning.

"I'm going away," he says.

"One of those programs? Like in the movies?"

"Something like that."

"Baby, I'm sorry."

"Me too."

I am so, so sorry.

The heavy bag jumps.

Pops on its chain and drops back as Malone cocks his left again and then lets go with a brutal body shot.

Again and again and again.

Sweat flies off his face onto the bag. He comes over the top with a right cross and then follows with a left to the liver.

It feels good.

Feels good to hurt.

The sweat, the burn in his lungs, even his raw and bruised knuckles as he works out bare fisted against the bag's rough canvas, flecked now with his blood. Malone's taking it out on the bag, taking it out on himself, they both deserve the pain, the hurt, the rage.

Malone sucks in some air and goes at it again, his heavy punches aimed at O'Dell, Weintraub, Paz, Anderson, Chandler, Savino, Castillo, Bruno . . . but mostly at Denny Malone.

Sergeant Denny Malone.

Hero cop.

Rat.

He finishes with a punch to the heart.

The bag jumps and then settles back down on its chain, swings gently like something that's dead but don't know it yet.

CHAPTER 32

n the morning, Malone walks down Broadway past a newsstand on the corner.

He sees his face on the cover of the *New York Post* with a screaming headline, TWO HEROES SHOT, a picture of Malone standing with Russo and Monty in the aftermath of Pena.

Monty's image is highlighted in a white oval like a halo.

The *Daily News* shouts ONE ELITE COP KILLED, ANOTHER WOUNDED and has a slightly different photo of Malone, and a photo of Malone from the Pena bust with a subline reading DIRTY DENNY? DID HE FEEL LUCKY?

The front page of the *New York Times* doesn't have his picture but a headline reads WITH LATEST BLOODBATH, IS IT TIME TO RECONSIDER ELITE POLICE UNITS?

The byline is Mark Rubenstein.

Malone hails a taxi and goes to Manhattan North.

Russo looks sharp.

Pressed Armani suit, white monogrammed shirt with cuff links, red Zegna tie, Magli shoes shined to a high polish. Summer, he ain't wearing the retro overcoat but he has it draped over his arm, making it awkward for O'Dell to cuff him.

At least he does it in front, not behind his back.

Malone lays the overcoat over the cuffs.

The media's outside Manhattan North. TV trucks, radio, print guys with their photographers.

"You have to do that?" Malone asks O'Dell. "Make him do the perp walk?"

"I didn't."

"Someone did."

"Well, it wasn't me."

"And you had to do it here," Malone says, "in front of other cops."

"Did you want me to do it at his house, in front of his kids?" O'Dell looks angry, tense. He should be—every cop in the station is eye-fucking him and the other feds.

Eye-fucking Malone, too.

He could have skipped this—O'Dell told him to—but Malone thought he had to be there.

Deserved to be there.

To watch them put bracelets on his brother.

Russo keeps his head up.

"Good-bye, you fucking donkeys," Russo says. "Have fun waiting out your pensions!"

The feds take him out.

Malone walks with him.

Cameras click like machine guns.

Reporters press forward but the uniforms keep them back. The guys in the bags are in no mood to take any shit. Seeing another cop go out in cuffs makes them sick and scared.

And angry.

After the cop shootings, the Blue went into the projects in waves and with bad intent.

The uniforms disabled the dash-cam systems on their cars so the video cameras wouldn't work and then went to town.

You had a warrant, a no-show parole date, a complaint for littering—you were going. You had as much as a roach on you, an old needle, a pipe with a grain of old rock in it, you're going. You resisted arrest, you talked smack, you as much as looked at a cop sideways, you caught a bad beating and then you got thrown in the car with your hands cuffed behind your back but your seat belt unfastened and the cops would speed up and then hit the brakes so your face smashed into the security screen.

The Three-Two went through St. Nick's twice—looking for weapons, dope, most of all information, trying to get someone to snitch, to drop a dime, to sell a name.

Da Force—what's left of the motherfuckers anyway—came in right behind and they weren't looking for collars, they were looking for payback, and the only way to stay out of the equation was to give them information and then you were stuck in a jam between Da Force and DeVon Carter and the thing is, Da Force is going to come and go.

DeVon Carter stays.

You got to catch a beating, you catch it with your mouth shut like it's wired, which it might well be by the time Da Force and their plainclothes dogs got done with you.

The people in St. Nick's were wondering why they were catching the shit when everyone knew it was the Domos who massacred those cops, all the way over on the other side of Harlem.

So when the word got out that a cop from Da Force was heading out in cuffs, an eager crowd gathered out on the street.

Hooting, hollering.

If the cameras weren't there, the uniforms might charge them, clean their clocks, shut their fucking mouths.

Russo slips into the backseat of a black car.

Waves to Malone.

Then he's gone.

Malone walks back into the house.

A few cops look at him sideways. No one talks to him.

Except Sykes.

"Clean out your locker," he says. "Then come to my office."

The desk sergeant looks down, cops turn their backs as Malone walks past.

He goes down to the Task Force locker room. Gallina is there with Tenelli and Ortiz, a couple of plainclothes sit on the bench, shooting the shit.

They shut up when Malone comes in.

Everyone finds a reason to look at the floor.

Malone opens his locker.

And sees a dead rat.

He hears suppressed laughs behind him and whirls around. Gallina is smirking at him, Ortiz coughs into his fist.

Tenelli just stares.

"Who did this?" Malone asks. "Which one of you assholes?"

Ortiz says, "This place has vermin. It needs an exterminator."

Malone grabs him and slams him into the opposite lockers. "Is that you, huh? You the exterminator? You want to start now?"

"Get your hands off me."

"Maybe you got something else you want to say."

"Let go of him, Malone," Gallina says.

"Stay out of this," Malone says. He gets right into Ortiz's face. "You got something to say to me?"

"No."

"What I thought," Malone says. He lets him go, cleans out his locker and walks out.

Hears laughter behind him.

Then he hears, "Dead man walking."

Sykes doesn't ask him to sit down.

Just says, "Your shield and your gun on my desk."

Malone takes off his shield, sets it on the desk, then puts his duty weapon beside it.

"I guess I always knew that you were a dirty cop," Sykes says, "but I didn't think the legendary Denny Malone was a rat, too. I had some respect for you—not much, but some—but now I don't have any. You're a crook and a coward and you disgust me. The King of

Manhattan North? You're the king of nothing. Get out. I can't stand to look at you."

"If it helps, I can't either."

"It doesn't," Sykes says. "My replacement is on his way. My career is over. You took it from me, just like you stole the reputations of thousands of decent, honest cops. I know you made a deal, but I hope they put you under the jail anyway. I hope you rot there."

"I won't last long in prison," Malone says.

"Oh, they'll keep you safe," Sykes says. "They store you at Fort Dix, haul you out to testify. You have three or four years of informing on your brothers before they put you in an actual facility. You'll be fine, Malone. Rats always are."

Malone walks out of his office and then out of the house.

Eyes follow him.

So does silence.

McGivern's waiting for him out on the street.

"Did you give me up, too?" McGivern asks.

"Yeah."

"What do they have?"

"Everything," Malone says. "They have you on tape."

"Your father would be ashamed," McGivern says. "He's rolling in his grave."

They reach Eighth Avenue.

Malone waits for the light.

It turns green and he starts to cross. He hears McGivern behind him, yelling, "You're going to hell, Malone! You're going to hell!"

No question about it, Malone thinks.

It's a slam dunk.

The receptionist remembers him.

"The last time I saw you," she says, "you had a dog."

"He pulled the pin."

"Mr. Berger will be right with you," she says. "If you'd like to have a seat."

He sits down and leafs through *GQ*. It tells him what the well-dressed man is going to be wearing that fall. A few minutes later, the receptionist shows him into Berger's office.

It's bigger than Malone's whole apartment. He sets the briefcase down by Berger's desk. The lawyer will know what it is.

"Would you like a drink?" Berger asks. "I have some excellent brandy."

"No, I'm good."

"You don't mind if I indulge," Berger says. "It's been a day. I understand that Russo is in federal custody."

"That's right."

"And you felt it necessary to be present," Berger says, pouring himself a drink from a crystal decanter. "Tell me, Malone, does your masochism know no bounds?"

"I guess not."

"I've heard," Berger said, "that something like two-thirds of the firefighters and police who ran into the Towers that day took Last Rites. I wonder if that's true."

"Probably."

"If you are going to be a star witness," Berger says, "you are going to have to be more prolix. That means—"

"I know what it means."

"Better already." Berger tosses down his drink. "I guaranteed O'Dell that I would surrender you by three o'clock. That leaves a couple of hours. Do you have any business to take care of? Anything you need?"

"I have my toothbrush, but we have some business," Malone says. "There's a woman named Debbie Phillips. She just had a baby, Billy O'Neill's son. Share of that money needs to be doled out to her, a little at a time. All the information's in there. Can you do that?"

"I can," Berger says. "Anything else?"

"That's it."

"Well, no time like the present then."

The receptionist sticks her head in. "Mr. Berger, you asked to be informed. They're about to make an announcement on the Bennett investigation."

Berger flicks on a television mounted to the wall. "Shall we?"

The DA appears behind a lectern, flanked by the commissioner and the chief of patrol.

"This was an unfortunate incident," the DA reads into a microphone, "but the facts are clear. The deceased, Mr. Bennett, refused Officer Hayes's lawful order to stop. He turned, advanced toward Officer Hayes while taking from his jacket what appeared to be a handgun. Officer Hayes discharged his weapon, fatally striking Mr. Bennett. Tragically, what Officer Hayes perceived to be a weapon was eventually determined to have been a cell phone. But Officer Hayes acted lawfully within the parameters of proper procedure. Had Mr. Bennett obeyed the lawful order, the tragic consequences would not have followed. That being the case, the grand jury has declined to press any charges against Officer Hayes."

"Judicially correct," Berger says, "but politically idiotic. Totally tone-deaf. The ghettos will be burning by sunset. Are you ready to go?"

Malone's ready.

Berger's driver takes them down to the FBI field office at 26 Federal Plaza. Who the fuck knew, Malone thinks, I'd go to hell in a chauffeured limo?

The building is a tower of glass and steel, cold as a dead heart. They go through the metal detectors, then up to O'Dell's office on the fourteenth floor, sit on a bench in the hallway and wait.

O'Dell's office door opens and Russo comes out.

Sees Malone sitting there.

"So you didn't put one in your head," Russo says.

"No." Should have, maybe, he thinks.

Didn't.

"That's okay," Russo says. "I did it for you."

"The fuck you talking about, Phil?"

"I told you last night," Russo says, "I was going to do what I had to do."

Malone doesn't get it.

Russo leans over, speaks right into his face. "You gave me up to save your family. I don't blame you. I'd have done the same thing. So I just did, Denny."

Then it hits him—Russo had only one card to play, and he'd laid it down.

"Yeah, Pena," Russo says. "I told them you murdered him. Shot that spic motherfucker in cold blood. Now I testify, I'm the star fucking witness at your trial, I walk, I go sell aluminum siding in Utah and *you* get the life without parole."

A fed comes out of the office, takes Russo by the wrist and starts to lead him away.

"No hard feelings, Denny," Russo says. "We each did what we had to do."

O'Dell opens the door and gestures for Malone to come in.

"Our deal is off," O'Dell says. "Your client will be charged with capital murder. His testimony will no longer be required as we have Phil Russo for everything we need. And Sergeant Malone will have to find new legal representation, as you will no longer be able to function in that role."

"How's that?"

"You'll be conflicted out," Weintraub says. "We'll call you as a prosecution witness to testify as to Malone's considerable personal *animus* against Diego Pena."

O'Dell cuffs Malone and takes him to the Metro Correctional Center down on Park Row and puts him in a holding cell.

The door shuts and just like that Malone is on the other side.

"Why did you have to kill him?" O'Dell asks.

CHAPTER 33

t was Nasty Ass who tipped Malone that something was wrong at 673 West 156th. This was back in the early days of the Task Force, a fetid August night, and the snitch didn't even want to be paid for it, not in cash or smack, and he looked shaken as he said, "I heard it's bad, Malone, really bad."

Malone's team went to check it out.

You go through a lot of doors on the Job. Most of them are forgettable, indistinguishable.

Malone would never forget this one.

The whole family was dead.

Father, mother, three young kids ranging in age from seven down to three. Two boys and a girl. The kids had been shot in the back of the head; same with the two adults, although they'd been chopped up with machetes first—arterial blood had sprayed all over the walls.

Russo crossed himself.

Montague just stared—the murdered kids were black and Malone knew he was thinking about his own children.

Billy O cried.

Malone called it in—five homicides, all AA—adult male, adult female, three minors. And step the fuck on it. It took maybe five minutes for Minelli from Task Force Homicide to get there—the ME right behind him with the Crime Scene people.

"Jesus Christ," Minelli said, staring. Then he shook it off and said, "Okay, thanks, we got it from here."

"We stay with it," Malone said. "It's drug related."

"How do you know?"

"The adult vic is DeMarcus Cleveland," Malone says. "That's his wife, Janelle. They were midlevel smack slingers for DeVon Carter. This wasn't a robbery—the place hasn't been tossed. They just came in and executed them."

"For what?"

"Slinging on the wrong corners."

Minelli wasn't going to get into a border skirmish on this one, not with three dead kids. Even the Crime Scene people were shook—no one made the usual jokes or looked around for something to put in their pockets.

"You have an idea who did it?" Minelli asked.

"Yeah, I do," Malone said. "Diego Pena."

Pena was a midlevel manager in the Dominicans' NYC operation. His job was to stabilize the otherwise chaotic retail business in the neighborhood, get the low-level blacks under control or move them out. Briefly put, you buy from us or you don't buy.

Malone's hunch was that the Clevelands had refused to get in line and pay the franchise fee. He'd heard DeMarcus Cleveland proclaim his resistance on a corner one night: "This is *our* motherfucking hood, Carter's motherfucking hood. We black, not Spanish. You see tacos around here? Brothers doing the fuckin' merengue?"

It got laughs on the corner, but no one was laughing now.

Or talking.

Malone and his team canvassed the building and no one heard anything. And it wasn't just the usual "fuck the cops, they won't do anything anyway" or the gangbanger "we take care of our own business" attitude.

It was fear.

Malone understood—you kill a dealer in a turf dispute it's just another day in the neighborhood. You kill the dealer and his whole family—his kids—you're sending a message to everybody.

Pónganse a la cola.

Get in line.

Malone wasn't taking "I don't know" for an answer.

Three dead children, shot in their beds, he went full Task Force on it. You don't want to be a witness? Cool, you can be a defendant. He and his team rousted every junkie, dealer and hooker in the hood. They popped guys for just standing there—loitering, littering, looking at them wrong. You didn't hear nothing, see nothing, you don't know nothing? That's okay, don't worry about it, we'll give you some time in Rikers to think about it, maybe something will come to mind.

The team filled up booking in the Three-Two, the Three-Four and the Two-Five. Their captain back then was Art Fisher—he had street brains and balls, and didn't give them any shit about it.

Torres did. He and Malone about got into it in the locker room when Torres asked him, "What are you busting your ass for on this thing? It's NHI."

No Humans Involved.

"Three dead kids?"

"If you do the math," Torres said, "that saves the city, what, about eighteen illegitimate *grand*kids on welfare?"

"Shut your stupid mouth or you won't be giving blow jobs for a month," Malone said.

Monty had to get between them. You don't go around Big Monty to get into a beef. He said to Malone, "Why do you let him get to you?" Meaning, *I don't, why should you?*

Who worked the case hard was Nasty Ass.

When he wasn't whacked out, the snitch worked the streets like he was cop. (Malone had to warn him more than once that he wasn't.) He went out of his way, took chances, asked questions of people he shouldn't have been asking questions. For some reason this got to him, and Malone, who had long since decided that junkies didn't have souls, had to reconsider his opinion.

But it turned up nothing they could use to get to Pena.

He just kept pushing the heroin—a product labeled Dark Horse—onto the street, and everyone was too afraid of him to get in his way.

"We have to go after him more direct," Malone said one night as they sat in the Carmansville Playground tossing back a few beers.

"Why don't we kill him?" Monty asked.

"Worth going to the joint for you?" Malone asked.

"Maybe."

"You got kids," Russo said. "A family. We all do."

"It isn't murder if he tries to kill us first," Malone said.

That's how it began, Malone's campaign to goad Pena into trying to kill a cop.

They started with a club in Spanish Harlem, a real nice salsa place Pena had a piece of, maybe laundered money through. They waited for a Friday night when the place was packed and went in like storm troopers on crack.

The security guys at the door tried to jump ugly when Malone and team walked right past the line, showed their badges and said they were coming in.

"You got a warrant?"

"The fuck are you, Johnnie Cochran?" Malone asked. "I saw a guy with a gun run over here. Hey, maybe it was you. Was it you, Counselor? Turn around, put your hands behind your back."

"I got my constitutional rights!"

Monty and Russo grabbed him by the back of the shirt and threw him through the plate glass window.

One woman had her phone on video and held it up. "I have everything right here, what you did!"

Malone walked over, knocked the phone out of her hand and crushed it under his Doc Marten. "Anyone else had their constitutional rights violated? I want to know right now so that we can rectify the situation."

No one spoke. Most people looked down.

"Now get out of here while you have the chance."

The team went into the club and busted that shit up. Monty took an aluminum baseball bat to the glass tables, chairs. Russo kicked in speakers. Customers scrambled to get out of the way. It sounded like a rainstorm on a tin roof as people dropped guns on the floor.

Malone went behind the bar and swept bottles off. Then he told one of the bartenders, "Open the register."

"I don't know if—"

"I saw you put coke in there. Open it up."

She opened it and Malone took out handfuls of bills and tossed them over the bar like leaves.

A big guy in an expensive silk shirt, a real *crema,* came up to him. "You can't—"

Malone grabbed him by the back of the neck and slammed his face onto the bar. "Why don't you tell me again what I can't do? You the manager?"

"Yes."

He took a handful of bills and shoved them into the man's mouth. "Eat these. Come on, *jefe,* eat. No? Then maybe you keep your fucking mouth shut, except to tell me where Pena is. Is he here? Is he in the back room?"

"He left."

"He left?" Malone asked. "If I go back into the VIP room and he is there, you and I are going to have a problem. Well, *you're* going to have a problem—I'm just going to go *Riverdance* on your face."

"Toss everybody!" Malone shouted as he walked to the stairs. "Call the uniforms! Tell them to bring a bus! Everyone goes!"

He went up the stairs to the VIP room.

The security guy at the door seemed unsure, so Malone made up his mind for him. "I'm a VIP. I'm the most important person in your world right now because I'm the guy who decides if you get thrown into a cage with a crew of spic-hating *mallates.* So let me through."

The guy let him through.

Four men sat in a banquette with their ladies, gorgeous Latinas in full makeup, big hair and beautiful expensive short dresses.

Guns lay on the floor at the men's feet.

430 /   DON WINSLOW

These were heavy, well-dressed guys. Very calm, cool, arrogant. Malone knew they had to be Pena's people.

"Get out of the booth," Malone said. "Lie down on the floor."

"What do you think you're doing?" one of the men asked. "You're wasting everyone's time. None of these busts will stand up."

Another grabbed his phone and pointed it at Malone.

Malone said, "Hey, Ken Burns, the only documentary you're going to make is your own colonoscopy."

The guy set the phone down.

"On the floor, lie down. Everybody."

They eased out of the booth, but the women were reluctant to lie down because their skirts rode up too high.

"You're disrespecting our women," the first guy said.

"Yeah, they have a lot of self-respect, fucking pieces of shit like you," Malone said. "Ladies, did you know your boyfriends kill little kids? Three-year-olds? In their beds. Yeah, I definitely think you should marry these honks. Of course, they're probably married already."

"Show some respect," the guy says.

"You open your mouth to me again," Malone said, "I'm going to bring a female officer in here to do an orifice search on your ladies, and while she's doing that, I'm going to be kicking your brains in."

The guy started to say something, but then thought better of it.

Malone squatted and said quietly, "Now when you make bail, you run and tell Pena that Sergeant Denny Malone, Manhattan North Special Task Force, is going to wreck his clubs, bust his dealers, roust his customers, and then I'm going to start getting serious. Do you understand me? You may speak."

"I understand."

"Good," Malone says. "Then you call your bosses down in the Dominican and tell them it's never going to stop. You tell them that Pena has fucked up and Detective Sergeant Denny Malone, Manhattan North Special Task Force, is going to hose their Dark Horse into the sewers as long as Pena is walking upright in New York City. You tell them they don't run this neighborhood. I do."

THE FORCE / 431

The uniforms were already downstairs when Malone got there—cuffing people, picking up vials of coke, pills, the guns.

"Everyone goes," Malone told the uniform sergeant. "Possession of firearms, cocaine, Ecstasy, looks like a little smack . . ."

"Denny, you know these aren't going to hold up," the sergeant said.

"I know." He shouted to the crowd, "Don't come back to this club! This is going to happen every time!"

As he and the team walked out the door, Malone yelled, "May Da Force be with you!"

The captain then, Art Fisher, wasn't a pussy, so he shouldered the weight.

The ADAs filed into his office screaming that they couldn't and wouldn't pick up a single case, the whole raid was a Mapp violation, a prime example of bad police tactics bordering on—no, crossing the line of—brutality.

When Fisher stonewalled them ("Are you afraid of some Chiquita suing you over an iPhone?"), the prosecutors went to their immediate boss, who in those days was Mary Hinman.

That didn't work out so well.

"If you don't want to take the cases, don't," she said. "But don't make onions, either. Grow a pair and buckle up, the ride is going to get rougher."

One of them said, "So we're just going to let that Denny Malone and his crew of Neanderthals run roughshod over Manhattan North?"

Hinman didn't look up from her paperwork. "Are you still here? I thought you left when I told you to go do your job. Now if you don't want the job . . ."

IAB took a weak swing, too.

They were catching heat from complainants and the Civilian Complaint Review Board.

McGivern shut that down. He pulled from his desk a crime scene photo of the three children shot in the head and asked them if they wanted to see this on the front page of the *Post* with the headline INTERNAL AFFAIRS HALTS PROBE OF CHILD KILLERS.

They didn't want that, no.

This was all before Ferguson, before Baltimore and the rest of those killings, and while the Latin community was offended by the nightclub raid, it had no truck with baby killers, and neither did the black community.

Malone kept at it.

His team hit bodegas, stash houses, cash houses, clubs and corners. The word got out on the street that if you were dealing or shooting anything but Dark Horse, the police were going to turn the other way, but if you had Diego Pena's product, Da Force was coming straight at you on a collision course, no skid marks.

And they weren't going to stop.

Not until someone gave them something they could use on Pena.

Malone, he took it to a whole new level, one that broke the unwritten rules that govern the relationship between cops and gangsters. A dealer going down on his third bust gave up where Pena was really living, and Malone found him up in Riverdale and staked it out.

He'd watch Pena's wife take their two kids to the ritzy private school. One day, as she was walking from the car to the house on the way back, he walked up to her and said, "You have nice children, Mrs. Pena. Do you know that your husband has other people's families murdered? Have a wonderful day."

Malone wasn't back at the station ten minutes before a civilian assistant came up to tell him there was someone downstairs asking for Sergeant Malone.

She handed him a card. *Gerard Berger—Attorney-at-Law.*

Malone went downstairs to see an elegantly dressed man who had to be Gerard Berger, Attorney-at-Law. "I'm Sergeant Malone."

"Gerard Berger," Berger said. "I represent Diego Pena. Is there someplace we could go to talk?"

"What's wrong with here?"

"Nothing," Berger said. "I just wanted to spare you potential embarrassment in front of your fellow officers."

Embarrassment? Malone thought. In front of *these* guys? He'd seen some of them have contests to see who could ejaculate the farthest.

"No, this is fine," Malone said. "Why does Pena need representation? Has he been charged with something?"

"You know that he hasn't," Berger said. "Mr. Pena feels that he is being harassed by the NYPD. Specifically you, Sergeant Malone."

"Gee, that's too bad."

"Go ahead and joke," Berger said. "We'll see how funny you think this is when we sue you."

"Sue away. I don't have any money."

"You have a home in Staten Island," Berger said. "A family to take care of."

"Keep my family out of your mouth, Counselor."

Berger said, "My client is giving you a chance, Sergeant. Cease and desist. Otherwise we will file a civil suit and an official complaint with the department. I'll have your shield."

"Well, when you get it," Malone said, "stick it up your ass."

"You're dog shit under my shoe, Sergeant."

"Is that it?"

"For now."

Malone went back up to his desk. The whole squad had already heard that the infamous Gerard Berger had paid a visit.

"What did that hump want?" Russo asked.

"He gave me the whole you'll-never-work-in-this-town-again speech," Malone said. "Told me to lay off Pena."

"Are you going to?"

"Absolutely."

What Malone did next will forever go down in the folklore of Manhattan North as "Dog Day Afternoon."

Malone went to see Officer Grosskopf of the K-9 squad and asked to borrow Wolfie, an enormous Alsatian that had been terrorizing Harlem for the past two years.

"What are you going to do with him?" Grosskopf asked.

He loved Wolfie.

"Take him for a ride," Malone said.

Grosskopf said yes because it was very hard, not to mention risky, to say no to Denny Malone.

Malone and Russo got Wolfie into the back of Russo's car and drove to a food truck on East 117th that was technically called Paco's Tacos but was generally known as the Laxatruck, where Malone fed Wolfie three chicken enchiladas with chile verde, five mystery meat tacos, and a giant burrito called the Gutbuster.

Wolfie, normally held to the strictest of diets, was thrilled and grateful and fell instantly in love with Malone, licking him enthusiastically and happily wagging his tail as he got back in the car, eagerly awaiting the next gastronomic surprise.

"How long will it take to get there?" Malone asked Russo.

"Twenty minutes, no traffic."

"You think we got that long?"

"Gonna be close."

It took twenty-two minutes, during which time Wolfie's joy turned to discomfort as the greasy food worked its way through his bowels and then demanded exit. Wolfie whined, giving the signal that Grosskopf would instantly have recognized as a need to get out.

"Suck it up, Wolfie," Malone said, scratching his head. "We'll be there soon."

"This dog shits in my car . . ."

"He won't," Malone said. "He's a stud."

When they got there, Wolfie was twisting in discomfort and headed straight for the strip of grass outside the office building, but Malone and Russo took him inside, into the elevator and to the seventeenth floor.

Berger's receptionist, a drop-dead gorgeous young woman that

Berger was probably banging, said, "You can't bring a dog in here, sir."

"He's a service dog," Russo said, staring at her boobs. "I'm blind."

"Do you have an appointment with Mr. Berger?" she asked.

"No."

"What's the matter with your dog?"

The answer became immediately apparent.

Wolfie whined, Wolfie whirled, Wolfie let loose an almost apocalyptic blast of steaming, chili-infused dog shit all over Gerard Berger's (previously) white Surya Milan carpet.

"Oops," Malone said.

Exiting to the sound of the receptionist retching, Malone patted the shamefaced but relieved Wolfie's head and said, "Good boy, Wolfie. Good boy." Then they took Wolfie back to the station.

The word got there ahead of them because they were greeted with a standing ovation, and Wolfie was lavished with pets, hugs, kisses and a box of Milkbone cookies tied up with a blue ribbon.

"The captain wants to see you," the desk sergeant told Malone and Russo, "as soon as you get in."

They returned Wolfie to a livid Grosskopf and went into Fisher's office.

"I'm just going to ask you this once," he said. "Did you take a police dog to shit all over Gerard Berger's office?"

"Would I do something like that?" Malone asked.

"Get out. I'm busy."

He was. His phone was ringing off the hook with congratulations from every precinct in New York City.

Grosskopf never really forgave Malone for abusing Wolfie's digestive system, a hostility that was exacerbated by the fact that any time Malone came within fifty feet of Wolfie, the dog would try to go to him, because Malone had given him the best afternoon of his life.

Malone kept at it. Nasty Ass—and only God knew where he got this kind of information—told him that Pena's wife was holding a surprise birthday party for her husband at Rao's, the famous East Harlem eatery.

Pena, he was sitting at the big table with his family, his friends, more than one business leader, a few local pols, and he was opening his presents and took out a big package that was a framed photo of three dead children with a note: *From Your Friends at the Manhattan North Special Task Force—No Happy Returns, Baby Killer.*

Malone heard about it—from the wiseguys on Pleasant Avenue. He got invited to a sit-down with Lou Savino, whom he'd known since he was a beat cop in the bag. They sat outside a café with cups of espresso and the capo said, "You piece of work, you. You gotta cut this shit out."

"Since when are you a message boy for the tacos?"

"I could be offended by that," Savino said, "but I'm not going to be. We leave wives out of our business, Denny."

"Tell that to Janelle Cleveland. Oh, that's right, you can't. She and her whole family are dead."

"This is a pissing match between two sets of monkeys," Savino said. "You got your brown monkey and you got your black monkey. What's the difference which gets the banana? It's nothing to do with us."

"It better not be, Lou," Malone said. "If any of your people are moving Pena's product, all bets are off, I'm coming after them, I don't care."

He knew what he was doing—letting Savino know that if he wanted to deal smack, it had to be with anyone but Pena. It might prompt him to put in a call to the Dominican.

The key to staying alive in any kind of organized crime outfit is very simple—make other people money. As long as you're making other people money, you're safe. Start costing people money, you're a liability, and crime organizations don't keep liabilities on the books for very long.

It's not like they can write them off on their taxes.

Malone was turning Pena into a liability—the man was costing his bosses money and trouble, and he was becoming an embarrassment, a guy who was letting himself be humiliated, his wife insulted, his businesses trashed; he became the subject of jokes.

You're running for toastmaster general you want to be a comedian. You're trying to take over the ghetto drug trade, last thing you want to be is funny.

You want to be feared.

And if people are going Celebrity Roast on you, even behind your back, they ain't scared of you. And if they ain't scared of you, and you're not making people money, you're just a problem.

Drug organizations don't have HR departments. They don't bring you in, counsel you, instruct you on how you can improve your job performance. What they do is they send someone you know, someone you trust, who takes you out to drinks or to dinner and tells you, *Cuida de tu negocio.*

Take care of your business.

"Just sit down with the guy," Savino said, "is all I'm asking. We can work something out."

"Three dead kids. There's nothing to work out."

"It's always good to talk."

"He wants to talk," Malone said, "he comes in and confesses to ordering the murder of the Cleveland family, then he writes a statement. That's the only way I sit down with him."

But Savino played his trump card. "This isn't him asking, this is us."

Malone couldn't refuse a direct request from the Cimino family. They were in business together, he had obligations.

They met in the back room of a small restaurant in the East Harlem neighborhood controlled by the Ciminos. Savino guaranteed Malone's safety; he, in turn, promised that there would be no bust and he wouldn't wear a wire.

When Malone got into the room, Pena was already at the table. White shirt, overweight, ugly, even in a thousand-dollar suit. Savino got up to hug Malone and started to pat him down. Malone knocked his hands away. "You patting me down? You pat *him* down?"

"He's got no reason to wear a wire."

"*I* have no reason to wear a wire," Malone said. "This is not a way to start this sit-down, Lou."

"Where's the wire?"

"Up your mother's twat," Malone says. "Next time you eat her out, don't say anything incriminating. Fuck you, I'm outta here."

"It's all right," Pena said.

Savino shrugged and gestured at Malone to sit down.

"Who you taking orders from these days?" Malone asked Savino. He sat down across from Pena.

"Do you want anything?" Pena asked.

"I'm not breaking bread with you," Malone said. "I'm not drinking with you. Lou asked me to meet, so here I am. What do you want to say to me?"

"This all has to stop."

"It stops when they stick the needle in your arm," Malone said.

"Cleveland knew the rules," Pena said. "He knew that a man puts not only himself on the line, but his entire family. That's our way."

"This is my turf," Malone said. "My rules. And my rules are that we don't kill kids."

"Don't try to be morally superior with me," Pena said. "I know what you are. You're a dirty cop."

Malone looked at Savino. "Is that it? We've had our conversation now? Can I go, get something to eat?"

Pena set a briefcase on the table. "There's two hundred fifty thousand dollars in there. Take it and eat."

"What's this for?"

"You know what it's for."

"No, you *tell* me what it's for, you piece of garbage," Malone says. "You tell me it's for giving you a pass for murdering that family."

"Pat him down," Pena said to Savino.

"You lay a finger on me," Malone said, "so help me God, Lou, I will wipe this floor with you."

"He's wired," Pena said.

"You are," Savino said, "you're not walking out of here, Denny."

Malone ripped off his sports coat, popped his buttons, opening his shirt, baring his chest. "You happy now, Lou? Or you wanna put on a glove, stick a finger up my ass, you wop faggot motherfucker?"

"Jesus, no offense, Denny."

"Yeah, well, I'm offended, by you and by this baby killer." Malone picked up the briefcase, threw it at Pena. "I don't know what you heard about me but I know what you didn't hear. You didn't hear I was going to let some mutt kill three children on my beat and walk away. You offer me that briefcase again I'm going to shove it down your throat and out your ass. The only reason I don't hook you up and haul you in right now is I promised Lou I wouldn't. But that don't extend to tomorrow or the day after or the day after that. I'm going to put you on a slab, if your bosses don't beat me to it."

"Maybe I'll put *you* on a slab," Pena said.

"Do it," Malone said. "Come after me. Bring all your people, though. You call the wolf, you get the pack."

Russo and Montague appeared in the door of the restaurant as if they'd been listening. They had—they'd been sitting out in a car taping the whole fucking thing with a parabolic ear.

"You have a problem, Denny?" Russo asked. He was sporting a smile and a Mossberg 590 shotgun.

Monty wasn't smiling.

"No problem," Malone called back. He looked at Pena. "And you, shitbird. I'll ass-fuck your widow on your coffin until she calls me Papi."

They geared up, heavy.

Started carrying freakin' artillery.

It could come from any direction, from Pena or even from the Ciminos, although Malone doubted a Mafia family would be reckless enough to kill an NYPD detective.

They took precautions. Malone didn't go home to Staten Island but cooped up on the West Side. Russo kept his shotgun on the passenger seat. But they still hit the streets, worked Pena's operation, worked their sources, chipped away.

And Malone took the tape to Mary Hinman.

"Berger will walk through this like shit through a goose," Hinman said. "You didn't have a warrant, you didn't have probable cause—"

"Police officers surveilled a fellow officer on an undercover operation," Malone said. "In the course of those duties they heard a man confessing to a multiple murder and—"

"You want me to charge Pena with the Cleveland homicides based on that?" Hinman asked. "Career suicide."

"Just bring him in," Malone said. "Get him in the room. Let Homicide play him the tape and work on him."

"You think Berger will let him answer any question other than his name?" Hinman asked.

"Try anyway," Malone said, so tight, so frustrated, he was about to break out of his skin. "You owe me."

How many convictions did you get from me testilying?

They brought Pena in.

Malone watched from behind the window as Hinman played the tape. *"Cleveland knew the rules. He knew that a man puts not only himself on the line, but his entire family. That's our way."*

Berger held his hand up to Pena to keep quiet, looked at Hinman and said, "I don't hear anything even remotely close to a confession to or even guilty knowledge of the Cleveland murders. I heard a man expressing an admittedly repulsive cultural norm that, while reprehensible, is not criminal."

Hinman turned the tape back on.

"There's two hundred fifty thousand dollars in there. Take it and eat."

"What's this for?"

"You know what it's for."

"So now you think you have my client for attempting to bribe a police officer," Berger said. "Except you don't have the money. Perhaps the briefcase was empty. Perhaps my client was merely taunting Sergeant Malone in admittedly misguided retribution for his endless puerile harassments. Next?"

"No, you tell me what it's for, you piece of garbage. You tell me it's for giving you a pass for murdering that family."

"Pat him down."

Hinman played the rest of the tape.

Berger said, "I heard nothing incriminating. I did hear an NYPD detective threaten a subject and say that he was going to 'ass-fuck' his wife on his coffin. You must be very proud. In any case, this tape is not only useless, it would be inadmissible should you be so foolish as to bring charges against my client. A grand jury might be impressed; a judge would indignantly toss it in the garbage where it belongs. You have nothing on my client."

Hinman said, "We have a line on the shooters and they'll implicate your client. His moment to get on the bus, spare himself the needle, is now."

It was a total bluff, but Pena flinched.

Berger didn't. "Do I hear whistling past the graveyard? Or a tacit admission that your 'case' presently amounts to nothing? I will tell you this, Counselor, your police are out of control. I will take that up with the Civilian Complaint Review Board, but I would recommend you save your career by taking action and culling the rabid dogs from your pack."

He stood up and gestured for Pena to do the same. "Good day."

Berger looked straight into the mirror, took out a handkerchief, smiled at Malone and lifted his shoe. He wiped the sole and tossed the handkerchief into the trash can.

The neighborhood started to turn on Pena.

It was subtle at first, a mere leak. But the leak became a stream that became a flood that cracked open the wall of Pena's invulnerability.

No one came into the house—there wasn't that kind of trust—but it was a nod, a flick of the head, the slightest gesture to let Malone know, as he cruised the streets, that a conversation was wanted.

Those talks happened on the corner, in alleys, in tenement hallways, in shooting galleries, in bars. Words about who killed them three kids, who Pena hired, who the shooters were.

Some of it was cynical; the informants wanted the flow of heroin to resume, the hassling to stop, Malone to shut down his relentless campaign. But a lot of it was conscience freed from fear as the tide started to turn.

A picture began to emerge that Pena had hired two ambitious up-and-comers who wanted to make their bones with him. And the community was especially angry because they were black.

Tony and Braylon Carmichael were brothers, twenty-nine and twenty-seven, respectively, with sheets that stretched back to the early teens for assault, robbery, dealing and burglary, and now they were looking to move up as wholesalers for Pena.

He had an entry-level job for them first.

Kill the Clevelands.

The whole family.

Malone, Russo and Montague crashed into the apartment on 145th with guns drawn, ready to shoot.

Pena had gotten there first.

Tony Carmichael was slumped in a chair, two entry wounds in his forehead.

Well, Malone thinks, we managed to execute one of the killers, anyway—indirectly, by telling Pena we were on the shooters. They searched the rest of the apartment but didn't find Braylon, which meant that their case against Pena was still alive.

Malone went to Nasty Ass. "Put it out on the street. He reaches out to me, I promise to bring him in safe. No beating. He makes whatever deal he can make for testifying on Pena."

Braylon was a dumbass—his late brother was the brains of the operation. But Braylon had to be smart enough to know that Pena was hunting him, Cleveland's friends were hunting him, and his only chance was Malone.

He reached out that night.

Malone and his team picked him up in St. Nicholas Park, where he'd been hiding in some bushes, and brought him into the station.

"Don't say a fucking word to me," Malone said as he cuffed him. "Keep your mouth shut."

He wanted to do this right. Called in and made sure that Minelli was ready to interview and that Hinman was present. Braylon didn't want a lawyer. He gave it all up, how Pena had hired him and his brother to kill the Clevelands.

"Is it enough?" Malone asked.

"It's enough to arrest him."

She got a warrant on Pena, and Homicide went to pick him up—Hinman strictly forbade Malone to go.

Pena wasn't there.

They missed him by minutes.

Gerard Berger had surrendered his client to the feds.

Not for murder, for narcotics trafficking.

Malone exploded when Hinman called him with the news. "I don't want him for trafficking! I want him for the murders!"

"We don't get everything we want," Hinman said. "Sometimes we have to settle for what we can get. Come on, Malone, you won. Pena turned himself in to save his life and go to a federal lockup where his own people can't kill him. He'll do fifteen to thirty, probably die there. That's a victory. Take it."

Except it wasn't.

Gerard Berger cut his client the sweetheart deal of all time. In exchange for providing intelligence on the cartel and testifying in a dozen standing cases, Diego Pena received two years minus time served, which meant that when he was finished ratting on the stand he would probably walk away.

A federal judge had to sign off on the deal and did, saying that the information Pena could provide would take tons of heroin off the streets and save more than five lives.

"Bullshit," Malone said. "If it's not Pena's heroin, it will be someone else's. This won't change a thing."

"We do what we can," Hinman said.

"What am I supposed to tell the people?" Malone asked Hinman.

"What people?"

"The people in the neighborhood who put their fucking lives on the line to bring this guy down," Malone said. "The people who trusted me to get justice for those kids."

Hinman didn't know what to tell him.

Malone didn't know what to tell them.

Except they already knew. It was an old story to them—the careers of a bunch of white suits were more important than the deaths of five black people.

Braylon Carmichael received five life sentences to be served consecutively.

Denny Malone lost part of his soul. Not all of it, but enough of it that when Pena got tired of the straight life and went back to dealing heroin, Malone was both willing and able to execute him.

alone's cell door opens and O'Dell stands there.

He asks, "You had your shower yet?"

"Yeah."

"Good," O'Dell says. "We're going uptown."

"Where?" Malone is content in his cell, with his own thoughts.

O'Dell says, "Some people want to see you."

He walks Malone outside, puts Malone in the back of a car and slides in beside him. O'Dell takes the cuffs off. "I assume I can trust you not to run on me?"

"Where would I run?"

Malone looks out the window as the car drives past City Hall and takes Chambers out to West Street and then up the West Side Highway.

After only one night in a cell, freedom already seems strange to Malone.

Unexpected.

Heady.

The Hudson seems broader, bluer. Its wide span seems to offer escape, the whitecaps off a stiff breeze tantalize release. The car passes the Holland Tunnel, then Chelsea Piers, where Malone used to go to play midnight hockey pickup games, then the Javits Center, the concrete and plumbing and windows and lighting of which saved the mob, then the Lincoln Tunnel, and Pier 83, where Malone always meant to take the family on the Circle Tour around Manhattan but never did and now it's too late.

The car turns east on Fifty-Seventh and that's when Malone sees that something's wrong.

The air to the north has a yellow tint to it.

Almost brown.

He hasn't seen that kind of air since the Towers came down.

"Can I roll down the window?" Malone asks.

"Go ahead."

The air smells like smoke.

Malone turns to O'Dell with the question in his eye.

"The riots started about five o'clock yesterday," O'Dell says. "Shortly after you went in."

The protests on the Bennett decision began peacefully, O'Dell tells him, then a bottle was thrown, then a brick. By six thirty storefront windows along St. Nicholas and Lenox were being smashed, shops and bodegas looted. By ten o'clock Molotov cocktails were being thrown at sector cars on Amsterdam and Broadway.

The tear gas and batons came out.

But the riots spread.

By eleven Bed-Stuy was in flames, then Flatbush, Brownsville, the South Bronx, and parts of Staten Island.

When dawn finally came, smoke obscured the hot July sunshine. City officials hoped the violence would end with the night, but it started again at around noon, as protesters massed outside City Hall and One Police Plaza and charged police lines.

In Manhattan North, firefighters trying to put out blazes were shot at by snipers from the towers of St. Nick's and then refused to answer any more calls, so entire blocks just burned.

Every cop in the city has been called in on riot duty. They haven't gone home, instead have grabbed combat naps in locker rooms and cribs. They're exhausted, mentally and physically played out, ready to snap.

"Volunteers"—biker clubs, militias, white supremacist groups, gun-rights crazies—have come in from other areas to help reestablish "law and order," making the job even tougher for the police now trying to prevent the riots from escalating into a full-out race war.

It's the fire this time.

The car drives along Billionaires' Row and pulls up alongside Anderson's building.

Berger stands outside the building, clearly waiting for the car. He steps up and opens Malone's door. "Don't say anything until you've heard them out."

"What the fuck?"

"That would be saying something."

They take an elevator to the penthouse.

It's quite a roomful, Malone sees.

The commissioner, Chief Neely, O'Dell, Weintraub, the mayor, Chandler, Bryce Anderson, Berger, and Isobel Paz. Malone's surprise at seeing her shows on his face and she says, "We've all come to a little arrangement. Have a seat, Sergeant Malone."

She points to a chair.

"I've sat plenty," Malone says.

He stays standing.

"Seeing as we have a previous acquaintance," Paz says, "I've been asked to emcee this meeting."

The commissioner and Neely look as though they'd just as soon set Malone on fire. The mayor looks at the coffee table, Anderson looks frozen, Berger smiles his smug smile.

O'Dell and Weintraub look like they want to vomit.

Paz says, "First of all, this meeting never happened. There are no recordings, no memos, no record. Do you understand and agree?"

Malone says, "Write any fiction you want. I don't give a fuck anymore. Why am I here?"

"I've been authorized to make you an offer," Paz says. "Gerard?"

"I thought you were conflicted out," Malone says.

"That's when it looked certain that we were headed to trial," Berger says. "That is no longer so certain."

"Why's that?"

"You may or not be aware of the social turmoil that has resulted from the unfortunate grand jury decision on the Michael Bennett case," Berger says. "Put simply, one more match will set the entire city, if not the country, aflame."

"Call the Fire Department," Malone says. "Can I go back to my cell now?"

"Certain rumors have reached the mayor's office," Berger says, "that a video clip, taken with a cell phone, exists of the Michael Bennett shooting, which purports to show Bennett running away when Officer Hayes shot him. If that tape were to be made public, it will make what is happening now look like Girl Scouts roasting s'mores."

"It can't be allowed to happen," the mayor says.

"What's it have to do with me?" Malone asks.

"You have relationships in the African American community in Manhattan North," Berger says. "Specifically, you have a relationship with DeVon Carter."

"If you want to call it that." *Someone wanting you dead is a relationship, I guess.*

"Cut the shit, Detective!" the commissioner says. "You and your whole unit were on Carter's pad!"

Not exactly, Malone thinks.

Torres and his team were.

But close enough.

"Our understanding is that Carter has the video," Paz says, "and is threatening to make it public. He has gone deep underground where we can't find him. Our offer is—"

"Can we quit fucking around?" the commissioner asks. "Malone, the deal is you get us the vid clip, you walk. It stinks to high heaven, if you ask me, but there it is."

"What about Russo?"

Weintraub frowns as he says, "His deal will stick."

"And no indictment on Montague," Malone says.

The commissioner says, "Sergeant William Montague is a heroic New York police detective."

"Do we have a deal?" Paz asks Malone.

"Not so fast," Berger says. "There is the matter of forfeiture."

"No," Weintraub says. "We are not letting him keep the money. No."

"I was thinking of the house," Berger says. "Malone agrees to transfer full ownership of their house to his wife, who I understand is starting divorce proceedings anyway, and she keeps the house."

Chief Neely says, "We're going to let the dirtiest cop in this city just walk away?"

Bryce Anderson finally speaks. "Would you rather the city burns down? I mean, do we really give a damn that a heroin dealer got what he had coming to him? Are we going to put that against the potential deaths of innocent people, not to mention the destruction? If three bad cops get a pass, well, they won't be the first, will they? If letting this guy go stops this city from burning, that's a deal I make every time."

It's the last word.

The man in the penthouse gets the last word.

Paz looks to Berger. "Are we good?"

"'Good' is not exactly the word I'd choose," Berger says. "Let it suffice to say we have arrived at a mutually satisfactory arrangement that we can all tell ourselves is for the greater public welfare. Do we have a deal, Detective Malone?"

Malone says, "I'll need my shield and gun."

He's going to be a cop again.

For one last time, he's going to be a cop.

CHAPTER 35

Manhattan North is under siege.

Malone runs the gauntlet of rioters pressing up from Grant and down from Manhattanville.

Squadrons of uniformed cops line MLK Boulevard, facing south; more are in position on 126th, facing north, creating a corridor in which the precinct house sits like a surrounded fort. The cops have lined squad cars up like wagons and stand behind them. Mounted cops sit on horses that prance nervously up on the sidewalk. Snipers man the rooftop of the precinct house.

Amsterdam Liquor Mart's been looted, its windows smashed in, its contents taken. On MLK, the C-Town Supermarket has been trashed. Ministers from Manhattan Pentecostal and Antioch Baptist are on the street, urging calm and passive resistance, while across 126th protesters gather in the little park next to St. Mary's as both sides seem to be waiting for sundown to see what happens next.

He goes looking for Nasty Ass.

The snitch is in the world of Nowhere to Be Found.

Malone checks all his usual haunts—Lenox Avenue in the Buck Twenties, Morningside Park, outside the 449.

A white cop walking alone in Harlem in the middle of a race riot, it was anyone but Malone, he'd probably be dead. But there's still his reputation, the fear, even the respect, and the people let him walk and leave him be.

It may be on fire, but it's still the Kingdom of Malone.

He does find Oh No Henry.

The man sees Malone and takes off like a freakin' gazelle. Lucky for Malone, junkies ain't exactly known for their proficiency in the hundred-yard dash, so Malone catches up with him and shoves him against an alley wall. "You run on me now, Henry?"

"Oh, no."

"You just did."

"I thought you was a gorilla."

"Yeah, I want to steal your dope," Malone says. "Where's Nasty Ass?"

"Can we take this somewhere private?" Henry asks. "If I get seen with you like this—"

"Then you better start talking fast," Malone says. "Tell me right now or I'll get on a bullhorn and walk down Lenox *announcing* you're my snitch."

Henry starts crying. He looks terrified. "Oh, no. Oh, no."

"Where is he?" Malone bounces him off the wall.

Henry slides down and lies on the ground in a fetal position. Hands over his face, crying hard now. "The school, the playground."

"Which school?"

"One Seventy-Five." Henry curls up even tighter. "Oh, no. Oh, no."

Oh No Henry is full of shit.

Oh No Henry was lying to him, because Malone can't find Nasty Ass on the playground outside PS 175. And it's weird—hot summer night, even during a riot, and the playground is empty, abandoned.

Like it's radioactive or something.

Then Malone hears it.

A moan, but not from something human.

Some hurt mewling animal.

Malone looks around, trying to find the source of the sound. It's not coming from the basketball court or the chain-link fence.

Then he sees Nasty leaning against a tree.

No, not leaning against the tree.

Nailed to the tree.

Spikes in his hands instead of his arms.

He's stripped naked, his arms stretched up above him, one hand over the other, nailed into the trunk, his skinny legs stretched out, the feet crossed, nailed into the trunk. His chin is dropped onto his chest.

They beat the fuck out of him.

His face is hamburger, his eyes loll crazily in their sockets. His jaw is broken, his twisted teeth smashed, his lips dangle like strips.

He's shit himself.

It's caked on his legs and the tops of his feet.

"Oh, God," Malone says.

Nasty Ass opens his eyes, as much as they can open. Sees Malone and whimpers. No words, just pain.

Malone grabs the thick nail through Nasty's feet and yanks it out. Then he reaches up and takes hold of the nail head embedded in Nasty's hands. He wrenches it and pulls, wrenches and pulls and it finally comes out and Malone catches Nasty and eases him to the ground.

"I got you, I got you," Malone says.

He radios, "I need a bus. Put a rush on it. One-Three-Five and Lenox."

"Malone?"

"Send it."

"Go fuck yourself, rat. I hope you die."

The bus isn't coming.

No radio car is coming, either.

Malone gets his arms under Nasty Ass and lifts. Carries him like a baby across Lenox to Harlem Hospital, to the E-room.

"Who did this to you?" Malone asks. "Fat Teddy?"

He can't make out what Nasty says.

"Where is he?" Malone asks. What he wanted to find out from Nasty in the first place, but he was too late.

"St. Nick's," Nasty whispers. "Building Seven."

Then he smiles, if you can call what forms on what's left of his mouth a smile, and says, "I heard something else, Malone."

"What did you hear?"

"That we the same now, you and me," Nasty Ass says. "We both snitches."

His head falls back into Malone's arms.

Malone carries him into the E-room.

Claudette's on duty.

"Jesus God," she says, "what did they do to this poor soul?"

They put Nasty on a gurney, start to roll him in.

"You have blood all over you," Claudette says to Malone.

She holds Nasty's hand as they roll him in.

Malone walks down to the men's room, wets a paper towel and does his best to get the blood and the shit off his clothes.

Then he goes and sits in the waiting room.

It's crowded, busy from the riot casualties. Cuts from the broken glass of storefront windows, bruises from fights, burns from setting fires or getting caught in them. Swollen red eyes from tear gas, contusions from the beanbags fired from police shotguns—the more serious gunshot wounds are already in ER or on the wards in the recovery rooms, or in the morgue waiting for transfer to the funeral homes.

"He's gone, baby," Claudette says.

"I figured."

"I'm sorry," Claudette says. "Was he your friend?"

"He was my snitch," Malone says reflexively. Then he reconsiders. "Yeah, he was my friend."

A violation of one of the first unwritten laws of police work: Never make friends with a snitch.

454 /   DON WINSLOW

But what else would you call a guy you shared the streets, the parks, the alleys with? Who you worked with, really, because he helped you make busts, take the really bad guys off the street, protect the neighborhood?

Never make friends with a snitch or a junkie, so a junkie snitch . . .

But yeah, Nasty was my friend and he always thought I was his. And look where that got him.

Claudette asks, "Did he have family?"

"Not that I know of." Not that I ever bothered to find out, Malone thinks. But yeah, there's probably a mother and father some-where. Maybe even a wife, who knows, maybe even a kid or kids. Maybe someone is looking for him, or maybe they gave up on him, wrote him off . . .

"So the body . . ."

"Call Unity," Malone says, naming the nearest funeral home. "I'll pay for the burial."

"You're a good friend," she says.

"I'm such a good friend," he says, "I never even bothered to find out his real name."

"Benjamin," Claudette says. "Benjamin Coombs."

She looks exhausted—the casualties from the riots have kept her on almost continual duty, with a few minutes for naps.

"You have a minute?" Malone asks. "Go outside and talk?"

She looks around and then says, "A minute. You know, it's slammed. The riots . . ."

They go out onto 136th.

"I thought you were going to jail," Claudette says.

"I thought I was too," Malone says. "I made a deal."

Maybe even dirtier than the last one.

"You told me one time," Malone says, "something about the *weight* of being black. You still feel that?"

"Well, I'm still black, Denny," she says.

"Does it still wear you down?"

"I'm not using," she says, "if that's what you're asking."

"No, I just mean . . ."

"What do you mean?"

"I dunno."

She looks down and shuffles her shoe along the concrete of the sidewalk, then looks back up at him. "I need to get back in."

"Okay."

"You did a good thing, bringing him in. I couldn't love you more." She wraps her arms around him. Her cheek is wet against his neck. "Good-bye, baby."

Good-bye, Claudette.

Hot summer night, the air-conditioning don't work, so the residents of St. Nick's are outside in the courtyards. There's no such thing as a white cop sneaking in, so he doesn't even try to be subtle.

Just marches in like he still owns the place.

Like he's still Denny Malone.

The whistles, hoots, shouts and insults start, so by the time he hits Building Seven all of St. Nick's knows he's coming and ain't no one thinking about no Christmas turkey giveaways.

They're just thinking about how much they hate cops.

A crew of Get Money Boys stands outside the door of Building Seven.

That don't surprise Malone.

It does surprise him that Tre is with them.

The rap mogul walks up to Malone.

"Slummin', Tre?" Malone asks.

"Just helping to protect my people."

"Me too."

"They think a brother kills a cop," Tre says, "they turn the world upside down. Not the same when a cop kills a brother."

"You want to protect your people," Malone says, "tell these guys to get out of my way."

"You have a warrant?"

"It's public housing," Malone says. "I don't need a warrant. Man with a law degree like you, I thought you'd know that."

"I'm sorry about your friend," Tre says. "Montague was cool."

"He still is," Malone says.

"This is not what I've heard," says Tre. "I've heard he's going to need a helper monkey."

"You volunteering?" Malone asks.

The GMBs think it's enough to go, move toward Malone with the intent to fuck him up good. They already know, the whole street knows, that no backup is coming in for him.

Tre gestures for them to be cool, then turns back to Malone. "What do you want here?"

"I need to talk with Fat Teddy."

Tre says, "You know Fat Teddy will let you beat him to death before he gives anything up. He has a mama, a sister and three cousins in St. Nick's and Grant's."

"We'll protect them."

"You can't even protect yourselves," Tre says.

"You're obstructing a police investigation, Tre," Malone says. "Get out of my way or go out in cuffs."

"See, I think what I'm obstructing is some private business between you and Carter," Tre says. "But if you want to play the obstruction card, put me in bracelets and let a fresh round of riots ensue."

He turns around and offers his hands.

"You'd love that, wouldn't you?" Malone says. "Deposit some needed street cred into your account."

"Do what you're going to do," Tre says. "I don't have all night."

Then Fat Teddy walks out the front door with his hands up. "My lawyer's on his way. What you want with me?"

"You're under arrest."

"I heard you weren't police no more."

"You heard wrong," Malone says. "Put your hands behind your back before I bust your fat head open."

"You don't have to do that, Teddy," Tre says.

"Shut your fuckin' mouth."

"Or what?"

"Or I'll shut it," Malone says. "Don't test me."

"Don't you test me," Tre says. "You see anything but brothers around here? You call for backup, Malone, what I hear is no one's going to come. You'd be the one dead cop they don't care about."

"But you won't live to see it," Malone says. Has to be twenty people holding their cell phones up on this. Looks like a rock concert, Malone thinks. He turns back to Teddy. "Hands behind your back. If I pull my gun, I *will* shoot you, then Tre here. What you all need to know is, I just don't give a fuck anymore."

Teddy must believe him, because he puts his hands behind his back. Malone walks him away from the door a few steps, pushes him against the wall and cuffs him. "You're under arrest for homicide."

"Who I kill?" Teddy asks.

"Nasty Ass."

Teddy lowers his voice. "I ain't kill him."

"No?" Malone asks. "Who did?"

"You did."

Malone feels the truth of it, but asks, "How's that?"

"Them guns," Teddy says. "Carter killed him because Nasty snitched on them guns."

"Carter nailed him to a tree."

"Ain't I know it?" Teddy says. "Why you think I tell you? That ain't right, what Carter did. Kill a brother, yes, if you feel you got to. But do *that* to him? He ain't gotta do that to a man."

"Where's Carter now?"

Teddy shouts it real loud, so it bounces off walls in the whole project. "I ain't know where Carter at!"

Malone leans close to Fat Teddy and whispers, "When I tell Carter *you* ratted him on the guns, he is going to kill you, your cousins, your sister *and* your mother."

"You do me that way, man?" Fat Teddy asks. "You do my *family* that way? That beneath you, Malone."

"I ain't got no bottom, Teddy," Malone says. "Not anymore. Where is he?"

The bottles start flying.

Airmail.

Bottles, cans, then burning garbage.

Fire fluttering from the sky.

Sirens go off, the uniformed bluecoat cavalry riding up urban canyons. Not to rescue Malone, God knows, but to kick some black ass before it pours out of the projects again.

"What's it gonna be, Teddy?" Malone says. "We ain't got a lot of time here."

"Four West 122," Teddy says. "Top floor. And Malone? I hope they do kill you. I hope your brother cops put two right in your face so you see it coming."

"That's right, you dumb fuck!" Malone yells. "Keep those fat lips glued together, see what it gets you!"

The crowd starts to move in on Malone. He backs off and retreats toward the car. It's not something he would have done, let the Jamaals chase him out of the projects, but he's never coming back anyway.

CHAPTER 36

It's the old Mount Morris neighborhood.

The old Harlem of graceful brownstones that once housed the doctors, the lawyers, the musicians, artists and poets.

The riots haven't touched this neighborhood.

Now Malone knows why.

DeVon Carter ain't having it.

Malone pulls up across the street from his building. Carter's sentries make him as soon as he gets out of the car. One of them says, "You got balls, white cop coming up here."

Malone says. "Tell Carter I want to see him."

"Why?"

"Why are you asking why?" Malone says. "All you have to do is go tell Carter that Denny Malone wants to talk."

The bouncer eye-fucks him for pride and then goes in. He takes about ten minutes, comes back and says, "Come on."

He leads them upstairs.

DeVon Carter is waiting in his living room. The apartment is large, open and spare. Bone-white walls feature large black-and-white photos of Miles Davis, Sonny Stitt, Art Blakey, Langston Hughes, James Baldwin, Thelonious Monk. A floor-to-ceiling bookcase, painted gloss black, holds volumes of mostly art books—Benny Andrews, Norman Lewis, Kerry James Marshall, Hughie Lee-Smith.

Carter wears a black denim shirt, black jeans, black loafers with no socks. He sees Malone glance at the book spines. "You know African American art? Oh, that's right, you have a black girlfriend. Maybe she taught you something."

"She taught me a lot," Malone says.

"I just bought a Lewis at auction," Carter says. "A hundred fifty K for an untitled work."

"You'd think for that kind of money they'd slap a title on it," Malone says.

"It's upstairs if you want to see it."

"I didn't come here to admire your art collection."

"What *are* you doing here?" Carter asks. "I heard you were behind bars. Something about you selling a large weight of heroin to the Dominicans. And here I thought we were friends, Malone."

"We're not."

"I would have paid you more," Carter says.

"You needed it more," Malone says. "Now you don't have the heroin and you don't have the guns, so you don't have the money and you don't have the people. Castillo is going to hose you off the street like the garbage you are."

"I got cops."

"The old Torres crew?" Malone asks. "If they haven't already gone over to the Domos, they will."

It won't be Gallina, Malone thinks. He doesn't have the brains or the guts.

It'll be Tenelli.

Carter knows he's right. He asks, "So what are you offering me? Your crew, or what's left of them? No, thanks."

"I'm offering you the whole fucking department," Malone says. "Manhattan North, the Borough, Narcotics, the Detective Division. I'll throw in the mayor's office and half the motherfuckers on Billionaires' Row."

"In exchange for what?"

"The Bennett video clip."

Carter smiles. Now it all makes sense to him. "So your bosses let their nigger out of his cage to come fetch it."

"That's me."

"What makes you think I have it?"

"You're DeVon Carter."

He has it.

Malone can see it in his eyes.

"So you want me to sell out my people," Carter says, "to buy whites' protection."

"You've been selling out your people since you put your first dime bag on the street," Malone says.

"This from a dirty, dope-slinging cop."

"That's how I know," Malone says. "We're the same, you and me. We're both dinosaurs, just trying to buy ourselves a little more time before we go extinct."

"Human nature," Carter says. "A man wants to breathe for as long as he can. A king, he wants to stay on the throne. We were kings, Malone."

"We were that."

"We should have worked together," Carter says. "We'd still be kings."

"We still can."

"If I give you that tape."

"It's that simple," Malone says. "You give me that tape, we'll run Manhattan North together. Nobody can touch us."

Carter stares at him, then says, "You know the best thing about these riots? They burn down things you wanted taken down anyway—slum buildings, dirty bodegas, shabby bars. Then you buy low, build nice things and sell high. Let me give you some advice, Malone. You take some of your dirty dope money, put it into real estate, you become a pillar of the community."

"Does that mean we have a deal?"

"We've always had a deal."

"I need to see the clip."

Carter has a beautiful flat-screen monitor.

He jacks an iPhone in.

The images are painfully clear.

Michael Bennett is a typical street kid in a gray hoodie, baggy jeans and basketball shoes. He stands in the middle of the street arguing with a uniformed officer, Hayes.

Hayes goes to cuff him.

Bennett turns and runs.

He's fast, like a fourteen-year-old, but he isn't faster than a bullet.

Hayes pulls his service weapon and empties it.

Bennett's body spins so the last two shots hit him in the face and the chest, the exact reverse of what the ME said.

Jesus Christ.

It's just murder.

Black lives matter, Malone thinks.

They just don't matter as much as white lives.

"You made copies," Malone says.

"Of course I did," Carter said. "Mrs. Carter didn't raise herself any stupid black babies. You tell your bosses that if anything happens to me, this clip will be released on fifty major media outlets and the Internet. Then the whole city will burn. Make the same deal for yourself, I don't mind. I want you back on the street."

He hands Malone the phone.

"The riots will die down, they always do," Carter says. "You and me, we'll go back to keeping the lid on, because we always do. Make Manhattan North safe for real estate. Now you run and go tell Massuh Anderson as long as I get room to make my play, he doesn't have to worry about the video."

Malone puts the phone in his pocket.

"Are we good?" Carter asks.

"Let me ask you something," Malone says. "Who was Benjamin Coombs?"

Carter looks puzzled. Searches his brain for the name, as if it's some African American painter he hasn't heard of. But it doesn't come to him, and he's annoyed when he has to ask, "Who?"

Malone pulls his gun.

"Nasty Ass," he says.

He shoots Carter twice in the chest.

CHAPTER 37

They're waiting for him at Anderson's penthouse.

The gang's all there.

Like a group portrait an artist has done on consecutive days. Same people, different poses, but all eyes focused on Malone as he walks in.

Chief Neely says, "Pat him down."

"Why?" Berger asks.

"He's a rat, isn't he?" the chief of detectives says as he walks over to Malone and starts to search him. He looks right in Malone's face as he says, "Once a rat, always a rat. I don't want to get rid of one recording just to get another even worse."

"I'm not wearing a wire," Malone says, raising his arms. "But knock yourself out, sir."

Neely pats him down, then looks at the rest of them and says, "He's clean."

"Did you get the clip?" Paz asks Malone.

"Don't worry, I got it," Malone says. "That was our deal, wasn't it? I get you guys the Bennett tape, you cut me loose?"

Paz nods.

"No," Malone says, his eyes boring through her. "I want to hear you say it. I want you to make a proffer, full fucking disclosure."

"That was our deal," Paz says.

"Yeah, that *was* our deal," Malone says. "That was before."

"Before what?" Anderson asks.

"Before I saw it," Malone says. "Before I saw our cop kill that kid. Shot him running away. It was pure murder. So now the clip is worth more."

"What do you want?" Anderson asks.

"I go back on the Job," Malone says. "I go back to running Manhattan North. That's my price. Carter's is a little steeper. He gets a free hand running his dope business. We go after the Dominicans and leave him alone. You're thinking of sending someone to clip him—or me, for that matter—forget about it."

"There are copies of the vid clip," Anderson says.

"Did you think you were playing with children?" Malone asks. "Dumb cops and jungle bunnies? He's your fucking real estate partner anyway, isn't he, Mr. Anderson? But don't worry, you keep your part of the deal, we keep ours."

The mayor says, "We cannot countenance—"

"Yes, we can," Anderson says, his eyes not leaving Malone. "We can and will. We don't have a choice, do we?"

"And everyone is in, right?" Malone says. He scans the room, looking from face to face. Like one of those old John Ford westerns his old man used to like, close-up after close-up of faces showing hope, fear, anger, anxiety, challenge. Except these aren't cowboy faces, they're city faces, New York City faces full of wealth, grit, cynicism, greed and energy. "Mr. Mayor, Mr. Commissioner, Chief Neely, Special Agent O'Dell, Ms. Paz, Mr. Anderson. All in, right? Speak now or forever hold—"

"Give us the goddamn clip," Anderson says.

Malone tosses him the phone. "This is the original. Carter's dead. The clip is probably already running on CNN, Fox, Channel Eleven, the Net, I don't know."

Paz stares at him in disbelief.

"Do you even know what you've done?" Anderson asks. "You've burned down this city. You've set fire to this whole country."

"I can't help you now, Denny," Berger says. "There is nothing I can do to save you."

"Good," Malone says. He doesn't want to be saved. "I loved the

Job. I loved it. I loved this fucking city. But it's wrong now. You fucked it up.

"Fuck you. Individually and collectively fuck you all. Eighteen years I spent on those streets, down those hallways, through those doors, doing what you wanted done. You didn't want to know how, you just wanted it done. And I did it for you and now I'm done. Now you live with what happens when guys like me aren't around anymore to keep the animals from busting out of their cages and marching down Broadway to claim what you've kept from them for four hundred years.

"You call me a dirty cop. Me and my partners, me and my brothers. You call us corrupt. Well, I call *you* corrupt. You're the corruption, you're the rot in the soul of this city, this country. You take millions in bribes on city construction, but you're going to set me free to cover that up. Slumlords get passes on buildings with no heat and toilets that don't work, and you look the other way. Judges buy their benches and sell cases to make it back, but you don't want to hear about that."

He looks at the commissioner. "You guys take gifts, trips, free meals, tickets from rich citizens to protect them from tickets, citations, violations . . . get them guns . . . and then you come down on cops for a free cup of coffee, a drink, a fucking sandwich."

Malone turns to Anderson. "And you, you built this penthouse laundering dope money. This whole fucking thing is built on a pile of white powder and the backs of poor people. I'm ashamed I ever worked for you, helped protect you.

"Yeah, I'm a dirty cop. I'm a wrong guy. I gotta answer to God for what I did. But not to *you*. Not to any of *you*. That drug war to you is a way to keep the niggers and the spics in their place, fill the courts and the cells, keep the lawyers and the guards and yes, the police, in full fucking employment, and you play with your numbers to make them what you want them to be so you can get your promotions and your headlines and your political careers.

"But *we're* the ones out there. *We* pick up the bodies, *we* tell the families, *we* watch them cry. We go home and cry, we bleed, *we* die, and you sell us down the river any time it gets tough. But we go out there and, no matter what—no matter what else we've done or what you think of us, if we get lost along the way—we go out there and try to protect those good people.

"Dirty cops? They're my brothers, my sisters. They may be dirty, they may be wrong, but they're better than you. Any one of them is better than any one of you."

Malone walks out the door, no one tries to stop him. He walks up Fifth to Central Park South, turns toward Columbus Circle and is halfway there before he looks over his shoulder and sees O'Dell coming behind him, his right hand inside his jacket. The agent is striding, fast, a man on a mission.

This is as good a place as any, Malone thinks.

He turns and waits.

O'Dell walks up to him, a little out of breath.

"Did you get it?" Malone asks him.

O'Dell opens his shirt, shows him the wire. "I'm on the next Acela to DC. They'll be coming after you, you know."

"I know. You too."

"Maybe once people hear what's on this tape . . ."

"Maybe," Malone says. "I wouldn't count on it, though. They got friends in DC, too. So take care of yourself, huh? Keep your head on a swivel."

People walk past them like water around a rock, stillness an obstacle in this city of motion.

"What are you going to do now?" O'Dell asks.

Malone shrugs.

The only thing I know how to do, he thinks.

CHAPTER 38

Now York, 4 A.M.

The city's not sleeping, just taking a gasping spell after another night of rioting that broke out with renewed violence when the Bennett video hit the screens.

Rioters came down Broadway from Harlem, smashing windows, looting stores first around Columbia University and Barnard, then down into the Upper West Side, turning over cars, robbing cabs, beating any whites who hadn't locked themselves in their buildings, setting fires until the National Guard formed a line on Seventy-Ninth and fired first rubber bullets and then live rounds.

Thirteen civilians, all of them black, were shot; two were killed.

And it wasn't just New York.

Protests turned into riots in Newark, Camden, Philadelphia, Baltimore and Washington, DC. By night—like embers flying in a ferocious wind—riots were touched off in Chicago, East St. Louis, Kansas City, New Orleans, Houston.

Los Angeles went up later.

Watts, South Central, Compton, Inglewood.

National Guard units were called in, federal troops sent to LA, New Orleans and Newark as the Michael Bennett riots turned into the worst since Rodney King, and the long hot summers of the '60s.

Malone watched it from a barstool at the Dublin House.

Saw the president come on and plead for calm. When the president finished up, Malone went into the men's room and chased the three Jamesons with four go-pills.

Going to need them.

He knew they'd be looking for him.

Probably already been to his apartment.

He left the bar and got into his car.

His own car, his beloved Camaro he bought when he was first promoted to sergeant.

Got the Bose cranked up now as he follows another car up Broadway.

The drive uptown is a trip through shattered dreams.

Decades of progress burned down in days of rage and nights of torment. Malone's been cruising these streets for eighteen years, seen them when they were ghetto wasteland, seen them bloom and grow, now sees them going back to boarded windows and charred storefronts.

Inside, people still have the same hopes, the same disappointments, the love, the hate, the shame, but the dreams, the dreams are on hold.

Malone drives past Hamilton Fruits and Vegetables, the Big Brother Barber Shop, the Apollo Pharmacy, Trinity Church Cemetery and the mural of a raven on 155th. Past the Church of the Intercession—but it's too late for intercession, Malone thinks—past the Wahi Diner and all the small gods of place, the personal shrines, the markers of his life on these streets that he loves like a husband loves a cheating wife, a father loves a wayward son.

He follows the car as it goes up Broadway.

Illmatic pumped up:

I never sleep 'cause sleep is the cousin of death
Beyond the walls of intelligence, life is defined
I think of crime when I'm in a New York state of mind.

Last time you drove uptown this time of the morning, Malone thinks, you were with your brothers, your partners—laughing, busting balls.

That was the night Billy O died.

Now Monty is as good as gone.

Russo, he ain't your brother anymore.

Levin, the one you were supposed to protect, is dead.

And your family, who you told yourself you did it all for, they're gone and don't want to see you.

You got nothin'.

It's 4 A.M. in New York.

The time for waking dreams.

The time to wake from dreams.

The car he's following turns left on 177th and drives west past Fort Washington and Pinehurst Avenues until it takes another left onto Haven Avenue, crosses 176th and pulls over on the east side of Haven, just uptown from Wright Park. Malone watches Gallina, Tenelli and Ortiz get out, not even bothering to disguise the assault rifles—M4s and Ruger 14s—as they go into the building.

The Trini lookouts let them in.

Why not? Malone thinks. They're on the same side now. Tenelli made the move and it was the smart bet.

He sees a black Navigator pull up in front of the building and Carlos Castillo get out of the backseat. Two shooters get out with him and flank him as he goes inside. Malone drives down the street, pulls off on Pinehurst Avenue and parks at the end of the cul-de-sac.

I lay puzzle as I backtrack to earlier times
Nothing's equivalent to the New York state of mind.

Malone has a Sig Sauer and a Beretta, the knife at his ankle, a flashbang grenade.

But no Billy O, no Russo or Monty, no Levin to take his back.

Climbing into his vest and Velcroing it tight, he wishes he could hear Big Monty bitch about the vest again. Tilt his trilby, roll his cigar.

He flips the lanyard with his shield over his chest. Then he grabs the Rabbit out of the trunk, walks through the park and into an alley beside Castillo's building.

He climbs the fire escape to the edge of the roof.

The Trini lookout is looking out the other way, toward the street. And he's not looking that hard—Malone can smell the weed.

Malone moves across the roof.

Wraps his left forearm around the Trini's throat and pulls him up, close and tight so he doesn't scream as Malone pumps two rounds from the Sig into his back. The body slumps and Malone lets it down easy.

No one is going to notice the shots—there's sporadic gunfire all over the city, the sector cars have stopped responding to the 10-10s— and the die-hard Fourth of July partiers are still setting off fireworks.

Malone looks downtown and sees the eerie orange glow of fires burning and thick black smoke rising against the night sky.

Then he goes to the roof door.

It's locked, so he jams the Rabbit in and squeezes. Wishes again that Monty were here because it's hard, but he keeps pressing and the lock finally gives it up and the door swings open.

Malone goes down the stairs.

My last vertical, he thinks.

He holds the Sig in front of him.

Another door, but this one's not locked.

It opens into a hallway.

A dim fluorescent light hanging from a rusty chain casts sick yellow light on the face of the surprised sentry outside the wooden door at the end of the hallway.

His mouth forms a vacant O.

Brain rushing to send a message that never gets to his hand because Malone shoots him twice and he crumples in front of the door like a rolled-up welcome mat.

The last door, Malone thinks.

Flashbacks to Billy O.

And Levin.

So many goddamn doors, so many things on the other side.

Too many dead.

Dead families, dead children.

A dead soul.

Malone presses himself against the wall and edges toward the door. Bullets come out. Heavy, spinning rounds shattering wood.

Malone hollers as if in pain and drops face-first to the floor.

The door opens.

His gun in front of him, Gallina's eyes are adrenaline wide, his neck swivels as he looks for the threat then sees the dead man at his feet.

Malone fires a burst into and through his chest.

Gallina spins like a top.

A sprinkler spraying blood.

The gun drops from his hand, clatters on the floor.

More bullets come out, splintering the wall above Malone's head. He rolls across the floor to the other side of the wall as a Trini gun peeks out from the doorway, searching for him.

Malone pulls the safety pin on the flashbang grenade and tosses it in and pushes his eyes into the crook of his elbow.

The noise is horrific, sickening.

The white light washes everything out.

He counts to five, then lunges to his feet and dives for the open door. His balance is fucked from the blast, his legs rock like he's drunk. A Trini staggers out, screaming, his face burned, the green bandanna around his neck on fire. Grabbing at his throat to rip off the flaming noose, he bounces off Malone, sending him to the floor. The Sig drops from Malone's hand and he can't see to find it so he pulls the Beretta from his waistband.

Ortiz looks down at him.

Ortiz raises a Ruger.

Malone shoots as he shuffles on his ass to get his back against a wall. Ortiz groans heavily and falls to his knees, the Ruger still out and pointed. Malone hits him with two more shots.

Ortiz falls on his face.

Blood pools beneath him.

The heroin, fifty kilos of Dark Horse, is stacked neatly on tables.

Castillo sits calmly behind one of them, behind his dope like Midas counting his gold.

Malone gets up, pointing the Beretta at him.

"I thought you'd be Carter," Castillo says to him.

Malone shakes his head. "You killed one of my brothers. Another one is brain dead."

"It's a dangerous game that we play," Castillo says. "We all know the risks. So what are we going to do here?"

Castillo smiles.

Satan's smile on meeting Faust.

A quick look tells Malone that the Dark Horse is all there. They were just cutting it to put it out on the streets.

His streets.

Last time he stood in this spot he made the worst mistake of his life. Now he says, "You're under arrest. You have the right to—"

Malone hears the two pops.

They drive him forward like punches and he falls face-first but rolls before he hits and looks up to see Tenelli.

His finger squeezes the trigger and keeps squeezing.

The four shots hit her low to high, running up from her groin to her stomach, her chest and then her neck.

Her black hair whips her face.

She swats at the wound on her neck like it's a mosquito.

Then sits down on the floor and looks at Malone with this funny little smile like she's surprised she's dying, like she can't believe she's stupid enough to let herself get killed.

A croak comes deep from her chest and her eyes pop and she's gone.

Malone pushes himself up.

The pain is awful.

He hollers and then spews vomit. Hunches over, pukes again and then looks down and sees blood coming out from the exit wound below his vest. He touches the wound and blood seeps through his fingers, making them red, hot and sticky.

Malone aims the gun at Castillo's head and pulls the trigger.

Hears the metallic click and knows it's empty.

Castillo laughs. Gets up from his chair and walks over. Puts his hand on Malone's chest and pushes him down.

It doesn't take much.

Malone's on all fours.

Like an animal.

A wounded animal that needs to be put down.

Castillo pulls a pistol from his jacket.

A slick little Taurus PT22.

Small, but it will do.

He puts the barrel against Malone's head. "*Por Diego.*"

Malone don't say nothing. He pulls the SOG knife from his ankle, raises up and stabs behind him.

The pistol goes off with a deafening roar but Malone is still alive in a world of red light and red pain as he gets up, turns, and slashes the knife up through Castillo's leg, severing the femoral artery.

He looks into Castillo's face, pulls the knife out and then plunges it into his stomach and rips up.

Castillo's mouth opens wide.

An inhuman sound comes out.

Malone pulls the knife out and lets Castillo fall.

His blood smears Malone's chest.

Malone staggers to the table and starts loading the bricks of heroin into duffel bags.

CHAPTER 39

This one time Malone took the family to the White Mountains in New Hampshire on the kids' spring break. They rented a little cabin in a canyon by a river and one morning he got up early and ran some water out of the tap so cold it almost hurt to drink, but it tasted so good and so clean he couldn't stop.

That was a good trip, a good vacation.

Now bachata music comes from a boom box somewhere as Malone comes out of the building onto the street.

Helicopter rotors chop the air.

Malone hurts and he's thirsty as he hefts the bags, walking—shuffling—west on 176th onto Haven. Blood follows him like a guilty secret as he crosses the street and staggers onto Riverside, then across, then into some trees and trips over a root and falls.

It would be nice to just lie there, just lie there and go to sleep warm and drowsy in the grass, but the pain stabs him anyway and he can't stay there—he has somewhere to go—so he struggles to his feet and keeps walking.

John, he caught a trout from the river and when Malone put it on a tree stump and started to clean it, John, he started to cry when he saw the guts come out and he cried because he was sorry he killed the fish.

Malone walks onto the Henry Hudson.

A car blasts its horn and swerves around him. A yell comes out the window, "Fucking drunk!"

Malone crosses the northbound lane, then the south and then he's in trees again and then he comes to some basketball courts, empty now in the early morning and even though he can see the river he leans against a post to rest and steady himself as he bends over and throws up again.

Then he starts again and comes to more trees and uses them to hold himself up until he makes it to some rocks by the edge of the river.

He sits down.

Unzips the duffel bags and starts taking out the bricks of heroin.

Billy O looks up and smiles at him.

"We're rich."

Then the dog snaps at the end of its chain.

Puppies mewl, a small knot of squirming life.

The day Malone graduated from the Academy was one of those spring days that New York occasionally produces, one of those splendid days when you know you don't want to be anywhere else in the world and you don't want to be anyone but you in this place, this city, this world unto itself.

And he was young, young and clean and full of hope and pride and belief, belief in God and belief in himself and belief in the Job, belief in the mission, to protect and serve.

Malone stabs the knife into the brick of heroin and slashes the plastic.

Then he tosses it into the river.

Does this again and again.

That spring day he stood in an ocean of blue, his brothers and sisters, his friends, his comrades in arms, and they were white and black and brown and yellow but what they really were was blue.

Sinatra sang "New York, New York," as they filed in and stood at attention.

I should call in a 10-13, he thinks now, Officer down, officer needs assistance, but he don't have his radio and he can't remember where his phone is and it doesn't matter anyway because they wouldn't come if they knew it was him and even if they did they wouldn't make it on time.

You should have called 10-13 a long time ago.

Before it was too late.

Claudette's skin is black against the white silk right there at that softest spot in the world, a world of concrete and asphalt, steel cuffs and bars, hard words and harder thoughts, her skin is dark and soft and cool so near the warmth of her.

He empties one bag of the junk and starts in on the next one, wants to get it done before he falls asleep.

Levin smiles up at him we're rich.

No that was Billy.

Or Liam.

So many dead.

Too many.

When John was born he took so long coming, when he finally slid out, Malone, he was so tired he climbed into the gurney and the three of them, they fell asleep together.

Caitlin, being the second, she was a lot faster.

Jesus, it hurts.

Malone in his new blue uniform, his new shield, his hat and his white gloves, his mother and his brother Liam and Sheila watching and he wished his father could have been there, could have lived to see this, he would have been proud even though he told Malone he didn't want this life for him, this was the life that his family knew, his father, his grandfather, this was their life, what they did, what they believed, through the pain and the sorrow this is what they did and he wished his dad were there to see him take the oath.

"I do hereby pledge and declare to uphold the Constitution of the United States and the Constitution of the State of New York and faithfully discharge my duties as a police officer in the New York City Police Department to the best of my ability, so help me God."

So help me, God.

No you won't, why should you?

The pain bites at his guts and he screams as he twists on the rocks.

John cried for that fish.

He cried.

The air smells like ash. Like the day that Liam died.

Ashes, smoke, shattered buildings and broken hearts.

Tears cut lines through charred cheeks.

Now the city is waking up.

He hears sirens wail like newborn babies.

Malone looks back at his kingdom in flames behind him, plumes of smoke rising as if from funeral pyres.

Slashes another bag and gives it to the river.

Then he throws his white gloves in the air as blue and white confetti showers him and his brothers and his sisters and they yell their lungs out as the crowd cheers and he knows at that moment that this is what he wants, what he always wanted, that this is how he'll spend his life, his blood, his soul, his being.

A pure fire burns in his heart.

It's the best day of his life.

No, that's not today, he remembers.

That's not now, that was then.

Heroin falls from the ceiling like it's snowing inside. Floats gently into Billy's wounds, his blood, his veins, soothes the pain.

Billy does it hurt anymore?

Does the hurting stop?

Does it end?

Our beginnings can't *know* our ends, our purity can't imagine its corruption. All he knew back then was that he loved the Job, in those early years walking or riding the streets in his bag, seeing the people see him, the innocent feeling safe because he was there, the guilty feeling unsafe because he was there.

He remembers his first collar the way you remember the first time you made love—a holdup thug who'd mugged an old lady and Malone found him and took him off the street and it turned out he was wanted in ten other robberies and the city was safer, the people were safer, because Malone was on the Job.

He loved the way that people looked to him to help them, save them from predators or from themselves. He loved that they looked to him for assistance, answers, even accusation and then absolution. He loved the city, loved the people he protected and served, loved the Job.

He couldn't imagine then that those streets could wear him down, that the Job could wear him out, that the sorrow and anger, the bodies, the heartbreak, the suffering, the foolishness, the cynicism would grind on his soul like a stone on steel, dulling not sharpening, leaving nicks and invisible, insidious cracks that would spread until the steel first broke and then shattered, until he understood what killed his father and left his blue coat draped across the dirty snow and Billy O lying on the floor strewn with dirty cash, his body and blood corrupted.

Malone's soul started shiny as his new shield, darkened as it changed to gold and now is black as night.

He drops the last brick into the water.

That's good, now none of it will hit his streets.

The job done, he lies back.

The old man died in a pile of dirty snow, Liam underneath a burned building, me on sharp rocks looking up at the sky.

The sky is gray, the sun will be up soon.

The sirens howl.

A radio crackles in his ear.

10-13, 10-13.

Officer down.

Then the sky is white and sirens stop and the radio goes dead quiet and he's making his first collar again, the guy who robbed the old lady.

All Denny Malone ever wanted to be was a good cop.

ACKNOWLEDGMENTS

Many police officers, active and retired, were incredibly generous to me, sharing their time, experience, stories, thoughts, opinions and emotions. I owe them a great debt, but it might be a disservice to them to list them by name. You know who you are, and I can't thank you enough. I also want to thank you for what you've done and what you do.

On the subject of thanks, this book had its origins in an early-morning phone call from Shane Salerno, my partner-in-crime-writing, colleague and close friend for coming on twenty years now. I thank him for the inspiration, creative input, unflagging support and the many much-needed laughs. It's been a ride, brother.

I would also like to thank David Highfill for bringing me into William Morrow and for his thoughtful editing of the manuscript.

To Deborah Randall, David Koll, Nick Carraro and everyone at the Story Factory.

To Michael Morrison, Liate Stehlik, Lynn Grady, Kaitlin Harri, Jennifer Hart, Sharyn Rosenblum, Shelby Meizlik, Brian Grogan, Danielle Bartlet, Juliette Shapland, Samantha Hagerbaumer and Chloe Moffett for their passionate support of this book and for working so hard to make it possible.

My appreciation also goes out to production editor Laura Cherkas and copyeditor Laurie McGee for their hard work.

To Ridley Scott, Emma Watts, Steve Asbell, Michael Schaefer and Twentieth Century Fox for their belief in this manuscript and for purchasing the film rights to this book after our successful col-laboration on *The Cartel*.

To Matthew Snyder and Joe Cohen at Creative Artists Agency.

To Cynthia Swartz and Elizabeth Kushel for their fantastic work on *Savages, The Cartel* and now *The Force*. Thank you for all of your hard work.

To Richard Heller, my attorney.

To John Albu for hauling me around.

The good folks at the Solana Beach Coffee Company, Jeremy's on the Hill, Mr. Manitas, The Cooler, El Fuego and Drift Surf for keeping me in caffeine, breakfast burritos, burgers, nachos, fish tacos and needed diversion.

The late Matty Pavis for his kindness and generosity, and my Staten Island *paisan* Steve Pavis for introducing me to his brother.

The late Bob Leuci, who was a prince anywhere.

I'd like to express appreciation to all my readers, old and new, for all their support and kindness over the years. Without them, I don't have this job that I love.

To my mother, Ottis Winslow, for the use of her front porch and for all those library books over the years.

To Thomas, my son, for his encyclopedic knowledge of hip-hop lyrics and for all the years of patience and support.

And, always, to Jean, my patient wife, for her tireless support and for taking this, and every other, journey with me. ILYM.